FEB 06

DATE DUE

5 9/d			
GAYLORD			PRINTED IN U.S.A.

THE
HIDDEN DIARY
OF
Marie Antoinette

Also by Carolly Erickson
in Large Print:

Lilibet

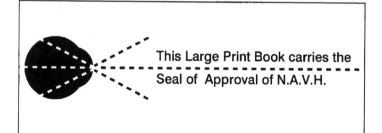

This Large Print Book carries the
Seal of Approval of N.A.V.H.

THE
HIDDEN DIARY
OF
Marie Antoinette

Carolly Erickson

WHEELER
PUBLISHING

Published in 2006 by arrangement with
St. Martin's Press, LLC.

Wheeler Large Print Hardcover.

The text of this Large Print edition is unabridged.
Other aspects of the book may vary from the original edition.

Set in 16 pt. Plantin by Minnie B. Raven.

Printed in the United States on permanent paper.

Library of Congress Cataloging-in-Publication Data

Erickson, Carolly, 1943–
      The hidden diary of Marie Antoinette /
by Carolly Erickson.
            p. cm.
      ISBN 1-59722-157-0 (lg. print : hc : alk. paper)
      1. Marie Antoinette Queen, consort of Louis XVI, King
of France, 1754–1793 — Fiction.   2. Louis XVI, King of
France, 1754–1793 — Fiction.   3. Fersen, Hans Axel von,
greve, 1755–1810 — Fiction.   4. France — History —
Revolution, 1789–1799 — Fiction.   5. France — History —
Louis XVI, 1774–1793 — Fiction.   6. Queens — Fiction.
7. Large type books.   8. Diary fiction.   I. Title.
PS3605.R53H53 2005b
      813'.54—dc22   2005028380

To Raffaello

As the Founder/CEO of NAVH, the only national health agency solely devoted to those who, although not totally blind, have an eye disease which could lead to serious visual impairment, I am pleased to recognize Thorndike Press* as one of the leading publishers in the large print field.

Founded in 1954 in San Francisco to prepare large print textbooks for partially seeing children, NAVH became the pioneer and standard setting agency in the preparation of large type.

Today, those publishers who meet our standards carry the prestigious "Seal of Approval" indicating high quality large print. We are delighted that Thorndike Press is one of the publishers whose titles meet these standards. We are also pleased to recognize the significant contribution Thorndike Press is making in this important and growing field.

Lorraine H. Marchi, L.H.D.
Founder/CEO
NAVH

* Thorndike Press encompasses the following imprints: Thorndike, Wheeler, Walker and Large Print Press.

PROLOGUE

Conciergerie Prison

October 3, 1793
They say the fearsome thing doesn't always work well.

It takes three or four chops to sever the head. Sometimes the poor wretches scream horribly, for a full minute, before their agony is ended with a single massive blow.

They say the amount of blood is remarkable. Streaming, cascading out, thick and dark red, more blood than you would imagine a person had in him. The heart goes on pumping it out, pulse after pulse, after the head is cut off.

The executioner walks proudly to the edge of the scaffold, holding up the bleeding head, the eyes staring in surprise, the mouth open in a silent cry. And as he walks, he is drenched in the gushing blood.

My husband had a lot of blood, they tell me. He was such a large, heavy man, strong and tough as an ox. A man of the outdoors, with a workman's big, competent hands. It would have taken more than one slice of the blade to kill him.

They wouldn't let me watch him die. I know I could have given him strength at the end, if only I had been there with him. We went through so much together, Louis and I, right up until the day they came for him and took him away from me. He didn't try to resist, that day when they came, the mayor and the others, to take him away. He merely called for his coat and hat and followed them. I never saw him again.

I know he died well. They say he was calm and dignified, reading the psalms on the way to the open square where the huge machine with its slicing blade awaited him. I am told he ignored all the shouts and cries from the crowd, and did not look for rescue, though there were those who would gladly have saved him if they could. He undressed himself and opened the collar of his shirt and knelt to offer his neck to the blade, refusing to let them bind his hands like a common criminal.

At the end he tried to say that he was innocent but they drowned him out with the noise of drums and rushed to drop the heavy blade.

That was nine months ago. Now they will be coming for me, their former queen,

Marie Antoinette, now known as Prisoner 280.

I don't know when it will be, but soon. I can tell by Rosalie's face when she brings me my soup and lime-flower water. She has given up hope that I will be spared.

At least they let me write in this journal. They will not let me knit or sew, because of the pointed needles — as if I had the strength to stab anyone! — but I am allowed to write, and my guards cannot read so what I write remains private. Rosalie can read some but she is discreet, she will not betray me.

Writing helps me to forget this horrible dark little airless room in which I am confined, that stinks of rot and mildew and human waste. This awful cold and damp, my wet shoes and sore leg that throbs now more than ever, despite the liniment that Rosalie rubs on it. The coarse guards that watch me and the others that stand outside my door, joking about me and laughing. The hard, cold cot I lie on at night, unable to sleep, crying my heart out over my son, my little chou d'amour, Louis-Charles. Or as I must call him now, King Louis XVII.

Oh, if only I could still see him! My dearest child, my little boy-king.

Until last August I saw him nearly every

day, if I stood at the window of my old cell long enough. The horrible old ruffian who guards him, Antoine Simon, took him past my cell on his way to walk in the courtyard for exercise, making gross jokes and teaching him to sing the Marseillaise.

Poor Louis-Charles, only eight years old, losing the father he loved and now deprived of his mother too. How I fought when they came to take him away from me. It took them nearly an hour. I would not let go of him, I yelled and threatened them. In the end I begged them, sobbing, not to take him from me. It was only when they said that they would kill both my children that I relented.

What will they do to my boy? Poison him? Or worse, turn him into a little revolutionary, make him believe their lies. They will try to deny him his royal heritage, of course. No kings for them! And no queens either. Only Citoyen Capet and Veuve Capet, and our son Louis-Charles Capet, citizen of the French Republic.

And what of my Mousseline, my Marie-Thérèse, my lovely daughter, only fourteen, so young. Far too young to be an orphan. I miss her, I miss all my children. Poor little Sophie, my baby, who was never well and who only lived a year. And my dearest Louis-Joseph, my firstborn, the poor crippled one, never strong, in his grave at Meudon. How many tears have I shed for him, for them all.

I know that I suffer from an excess of emotion. It is because I am unwell, and because they give me so much lime-flower water and ether to drink. I do not have enough strength to keep my composure. I live on soup and bread, and I have become very thin. Rosalie has had to alter both my gowns to make them smaller. I bleed so much, and so often, that I know something is wrong, though they will not let me see a doctor.

I am tired and full of tears and blood, but still I have not given up. In the messages Rosalie slips under my plate of soup, messages I read when I sit on the chamber pot, partly hidden from my guards by a screen, there is much hopeful news. The armies of Austria and Prussia are coming nearer, they are winning battle after battle against the rabble revolutionary forces. The Swedish may yet send a fleet to invade Normandy. Peasant armies in the Vendée — oh, thank heaven for the ever faithful Vendéans! — are fighting to restore the throne.

It may yet happen, and I may live to see

it. Paris may come under attack, and the revolution may be destroyed. My Louis-Charles may yet sit on his father's throne.

I am weary, I can write no more. But I can read, until they come for me. I can read this journal, the only thing I have left from my youth. I like to reread it, to relive those happier times, before I learned how cruel the world can be. Before I became Queen Marie Antoinette, when I was simply Archduchess Antonia, living at the court of my dear mother Empress Maria Theresa in Vienna. With all my life ahead of me . . .

ONE

June 17, 1769

My name is Archduchess Maria Antonia, called Antoinette, and I am thirteen years and seven months old, and this is the record of my life.

Writing in this journal is my punishment. Father Kunibert, my confessor, has told me to write down all my sins in this journal so that I may reflect on them and pray for forgiveness.

"Write!" he said, pushing the book toward me, his thick white eyebrows going up, making him look ferocious.

"Write what you have done! Confess!"

"But I have done nothing wrong," I tell him.

"Write it down. Then we will see. Put there everything you did, starting with last Friday. And leave nothing out!"

Very well, I will put down in this book all that I did on the day I went to see Josepha, and what happened afterward, and then I will show Father Kunibert what I have written and make my confession.

Tomorrow I will begin.

June 18, 1769

It is very hard and sad to write what happened, because I am so very sorry that my sister was in such pain. I tried to tell Father Kunibert this, but he just opened the journal and handed me the box of sharpened quills. He is a hard man, as Carlotta says. He does not listen to explanations.

On Friday morning, then, this is what I did.

I borrowed a plain black cloak and hood from my maid Sophie, and put a silver crucifix around my neck such as the Sisters of Mercy wear. I prepared a basket with fresh loaves and a ripe cheese and some strawberries from the palace garden. Without telling Sophie or anyone else where I was going, I went at night to the old abandoned stables where I was sure my sister Josepha was being kept.

Josepha had been missing for a week, ever since she became hot with fever and began to cough. No one would tell me where she was, so I had to find out by asking the servants. Servants know everything that happens in the palace, even what goes on between the master and mistress in the privacy of their bedroom. I found out from Eric, the stable boy who grooms my riding horse Lysander that there was a sick girl in the basement of the old riding school. He had seen the Sisters of Mercy going there at night, and once he saw our court physician Dr. Van Swieten go in and come out again very quickly, holding a handkerchief over his mouth and looking very pale.

I was sure my sister Josepha was there, lying in the dark probably, sick and lonely, waiting to die. I had to go to her. I had to tell her that she was not forgotten or abandoned.

So I wrapped the black cloak around me and went out. The candle I carried guttered in the wind as I crossed the courtyard and made my way along the arcaded walkway and out into the stable yard. There were no lights in the old riding school, no one ever went there and no horses were kept tethered in its stalls.

I tried to keep my thoughts on Josepha, but my fear rose as I entered the dark building with its high domed ceiling. Dim shapes loomed up amid the darkness. When I shone my light on them they turned out to be cupboards for harnesses and empty bins that had once held hay.

All was silent, except for the creaking of the old timbers in the roof and the distant calling of the palace sentinels as they made their rounds. I found steps leading down into more darkness. I started to go down, praying that my candle would not go out, and trying not to think of the stories Sophie liked to tell about the palace ghost, the Gray Lady who walked weeping through the corridors at night and sometimes flew in at the windows.

"Don't be foolish, Antonia," my mother would say when I asked her about the Gray Lady, "there are no ghosts. When we die, we die. We do not live on as disembodied spirits. Only peasants believe such nonsense."

I respected my mother's wisdom, but I wasn't sure about the ghosts. Sophie had seen the Gray Lady several times, she said, and many others had seen her too.

To keep my mind off ghosts I called out to Josepha as I descended the stairs.

I thought I heard a weak cry.

I called out again, and this time I was sure I heard an answer.

But the voice I heard was not my sister's. Josepha had a strong, laughing voice. The voice I heard now was pinched and thin, and terribly anxious.

"Don't come any nearer, whoever you are," it said. "I have the pox. If you come near me you will die."

"I hear you, I'm almost there," I called out, ignoring the warning.

I found her in a small, cell-like room where a lantern hanging from a nail in the wall gave the only light. I could not help but gag, the stench in the room was so overwhelming. A powerful, cloying odor, not the odor of decay or dirt but a sickly, ghastly stench of rot.

From where she lay in her narrow bed Josepha lifted one weak arm as if to ward me off.

"Please, dearest Antonia, turn back. Go back."

I was crying. What the weak lantern-light showed me was monstrous. Josepha's skin was purple, and full of blisters. Her face was swollen and red, her cheeks puffed out grotesquely, and there was blood dripping from her nose. Her eyes were bloodshot.

"I love you," I said through my tears. "I am praying for you." I put down the basket, wondering whether rats would come and eat the food I had brought. But then I thought, the smell in this room is so terrible not even rats would come near.

"I am so thirsty," came the voice from the bed.

I took from my basket the bottle of wine

I had brought and set it beside Josepha's bed. With difficulty she raised herself, reached for the bottle and drank. I could tell she was having trouble swallowing.

"Oh, Antonia," she said when she had put the bottle down, "I have such terrible dreams! Fire coming down, and burning us all up. Mother on fire, screaming. Father, laughing while he watches us all burn."

"It is only the sickness that makes you dream such things. We are all safe, there is no fire." But there is, I thought. There is the fire of the cowpox, that makes Josepha burn with fever and turns her brain to madness.

"You must have medicine, you must get well."

"The sisters give me brandy and valerian, but it doesn't help. I know they have given up on me."

"I have not. I will come back, I promise."

"No. Stay away. Everyone must stay away."

Her voice grew fainter. She was going to sleep. "Dear Antonia . . ."

My tears were falling fast, but I knew I couldn't stay. I couldn't risk being missed. No one knew where I had gone, I hadn't even told Carlotta, with whom I share my bedroom.

So I left Josepha, and went back up the dark stairs and out through the old riding school and back along the torchlit arcade to the palace.

The next day I was in the room when Dr. Van Swieten came to see my mother the empress. My brother Joseph, who is twenty-six and who has just buried his second wife, was also there. Ever since our father died, our mother has looked to Joseph for help in governing her many lands. One day after she dies Joseph will rule them all, so he needs to learn. Already he has the firmness that my mother says all rulers need. But I have heard her say to Count Khevenhüller that Joseph does not yet have the necessary compassion and concern for people that he will need if he is to rule well.

"What of Josepha?" my mother asked the doctor as he bowed and murmured "Your imperial highness."

"It is the black pox."

I saw my mother blanch, and Joseph turn his face away. The black pox was the severest kind of cowpox. No one ever survived it. When there was black pox in Vienna we children were always taken away at once into the country, so that we would not become ill. Servants with black pox were turned out of the palace and sent as far away as possible. None ever returned. And now my sister Josepha was dying of it too.

"It is perfectly horrifying," the doctor was saying. "I have seen it often before. There is no point in trying to preserve life once the pox takes hold. The archduchess cannot be saved. She can only make others ill."

"Is she receiving every care?" I heard my mother ask.

"Of course. The Sisters of Mercy visit her, and the dairymaids." It was well known that dairymaids were spared from being struck down with the cowpox. For some reason, they could care for sick people without fear of becoming sick themselves.

"No one must know who she is," Joseph boomed out. "No one from the court must be allowed near her. We cannot have another outbreak of Pox Fear, like last summer."

Whenever the cowpox appeared, people panicked. The entire town caught the Pox Fear. There were frenzied efforts to escape the sickness. Terrified householders, trying to flee, were trampled or crushed to death.

No one wanted the Pox Fear to invade the palace, where hundreds of servants and officials lived in close quarters and served the empress and our family.

"That is understood," Dr. Van Swieten said. "The archduchess is being kept where no one will find her."

I almost spoke up then, but managed to hold my tongue. Standing beside my mother, I heard her black silk skirts rustling, and was aware that she was trembling.

"I can't lose any more of my children," she was saying. "First my dear Karl, and then Johanna, only eleven when she died, poor girl, and now my lovely Josepha, so young, and about to be married —"

"You have ten of us left, maman." Joseph's voice was cutting. He knew that although he was the eldest son, and our mother's heir, she had preferred Karl, and loved him more. "Surely ten children is a sufficient number."

I am fond of my brother Joseph, but he does not understand what it is to love someone. When our father died four years ago he did not weep, but snorted with contempt.

"He was a lazy do-nothing, surrounded by idle hangers-on," I heard him say. He refused even to lay a wreath on father's grave, though he did offer his arm to mother at the funeral.

Joseph is twenty-six, and has been married twice, but he did not grieve for either of his wives when they died, or for the poor little dead baby his first wife gave him. Joseph is hard for me to understand.

"How much longer will she live?" Joseph asked Dr. Van Swieten.

"A few days perhaps."

"When she dies, have the body taken away quickly. Let there be no announcement. She will not be missed. One excess daughter more or less —"

"Joseph! That will do." My mother spoke firmly, but I could hear the panic in her voice.

But my brother, in his bitterness, went on.

"And I want the body burned. Along with all her clothes and effects."

"Enough! What you propose is unchristian. I will never allow it. You forget yourself."

"Such foolishness!" I heard Joseph mutter. "To believe that some day all the bodies of the dead will sit up in their graves, and come back to life. A priest's fairy tale."

"We will abide by the teachings of the church," my mother said quietly. "We are not heathens, or sectarians. Besides, Josepha is still alive. And while she lives, there is hope. I will retire now to my chapel to pray for her. And I recommend that you do the same."

To the doctor she said, "I want to be informed if there is any change in her condition."

At this I could keep still no longer.

"Oh maman, there is such a terrible change in her. You would not believe it!" Tears ran down my face as I spoke.

My mother looked down at me, her eyes grave. Joseph glared at me in fury. Dr. Van Swieten gasped.

"Explain yourself, Antonia," said mother calmly.

"I have seen her. She is all puffed up, and black and purple, and she smells horrible. And they keep her in a dark rathole under the old riding school, where no one ever goes." I looked up into my mother's eyes. "She's dying, maman. She's dying."

Instead of enfolding me in her black silk skirts, as I expected her to do, my mother took several steps back from me, so that I could no longer smell her familiar smell, a combination of ink and rosewater.

"Your imperial highnesses must withdraw," Dr. Van Swieten said to my mother and Joseph, who were both putting more distance between themselves and me. "I will take charge of her. She will be watched for signs of the black pox." He motioned to one of the tall footmen standing at the back of the large room, waiting for orders.

"Send for my assistant, at once. And the dairymaids."

I was taken to the old guards' quarters and kept there, watched by two village women, one old, one young, until they were certain I was not going to become sick like my sister. All my clothes were taken away and burned, and Sophie sent new clothes. When I was putting them on a note fell out. It was from my sister Carlotta.

"Dearest Antoinette," she wrote, "how brave you were, to visit poor Josepha. Everyone knows what you did. We all have to pretend to disapprove but we admire you. I hope you don't get sick. Joseph is angry. I love you."

July 3, 1769
I have decided not to show this book to Father Kunibert. It will be my record, my private journal, of my life. Mine alone.

So much has happened to me in the past

several weeks. I have been kept away from poor Josepha, who died on the third day after I visited her. I try not to think of her in her suffering, but I know I will never forget how she looked, there in her cot, when I found her.

Father Kunibert says I must reflect on my disobedience, and pray to be forgiven. He says I must be grateful to be alive. But I do not feel grateful, only full of sorrow. I was not allowed to attend the brief funeral mass for Josepha, because I was still being watched by the dairymaids, who inspected my hands and arms and face every morning and evening for pox blisters and murmured to one another and shook their heads over me.

I have thought about death, and how Josepha only had seventeen years on earth, so brief a season! Why do some die and some live? I can write no more about this, I am too full of sorrow.

July 15, 1769
Finally Dr. Van Swieten has let me return to the apartments I share with Carlotta. I do not have the cowpox.

July 28, 1769
This morning Sophie got me up early and

dressed me with extra care. I asked her why but she wouldn't tell me. I knew it had to be something important when I saw her bring out my pale blue silk ball gown with the silver lamé trim and the pink satin rosettes on the bodice.

My hair was brushed and pinned back from my face and a silver-gray wig put over it. The wig was becoming, and made me look very old I thought, especially when Sophie threaded pearls through it.

I have always been told that I look like my father, who was very handsome. Like him I have a wide forehead and large eyes set far apart. My eyes are light blue like my mother's and she likes me to dress in blue to bring out their color.

I could tell, as Sophie dressed me, that she was satisfied with the effect. She smiled to herself and hummed as she worked. Sophie has been my maid ever since I was seven years old and she was fifteen, and she knows me better than anyone, better even than my mother and Carlotta.

When I was ready I was taken into the grand salon where my mother was. There were several men with her, and they all stared hard at me as I entered the room and walked to my mother's side.

"Antonia, dear, this is Prince Kaunitz and this is the Duc de Choiseul." Both men bowed to me and I inclined my head in acknowledgment, feeling the unaccustomed weight of the wig as I did so.

My dancing master Monsieur Noverre came forward and signaled for the court musicians to play. He led me in the polonaise and then the allemande as the gentlemen watched closely. My harp was brought forward and I played several simple tunes — I am not a very accomplished harpist — and I sang an aria by Herr Gluck who had taught me to play the clavichord when I was younger.

Trays of coffee and pastries were brought in and I sat with my mother and the prince and the duke talking of one thing and another. I felt rather foolish in my ball gown but we passed a pleasant half-hour chatting, and I did my best to answer the questions put to me, questions about everything from my religious education to my knowledge of geography and history to my ideas about marriage.

"Naturally you hope to marry one day," Prince Kaunitz said amiably. "And what is your idea of the perfect wife?"

"One who loves her husband dearly, as my mother loved my father."

"And presents him with sons," the Duc de Choiseul added.

"Yes, of course. And daughters too, if the lord wills it."

"To be sure. Daughters too."

"Do you believe, archduchess, that a wife must obey her husband in all things?"

I thought for a moment. "I hope that when I marry, my husband and I will decide together what is best, and act as one."

The two men looked at one another, and I thought I saw a faint look of amusement in their faces.

"Thank you, Archduchess Antonia, for your frankness and your courtesy."

My mother and the men rose and walked the length of the enormous room, deep in conversation.

"Physically, she is perfect," the duke said. "Her education has been inadequate, but she can be taught. There is great charm —"

"And a good heart, a very good heart," I heard my mother add.

They took their time, walking and talking, Prince Kaunitz gesticulating, the duke more measured, more calculated in his movements and his tone.

"This is the alliance we have long hoped for," I heard my mother say. "The union of

Hapsburg and Bourbon will secure our fortune, long after I am gone."

"Austria is not our enemy," the duke said. "Britain is. We must fortify ourselves against Britain."

"And we must fortify ourselves against Prussia," Prince Kaunitz countered. "The interests of both Austria and France will be served by this marriage. And the sooner it is made, the better."

August 1, 1769
I am to marry the dauphin Louis, heir to the throne of France.

The Duc de Choiseul brought me his picture. He is ugly, but the duke assures me that he is very pleasant and well-mannered, though a bit shy.

August 5, 1769
I can't think of anything except going to France. Carlotta and I talk and talk about our futures. She is betrothed to Ferdinand of Naples — the prince Josepha was to marry — and poor Josepha's trousseau is being altered to fit Carlotta, who is much stouter.

We promise to write to each other often after we are married, but how often will we see each other, once I am in France and she is in Naples?

We are both very curious about what it will be like, sleeping with our husbands. We know very little, but we know it has to do with having babies and with what Father Kunibert calls the wickedness of fornication.

"What is fornication?" I asked Father Kunibert one day.

"Wicked carnality. Sinful congress between people who are not married — or who are married to others."

"But what is it exactly?"

"Ask your mother," he told me curtly. "After fourteen children, she is an expert."

But my mother was very vague on the subject when I asked her, talking of a wife's loving obligation to please her husband, whatever he asked of her.

"What will he ask of me?"

"That is between you and Louis."

It was no use. I tried asking Sophie, but she merely shook her head and said "You will find out."

Finally I decided to ask the servants. One day after I had returned from riding on Lysander, and was in the stables watching the horse receive his rubdown, I approached Eric.

Eric is eighteen or nineteen, strongly built and with dark hair and deep blue eyes. I like him and feel safe when I am with him. Once, when Lysander had bolted, Eric had come after us and stopped the runaway horse and I have always been grateful to him for that. He also told me where to find Josepha, something I have never confided to anyone — not my mother, not Father Kunibert when I made my confession to him, not Joseph when he came to me and demanded to know how I had discovered where our poor sick sister was being kept.

So I said to Eric, as he was brushing Lysander, I am to be married soon, and no one will tell me what to expect. Will you tell me?

Eric stopped brushing the horse, letting the brush rest against Lysander's powerful brown haunch. Without meeting my gaze, he said, "That is not for me to tell you, your highness."

"But you've always answered my questions before. I count on you."

He trembled and dropped the brush into the straw. Quickly, before I had time to realize what was happening, he reached for me and kissed me.

I was on fire. I could not think, or breathe, or react. It was the most delicious moment of my life.

31

He released me. "There," he said, breathless, "that is what you can expect. That and more. And if you tell anyone about this" — he bent and picked up the brush and began brushing Lysander's coat again — "I will be dismissed — or shot by the guards."

"I won't say anything." I was smiling. I wanted him to kiss me again.

August 10, 1769
Eric will be accompanying me to France, along with Sophie and my laundress and my new tutor, Abbé Vermond, who is teaching me to speak proper French instead of the court French we speak here in Vienna. The abbé says we all have thick German accents.

As for who else will go with me, I will not find out for many months. Mother says I am expected to leave my old life behind when I go to France. I must become a Frenchwoman, so that my husband's subjects will find me acceptable as their queen.

"You must become as much like the French as possible," maman told me, "but in your heart and blood you will always be a Hapsburg. By your marriage you will save Austria. As long as Hapsburg and Bourbon are allied by marriage, the Monster Frederick of Prussia will remain at bay. He cannot devour us while we have the loyal support of the French."

Abbé Vermond is doing what he can to make me understand these high matters, but I confess that what interests me far more are the French styles.

Every week I receive dozens of dolls from Paris, dressed in the fashions to be worn next spring. From these I am expected to choose my trousseau.

Carlotta is very jealous. Her trousseau will not fill more than ten trunks, while mine will easily fill a hundred, maman says. I have lined up the dolls underneath the windows of our bedroom and each day, after I have heard mass and had my lessons with Abbé Vermond, I walk in front of the long row of dolls and pretend that they are court ladies, bowing to me.

September 7, 1769
A few days ago we came here to Greifelsbrunn, one of our hunting lodges. My brother Joseph is a great hunter and my mother follows the hunt in her carriage. Every night the animals killed that day are laid out on the grass for all to see, stags and boar and aurochs, their antlers and tusks gleaming in the torchlight.

I go for long walks with Carlotta. The air is crisp in the forest and already the leaves on the great trees are turning gold and red.

I am growing taller. Sophie measured me. I have put on weight and the dressmakers in Paris who are creating my trousseau have been told to make the bodices of my gowns wider and longer.

I am growing, but General Krottendorf still has not arrived. (General Krottendorf is the name we give to a woman's menstrual period in my family.) My mother is anxious about this because I cannot be married until I am ready to have babies, and I am to leave for France in only seven months. Carlotta got her first visit from the general when she was fourteen. Josepha was fifteen.

I hope that all the exercise I am getting here at Greifelsbrunn will have a good effect, and make me grow up faster. I go riding with my mother or Carlotta and feel quite invigorated afterwards. I linger in the stables in order to see Eric. I have told no one about his kissing me, but I think about it often. I want to be alone with him, so that he can kiss me again.

I know Father Kunibert would disapprove, especially now that I am betrothed to Prince Louis. But I can't help it. My feelings are strong.

September 10, 1769
We are still here at Greifelsbrunn and it is a warm autumn night with a light rain falling outside. I am alone, Carlotta is sick and maman sent her back to Schönbrunn this morning to consult Dr. Van Swieten.

I went riding today with Eric. I was going to go alone, Carlotta being gone and the others off hunting, but the stable master stopped me and said that the woods could be dangerous and I needed an escort. He ordered Eric to go with me.

My heart was pounding, but I tried not to look too pleased as Eric brought his horse up and we set off.

I challenged him to a race and won — of course he let me win, I imagine. We rode through deep woods and then came to the shore of a tranquil green lake. I had never before ridden so far from the lodge and didn't know that this lake existed.

Eric dismounted and then lifted me down off Lysander's back. The feel of his strong, warm hands made me almost dizzy with happiness.

We walked the horses along the lake shore. It was a tranquil scene, the calm of the dark limpid water and a screen of yellow-leaved maples on the far bank. The sky was overcast, and soon raindrops began plashing into the water.

"Here, let's take shelter here," Eric said, leading me into a thicket. The rain began to fall harder, and my skirt was getting muddy. Already my shoes were nearly ruined.

An outcropping of rocks led into a dim cave, and I pulled Eric inside. There was no sound but the noise of the rain. I looked at him, willing him to kiss me, wondering if I had the courage to kiss him.

"Your highness," he said softly, "I long to possess you. But I must not — we must not."

"Only this once," I told him. "Then never again."

I sat down on the soft moss and pulled him down beside me. Then he kissed me again and again, and I thought, I want to die, I can't bear this excitement, this joy. We kissed and kissed, but that was all. There was none of what Father Kunibert would have called fornication.

Eric was very tender, and confessed that he had loved me for a long time. He told me I was beautiful, and kind, and that he was not worthy to hold my horse, much less be my lover. He confessed that he met girls from the castle, chambermaids and kitchen girls, from time to time and slept with them and that once he had slept with an older married woman who was one of my mother's ladies-in-waiting.

"Which one?" I asked him, but he would not say.

"Your highness," he said at length, getting up and helping me to my feet, "you are far too young and far too highborn to become infatuated with a servant. You must save your desire for your husband."

I confess I cried then, remembering the picture I had been sent of Prince Louis.

"But he is ugly!" I burst out. "He looks like a pig!"

Eric laughed. "Pig or not, he will be a great king."

"But that is nothing to me." I knew even as I said the words that that was not quite true.

"It is a great deal to your family."

I didn't want this beautiful, spellbound afternoon to end. We rode back to the lodge slowly, and when at last we reached the stables Eric helped me dismount with unusual gentleness. He took my hand and kissed it.

"Your highness," he said, bowing, and led the horses toward the stalls.

I made my way to the lodge, aware that my skirts were wet and mud-stained and my hair, which Sophie had dressed simply that morning, was in disarray.

As soon as she saw me Sophie got a knowing look in her eye, but said nothing. She merely helped me out of my wet clothes and ordered the groom to bring hot water for my bath.

I am still wrapped in a warm cocoon of contentment. I wonder whether Eric is thinking of me. I am sure that he is.

When Josepha died, I thought to myself, how sad that she had to die before ever having known love. Now I realize that if I die tomorrow, I will not be like my sister. I have known love, I do know it, and nothing else matters.

October 11, 1769
There is to be a ball at court to celebrate my engagement. I will be the center of attention. It will be a sort of rehearsal for the balls and court ceremonies I will face once I get to France.

Maman says I must become accustomed to being stared at and judged, especially by the French who think they are superior to everyone else.

The truth is, I like being watched and admired, I don't mind it at all. I love balls and parties, getting dressed up and hearing the orchestra play and dancing. I'm sure it is wicked to think this, but the truth is, I know that I am very pretty and am becoming prettier all the time. I am the most beautiful of all my sisters, that has been everyone's opinion for years.

Among the loveliest of the ladies at my mother's court I would not stand out, but in a few years, I imagine, I will be a worthy rival to them. The Duc de Choiseul says that the women of the French court are far more beautiful, and more sophisticated and stylish, than those of Vienna. We will see.

Everyone refers to me now as "the dauphine," and I wear a ring my fiancé sent me, along with another picture of himself for me to wear around my neck. I dislike being reminded of his looks.

November 1, 1769

My ball was a great success. Afterwards I was so worn out that I slept for nearly an entire day.

The gown I wore, which was of pale green silk with rows of cream-colored lace, was sent from Paris and was much admired. The bodice was lined with whalebone and made my waist look even smaller than it really is.

Prince Kaunitz danced with me.

"Madame la dauphine, you do great credit to the House of Hapsburg," he said, bending to kiss my hand. "You have become a most polished and gracious young lady."

"Regal, very regal," I heard the Duc de Choiseul murmur as he came to pay his respects. "But you must be sure to wear that device the dentist made for you every day." A dentist from Versailles has been working on my teeth and he is very rough and cruel. I dislike him and swear at him in German, which he does not understand.

My looks and behavior at the ball pleased maman, who smiled her approval. When Joseph came up to dance with me he had a smirk of satisfaction on his often sour face.

"I salute you, sister," he said as he led me in the polonaise. "I had not thought you capable of such poise."

There were so many people at my ball that I could not possibly greet them all, but I spoke to as many of them as I could, and accepted their compliments and good wishes. I wore the ring the dauphin Louis had sent me, and this was much remarked upon.

I wished that Eric could have been at the

ball, dressed as a captain of dragoons perhaps in a fine uniform. He would have outshone even the most handsome of the Poles. How I would have loved to dance with him!

November 5, 1769
Carlotta is leaving. The courtyard is full of coaches and wagons being filled with her trunks and boxes.

We embrace and cry, and I tell her I will always be thinking of her and will write often.

"Oh, Antonia, I am so afraid! What if he hates me and rejects me?"

It was unlike Carlotta to show weakness. I felt sorry for her.

"He cannot reject you, you are Archduchess Caroline of Austria. Your birth is higher than his."

"But he may not find me pleasing. I may — offend his eyes."

I did not know how to answer that. Carlotta and I both knew that she was short and very plump, with features that could not be called anything but plain.

"If he has any sense he will value you for your shrewdness and strong will. Together you will make healthy children."

She blanched. "I hope so."

I was allowed to ride in the coach that escorted Carlotta for five miles along the road that led south toward the mountains dividing the Hapsburg lands from Piedmont. When we reached the point where the family coach had to turn back, I got out and went over to embrace Carlotta one last time.

"Be happy, dearest sister. Write me long letters. Tell me everything."

She clung to me, then forced herself to get back into the coach. We stood and watched, waving, as the horses picked up speed and took her from us.

I will be waiting for her first letter.

November 19, 1769

With mother's help and Sophie's I have at last ordered my trousseau. I am to have forty-seven ball gowns in silk and embroidered brocade, and an equal number of afternoon dresses. Twenty court gowns are being prepared, with more to be made for me once I arrive in my new home. French fashions change so rapidly that there is a danger my entire trousseau will be completely out of style by next spring.

The cruel French dentist, who talks ceaselessly while he torments me, says that only certain colors are acceptable each season in Versailles, so that if my gowns are in the wrong colors I will seem unstylish.

"It is for the dauphine to set the style, not mimic it!" I told him, speaking with some difficulty as he had his fingers in my mouth at the time.

"Spoken like a Frenchwoman!" he answered with some spirit, amused at me. "Perhaps there is hope for you, little archduchess."

January 14, 1770
General Krottendorf is here. Now I can be married. The dauphin sent me a gift. I opened it when I was alone, thinking it would be a love token of some kind. It was a gold filigree box of dried mushrooms.

February 20, 1770
Poor Carlotta is miserable. She wrote me a long letter, full of homesickness, about how much she missed me and all the family.

She says Ferdinand is cold to her, and her relatives hate her and think she is haughty and superior. She has no one to speak German to, not even a priest. The entire court condemns her because she is not yet pregnant. On that subject she writes guardedly, probably she fears that her letters will be read by spies. Yet it is clear from what she writes that her wedding night was horrifying, and she hates being married almost as much as she hates being away from Vienna.

At least the Bay of Naples is beautiful, she says, and it is sunny and warm there all winter long. She has a lovely place to be wretched in.

February 25, 1770
Finally I have learned about what happens between husband and wife when they are in bed together.

My brother Joseph came to me and said that he heard I had been asking the servants about what to expect on my wedding night.

"Asking such things of servants is not proper," he said. "On matters of sex you must speak only to your husband or your relatives, your doctor or your priest."

"But priests know nothing of sex. It is forbidden to them."

"If only that were true," Joseph said ruefully, raising his eyebrows in disapproval. "But don't let us become distracted. Here is what you need to know. It is all about the sword and the scabbard."

He touched the elaborate gold handle of

the ceremonial sword he wore at his waist and slowly drew it from the long thin leather scabbard that held it.

"You see how perfectly the sword fits in its scabbard, how easily it can be put in and drawn out?" He illustrated his point by taking the sword out completely and then replacing it, several times.

"Now, men and women are made just like that. Men have swords and women have scabbards. They fit perfectly — well, usually they do."

"The very first time the sword is put into its scabbard there is a slight hindrance, and a little blood. But that is soon over, and the entire operation goes smoothly."

He smiled with satisfaction at his own cleverness in expounding the mystery of sex with such dispatch.

"Oh, and there is much pleasure to be had from the entire experience," he added. "And babies are made."

"If it all goes so well, why is Carlotta miserable?" I showed Joseph our sister's letter. He read it, then shrugged.

"You must keep in mind, Antonia, that Carlotta is ugly, and very disagreeable. No doubt Ferdinand dislikes her. I was afraid this would happen when we arranged the match. Josepha would have been much more to his taste — to any man's taste. When a husband dislikes his wife the sword is not strong and firm but limp and weak. It cannot be put into the scabbard."

"And will Prince Louis like me, do you think?"

"I have no doubt that he will. Any man would."

I asked my brother about the gold box Prince Louis sent me with its puzzling contents of dried mushrooms.

"Maybe it's an aphrodisiac," he said, half to himself.

"What's that?"

"Never mind. You can ask the prince when you see him. It won't be long now."

March 5, 1770
Goose-Droppings. That is the color of my new gown for the welcoming supper we are giving for the French from Versailles.

It is the latest fashion craze at the French court, I am told, to wear gowns in the colors of animal droppings. Imagine! One of last season's colors was Squashed Toad.

March 14, 1770
All Vienna is decorated with torches and colored lanterns. Lit candles make the windows

gleam, and there are fireworks at night and music and dancing. Night and day the palace kitchens are busy with baking and roasting, pastry-making and stewing. Chickens, lambs, pigs and geese turn on dozens of spits over high-banked fires, and the air is full of the rich scent of cooked meat.

There are banquets nearly every night and during the day I am brought before the judges and notaries to sign the documents that are turning me from a subject of my mother into a subject of my future husband's grandfather, the king of the French, King Louis XV.

Six months ago I barely knew the name of the King of France. Today, thanks to my studies with Abbé Vermond, I can recite the lineage of King Louis going back three hundred years and the significant events of his ancestors' reigns.

I know the names of most of the French provinces and can locate them on a map of France that hangs on the wall beside my bed. I can tell the story of Jeanne d'Arc, of the saintly King Louis IX and the cynical King Henry IV, who said "Paris is worth a mass," and became a Catholic though he was a Protestant before. I know that the River Seine runs through Paris and that the great cathedral in the city is called Notre Dame, Our Lady.

Soon I will see it all for myself.

April 21, 1770

Eric has sent me a gift, a little dog. I call her Mufti. She is so small she fits inside my sleeve.

March 21, 1770

April 1, 1770

Tonight was my wedding. Instead of a groom I had my brother Ferdinand who stood beside me in the candlelit church and recited the vows that Prince Louis will recite when I get to France.

All the court was present at the ceremony, which was very beautiful and solemn. Mother took me down the aisle, limping on her sore leg which has been hurting her since Christmas but happy nonetheless. I had a beautiful silver gown and wore a long lace veil sent from one of Prince Louis's aunts. It was to have been her wedding veil but she never married. I wonder why.

Mother says I can take Lysander and Mufti to France with me.

April 6, 1770

This afternoon I had a sad visit with mother

who summoned me to talk to her about my new life in France.

She rose from her desk, smiling, and kissed me when I came into her private study. As usual her desk was piled with papers. Her old yellow cat slept between two of the piles, on a length of soft wool she keeps there for his comfort.

I was suddenly overcome with sorrow, and could not help crying. I embraced mother and smelled her rosewater scent.

"Oh, maman, I can't bear to leave you! How I will miss you. Now I know how Carlotta felt when she left, why she cried herself to sleep so many nights."

Mother led me to the wide bow window and we sat together looking out at the garden. The earliest roses were just beginning to bloom, red and pink and yellow, and the fruit trees were almost in full leaf.

"I know what you are feeling, Antonia," mother said at length. "When I married I had to leave behind much that was familiar. It was a step into the unknown."

She reached for my hand and held it in her lap as she talked, occasionally patting it absentmindedly. It was unlike her to do this, and I knew it meant that she was allowing herself to show how much she loved me. It was only because I was leaving that she unbent this way, I was sure. Usually she stayed strong, and affectionately detached.

"You must remember three things, my dearest child. Go to mass regularly, always do as the French do, no matter how outlandish their customs seem, and make no decisions without asking advice."

"Whose advice, maman? Prince Louis's?"

Her mouth turned down and for a moment a troubled look came into her eyes.

"The prince is still young, as you are. He is not yet — seasoned. Ask the Duc de Choiseul, or Count Mercy, or one of the Austrians. Kaunitz will give you some names of those he trusts at the French court before you leave.

"Oh and be careful whom you speak to in confidence, among the servants. Many are paid informants."

"I will speak only to Sophie."

Mother sighed and patted my hand.

"You will overcome any obstacles you encounter, Antonia. You have a good heart, and stout Hapsburg courage. Never forget who you are and whose blood runs in your veins. Be proud. And try, for all our sakes, to be prudent."

"I will, maman. Truly I will."

After I left mother I went out for a walk, to take a last look at things I have loved. I went out into the pasture beyond the dairy and smelled the scent of the rich loamy earth. I visited the old riding school and said a prayer for the soul of Josepha, trying in vain not to picture her as she lay, grotesque in her pain, on her deathbed. I looked under the eaves for the nests of starlings and heard the tiny cries of the baby birds. It made me very sad to realize I would not be there to watch them grow and see them fledge as I always had before.

Now it is I who am the fledgling.

TWO

April 23, 1770
I can hardly write, the coach is shaking so violently back and forth.

We are in the third day of our long journey. I miss my family. I have Sophie with me, and Mufti, and Eric, who as Lysander's groom was included in my traveling party. When I lean out the window of the coach I can see him, at the far end of the long procession of coaches and wagons, riding with the other stable servants. Every time I hug Mufti I think of Eric — though I am trying now to think of Prince Louis, since I am married to him and will be with him before long.

Last night we stayed with the monks of Himmelsgau Abbey, a place too small for all of us. Most of the servants had to sleep under wagons and tents in the courtyard, and it rained, and everyone was uncomfortable. The abbot was very unfriendly to the French dignitaries and they took offense. We were given very little to eat and I am hungry.

April 30, 1770
We have been traveling for ten days and it is

very tiring. At night I fall into bed, my muscles aching from the constant jolting of the coach along the rough roads. Sometimes we have to get out and walk, as the roads are so muddy our coach cannot take the extra weight of passengers without becoming bogged down.

We broke an axle two days ago and had to wait for several hours while it was repaired.

The countryside through which we are journeying is very beautiful, with good dark rich farmland and stands of fine trees. The farmers are ploughing and sowing new seed. They stop to watch us pass, staring in wonderment at the painted coaches and servants in their blue velvet livery — dirtied by the rain and mud, but elegant nonetheless.

We are still in German-speaking lands but the villagers here speak differently and I have trouble understanding them. We are almost in France now.

May 15, 1770

It is evening now, and I am here in the chateau of Compiègne. I have an hour to myself. I must set down what happened yesterday while it is still fresh in my mind, because it was all so strange. So very different from what I had expected.

Yesterday I met Louis.

My traveling party arrived at the edge of a great forest. It was late in the afternoon, and we had been on the road since early morning. As usual I was sore and bruised from the punishing rocking and heaving of the coach.

We stopped at a bridge and I could see that there were a number of coaches and riders already there, waiting for us. I got out of the coach and one of the French officials approached me, making a low bow.

"Madame, I am to take you to the prince."

"Just as I am? So bedraggled from riding all day?"

"He prefers to meet you informally. He dislikes ceremony."

I remembered what my mother had said, do as the French do, no matter how odd — or did she say outrageous? Tucking Mufti into the sleeve of my gown, where she customarily rode when I went out, I went with my escort over the bridge and into the forest, leaving behind the others, who were watching us while pretending not to.

All around us was silence and dimness. The immense old oaks and chestnuts spread their branches to make a canopy over our heads, while at our feet spread new green shoots and the first spring flowers. I was charmed, it was like something out of a storybook.

"The prince comes here," my guide explained, "when he desires to be away from the cares and burdens of court life. He has built himself a small house. A retreat, if you like."

I could see, among the trees, a low wooden hut with a thatched roof. Gray smoke curled upward from the chimney.

"I must caution you, your highness," the Frenchman said to me as we approached the dwelling, "that the prince, who is of a retiring disposition, is somewhat wary of strangers —"

As he spoke I saw, through the one window of the low hut, a round, frightened face peering out at us. It was Prince Louis. I recognized him at once from the portraits I had been sent. The face disappeared almost immediately.

"He does know that I am coming?"

"We thought it best not to tell him the exact day of your arrival, as he tends to become — agitated, at the thought of meeting new people."

An awful thought occurred to me. "But he does know that I am coming, that we are to be married." Indeed we were married already, for I had gone through the wedding ceremony in Vienna, with my brother taking Prince Louis's place.

"Oh, of course. He has been expecting you these many months."

We came to the low door of the hut.

"Your highness, it is I, Chambertin. I have brought you a visitor. A very special, charming visitor."

Silence. Then, as if from far away, a choked voice.

"Go away."

My companion waited for a moment, his composure unruffled by the curt response, then called out again.

"She has come a very long way, just to see you. Please let us in."

Again the choked voice from the other side of the door. "I am busy. Come back next week."

I turned to go. "The prince is occupied. I can return tomorrow, after I have had a bath, and some food —"

"Please, your highness. I know how to deal with his moods."

Chambertin lifted his hand to knock on the door, and at the same instant Mufti, who was in my sleeve, emerged from the froth of lace and barked sharply.

Almost at once the door opened a crack, and Louis peered out.

"Is that a dog? I like dogs."

"This is Mufti, your highness. I brought her all the way from Vienna." I held her out toward the prince, who opened the door to let us in.

The interior of the hut was dark, save for a fire in the hearth and lantern on the wall. On long tables were twigs and stems and bits of bark and leaves, each accompanied by a sheet of paper with careful hand-writing. Shelves on the walls held jars and baskets, and in a glass-fronted cabinet were displays of moths and butterflies. The remains of the prince's dinner — a plate of cold meat, a hunk of cheese with the knife still in it, a loaf of black bread and a mug of beer — were on a low bench by the fire.

Prince Louis stared at us, wide-eyed, taking in my high-piled blond hair, coming loose here and there as a result of the day's wear and tear, my blue silk day-dress and pearl necklace, my finery in sharp contrast to the bare, rough interior of the hut and to his own attire. He was dressed like a farmer in pantaloons and a tunic of coarse brown cloth.

I held Mufti out to him and said, "She won't bite."

Some of the alarm in his face receded as he took the little dog in his arms and stroked her. He smiled — a lovely, child-like smile. I was touched.

"I know who you are," the prince said after a long pause. "I sent you some mushrooms. Did you receive them?"

"Yes. Thank you."

"I am making a grand catalog of all the plants in the forest. When it is completed I shall go on to make a catalog of the insects. No one has ever done it before."

"What a worthy endeavor."

"My grandfather doesn't think so." Louis's tone was bitter. "He thinks little of me. But he will like you, you are pretty."

"I'm glad you think so. Will you show me some of your plants?"

Prince Louis seemed to lose his shyness as he led me around the hut, pointing out one bit of foliage after another. He showed me drawings he had made, dozens of them, and I said I thought they were very good.

"I suppose I will have to marry you," he remarked after a time, looking at me balefully.

"It is expected of us."

For one alarming moment I thought he might cry. But he only reached for my hand and put it to his lips.

"Then I shall."

"If your highness is ready, we ought to rejoin the others," said Chambertin.

Louis sighed, then handed Mufti back to me. He doused the fire and put on a frayed black greatcoat that hung on a peg by the door.

"Very well then," he said, squaring his shoulders, "let us go."

It was all so surprising to me, I am still pondering the experience. This cold, sad boy is to be my husband, and to rule France?

May 18, 1770

I am now dauphine. Louis and I were married yesterday by the Archbishop of Rheims, with a great crowd looking on in the chapel at Versailles.

My heart went out to poor Louis, who was so ill at ease and restless. I held his hand as we walked through the long galleries of the palace between rows of onlookers and I could feel him trembling. He repeated his vows before the archbishop in a low voice, stumbling over the words. I said my vows clearly and did not falter. Maman would have been proud of me.

May 24, 1770

I am a wife — yet not a wife. Louis comes to my bed each night as he is bound to do, but turns his back to me and snores. I am lonely. I am afraid I do not please him. What am I to do?

June 15, 1770

Everyone has descended on me at once. I was awakened this morning not by Sophie, who usually brings me my morning chocolate, but by the Comtesse de Noailles, who told me to put on a dressing gown as Dr. Boisgilbert was coming to examine me.

At the sound of Dr. Boisgilbert's name Louis, who had been sleeping restlessly beside me, sat up quickly and, without waiting to summon Chambertin, who usually dressed him, quickly put on his trousers over his nightshirt and ran out of the room.

I was spared no embarrassment. The doctor quickly determined that I was not pregnant ("The hymen is intact," he remarked matter-of-factly to the countess), and gave his opinion that my failure to experience my monthly bleeding was due to nervousness.

"Your royal highness," he said to me when I had refastened my dressing gown and recovered some of my dignity, "I am informed that the prince shares your bed each night. The king has asked me to ask you whether he has attempted to consummate your marriage."

"We are — as friends, as brother and sister," I told him.

"It is as I thought. The boy is as yet too young. He must mature."

Soon after Dr. Boisgilbert left I received a message that the Duc de Choiseul would be calling on me. I summoned Sophie, who dressed me and hurriedly arranged my hair.

"Monsieur," I began when the duke was ushered in, "I am aware that everyone is disappointed that I am not yet pregnant. But it is not my fault. Louis is still a boy. He acts like a boy, not a man."

"I fear he may always be a boy — unless he is led in a more desirable direction. It is up to you to lead him. There must be a son. Several sons. Entice him. Seduce him. It is what I brought you here for." Having delivered that abrupt message, he left.

Count Mercy, who came later that afternoon, was more practical. As my mother's representative at the French court he was used to solving problems. And unlike the duke, he was sympathetic to me.

He bowed, then came to sit beside me, ignoring the strict rules prevailing at Versailles about who could and who could not sit in the presence of royalty.

"Dearest Antonia," he said, speaking in German, "how very distressing and awkward all this must be for you. In a strange place, among strangers, with so much expected of you. It is a great deal to take on, at so young an age." He put a consoling arm around me, and I began to feel a little less alone.

"I have spoken to Dr. Boisgilbert," the count said, "and I think I understand what is going on. Prince Louis is unable to take the lead, as a man needs to, in the combat of love. Am I right?"

I nodded.

"So you, madame, must learn to take the lead for him." He patted my hand and stood up. "I know a lady who can help you in that task. You will meet her tomorrow. Her name is Madame Solange, and she is very charming. I know you will like her. She belongs to a world you know little of, I think. The French call it the demimonde. She is not respectable, but in her own arena she is without peer. Pay close attention and you will learn a great deal from her."

June 16, 1770

What an afternoon I have spent! I am quite enraptured by Madame Solange, who is one of the most beautiful and delightful women I have ever met. I know my mother would not approve of my friendship with her, my mother disapproves of courtesans and orders her Chastity Commission to fine them and send them away from Vienna. But I like Madame Solange very much and hope to see her again.

She invited me to her apartments which were small but tastefully decorated in white with gilded moldings. A flowery, spicy scent filled the rooms which were lit by dozens of glowing candles, the curtains being drawn against the afternoon glare.

I felt myself relax, basking in the delicious scent and soft light and in the warm, caressing voice in which the smiling Solange spoke to me.

"Madame la dauphine, you do me honor. Please join me." She led me into her boudoir, where an ornate bed of carved mahogany with a red velvet canopy stood against walls hung with glimmering pale silk. Madame Solange opened a wardrobe of polished wood and brought out a nightgown gossamer sheer and trimmed with fine lace and pink ribbons.

"This would be lovely on you, I think," she said, handing me the delicate garment, which when I took it, weighed almost nothing. It was much more immodest than anything in my trousseau, and at the thought of wearing it I blushed.

"Pink cheeks become you, your highness. With your blond hair and blue eyes and smooth white skin, and your trim figure, you are like a little love-doll, every man's dream of pleasure."

"But not my husband's," I said.

"That will change, I hope. We must make you irresistible."

She talked to me then, at some length, about matters of love and lovemaking, describing to me ways of stroking and caressing a man, of playfully teasing him, making him want me. As she spoke I could not help thinking of Eric, and the desire I had seen in his eyes and the feel of his lips on mine. Try as I would, I could not force myself to think of Louis, with his ungainly, overstuffed body and sad, plain features.

But I listened, and asked questions, and by the time the afternoon was over I felt much older and wiser in the ways of the world. Merely being in the presence of so experienced a woman as Madame Solange was a lesson in worldliness, for she spoke with such frankness about the body and its natural needs, as if sex were as normal as eating or sleeping.

I thought of Father Kunibert and his talk of wicked carnality, and remembered too my mother's cautions about the French, how they are candid and liberal-minded and how this can seem welcome yet be very dangerous.

I am determined to use what I have learned, to make my husband desire me. If only I could talk to Carlotta, how much I would have to tell her! I don't dare put my thoughts down in a letter to her, as all our correspondence is read by spies.

I have begun locking this journal because Count Mercy warned me not to trust my French chamberwomen, who are paid by Choiseul to find out everything they can about my private life. Of course, I imagine that most of them cannot read, and so could not decipher what I write here.

June 18, 1770
Last night Madame Solange helped me prepare myself and my bedchamber for my husband's nightly visit. I put on the revealing nightgown, loosened my hair so that it fell in long curls down my back instead of letting

Sophie braid it as she usually does, and together we scented the room with a potpourri of cloves and vanilla.

We lit small candles and madame made me a gift of some slippery satin sheets for the bed. Madame Solange tinted my lips and cheeks with rouge, which made me look very grown up.

Then she left and I waited for Louis to arrive.

He did not come until after ten o'clock, and I was very drowsy. He was dirty and sweaty, as he had been working alongside some laborers who were digging a new wine cellar. His clothes were full of mud and he dropped them on the carpet and clumped heavily over to the bed, pulling on his nightshirt.

"What's that smell?" he asked me. "It makes me want to sneeze."

He started to lie down and then caught sight of me in my thin nightgown, lit by the soft candlelight.

He fairly leapt out of bed, startled.

He shouted an obscenity. "Cover yourself! And take that paint off your face! What are you, a common whore?"

I wanted to flee, I felt so confused and ashamed. But I am not a coward. I stood my ground.

"I only wanted to please you, Louis. So that there will be love between us." I found a handkerchief and wiped my face, and tied on a dressing gown over the beautiful nightgown.

Louis climbed back into bed. I got in beside him, hardly knowing what to do or say. Had I made everything worse by trying to seduce him? I had earned his trust; had I now forfeited it?

We lay side by side, in silence, for what seemed like an hour. I couldn't sleep. I wondered if Louis was awake. He wasn't snoring, so I assumed he must be awake too.

The candles began to gutter in their holders, then to burn out. In the dimness, I felt Louis stir. He sat up in bed, resting against the pillows.

I heard his breathing.

"Are you awake?"

"Yes."

I felt his large hand on my shoulder. It was an affectionate gesture he sometimes made, almost a comradely one, resting his hand there. After a long pause he began to talk.

"It was never supposed to be me, you know. It was supposed to be my father. He was the next heir."

I knew what he meant, for Abbé Vermond had taught me the family tree of the Bourbons. The king, Louis XV, had a son who died young, making his eldest surviving son, my husband, heir to the throne.

"But he died. All I have left of him is his old black coat, the one I wear when I go into the forest. He never taught me to take his place. He didn't expect to die, you see."

"Yes, I understand."

"I can't do what they all want of me."

"You can — we can together. I will help you."

"Not everyone can be a king."

I sat up myself then, and looked over at my glum husband.

"You could give up the throne, I suppose. It has been done before."

Louis snorted. "They would never let me. My grandfather, Choiseul, all of them. They would sooner I died."

"We could run off to America. Disguise ourselves. You could become a lieutenant of artillery and I could be your laundress."

He laughed.

"General Lafayette is looking for volunteers."

"But if you went to America you couldn't finish your catalog of the forest."

"I want to stay," Louis said decidedly. "I

just don't want to be king."

"It may not happen for some time yet," I said.

"My grandfather is growing old. Boisgilbert says he cannot last long."

I decided to risk asking about the thing I was most anxious about.

"Louis, do you dislike me?" He turned his face away.

"No," he said, his voice very low.

"Then why —"

"I cannot. Do not ask me why. I cannot." The anguish in his voice was enough to silence me. After a time I said, "I didn't mean to shock you tonight, only to entice you."

"I know."

We went to sleep, curled together like puppies, his hand on my shoulder. Soon I heard his heavy breaths turn to snores. I am growing used to the sound.

August 27, 1770

For months I have been afraid to write about Eric, but now that I keep this journal under lock and key, and keep the key with me at all times, I am going to risk putting down what has happened.

I have seen Eric often since coming to France, but we are never alone. I am chaperoned everywhere, either by my official watchdog the Comtesse de Noailles or by one of my husband's aunts or by someone sent to spy on me by Choiseul or Mercy. So when I am in the stables or out riding Lysander with Eric and others as escort, every word we speak to each other is overheard.

He speaks respectfully to me, and I acknowledge his words and his aid with my horse just as I should, as the dauphine ought to speak to a groom. When our eyes meet, however, there is an unspoken warmth, a secret communication between us.

I am sure Eric knows, for it is common gossip throughout the court, that Louis and I are not married partners in the true sense. Sometimes I imagine that I see a flicker of pity in his eyes, but I am not sure. He is careful to hide his emotions. He is pleasant and deferential to me, and that is all.

Yesterday I was riding with Yolande de Polignac and Eric was with us as escort. We were part of a larger group, including Louis's two brothers and their grooms, but Yolande and I were racing and we got some distance ahead of the others. Lysander stumbled and I was thrown. I was not hurt, merely bruised a little. In a moment Eric had dismounted and was kneeling beside me. I assured him that I was all right, and as he helped me to my feet he whispered to me.

"Your royal highness, I must speak to you."

"Of course, Eric. Come to my levee, I will tell the chamberlain to admit you."

"I mean, I need to speak to you alone. The levee will be full of people."

I thought for a moment.

"I will wait after mass tomorrow to make my confession. When I come out of the confessional, I'll look for you."

Today after mass I made my confession and when I emerged from the side chapel where the confession box is Eric was waiting in the dim vestibule. He looked distracted.

He came toward me, bowed and murmured, "Your royal highness, I am to be married. My father has urged me to marry a Frenchwoman and the stable master has promised that when I marry he will make me an equerry with lodging for myself and my wife."

It took me a moment to realize what I was hearing. My handsome Eric, who loved and wanted me, was marrying someone else. Another woman would have all his ardor, all his sweetness. I envied that other woman, whoever she was.

I composed myself as best I could. "If that is what you truly want, Eric, then I am happy for you — and your wife-to-be, of course."

"It is not what I truly want," he said, his eyes full of anguish. "But that I cannot have, as you know better than anyone."

I looked away, not wanting Eric to see the tears starting in my eyes. I became aware that Madame de Noailles was approaching. I did not worry about her overhearing what we said, as we were speaking in German. But I did not want her to think I was being overly familiar with a servant. She had chastised me several times for that fault.

"Then neither of us has what we want," I whispered, and reached out to squeeze Eric's arm, turning my body so that the countess would not be able to see the gesture.

"Please understand, your royal highness. She is — we are expecting a child. I could have made other arrangements for her, she and the child would have been taken care of without my marrying her. But I am fond of her and when I become an equerry I will be able to provide for a family."

"Madame la dauphine, is this man annoying you?"

"No, countess. He is just telling me the good news that he will soon be married."

The Comtesse de Noailles surveyed Eric from head to toe.

"He is one of your Austrians?"

"Yes. A servant from my mother's court."

"I remind you that her highness Princess Adelaide is waiting for you. You promised to come for a game of piquet this afternoon."

"Of course." I extended my hand to Eric, who took it and kissed it. I turned to follow the countess, who was on her way out of the church, then turned back.

"By the way, you did not tell me the name of your bride."

Eric hesitated. "It is Amélie, your highness. Your chambermaid."

I was so stunned I had to sit down in the closest pew. My own chambermaid! A member of my household appointed by Choiseul, and undoubtedly Choiseul's spy.

Amélie was a sly, self-aware girl, pretty but with an air of challenge about her. Like the other chambermaids, she snickered and joked when she changed the linen on my bed, ignoring the frowns of the Comtesse de Noailles and smirking at her behind her back.

So Eric and Amélie were lovers, and Amélie had become pregnant — while laughing at me because I was still a virgin. I heard the countess calling to me, but could not gather my strength to go with her.

Eric and Amélie, Eric and Amélie. The thought of them stayed with me all afternoon, while I played cards with my husband's aunt Adelaide and attended a reception in the apartments of Madame de Polastron. I was distracted, and I'm afraid my distracted state was noticed and commented on.

I still ponder this unexpected turn of events. Here am I, dauphine, married to a prince who must have sons and cannot beget them, while my chambermaid Amélie is pregnant — and by the man I most desire!

September 15, 1770
A cruel song is being sung at court.

> Little maid, little maid
> What have you been doing?
> Belly big, belly big,
> Who have you been wooing?

Little queen, our dauphine
What have you been doing?
Dancing here, flirting there
When you should be screwing!

The song was about me and my chambermaid, and everyone knew it. I forbade my servants to sing the insulting song.

But Amélie was not the problem; it was the king's grasping, vulgar mistress Madame DuBarry, author of the nasty little ditty, who was my enemy.

I refuse to greet Madame DuBarry, or converse with her, or even admit that she exists. Even if my mother and Count Mercy had not told me to act this way, I would, because courtesans such as Madame DuBarry must not be allowed to run things.

What would life at Schönbrunn have been like if my father's mistress Princess Auersperg had been allowed to influence imperial decisions and govern court society?

Of course Princess Auersperg, who was a gentle and sweet woman, was nothing like Madame DuBarry, with her painted face and vulgar low-cut gowns. And the princess was always discreet, remaining in the background and never pushing herself forward.

I cannot avoid Madame DuBarry entirely, for Louis and I must be in the presence of the king quite often and where the king is, his mistress is — usually in his lap, or draped over the edge of his chair. She struts through his reception rooms in gowns sprinkled with diamonds, and even has clusters of small diamonds on the heels of her shoes, as she shows us proudly, lifting her skirts and circling her feet in the air lasciviously.

The king, who is almost senile, showers her with jewelry, and she shows off each new bauble in the most tasteless way.

One night just to spite her I wore the diamond we call the Hapsburg Sun to a card party in the royal salon. It is an immense yellow diamond, brought from India, and it flashes with a brilliance that outshines torchlight.

When Madame DuBarry saw the remarkable gem at my throat she stared, and then remarked, loudly enough to be heard by everyone, "It takes a real woman to wear a rock like that."

"Or a real lady," I remarked, addressing my companions. "But then, some people know nothing about how ladies ought to dress, or behave. They act like common streetwalkers."

"Does anyone here know a streetwalker who walks her dogs on a ruby leash? Or who sleeps in a solid gold bed? Or who has an income of more than a million livres a year?" DuBarry spoke to the entire company in the room, looking right past me, and no one met her gaze.

"A rich streetwalker is still a streetwalker, wouldn't you say, countess?" I said to the Comtesse de Noailles, who was frantically signaling to me to stop challenging Madame DuBarry with my remarks.

With that Madame DuBarry swept past us all, glittering and shimmering in her finery, and sat down beside the king, who had been drinking a good deal earlier in the evening and now sat in a stupor, a vapid grin on his once handsome face. Coyly his mistress ran one plump, pink-tipped finger down his wrinkled cheek.

"Louis dear, will you buy me a big diamond?"

"Anything, anything," he said, his grin widening. "Take all you want."

She got to her feet and bawled out the name of the royal treasurer, who came forward out of the crowd and bowed to the king.

"Give her what she wants," King Louis

said with a wave of his hand.

"I will attend to it tomorrow, sire."

"Tomorrow!" cried Madame DuBarry, her voice raucous with irritation. "Tomorrow isn't good enough! I want it now!"

"Your majesty," murmured the treasurer, deeply perturbed, and left the room as rapidly as his dignity allowed.

"I believe the Hapsburg Sun is about to go into eclipse," said my witty brother-in-law Stanislaus, the dauphin's eldest brother.

"Perhaps, but there is a new dawn on the horizon" was my rejoinder, and there was a low murmuring in the room, for my meaning was clear. For the moment Madame DuBarry ruled the king, but the king's days were numbered, and before long I would be queen, and would relish banning her and all those like her from court.

THREE

October 9, 1770

There is a definite chill in the air, and not only because summer is turning to fall and there is frost on the grass when I go riding in the early morning.

My husband's brother Stanny — Stanislaus Xavier — is whispering to everyone that he and not Louis should be the heir to the throne.

Stanny is a big, tough boy, nearly as tall as Louis and a bully. He goads Louis, teasing him about his fear of strangers and his love for the forest.

"Off hunting mushrooms again, are we?" he called out to Louis the other day as Louis was going out in his shabby black overcoat.

"None of your business," Louis mumbled.

"This sudden urge to go away couldn't have anything to do with the arrival of my future bride, could it?" Stanny teased. "We all know how much you like women."

At this there were several snickers from others in the room, and Louis, who had been nearly out the door, turned back.

"Explain yourself."

"I merely meant that you seem — a little shy — around your wife. Perhaps you would rather avoid meeting my Josephine."

Now the laughter in the room, though muffled, was unmistakable. I rushed to defend my husband, walking up to him with a smile and taking his arm affectionately. "Louis and I are perfectly comfortable with each other, aren't we dear?"

He gave me a grateful look and squeezed my arm. "Yes," he said, glaring at Stanny.

"And when are we to expect the, ah, fruits of this comfort to become evident?"

"Children are from the lord," I said. "They come when He sends them."

"Well the lord is sending me a bride today, all the way from Italy, and I do not intend to be the least bit shy with her once she gets here." Loud male laughter greeted this. "In fact —" he added, striding up to Louis, who let go of my arm and gently pushed me to the side as his brother approached, "I'll make a wager with you, Mushroom Boy. I'll bet my Josephine gives me a son before your wife even begins to stretch out her corset stays."

Louis shoved Stanny hard, so that he nearly fell backwards. When he recovered his balance Stanny put his head down and rammed Louis in the stomach, making him bellow like a wounded bull.

It took two tall strong footmen to separate the boys, and later on that day, after supper, Louis went into Stanny's rooms and broke one of his rare Chinese vases.

They fight a lot, and sometimes their younger brother Charles — Charlot — joins in, always on Stanny's side. Stanny is only fifteen, and Charlot thirteen, but already they strut about like bantam roosters, challenging each other and eager to scuffle.

Stanny thinks that if he and his wife have children, and Louis and I have none, that the king will make Stanny his heir. After all, Louis is odd, and tongue-tied in public, and appears dull-witted while Stanny is much more normal and quite intelligent. If, on top of all that, the king becomes convinced that Louis and I will never have a son to become king and carry on the royal line, then perhaps Stanny would be a better heir after all.

There, I've written it. I have to admit, in the privacy of this journal, that it might be true.

October 12, 1770
Marie-Josephine of Savoy, Stanny's fiancée,

has been here for three days now and everyone is talking about how ugly she is.

Not only is she short and fat, but she has a black mustache on her upper lip and horrid thick eyebrows like Father Kunibert's. Her complexion is pockmarked and red, and her hair is dressed in a style no one at our court (I am beginning to call it "our court" now) has worn for at least a year.

"My future wife may not be the most attractive woman at court, but I am assured by all her relatives that she will be the most fertile," Stanny remarked when he heard his fiancée criticized. "Josephine's mother had fourteen sons and daughters, and her grandmother had nineteen."

"And were they all ugly," Madame DuBarry retorted, "or only this one?"

Stanny glanced at his grandfather's mistress, his gaze as scornful as his voice.

"They were all royal," he said with emphasis. "And not a whore in the lot."

The king took little notice of Stanny's future bride other than to remark, to no one in particular, "She ought to wash her neck."

Remembering my own awkward and lonely early days in France, I invited Josephine to play piquet and lent her some of my jewels as she had few of her own and Stanny has not been generous with his gifts to her. It seems the wealth of the ruler of the Savoy is in children, not jewels or gold. There is a rumor that Josephine's dowry is only fifty thousand silver florins, and that most of it will never be paid.

So far we like each other, Josephine and I, though she is very quiet and speaks French with a strong Italian accent. When she does say anything it is very humdrum, such as "Please pass the tea cakes" or "How precious your little pug dog is." I have two new pug dogs and have promised her a puppy from their next litter.

October 28, 1770
Eric's wife is getting bigger and bigger. Every time I look at her and remember that she is carrying his child, I feel a pang.

November 4, 1770
Louis gave a ball tonight to celebrate my fifteenth birthday. He put on one of his fine suits of silver cloth to honor me, and tried to dance. He has been attempting to learn the steps of the polonaise and taking lessons once a week, and in order to please me he makes an effort to keep time with his poor shambling feet when the fiddler plays the

tunes. I am grateful for his efforts. I know how he hates dressing up and dancing. I know he did his best tonight but he was very awkward and everyone tried not to look at him when he danced.

Stanny and Josephine were there and when Stanny cruelly imitated Louis's poor dancing behind his back there were titters of laughter. Someone, I could not tell who it was, began singing in a low voice a nasty little song about Louis.

> Tick tock
> Where's your cock?
>
> Never seen
> In the dauphine
>
> Clock strikes one
> Where's your son?
>
> Clock strikes four
> Dauphine's a whore

Louis was so upset by it all that when the food was brought in at midnight he stuffed himself with roast pig and truffles and turtle soup and custards until he got sick and vomited all over the floor.

Stanny laughed and the Duc de Choiseul

stood up and said very loudly that the ball was over and made the musicians stop playing. Everyone left in a hurry. My ball was ruined.

November 19, 1770

Count Mercy came to see me today. I could tell from his expression that he had something important on his mind and I cringed inwardly. His manner is always kind but he knows what matters most and does not let things slide. I have come to dread our talks.

"Dearest Antonia, I trust you are fully recovered," he said when he had made himself comfortable in my sitting room, sending the servants out with a wave of his hand.

"I am, thank you count."

He nodded affably, taking his time in saying what he had come to say. I waited patiently.

"Antonia, I have been thinking about a solution to your dilemma — yours and Louis's. It is, as you realize, imperative that you present Louis with a son. Two or three sons would be best. And since he seems unable to beget these children himself, it seems to me that we might engage in a harmless deception — for the benefit of the family, to preserve the succession."

"A deception? What sort of deception?"
I asked him.

"To be blunt, we would find another man to take your husband's place."

I blinked. I did not know what to say.

"There is much at stake here, you realize. The union of Austrian and French interests must be made firm and lasting by the birth of children. The two dynasties must merge into one. Otherwise our enemies will be encouraged.

"I cannot hide from you the fact that there has been talk of annuling your marriage and sending you back to Vienna."

At this my heart leapt. How I would love to return home, to maman and Joseph and all my family. But of course I would be returning in humiliation; a failure. I would bring dishonor on the family. And according to Mercy, political disaster as well.

I struggled to understand.

"If our marriage were annuled, would it mean war?" I asked at length.

"Very possibly."

"Mother would hate having to send our armies into battle again."

"It is always preferable to find an alternative. And an alternative is what I am proposing. I suggest that we find a strong, healthy and discreet young nobleman, one much like your husband in build and coloring, who will agree to take his place in your bed. When your children are born they will resemble Louis, even though they are not his. No one will ever know the truth except myself, you and Louis — and the nobleman himself."

"But it would be a lie."

"A good lie, yes."

I looked at Mercy. "Are lies ever good?"

"I assure you as a lifelong diplomat that they are."

There was a long silence while I pondered what the count was saying. That for the sake of preserving my marriage and serving the needs of Austria, my beloved homeland, I should break my marriage vows and bear another man's children. And then lie about it to the world, and to my sons and daughters and all my family, for the rest of my life.

Then I had a sudden thought. Eric! Why couldn't Eric be Louis's replacement? He was not a nobleman, but he was strong and healthy, and I love him. For a moment I allowed myself to dream of being in Eric's arms, loving him, desiring him, letting him love me as a husband loves his wife. How happy that would make me! But Eric was married. It would mean his having to deceive Amélie. I felt certain he would not agree to that. And the longer I thought about it, the more I realized that I couldn't agree to such a deception either.

I did not say that to Count Mercy. Instead I said I needed to write to my mother and get her advice.

"I shouldn't do that," the count told me. "She wouldn't understand. Between ourselves, this is a matter for gallic subtlety and sophistication, not German rectitude. You must act as a Frenchwoman would. Your mother would never be able to do that. Yet she sent you here to become as much a part of this court, and its ways, as you could, so in a sense she has given permission already for what we may decide to do."

That was true. However, maman had also warned me against French liberal views and French subtleties. And she had told me always to remember who I am and where I come from.

"I will ponder your suggestion, Count Mercy," I said, extending my hand for the diplomat to kiss, indicating that I was ending our interview, "but at present I cannot follow your advice. Thank you for offering it."

He pressed dry lips to my wrist and,

bowing, walked toward the doorway. Before he reached it he turned.

"Antonia, I have only your best interests and those of Austria at heart."

"I never doubt that, count."

But I have begun to doubt it. Thinking over our talk now, after several hours have passed, I realize that the count is prepared to sacrifice me — my honor, my morals, my very body — for Austria's sake. The realization sends chills up my spine.

Who is there to protect me against the dark and complex intrigues of this world?

November 29, 1770
My little pug had nine puppies last night. So far all have survived, even the tiny runt, no bigger than my fist. Four are all brown, one brown with two white feet and three brown with four white feet. One is a milky color, as if it came from a different litter altogether. I have made a nest for them in a basket beside my bed. Louis is very tolerant of their squeaking.

December 5, 1770
Stanny and Louis quarreled and fought during the Advent Mass today and the king, who was near by, was annoyed. He didn't object to the sacrilege of fighting in church,

only to the noise and disruption. He likes to be able to sleep through the entire service undisturbed.

I went to a ball and wore the Hapsburg Sun which I know makes Madame DuBarry envious. My pale yellow gown was much admired, and when I glimpsed myself in a mirror I saw the huge diamond at my throat flashing like fire. I showed it off, dancing with the Comte de Noailles and Count Mercy and several others. Louis will not dance in public any longer, not even at balls in my apartments.

There were whispers that I was enjoying myself too much, but I ignored them. I was having a wonderful time, and was sorry when Louis stood up at eleven o'clock and beckoned to me that it was time to go. Everyone bowed and curtsied as we passed, and I was reminded of how, two years ago at Schönbrunn, I used to line up my dozens of fashion dolls in rows and then walk in front of them, pretending they were court ladies.

How long ago it all seems now!

December 18, 1770
Yesterday Amélie began having pains and I summoned Dr. Boisgilbert who examined her as she lay on a sofa in my sitting room.

He sent for the midwife.

I sent a page to fetch Eric and he came right away, sitting on a low stool beside the couch where Amélie lay and taking her hand in his.

"False labor," the midwife told him after she had examined Amélie. "Too early for the real thing." She left, and we all relaxed a little. The crisis was over.

I went out into the adjoining room to wait for Josephine, who was coming to see the puppies. I had promised to give her one as a Christmas gift. She soon arrived, smelling like strong cheese and in need of a bath.

While we talked and Josephine made her choice from among the dogs I could hear Eric and Amélie quarreling.

"Why didn't you come sooner?" she was shouting. "I could have died. I was in terrible pain. Terrible pain, don't you understand?"

"But my dear, I came as soon as I could. The king —"

Amélie swore. "Always the king, and the prince, and your little favorite the princess! I wish they were all —" She broke off, her voice muffled. I imagined that Eric had put his hand over her mouth, to protect her. To speak ill of the royal family could be very dangerous, as she would have realized had she been less angry and outspoken.

They continued to argue, but in lowered voices. Then in a few moments Eric came in where Josephine and I were, carrying the limp Amélie in his arms.

"She's exhausted. With your highness's permission, I would like to take her home."

"Yes of course you have my permission, Eric. I hope she will be stronger in the morning."

"Thank you, your highness."

This morning Eric returned to my apartments at the hour when I had my hair dressed and my rouge applied. There were often dozens of people in the room for this daily ceremony, watching, hoping to say a word to me or hand me a written appeal of some sort. But this morning the number of visitors was small, only a knot of Hungarians on an embassy from my mother's court and a dozen or so onlookers who stood observing me sitting at the center of the room before the tall mirror and low table where my combs and brushes and pins were laid out, my silvery white wig on its gilded stand.

André was combing out my long hair when Eric came in, looking very handsome in his livery of pale blue velvet, a white foam of lace at his neck. I nodded to him and he approached the toilette table, sitting on a low footstool near me. He looked tired.

"How is Amélie?" I asked him in German.

"Still complaining of soreness, your highness. She did not sleep well."

"I'll order the midwife to visit her again," I told Eric.

"You were very good to Amélie yesterday. I came to thank you."

"I know how important she is to you."

Eric's face fell. "If only you knew how it really is between us. How much I regret — the step I took last summer."

He spoke softly, almost in a whisper, his eyes downcast. I knew that he meant he regretted marrying Amélie, and his admission made me glad.

"I only did it because my father was urging me to marry, and because the stable master insisted that I take a wife before becoming a royal equerry."

"I remember well." At these words he looked up at me, and the warmth and sadness in his eyes made me feel an instant sympathy for him. Sympathy and, I must admit, love.

"How I wish that things were different," I went on, speaking very softly so that only Eric and André could hear me — and certain that André could not understand German. "Different for both of us."

"But your highness is a great success. You are gracious and poised — and so very beautiful."

"And very lonely."

"If ever I may offer your highness company, you have only to ask."

"Thank you, Eric. I may do that. It is good to be able to speak my own language, and hear it spoken."

"I came about one thing more," Eric said. "Amélie has asked that, when our child is born, you will be godmother at the christening."

Had Eric not confessed that he was unhappily married, this request would have given me pain. To take part in a ceremony celebrating Eric and Amélie's happiness as parents would surely wound me — but knowing that there was strife and disappointment between them made the prospect of being present at the child's christening much easier. In fact, I almost looked forward to it. I told Eric so, and he kissed my hand, lingering over it, I thought, and left.

December 28, 1770

I have decided not to wear corset stays any longer. They pinch, and make me short of breath. Madame de Noailles insists that I wear them. I tell her no, definitely and firmly, and my bedchamber women obey me. They are fond of me and dislike Madame de Noailles. When they dress me, they leave off the stays.

January 4, 1771

My little rebellion over the corset stays has caused a great stir at court.

Madame de Noailles, in a huff, went to Count Mercy and complained that I was disobedient and that my behavior was an affront to the king, who had appointed her to advise me. Choiseul heard of the conflict between me and Madame de Noailles and sent me a curt note ordering me to put my corset stays back on at once. Abbé Vermond, who along with Louis was one of the few who saw the humor in the situation, came to ask me with a smile about the "war of the corset" and to remind me that my mother had told me to follow French ways in everything. If French ladies wore corset stays then so should I.

For a week all eyes were on my waistline, which happens to be very small whether or not it is laced up in whalebone.

"Is she or isn't she wearing them?" was the whisper heard from one end of the long galleries to the other.

I remain aloof from the criticism. I have made my decision, and I will not change my mind, no matter how loudly Madame de Noailles sniffs her disapproval and how harshly she glares at me.

Battle lines have been drawn. I have decided to fight back.

January 6, 1771

I have decided not only to rid myself of corset stays, but to rid myself of Madame de Noailles as well.

I have a plan. It will require some guile and some luck, but I think it will work.

January 9, 1771

My apartments are in such an uproar that I have come with Louis to an ancient wing of the palace where he and some laborers are laying bricks to build a wall.

I have found a small quiet room near the bricklaying to sit in, and now that the footman has lit a fire in the hearth the little room is quite cosy. Sophie is with me. She is sitting before the hearth winding skeins of red wool into balls.

I need some peace, for Madame de Noailles is causing havoc in my apartments, giving orders and bustling around, shouting at the servants in her anger. Her things are being packed into trunks. She has been sent away from court.

I arranged her departure in this way. For some months I have known that the king and Madame DuBarry go out in the garden each day when the weather is fine. This morning I went walking there too, accompanied by my sister-in-law Josephine and several of my ladies. As we approached the Neptune Fountain I saw that Madame DuBarry and the king were on the far side of the fountain. He was being pushed in a wheeled chair as he is not very steady on his feet, and he had gone to sleep, his head lolling forward on his chest.

Standing by the rim of the fountain to admire the falling water, I remarked to Josephine, loudly enough for Madame DuBarry to hear, that I was giving a ball the following night and wanted to invite the king "and his good friend."

Making sure that I was overheard, I said that I had often wanted to invite the "good friend" in the past, but Madame de Noailles had refused to allow it.

"If only she were not there to restrict

me, I could choose my companions freely," I remarked. "There are certain people at court I would like to know much better. I may have misjudged them in the past."

I could imagine what the object of these remarks must be thinking, and how surprised and pleased she must be to hear that I wanted to know her better. Madame DuBarry craved acceptance and recognition by the court elite. No matter how many jewels and precious things the king gave her, this one thing was denied her: to be included in high social circles. Now I was offering her entrance into that elite group, or so I wanted her to think.

I sighed loudly. "If only someone would rid me of Madame de Noailles!" We moved on past the fountain and resumed our walk, taking a path that led away from Madame DuBarry and the dozing king.

I wondered how long it would take for the royal mistress to act. I did not have long to wait. By midday Madame de Noailles received a message from the master of the king's household informing her that she was being dismissed as my adviser.

I heard a howl of dismay, followed by a stream of angry shouts and curses. I pretended to know nothing about what had happened, but I could tell by the furious and knowing look in Madame de Noailles's eyes when she confronted me that she realized I had been involved in her dismissal.

"That will be all, madame," I told her icily when she came to me and accused me of causing her departure. "Thank you for your service." I swept past her out of the room, and went to look for Louis, who was just leaving to rejoin the bricklayers.

It is pleasant and restful here by the fire. I don't want to leave. Louis often works late into the evening, as he is strong and tireless. I may still be here at midnight, nodding over this journal and smiling at the thought that Madame de Noailles is now out of my life forever.

February 1, 1771
Stanny and Josephine were married two days ago and the entire court attended the wedding in the royal chapel. They were an ugly couple.

March 1, 1771
When Louis came to visit me this afternoon I saw at once that his lip was bleeding and one eye was swollen and starting to turn blue. He staggered as he lurched into my sitting room and sat down heavily on a bro-

caded chair. He reeked of drink.

"It's Stanny again, isn't it?" I said, beckoning for Sophie and telling her to bring a cloth and some ointment for Louis's cuts.

"He bet me ten silver florins I couldn't drink an entire bottle of port in five minutes. I almost did too. But then I threw up. I couldn't help it. Then I hit him."

Louis held still obediently while Sophie wiped the blood from his face and applied salve to his lips and swollen eye and I stood by looking down at him, glad that Madame de Noailles was no longer there to insist that I must sit if the dauphin was sitting. How relieved I am to be rid of her!

"You have to learn to ignore him when he dares you to do things, and when he insults you. You know he only does it to rile you. It amuses him. He's mean."

Louis hung his head. "I know."

I murmured to Sophie, "Send for Chambertin."

"Do you know what he told me?" Louis whispered, looking up at me with fear in his eyes. "He says his wife is pregnant."

"So soon?"

Louis nodded. "It is to be announced at the next meeting of the royal council."

I thought again of Count Mercy's suggestion, that I take another man into my bed. It would save the succession, and allow Louis some peace. Eric. Eric. Oh, if only!

Chambertin arrived, gentle and concerned as always, and with an apologetic nod to me, led Louis off to his own apartments. Next to me, I think, Chambertin is the one who cares about poor Louis most. He is valet, equerry, footman all in one. He does whatever needs to be done, and keeps a close and indulgent eye on his master.

March 28, 1771
I have seen Eric and talked to him — and he still loves me! I cannot write more now. All I can do is sing, and wrap my arms around myself and twirl, and go out and ride Bravane, the new horse the king has sent me, until I am quite spent.

I want to shout, Eric loves me! To the world. But all I can do is write it here. Eric loves me. Eric loves me. Eric loves me.

April 5, 1771
It has been a week now since my long talk with Eric in the little kiosk among the hornbeams, in the palace gardens.

It was right after the christening, when I went to the royal chapel to take my place as godmother to Eric and Amélie's new baby. She was christened Louise-Antoinette-Thérèse, named for Louis and myself and my mother.

I held her in my arms at the font as the priest poured water over her little head, wetting the lace christening cap I gave Amélie for her, but she didn't cry. She felt warm and smelled like milk. She is a hefty little girl and kicked her legs and waved her tiny arms with vigor.

I noticed that Amélie was avoiding Eric throughout the ceremony, never looking at him and keeping her distance. When it was over, and the priest had given baby Louise-Antoinette his final blessing, I handed her back to Amélie who thanked me briefly with a curtsey and then immediately left the chapel with two other women. I think they were her sisters. She did not wait for Eric.

The chapel emptied quickly. There had been only a few people at the christening and I had brought only two of my ladies with me. Eric was speaking to the priest and handing him a purse of coins. I told my ladies that I wanted a walk in the garden before the midday meal and that I preferred to be alone. They left me.

Eric caught up with me as I was making my way along a path between banks of rosebushes, just beginning to bud.

"Your highness, may I walk with you?"

"Of course Eric. You know how I look forward to your company." I spoke formally, in case anyone overheard me.

We made our way up into the part of the garden called the Heights of Satory, a natural woodland where great hornbeams shaded the paths. Few people came here I knew, and I felt alone with Eric, especially when we entered a small white-painted kiosk and sat side by side.

Without a word being spoken we kissed, long and thirstily, and when the kiss ended Eric took my hand and held it between both of his. I felt too happy to speak, overjoyed simply to be with him, and once again to feel his lips on mine.

How long we sat like that, without speaking, I cannot say. He kissed my hand and pressed it to his bowed head.

"How I wish we were still in Vienna," he said eventually, his voice rough with feeling.

"I often wish it too. I long to be happy with Louis, but it is no use. You are the one I think of, every day and every night."

"Amélie is envious of you. She had a dream that I left her for you. In a way her dream was right. I will never abandon her or our child, but in my heart I left a long time ago."

"Does she love you?"

"She wants very much to possess me. To make certain no one else possesses me."

"That isn't love, it's greed."

"Amélie is greedy. And spiteful."

"Louis is only greedy when he eats," I said, laughing. "And I have never seen him be spiteful. He really means to be kind, but he can't seem to learn how to show kindness. He frightens people, he is so odd."

"Does he frighten you?"

"No, we are friends. But he cannot give me the love I need. For that I dream of you."

"Dearest Antonia."

For a while we did not speak, and he kissed me again. I felt myself opening to him, as a flower opens trustingly to the sun. I am his, that is all.

"I need to know that your love is there, for me to think of, and to rely on," I told him.

"I will be your loving friend for life." He spoke these words with such solemnity, like a pledge or a vow. I can hear the sound of his voice, saying them now, as I write this.

From a distance came the noise of

people approaching, along the forest path.

"If we are seen together there is sure to be gossip," Eric said, kissing my hand once more and standing up.

"I will be sure to walk this way again," I told him. "To this pavilion."

With a final glance and a smile he was gone, and I took out of the pocket of my gown the book I had brought along, so that when the passers-by saw me I was reading, and they did not disturb me.

I was not actually reading, of course. I could not read, or think, or do anything but sit, letting the memory of all we had said wash through me again and again.

After half an hour of this most delicious confusion I left and returned to the palace to dine with Louis and his aunts. I was far too elated to eat much, though, and Aunt Adelaide scolded me for picking at my food.

July 1, 1771

A few days ago Louis brought a dairymaid to court. She was a sweet, fresh-faced girl, plump and pink-cheeked, her hands rough and chapped from pulling on the cows' udders. She blushed and looked down at the marble floor, hardly ever raising her eyes to look at any of us, very ill at ease to find herself in a palace. It was not long before members of my household began gathering around to gawk at her. Most of them had never seen a dairymaid at such close range before.

"She has brought her cow," Louis told me. "It is out in the courtyard. I want you to go out there with her and let her teach you how to milk it and churn butter."

I laughed.

"But I know perfectly well how to milk a cow already! Mother taught us all how to do it when we were children, and I've watched the dairymaids at Schönbrunn many times. As for churning butter, I've helped to churn it — it takes hours and hours, you know. But why should I spend my time on such tasks when there are plenty of servants to do them?"

"Because it would be good for you," Louis said in a voice I rarely heard him use, a sort of fatherly voice, only more like a stern father than a kindly one.

"You spend far too much time on frivolous pastimes, pastimes that do nothing to improve your character. I see the dressmakers come and go, nearly every day. You waste your time ordering new gowns, trying them on, having them altered endlessly and chatting with your foolish empty-headed friends about them. You spend half your life going to balls."

"I like to dance and enjoy myself. Is it not expected of the dauphine to lead others in the dancing?"

"It is a question of finding a proper balance between light pleasures and serious work. I go hunting for pleasure, but I also lay bricks and dig cellars and study specimens and learn how to make clocks. You, on the other hand, madame, invent new styles and make up new names for stylish colors. I hear you talking about them — Burning Ashes, Gudgeon's Belly, Unripe Pear, Dirty Rain! What silliness! Does this dairymaid wear aprons in such colors?"

He pointed to the girl, who blushed the color of Pigeon's Blood, aware that we were all staring at her.

"No! She wears the same plain dark gown every day, and a clean white apron and cap. Isn't that right, my dear?"

"Yes, sire." Her voice trembled.

I went to the cabinet where I keep my needles and thread and brought out the garment I was working on.

"I have many practical skills," I said to Louis, holding out the colorful satin vest I was making for the king, embroidered with gold and silver fleurs-de-lis and an elaborate royal monogram. "See, I have nearly finished this gift for your grandfather."

"You have been playing at that embroidery for two years! And it is still not finished!"

"But your grandfather is delighted with it. 'Bring me my vest, my little doll,' he says when he sees me. 'Where is my vest?' And you know how generous he is with me, giving me jewels that belonged to his first queen and paying all my dressmaker's bills. He never asks me whether or not I can milk cows!"

I saw that the poor dairymaid's shoulders were shaking and went up to her.

"I do like cows," I said soothingly. "Very much. Would you please show me the one you brought?"

I let her lead me out into the courtyard, many of the courtiers following us, where a carefully brushed brown cow with blue ribbons braided into her tail was tied to a post.

"She's quite handsome. Have you had her long?"

"Three years, madame. I raised her from a calf. She has won prizes at the Giverny agricultural exhibition." The girl's face shone with pride.

"Has she? Her milk must be very rich, I imagine."

I went on talking to the dairymaid, while the cow twitched her tail and the onlookers, beginning to be bored, wandered off. Evidently Louis wandered off as well, for when I looked around to find him, he was nowhere to be seen.

November 14, 1771
Stanny almost knocked me down this afternoon, running along the corridor toward the king's salon.

"It's here, it's here!" I heard him shout. "My son has been born!"

Loulou and I followed the sound of Stanny's excited shouts and I heard him tell the king's major-domo about the baby.

"I must see the king! I must announce this news to him myself!" Stanny's face was purple and he was out of breath.

The major-domo, impassive, stood in the doorway of the salon blocking Stanny from entering.

"The king," he said, brushing a speck of dust from his gold livery, "is taking a purge. He has given orders that he is not to be disturbed."

"But he knows that my wife is in labor. He will want to know about her delivery as quickly as possible!"

"He has yet to acquaint me with that desire," said the major-domo, who shut the salon door in Stanny's chubby face.

Hours later I was summoned to the king's apartments. He likes me to visit him. He says I cheer him up and make him feel young.

When I arrived Stanny was still sitting on a bench in the corridor, alongside several of the young pages who were waiting to carry out any order the king might give. Evidently Stanny had not yet delivered his good news.

The major-domo opened the door to me and admitted me but kept Stanny out, which infuriated him.

When I asked the king if he knew about Stanny and Josephine's new baby he waved his thin old hand in the air in a dismissive gesture.

"Only a sickly weakling," he said. "And probably just as ugly as its parents."

August 18, 1772
The king is aging more rapidly than ever. He looks small and shrunken in his velvet coat and silk waistcoat. The vest I made for him is too large for him now, but he wears it anyway.

One night after Louis and I had returned from an evening of card games in the king's apartments, Louis suddenly burst into tears.

"Oh, I don't want it! I don't want it! It's coming soon, I can feel it."

I had become accustomed to such outbursts and knew that if only I waited patiently, he would become calm and we could talk. When he stopped crying he began pacing fretfully.

"Did you see how frail he is getting? He can't remember how to play piquet any more, and he falls asleep every ten minutes. I heard Choiseul say the other day that he couldn't last six months."

"And I have heard Dr. Boisgilbert say," I told Louis, "that he may live for years. Didn't his father live to be seventy-five?"

"How do I know?"

"Look it up, it must be in one of those books of yours."

"What does it matter? All I know is, I don't want the next king to be me!"

"Louis the Unwilling, is that how you want to be remembered?"

"Better that than Louis the Miserable."

I knew better than to argue with my husband over this continuing fear of his. I believe that when the time comes, he will do what he must. And I will help him. Meanwhile there is to be a grand ball in a week's time, and I am to have a new gown in the color of Rusty Sword, and I will do my best to forget our troubles and dance until sunrise.

FOUR

April 23, 1774
I am now fairly certain that within a few days or weeks I will be Queen of France. The king collapsed suddenly two days ago and had to be carried to bed. Louis and I were informed and we went at once to the royal apartments where the surgeons and apothecaries had gathered. There were eight of them and they all looked very grave and purposeful.

We have not been allowed into the king's bedchamber, only Madame DuBarry is there. Dr. Boisgilbert says we cannot see the king because he is too ill, he has catarrhal fever and cannot recognize anyone.

Louis and I are waiting here, hour after hour. Louis clutches my hand and says, "Will he die? Will he die?" I try to calm him and together we pray for the lord's will to be done.

May 2, 1774
We are still keeping watch here in the king's apartments. He is worse. We know that because Dr. Boisgilbert avoids answering our questions and because of the worried looks

on the faces of the surgeons and apothecaries when they go and come during the
day. There are ten of them now.

To pass the time I have decided to begin
writing in this journal again. I stopped last
year because one of Count Mercy's spies
found the journal and broke the lock and
read it.

All my secrets became known to the
count, who lectured me on how I had to
grow up and do what was expected of me
and not see Eric any more.

I know where I will keep the journal now
that I have begun to write in it again. A
better hiding place.

May 3, 1774
My dressmakers are sewing my black
mourning gowns. The king has called for the
Archbishop of Paris to hear his confession.
Everyone is amazed. He has not made a con-
fession in forty years.

May 4, 1774 afternoon
King Louis is dying. He has made his confession. The servants are betting with each
other what day and hour he will die. Some of
them, the ones who have served him longest,
are crying.

I have asked Dr. Boisgilbert several

times if I may be allowed to see him. So far he has said no.

May 4 midnight
I have had a horrible fright.

Tonight Dr. Boisgilbert, who is worn out from days of watching by the king's bedside, came out into the anteroom and beckoned to me. Louis was asleep on a sofa and snoring loudly.

"He has little time left," the doctor said. "You can look in on him. Don't touch him." He left and I went to the door and softly opened it.

At once a terrible smell assaulted me and I immediately remembered where I had smelled it before: when my poor sister Josepha was dying. In the candlelight I could see the king's face, black with the pox and covered with sores. His eyes were closed and I could hear him struggling to breathe.

Madame DuBarry was beside the bed. At first I thought she was holding the king's hand but then I realized that she was trying to remove his rings.

"Get away!" I shouted. "Get away, you thief! You hag!"

I called for the guards and ordered them to remove Madame DuBarry, whose shrill, grating cries of protest were truly alarming.

"Why shouldn't I have his rings?" she yelled at me, with a curse. "He doesn't need them any more! I've earned them!"

"All you've earned," I said with fury as the soldiers took the royal mistress out of the room, "is a dungeon cell. Now get out of my sight."

When she was gone I moved as close to the king's bed as I dared. "God bless you, old man," I whispered. "God spare you pain."

With a groan the king opened his red-rimmed eyes. He saw me, and knew me.

"My little doll," he murmured, then drifted again into sleep.

I was trembling as I left the room. I wonder if I will be able to sleep, remembering his hideous face, and the terrible stench, and the sight of Madame DuBarry, greedy and thieving, stealing the rings from his thin white hands.

May 10, 1774
Today I am queen and Louis is king. The old king is no more, God rest his soul.

May 11, 1774
We are on our way to Choisy. Everyone re-

fers to me as "Madame the Queen" now and not "Madame the Dauphine" any longer, even Sophie. We had to leave Versailles because it is forbidden for the new king to stay in the palace where the old king has died. Also we know now that he had the pox, not catarrhal fever as Dr. Boisgilbert tried to make us believe. Everyone fears the pox so the palace has emptied quickly.

As soon as the news of the old king's death was whispered along the corridors there was a rush of people to Louis's apartments. The rooms are choked with servants and officials who all want new appointments. When they cannot see Louis they try to obtain an audience with me. I cannot possibly see everyone and answer all requests, so I escape.

Louis promises me my own private retreat. When we return to Versailles he says he will give me the Petit Trianon, an adorable little house in the palace gardens, for my very own.

May 25, 1774

All is confusion. There is no order any more. Nothing operates smoothly. Nerves are on edge, we are surrounded by conflict.

I am beginning to see what is happening, though I am not yet certain. I think that before the old king died, the Duc de Choiseul and Madame DuBarry governed everything. They were enemies, but together, between them, they governed the king and therefore all the ministers and royal servants did what was expected of them, more or less.

Now that Choiseul has been deprived of office and sent away and Madame DuBarry, at Louis's and my insistence, is living in exile on one of her ill-gotten estates, there is no one left to rule the court and make things run smoothly.

Sometimes I feel as if a whirlwind were sweeping through the palace, sending people and things flying in all directions. It is all I can do to hold tightly to some heavy thing like a marble pillar or an iron statue and wait for the roaring wind to pass.

June 1, 1774
In the crush of people at yesterday's levee someone cut off all the golden tassels from the curtains.

June 9, 1774
Louis has become obsessed with saving money. The finance minister Monsieur Turgot has impressed on him that there is little money left in the treasury. So Louis

wanders through the palace muttering "Economy, economy" and issuing orders to people to lower their costs.

He burst into my apartments when I was with my dressmaker Rose Bertin, having a fitting on my new silk gown in the color of Flea's Thigh. Loulou was there, as I have appointed her head of my household. Louis came up to Loulou and stared so intently into her face that she took a step backward.

"Your majesty," she said, and curtseyed.

"I know you," he announced. "I saw you at a ball. You were overdressed. You spend too much on gowns."

He turned to me. "That is why I have come," he told me, addressing me formally. "It has come to my attention, madame, that all your linen is replaced every three years. Is this true?"

"It is the custom, I believe, and has been since your great-grandmother's time." I did not know this to be true, but I said it anyway. If Madame de Noailles were still here, supervising my household, she would have known.

"Tell me this, do you truly need new undergarments so often? Do the laundresses wash your linen so roughly that it wears out every three years? No! The answer is no. From now on it shall be changed only every seven years!"

"But your majesty," said Loulou, "would you have your wife wear rags under her lovely gowns?"

I knew that she was teasing Louis and I could hardly keep from laughing. Rose Bertin, kneeling on the floor, her head bent over the hem of my gown, was smiling.

"Better she should go about in rags than that the state go bankrupt," was the king's pronouncement.

"And while we are pursuing economy in matters of dress, I have another command. Those basket things you women wear under your dresses."

"The paniers," I said.

"They have become too wide. From now on they shall be limited to — to — six feet."

"Six feet! But the current fashion is now for skirts to be at least twelve feet wide. Surely your majesty does not wish to dictate fashion."

The king fixed Loulou with his near-sighted stare.

"And why not? My ancestors ordained sumptuary laws in past centuries, regulating what fabrics could be worn, and what furs, and so forth. Well, these are my sumptuary laws. No baskets wider than six feet!"

He lumbered off, leaving us to laugh. It is all so absurd, that Louis should presume to interfere in what we wear. He goes to sleep at eleven every night, just when our good times are beginning. I go to Loulou's apartments, or we visit Yolande de Polignac who gives balls even on holy days or we take torchlit walks through the gardens. Loulou deliberately leads us all into the Heights of Satory where I occasionally meet Eric and when we get there she pokes me in the ribs and laughs. She alone knows my secret about Eric and I worry that others may guess it. So far they have not.

June 22, 1774

Late last night Chambertin came to my rooms with a servant, a young boy who was clutching his side in obvious pain. His face and arms were bloody and his blue velvet jacket and trousers were stained and torn. Despite his injuries the boy bowed deeply to me and would not raise his eyes to my face.

Though it was long past midnight I was still dressed. I had been to a ball and then went to Yolande's suite for a cup of chocolate. I was tired and a bit giddy from the pleasures of the evening. It took me a moment to realize that my husband's valet had come on an urgent errand, and needed my help.

"What is it, Chambertin? Has there been an accident? I know it can't be Louis, he has been in bed for hours."

"No, your majesty. Please forgive my intrusion at this late hour, but I did not know where else to turn."

"Please come in. I'll call for Dr. Boisgilbert to see to the boy."

"No, no, don't summon the doctor. This must be a private matter."

Sensing Chambertin's unease I took him and the servant into my bedchamber, where a startled Sophie, who had been napping on a sofa, put on her dressing gown and looked at me expectantly. The pugs came yapping happily toward me but I shooed them back to their corner.

Chambertin led me to an alcove.

"Your majesty, this boy has been a page to Prince Stanislaus. But he cannot return to that service. If he does he will be killed. I'm certain of it."

I looked over at the boy, standing with head bent, his face contorted in pain. He was quite young, perhaps thirteen or fourteen.

"He can stay here." I went to the boy, asked his name, and assured him that we would look after him. At a nod from me Sophie got her box of salves and ointments and bandages. I told her to take the boy up to Louis's carpentry shop in the attic where there were empty rooms and odds and ends of old furniture.

"Thank you, your majesty."

"Tell me what happened."

"As you know, the prince is very fond of good-looking young boys. Some of them return his fondness, but others do not. He becomes angry and beats them. He has beaten this boy before, but never so severely. If I had not happened to be passing, and heard the boy's cries for help, I'm afraid —"

"Yes, I see." Stanny. Angry, frustrated Stanny. Stanny who, as the rumor went, preferred boys to women. Now that his hopes to take Louis's place had come to nothing, he was taking out his anger on his pages.

"I didn't want Dr. Boisgilbert to find out. He would announce the incident to the entire court."

"No, of course not." I thought a moment. "The question is, where will he be truly safe? If the prince finds out that I have taken him into my household, as my page, he will be furious."

"Prince Stanislaus bears many grudges," Chambertin said. "He does not forgive."

"Then the boy must go to Vienna. I'll send him with Count Mercy when he leaves for Schönbrunn in September. Until then he can hide up in Louis's workrooms. Stanny never goes there."

Sophie says young Monsieur de la Tour is resting comfortably today. He has a broken rib and many bruises, which are all sore, but she bound up his chest and gave him an opiate for the pain. He is so relieved to be out of Stanny's reach and is overjoyed to learn that he will be going to Vienna. He told Sophie he wants to see the world and become a soldier.

Someone should punish Stanny and keep him in line.

August 1, 1774
Louis told me last night that two noblemen brought him a beautiful young actress from the Comédie-Française in hopes that he would make her his mistress. He laughed at them and sent the girl away.

I have sent young Monsieur de la Tour to Vienna with Count Mercy. The boy has been concealed from Stanny and no one will know where he has gone or why.

January 16, 1775
Finally I have this journal back!

I kept it locked in a wooden chest and last fall the chest got moved to Fontaine-bleau without my knowledge and only yesterday it was brought back. The court moves so often and I can never be sure what is to be taken and what is to be left. I must find a better hiding place for my journal.

January 24, 1775
It has snowed heavily for the past week and this morning when the sun came out Yolande, Loulou and I went to take some exercise in the palace gardens.

We slid down hillsides and made snow people and broke icicles off the roofs of the garden sheds. As we were walking through the rose garden we stumbled over two hard objects and, looking closely, we realized that they were bodies. We scraped away the snow and saw that two old women had frozen there, huddled together for warmth, a single scrap of blanket between them.

None of us said anything at first. We were too affected by the shocking sight.

"And to think," I said eventually, when I had begun to recover a little, "that last night while these poor women were out

125

here freezing, we were dancing at Madame Solange's ball."

I went to Abbé Vermond and arranged for a funeral mass for the two women but as we had no idea who they were, they had to be sent to the pauper's cemetery in Ste. Sulpice for burial.

March 3, 1775
We have had a harsh winter and Loulou, Yolande and I have been collecting money from our friends and palace officials to buy bread to feed the poor. Maman used to do this at Schönbrunn. Abbé Vermond is in charge of ordering the loaves from the palace kitchens and supervising the distribution at the palace gates early in the morning.

Louis scoffs at me, though he always puts ten or twenty silver florins in my gold collecting box when he thinks I am not looking.

March 19, 1775
There is unrest in Paris because of the bad weather and hunger and several bakeries were broken into. This would never happen in Vienna, the soldiers would prevent it.

April 5, 1775
Count Mercy has come to see Louis and

asked me to be present at their talk, which annoyed Louis.

The count has recently come back from Vienna where, he says, Joseph now rules more than maman does. Joseph is forcing his ideas on everyone and I can tell that the count thinks they are bad ideas, though he did not actually say so.

"At least there is no famine in the Austrian lands this spring, God be thanked," Mercy told us. "The finances are not managed well, but they are managed. Unlike those of France."

At these words Louis, who had been pacing nervously and looking at his watch, stopped where he was and glowered at Mercy.

"Monsieur Turgot has made great progress in bringing in revenues, which were sadly neglected during my grandfather's reign."

"Monsieur Turgot has wrecked the economy."

Louis, who usually slouches, now pulled himself up to his full height. "We have eliminated much waste. I myself fired two under-gardeners and reduced the hunting staff by seven."

"But you found all the men positions in the kennels and the kitchens," I reminded

Louis, who gave me a furious look and muttered, "Both were understaffed."

"The problems of your highness's treasury extend far beyond the royal household. Though palace costs are undoubtedly excessive. I am told that certain balls cost in excess of one hundred thousand silver florins."

I kept silent at this. I had no idea what our balls cost, but I was sure it was a lot.

"My purpose in speaking to you both is to bring you a message from his imperial highness." He meant Joseph. "He speaks to you, sire, as a fond brother, which he is by marriage, and to you, madame, as his favorite sister. He wishes you both a prosperous and successful reign. He offers you a list of suggestions which he urges you to follow."

Mercy took a sheet of paper from his leather portfolio. It bore the imperial stamp.

"Please give thought to these principles of monarchical rule, and apply them to your decisions."

Louis took the offered document with an ill grace.

"One final word of advice. These disturbances in the capital. Don't let them get out of hand. I am told two flour mills have been attacked and all the grain seized."

Louis shrugged. "There is food rioting every spring, when the winter reserves are gone. It is inevitable."

"This spring is different, your highness. Two things move the people: hunger and anger. Hunger can be controlled by lowering the price of bread, which I urge your majesty to do as soon as possible. But anger, the kind of anger that is spreading through the capital and out into the country villages this winter, that cannot be counteracted so easily.

"The people blame your majesty's ministers for the shortage of food. And though they do not understand all of M. Turgot's regulations, they are right. When hunger and anger combine, there can only be disaster."

After Count Mercy left I thought about what he had said. I was still thinking about it when I went out riding Bravane, though it was hard to keep my thoughts on serious things when the sun was so warm and the air so balmy, and the scent of the budding apple trees was so very fragrant with the promise of spring.

April 19, 1775
Louis has ordered all the bakers to lower the price of bread.

May 2, 1775

I was awakened early this morning by a sound like a herd of cows mooing. Sophie, who sleeps at the foot of my bed when Louis is not there, was already up and pulling on her dressing gown.

"What is that noise?" I asked her. She went to the window and pulled back the curtain, and beckoned for me to join her. We could see, in the courtyard below, dozens of servants shouting and rushing in and out of the palace and a squadron of guardsmen assembling with a mounted officer giving them orders.

Then in addition to the loud mooing sound I heard a terrific crash, followed by shrieks from elsewhere in my apartments and increased activity in the courtyard. I heard someone shout, "It's the gate! They've knocked over the gate!"

I hurriedly put on a morning gown and went out into the sitting room where my maids and chamberwomen were huddled together. Some of them were crying and all of them were very frightened. I told them not to worry, that whatever happened, we would all be safe because we had the protection of the king my husband and of the Garde du Corps, the royal bodyguard.

Sophie helped me gather up the dogs

and together we all made our way to Louis's rooms where there were guards at every door and more in the hallways outside. I saw M. Turgot, red-faced and looking very grim, go out with the Colonel of the Home Guard and several other ministers were trying to get Louis's attention.

Louis was still in his long white nightshirt, his old green slippers on his feet, examining one of the muskets a guardsman had handed him and trying to adjust the firing mechanism.

I don't know how long we waited there, in Louis's apartments, while soldiers came and went and equerries rushed in and out, bringing messages to Louis and the household officers. It seemed as though everyone was talking at once, there was such a din and commotion. We were in the way. We took an alcove for ourselves and watched everything that happened.

Soon we began hearing musket fire outside and screams and shouts. In the midst of all the confusion a servant from the palace kitchens appeared with a large basket of cakes and pastries and we ate greedily.

Before long we heard the roar of cannon. They were firing from the roof of the palace. With each loud boom the floor shook under us and I wondered if the old building could stand all the shaking. We all said our prayers and some of my maids, the younger and more timid ones, began crying again. The booming stopped after about a quarter of an hour and it seemed as though there were fewer people and less confusion in Louis's rooms. He withdrew to get dressed and when he came back, wearing the uniform of a cavalry commander, he looked more like a king than I had ever seen him look before.

By about three in the afternoon the noise and shouting and musket firing had died down. We still heard horses clattering in and out of the courtyard, and agitated servants came and went, delivering messages to Louis and leaving on errands. However, the usual patterns of life in the palace began to come back. I took all my maids and ladies and dogs back to my own apartments where some collapsed and went to sleep and others resumed their duties, after a fashion. I had my hair dressed by a trembling André, who had spent the past few hours under my bed, and then made my toilette as usual.

I was trying to keep everyone calm but of course I wanted to know what had happened. Were we at war? Would all the noise and fear come back later on? Should we move to another palace where we would be safer?

Finally after supper I learned what had gone on. Villagers from nearby Saint-Paul-d'Avray and Saumoy had come to the palace gates in the early morning as they always did, to receive their distribution of loaves and food scraps from the Bouche du Roi, the king's private kitchen. Abbé Vermond had been there to hand out the loaves I contributed.

But instead of taking the food and leaving, the villagers stayed on and demanded more. The crowd at the gate grew larger and larger. They shouted at Abbé Vermond and insisted that he bring out more loaves. He told me that it made him angry, and he shouted back, "Who am I, the Lord Jesus Himself, that I can multiply the loaves?" They jeered at him and called him a creature of the king, who wanted them all to starve so that he could take their lands.

They spat at him and tore his clothes. As he hurried back to the safety of the palace, the villagers, now hundreds of them, took hold of the iron gates and tried to pull them down.

Abbé Vermond is a mild man, highly intelligent and educated, completely unlike the gruff and irritable Father Kunibert. I have almost never seen Abbé Vermond angry. But he was angry tonight when he came to talk to me and pray with me for the souls of those who died today. He said that the villagers were ungrateful for all I did for them, and for the protection they enjoyed living so close to the great palace of Versailles.

"Don't they know that the king's soldiers protect them from bandits, and keep marauders from destroying their crops? Doesn't the king offer to take their sons into his army, and give their daughters work in his dairies and even in the palace itself? Why, the head gardener allows them to gather acorns in the fall to feed their pigs and to help harvest chestnuts and apples and cherries."

"Count Mercy always says that the only thing the villagers know is that the king's tax collectors take everything they have, and the king's bakers charge them too much for their bread."

"Ignorant people despise their betters. They obey them, they are frightened of them, and deep down, they despise them."

We said our prayers for the dead. There were many who died, for the cannon had fired into the crowd of people as they milled in the outer courtyard and later the cavalry had ridden into their midst, the soldiers slashing at them right and left with their sharp swords. All afternoon carts came and went, loaded with bodies. Fresh sand was sprinkled in the courtyard to cover the blood. Tomorrow, Abbé Vermond told me, the gate will be repaired and soon there will be no signs left to show that anything at all went on today.

There will be no signs, but I will remember.

June 28, 1775
How hot it is! I long to plunge into a cool lake wearing nothing but my chemise but I can never do that here. One afternoon Loulou and Yolande and I escaped to the Petit Trianon and ran in the fountains.

July 11, 1775
André has created a new hairstyle for the coronation. He has been practicing on my ladies, and this afternoon he tried it on me for the first time. He combed and fluffed my poor hair for half an hour, thickening it with paste, and then wrapped it over two thick horsehair pads and added more and more lengths of false hair until the whole elaborate

tower was nearly two feet high. Miniature gold crowns with diamonds were braided into the strands so that they sparkled.

The effect is beautiful but I can hardly turn my head and the pins that hold the whole tower together keep pricking my head. My scalp itches from all the pomade. Worst of all, I have to sleep in this Coronation Pouf until the ceremony itself, which is not for several weeks.

July 29, 1775

At last I am able to write about Louis's wonderful coronation, which left me so tired that I have done almost nothing but sleep ever since.

He dreaded it so much that for days before the ceremony he made himself sick by overeating. He drank camomile tea constantly to calm his nerves but still he couldn't sleep. He kept me awake with his pacing.

I thought he might disappear to his favorite place, his hut in the forest of Compiègne, so that he could avoid being crowned, but he was courageous and went through with the ceremony. I was very proud of him.

He sat on the golden throne in the great Cathedral of Rheims and the archbishop put the crown on his head and everyone in the church shouted "May the king live forever!" and clapped and clapped. They clapped for me too, and reached out to touch my gown as I passed. So many grimy hands, clutching at my skirts. So many grinning faces, toothless mouths, calling out and cheering.

On our way back to Versailles Louis snored in the carriage, still wearing his ermine and velvet. There were poor people kneeling by the side of the road calling out "Give us bread, your majesty!" but we had no bread to give them, and rode on.

FIVE

April 13, 1777

Joseph is here! I have not seen him in so long, I want to be near him every minute. I can't get over how much he has changed. He has gotten old-looking and is almost bald, like the paintings of grandfather in maman's study. His clothes are out of fashion and he says he doesn't care. Father Kunibert is with him and I am trying to stay out of his way, so he doesn't lecture me.

April 17, 1777

I lied to Father Kunibert. I told him I no longer wrote in my journal and that it was lost years ago. He says I look like the Whore of Babylon in my high-piled hair and silken gowns.

"Oh no, father," Joseph corrected him with a smile. "The Queen of Babylon, surely."

"You babble on a good deal yourself, brother," I said, making Joseph laugh so that all the lines around his eyes creased deeply. "Please tell me all about maman and the others."

He obliged me, and described the many changes at our court in Schönbrunn since I left. There was much to tell, and Joseph does like to talk. Finally he came to the subject closest to my heart.

"How is maman?" I asked him. "Tell me truly."

He patted my hand. "Our dear maman is growing old. It is as simple as that. Her strength is declining. There are the usual aches and pains of old age, but something else eats away at her and is a deeper pitfall for her to surmount. She is fearful."

"She fears the pains of hell," Father Kunibert put in. "She is a sinner."

Ignoring him, Joseph went on. "As she grows weaker, she fears losing her power. She gives more and more of it to me, yet she resents me for accepting it. She fears that I will change our empire, and she is right. I shall change it.

"Despite her old-fashioned ideas, she is a very wise and farsighted woman. She has glimpsed the future, and it frightens her, for she knows she will not be here to prevent it."

I do not know what Joseph means by this, but just hearing him talk about it is enough to frighten me.

"The future, hah!" spat out Father

Kunibert. "It is all right there, in the Book of Revelation. This world has no future. It is going to end, and soon. All the signs are here. Plague, pestilence, wars and rumors of wars —"

"Is there going to be a war?" I interrupted, asking Joseph. "Count Mercy is always saying so."

Joseph looked at me. "Our mother sent me here to help preserve the peace. By talking to you, as she would if she could travel so far, and if she could be spared in Vienna, which she could not.

"If I may be blunt, Antonia, and I hardly know how to speak otherwise, your frivolous behavior, and your failure to have a son, are harming Austria far more than you imagine. The result may well be war."

"They call me the Austrian bitch."

"And worse."

"What could be worse?" I asked.

"The Whore of Babylon," said Father Kunibert, and shuffled out of the room, shaking his head.

Joseph and I dined together in private, with Dr. Boisgilbert as our only guest. We discussed Louis.

"He has a slight deformity of the foreskin, nothing more," the doctor told Joseph. "Antonia knows all about it. I explained the problem to her. Two or three swift incisions would correct it. But he cannot face the pain. One look at my knives and he practically faints."

"Why not let him faint, and then perform the operation?"

"I could hardly do that, merely on my own initiative."

"No, of course you couldn't," Joseph said, suddenly thoughtful. "But what if I authorized it — indeed insisted on it?"

"Then, I suppose, I would have no choice but to obey."

"What if," Joseph went on, his fork poised in midair, "he were to injure himself, and faint, and while you were setting a bone or bandaging a wound you brought out your knives and took care of the other small problem?"

"I suppose it could be done, under the right circumstances."

"Are you a hunter, doctor?"

"Certainly."

"Then let us join the king when he goes after deer, or boar, or whatever tiresome animal it is we are supposed to slaughter at this season. Perhaps he will have an accident."

"Not a serious accident," I said, alarmed at what Joseph might be planning.

"If he is as clumsy on a horse as he is on

the dance floor, he can hardly avoid falling off."

It was true, Louis often fell when riding. Once he hit his head and was without sense or feeling for at least half an hour.

"When does he hunt again?"

"Now that the weather is fine, he goes nearly every day," I said. "He brings me back trophies." I had a cabinet full of ears, horns and stinking tails my husband had given me over the years, proofs of his skill as a hunter.

"Then there is one more trophy to be won." Joseph smiled. "A slice of the royal foreskin. Venery for venery, eh, doctor?"

April 27, 1777
They have done it.

Joseph and Dr. Boisgilbert went along on a hunting party, got Louis so drunk he tried to jump a fence and fell. He was in a lot of pain from bruises on his legs and back and the doctor gave him a strong sleeping draught. He hardly struggled at all when they lifted him onto a farmer's cart to bring him back to the palace. Along the way they stopped to put up a canvas over the cart because it was beginning to rain. Under the canvas the doctor hurriedly performed the surgery.

Louis is still in pain today and resting.

May 2, 1777
At last.

May 10, 1777
Everything has changed. I am a woman now and I hope to be a mother soon. Louis is as delighted by sex as a child with a new toy. I blush to write the infantile things he likes to do. Fortunately I have Loulou and Yolande to talk to and Madame Solange as well though Joseph has cautioned me that I must never be seen speaking to her as it reflects badly on me. I tell them everything and they laugh and reassure me that my husband is acting like an inexperienced new bridegroom, which is exactly what he is.

I am certain that Louis is performing adequately to make me pregnant and he performs often so that is also likely to produce a good result. Sophie says little but I notice she is smiling more these days and watching my belly when I dress. Joseph too is smiling these days and he has made me promise that my first son will be called Louis-Joseph.

August 3, 1777
This afternoon I waited for Eric in the

Temple of Love at the Petit Trianon. He was late, which was unlike him, and while I waited for him I fanned myself and loosened the sash of my white lace gown. The pillows on the wooden bench where I sat were soft, and I felt drowsy, sitting there in the midst of the garden, with the scent of roses and laburnum in the air. I lay back against the pillows and let my eyes close.

I must have dropped off to sleep when the sound of Eric's voice awakened me.

"How lovely you look, lying there," he said softly.

"Come, there is room for two."

"I long to, you know how I long to."

"My dear Eric." I sat up and he settled into a bench next to me. He smiled but I noticed lines of worry on his handsome forehead, and a look of anxiety in his fine dark eyes as he leaned over to kiss me.

It was hard for me to restrain myself, and I kissed him back passionately. After a time he released me, as he invariably did, his will being stronger than mine.

"I think Amélie suspects that we meet like this, in secret. I must not see you for a while. I'm going to pretend, for your sake, that I am in love with someone else. Then Amélie can be jealous of her, and not of you."

He kissed my hand, and then my cheek,

which was wet with tears.

"I understand," I managed to say. "You are right, of course. There must be no doubt about my fidelity, no gossip. Already there are rumors enough."

It was true. People said I was the mistress of Comte d'Adhemar, and the Prince de Ligne and the rich Hungarian Count Esterházy, and even Louis's youngest brother Charlot, whose company I enjoy and who was known to be the lover of many women of the court.

Eric and I took a tender leave of one another and I do not expect to see him alone for some time. Of course I see him often when others are present, since his duties as equerry bring him to my apartments or my husband's frequently. He is also in charge of my stables at the Petit Trianon. It is tantalizing to be so near him so often, to feel the thrill that his presence always arouses in me, and yet to have to keep my correct and formal distance.

It is tantalizing, it is unnatural. It is cruel. If only Eric were my husband instead of Louis, how happy my life would be. Meanwhile I worry, and wait.

August 27, 1777
Amélie is pregnant again. She brought me a

medal of Ste. Lucille which she says I must put under my pillow to bring me a child.

She curtseyed when she offered it to me, and looked up slyly with a half-smile.

"Ste. Lucille will bring you a child," she said, her voice sharp, "if you are faithful to your husband only, and leave other women's husbands alone."

"Our mistress is a faithful wife," said Sophie tartly.

"I hope that may be so," Amélie retorted. "Even you cannot observe her every moment of the day."

"You forget yourself, Amélie. Resume your duties."

"I will resume mine, your highness, if you will do yours."

"You should dismiss that impertinent girl," was Sophie's advice after Amélie had sauntered off. But of course I could not dismiss Amélie. I could not take the risk that she would spread spiteful gossip, or that she would force Eric to leave the court.

"She does her work well enough," Loulou remarked, knowing the reasons that I wanted Amélie to remain in my household. "I will insist that she speak respectfully."

October 20, 1777
We are all wearing a new hairstyle. It is

called the American Pouf. Red, white and blue ribbons and little American flags are entwined in mounds of hair and hairpieces. I began the fashion when the famous American Benjamin Franklin was brought to my husband's levee by Joseph and Louis and Mr. Franklin talked on and on about his inventions.

We are giving the Americans arms and food to help them fight the British but it is all done in secret.

December 14, 1777
Winter is dreary already and I am in low spirits. I think now that I will never have a child. Maman has sent me a girdle blessed by Ste. Radegunde, to wear to bed. It is a precious relic from the abbey of Melk embroidered with secret prayers and occult symbols and she says it has never been known to fail.

Loulou and Yolande look at me with pity in their eyes. They know how much I want and need a child. Mercy says there is new talk of finding a way to have me put aside and marrying Louis to someone else. No one wants Stanny to become king and if Louis were to die Stanny would rule. If Stanny died then it would be Charlot, and after Charlot would come his sons. Charlot and his foolish wife Thérèse have three children already.

When will my prayers be answered?

January 3, 1778

A thousand candles lit the long staircase at Yolande's ball last night, and as I began to go up the stairs the musicians were playing a sweet Viennese tune.

I remember thinking, they're playing that song just for me, because they know I love it, and then I remember glancing up the staircase, and then — oh, then — my memory folds in and out on itself like a kaleidoscope and the images grow blurry in my mind.

For I saw, coming down the staircase toward me, the most beautiful man I have ever seen. He was wearing a white uniform, and he looked so tall and slender and regal — no, more than regal, almost like a marble statue of a Greek god come to life. He had blond hair, a little ruffled by the wind as he came in from outside I suppose, and he smiled, not just with his lips but with his beautiful blue eyes and his whole face.

I stopped breathing and stared, forgetting everything else around me, as he came down the stairs toward me. The musicians must have been continuing to play but I did not hear their music. All around me people must have been coming and going, others dancing and talking on the dance floor below. But I was unaware of any of it. I saw only the smiling blond man in the white uniform, holding out his hand to me in friendship, walking toward me with the slowness of a dream.

"Your highness," he said, his voice deep and inviting.

I held out my small hand to him. He took it in his much larger one and pressed his warm lips to my wrist. I felt a spurt of flame ignite at my wrist and spread up my arm, across my chest, into my neck and cheeks. I could not speak. I could not move or think.

Somehow the moment passed, and the next thing I knew I was standing in a circle of friends, whispering to Loulou, "Who is that beautiful man?"

"That is Count Axel Fersen. He's just come from Sweden. His father is Field Marshal Fersen of the Swedish Army."

"Tell me he isn't going back to Sweden right away."

"Shall I find out?"

"Yes. No. Oh yes, please find out. Invite him — invite him to a late supper in my apartments tomorrow night."

Out of the corner of my eye I watched Loulou make her way through the crowded room to where Count Fersen stood, taller than most of the men around him, his fair hair gleaming in the candlelight. They spoke together briefly, then Loulou turned and left him to return to me. At that moment he looked in my direction, fleetingly, and before I turned my head away I thought I saw the merest glimmer of a smile on his lips.

Tomorrow I will see him again. Will I be able to sleep tonight?

January 5, 1778

Last night Axel came to supper and as soon as he entered the room I felt once again the strange and wonderful impact of his presence. Our eyes met and even though he was not near me I saw, or thought I saw, a look of recognition on his handsome face. Not the recognition of me as Antoinette, but a different kind of recognition entirely, as of someone close to him whom he had known for a long time. I cannot describe it, but I felt it, and I knew that he felt it too.

We were twelve at supper. Louis was absent. He never came to my late suppers, preferring to eat an early supper served to him by Chambertin and then retire to bed with a box of bonbons.

Axel sat across the table from me, between Yolande and the old Duchesse de Lorme, who is seventy and quite hard of hearing. He spoke wittily and very graciously to both of them, nodding patiently when the duchess misunderstood him and turning aside Yolande's flirtatious compliments with jokes and light banter.

Through it all, in passing, he glanced at me again and again, each glance a thrilling reminder to me of our unspoken closeness. For I did feel very close to him throughout that long supper, as aware of him there across the table as I was aware of my own breathing, my own heartbeat. We did not speak directly to each other, yet how much was said without words! How much was felt!

When the evening ended and he took my hand to kiss in parting I felt him slip a note into my palm.

"Good night, your majesty," he said. "And au revoir."

"Good night, count. I look forward to seeing you again soon."

I could hardly wait to read the note.

"Shall I come to you tomorrow afternoon at the Petit Trianon?" he wrote. "Please say yes."

I sent a page to Axel's lodgings with a note that consisted of only one word.

"Yes."

January 7, 1778

I can think of only one thing: Axel. Axel. Axel.

My world has been turned upside down and I am happily spinning and reeling with the impact. What glorious confusion!

I hardly know what words to put here, for there are not words to describe what is happening to me. It is as if I am newly born. As if I have crossed a threshold into an unknown land, the land of the heart.

Abbé Vermond has read to me about the Beatific Vision, when a saint glimpses the face of God and a new world opens before him. I too have had my Beatific Vision. I have glimpsed, as if for the first time, the face of love.

Axel came to me yesterday at the Petit Trianon and I told Loulou to send him up at once to my private rooms. He stepped across the threshold, held out his arms and I rushed into them, letting him enfold me as if he would never let me go.

"How can this be?" I said to him wonderingly when at last he released me and we stood, hands clasped tightly, regarding each other. "How can I love you so, when I don't even know you?"

I spoke without thought, and was surprised at the boldness of my own words. Yet they were true. Why not speak them?

"My little angel, I am hardly the one to ask for an explanation. All I know is, I am enraptured with you."

He kissed me then, long and fervently, and for the next hour I was lost in a sweet haze of joy and pleasure. He was a skillful and tender lover, and told me again and again how beautiful I was, calling me his little angel. When he stroked my cheek and smoothed my hair his hands were very gentle, and when we looked at each other I could not look away, so caught up was I in the beauty and depth and infinite sweetness in his fine blue eyes.

I made certain we were alone all afternoon, and we dined on sweet cream and strawberries and goose liver paté while Axel told me all about his life, bending over me from time to time and kissing me as he talked. I love listening to him talk. He speaks French and German very well but with a funny Swedish accent. His voice is low and deep and he talks slowly, everything he does is unhurried and full of grace.

His father is an important nobleman in Sweden and an adviser to the king. Axel expects to be like him. He has many military honors and decorations and has been in battles before. He jokes about it but I am sure he is very brave.

I cannot think of anything but Axel. I feel swallowed up by love for him, afloat on a vast sea of love, basking under the warm sun of love. They say that love between two people grows slowly over time and becomes deeper and richer with the years. That is nonsense. I now know that real love sweeps into one's life with the fury of a sudden storm. It is instant and powerful. Nothing else matters. Reason, restraint, judgment are swept away with the force of a swollen river surging past its banks, and nothing — not thought or feeling, sensations or life itself — can ever be the same again.

January 15, 1778
Axel is to be here only a short time. He is going to America with General Rochambeau. They are taking troops to help the Americans defeat the British, our enemies. They will fight in the savage wilderness, with the wild animals. There will be terrible danger. I am worried about his safety

but he only laughs and says he thinks the court of Versailles is not a very safe place either.

He attended Louis's levee in full uniform and when he was introduced, Louis stared at his chest with its expanse of ribbons and gleaming stars and gold medallions. I stood by, saying nothing.

Louis stepped very close to Axel and said quite loudly, "How did you get all those? Did you steal them?"

Axel smiled. "They gave me this one for ducking well under fire," he said, pointing to one of the shining medals. "And this one for staying out of artillery range."

Louis's loud laugh could be heard all across the large salon. He clapped Axel on the back roughly. "That's good. I'll remember that. For staying out of artillery range. That's good.

"I've never been near a battle myself," Louis added, watching Axel as he spoke to see how he would react.

"Your highness is much too important to the realm to be risked in combat," was the deft reply. "You are needed to direct the course of battles, not fight in them."

"I suppose so. In fact I would probably be in the way," was Louis's frank admission.

"I am told your majesty has a fine collection of maps," Axel said, avoiding the awkward subject of Louis's questionable value on the battlefield. "Have you any of the British colonies in the Americas? I would very much like to study them."

I moved away to talk to some Italian dignitaries and did not hear any more. I felt uneasy standing there, so close to both my husband and the man I love most in the world. I hoped I was not growing red in the face with embarrassment. At this court, as at Schönbrunn, women socialize with their husbands and lovers in a very relaxed and matter-of-fact way. However, this deception is new to me. I never felt any awkwardness or embarrassment about my infatuation with Eric, because he was only a servant. No servant could ever be a true rival to the king. But Axel, so highborn, so much at ease in the splendors of Versailles, he was a different matter entirely. And I must admit that my love for Axel is as far above my love for Eric as the heavens are above the earth.

January 24, 1778
He is to leave in three weeks. I cannot bear the thought of parting from him. What will I do?

January 27, 1778

This afternoon Axel and I lay naked in front of the fire on a thick bearskin rug, while it snowed outside. We have had a severe storm and there is deep snow everywhere. The view from my windows is all white. Only Loulou knows that Axel is here with me, and she brings us our food and keeps the other servants away, especially Amélie.

It was so warm and cosy by the fire, and the crackle of the logs as they burned was soothing and restful. I could almost forget, as I lay in his arms, that he will soon be gone. Almost — but not quite. When we made love I clung to him, as if by holding him as tightly as I could I might be able to keep him with me forever.

Afterwards, while he drowsed, I traced the long lines of his beautiful lean body with my fingertips, admiring each curve and hollow, each strong muscle, the curling blond hair on his broad chest, the smooth belly and taut loins, the entirety of him. He opened his eyes, took my hand and kissed my fingertips.

"I could never have imagined, when I left Vienna, that I would meet anyone like you. That I would feel as I do now. For a long time I wished, secretly, that I had never come to France at all. Nothing here has gone as I hoped — as my family hoped. As a wife I am a failure."

"Surely not. The Swedish ambassador has told me how good you have always been to your husband. How you have helped him and understood him when no one else could have."

"But I have failed. I have not given him a son, an heir to the throne of France."

"Not yet, perhaps. But you may be a mother in the future — unless Louis is incapable. Has he any bastards?"

"No. I'm sure he hasn't."

"Then the fault may lie with him, not with you. You mustn't blame yourself."

"Count Mercy used to tell me to take a lover, some nobleman who looked like Louis, and have children with him. But I couldn't imagine doing that, lying about who the real father was."

"No. Besides, the truth would be bound to come out sooner or later."

"Axel," I said a little hesitantly, "there is something I need to confess to you."

"What is that, my little angel?"

"There is someone I loved before I met you."

He smiled indulgently and stroked my hair. "Yes? And who was this lucky man? Don't worry. I may envy him but I won't challenge him to a duel."

"My groom, Eric." My voice was very low. "We never actually made love, but —"

"Yes, yes, I understand. It was a beautiful, innocent young love. I'm glad you told me. And I too must confess, dearest angel, that I have had loves of my own."

"Have there been many women in your life?"

"Many. But only a few whom I have truly loved."

"And did you never want to marry?"

At this Axel's face grew grim, his mouth set in a firm line.

"It is expected of me. One day, I suppose, I shall have to fulfill those expectations. Meanwhile, I have a — a friend, a very dear friend, Madame Eleanora Sullivan, who lives in Paris and whose company I treasure. She is a courtesan, and I have known her for a long time."

"A courtesan like my friend Madame Solange."

"Madame Solange is very lovely. Eleanora is far less lovely, and much more seasoned, but she has a warm heart and a generous spirit. Unlike so many people in this world, she has truly lived. She has been many things, a wife, an entertainer, an acrobat in the circus. She is fearless, and always completely herself. I admire her very much. She has taught me a good deal about life."

He saw that I looked crestfallen, and hastened to reassure me.

"Ah, my little angel, I would never want you to think of Eleanora as a rival." He took my face in his cupped hands, looked at me fondly, and kissed me. "I have never treasured any woman the way I treasure you now, this moment. You are all I think of, all I want. If only I didn't have to leave you —"

We stopped talking then, and made love again, and slept, and ate, and then talked some more, until Loulou came to light the lamps and Axel had to go.

Oh, how I love him! I would walk through fire for him. I would go, if he asked me, to the ends of the earth to be with him. If only he did not have to leave for America, and risk his life there. If only I could make him stay here, in this warm room, his long, lean white body gleaming in the firelight, his soft blue eyes full of love.

February 20, 1778

Axel is gone and I am in mourning. I could not bear to see him go. I was in tears when he came with General Rochambeau for his formal leavetaking. His sister was there, Baroness Piper. She wept and he embraced her very tenderly. He did not dare embrace me, he merely kissed my hand and pressed a note into it. Later I read it.

"My darling little angel, I carry your love with me. Keep mine in your heart until I return."

Where is he now? How soon will he come back to me?

April 12, 1778

I am going to have a baby. Sophie thinks all the signs are there. General Krottendorf is late, my breasts are tender and sore and I am sleepy all the time.

Louis is the father, of course, not Axel. Axel was very careful when we made love. He told me he wanted to ensure that there were no consequences.

Louis says we must wait another month before we announce my condition to the world, and Dr. Boisgilbert agrees. I have not written the good news to maman yet. How very happy she will be to hear it.

April 21, 1778

Our soldiers are gathering by the thousands in the camps in Brittany and Normandy.

Mercy says we may invade England, which has declared war on us because we made an alliance with the American colonies. Louis spends a great deal of time going over lists of supplies and provisions for the troops and writing letters to the arms manufacturers pointing out defects in guns and cannon. He hates meeting with the ministers and complains to me that they ignore him and do the opposite of what he thinks is best.

I remind him that they have been chosen for their wisdom and knowledge, which is greater than his. But he becomes stubborn when his vanity is injured, which is often.

I throw up every morning and sleep every afternoon. I am assured that this is normal. I am carrying the next heir to the throne of France, and his safety is all that matters.

May 3, 1778

Axel has come back to court and I can see him often. His expedition with General Rochambeau is postponed. I could not be happier to have him here except that I know he goes to Paris to visit Eleanora Sullivan. I spend my days being sick and being sleepy and wondering where Axel is when he is not with me and sometimes going with Louis to confer with our foreign minister the Comte de Vergennes who hates Austria and hates me.

I am helping Axel obtain a regimental command.

June 7, 1778
Dr. Boisgilbert says I must not fret over anything. I am learning to make net purses. Louis's Aunt Adelaide is teaching me. I know Paris is full of jokes that Charlot is the real father of my child. I ignore these slanders.

Abbé Vermond's brother is to be my accoucheur. Maman does not approve. She says he is a bungler. He came to see me and made me very uneasy. He is nothing like the abbé, whom I have known all my life and who is soft-spoken and highly intelligent. Dr. Vermond is nervous and cannot hold still. When he touches me I feel his sweaty hands tremble.

How can I help but fret when there is war and nasty gossip about me and I am to have a nervous accoucheur? And when it is all I can do to stay cool in the midst of this heat wave?

July 9, 1778
We are here at Compiègne and I walk every day in the cool of the forest under the great

trees. The baby kicks me a lot. He is an ath-lete, Louis says. He will be a great warrior.

"A great worrier, more likely," I tell Yolande, who walks with me in the after-noons. "His father is the greatest worrier who ever lived."

Louis is apprehensive over the war, which has been declared but isn't yet being fought, over his ministers, who won't listen to him and do what they please, over the lack of money in the treasury and the growing number of rabbits in the forest. He shoots the rabbits and swears under his breath that he wishes he could shoot all the ministers.

He is excited about the baby yet stub-born about Dr. Vermond. Everyone says English accoucheurs are the best and I ought to have one. Queen Charlotte, the English King George's wife, is German but is having all her babies delivered by an English doctor. I believe she has had many children and nearly all of them lived. Axel has sent for a Swedish doctor who studied in Edinburgh and he will be on hand when I go into labor. Sophie has promised that there will be a good midwife present as well, she will see to it. I feel better. Of course the baby will not be born for many months.

August 4, 1778

I have made net purses for maman, Carlotta, Loulou and all my sisters and nieces. I cannot force myself to tie another knot! I am embroidering clothes for the baby now, though he already has entire chests full of blankets and nightclothes and knitted stockings. Gifts for him arrive daily.

Abbé Vermond reads to me while I rest. Axel is away a lot with the soldiers in camp near the coast. My life is very dull and my belly is growing larger every week. Surely after this I will never have a small waist again.

September 1, 1778

Versailles is full of nobles. They are coming in from the country, ignoring the hunting season and moving into any rooms they can find, even the tiny cold ones in the attic. They want to be here for the birth of my child. He is not due until December but babies sometimes come early as everyone knows.

Dr. Vermond has ordered my bedchamber sealed tight so that it will stay warm for my delivery. The windows are fastened shut and all the cracks filled with glue and paint. The doors of the room are all nailed shut except for one which is left open for people to come and go. Tall screens are being put in place all around my bed, to preserve at least a bit of privacy.

It is very important that the birth be witnessed and I am prepared for that. I was present with Louis and dozens of others at all three of Thérèse's births and we saw clearly that her babies came out of her body and were not secretly brought in from outside and placed in the cradle. There must be no impostors in the royal family of France.

Thérèse screamed and swore and was cowardly during her labor, all three times. I will be brave. I will not make such a spectacle of myself. I want my son to be proud of me. One day when he is king I want others to tell him, "Yes, I was present the day you were born. Your mother bore you bravely. She hardly uttered a sound."

November 2, 1778

I did not know it was possible for one small woman's belly to stretch so far. I no longer walk, I waddle. I am twenty-three years old today but no one except maman takes any notice of my birthday. They are all watching me, eager to see a look of pain cross my forehead, or to hear me gasp and clutch my stomach.

The servants have a lottery under way, betting on what day my baby will be born. Louis has forbidden it but they buy and sell their tickets anyway, even Chambertin.

November 18, 1778
A brick crashed through a window in my sitting room today. Wrapped around the brick was a foul pamphlet with crude drawings of me having sex with other women. "Down with the Austrian bitch!" was written on the back of the pamphlet. Sophie threw it away, but Amélie found it and brought it to me to read. It is very odd that now that I am in love with Axel and see Eric only rarely, Amélie hates me more than ever.

December 20, 1778
Yesterday morning early I woke up with a terribly sore back and the pain did not go away even when Sophie brought me willow bark tea which usually eases my backaches.

Dr. Vermond was called in from the next room and at once ordered me into the labor bed. I was helped into bed and soon began to sweat as the fire in the hearth was blazing very high and the room was very warm.

The pain spread to my belly and I realized I must be in labor. Sophie strapped on the holy girdle blessed by Ste. Radegunde from Melk Abbey and I clutched my rosary of ivory beads, the one maman gave me when I was a little girl at Schönbrunn. I tried not to think of all the women I have heard of who died giving birth. I remembered what Dr. Boisgilbert told me, that I was a sturdy girl who could stand up well to labor and childbirth. I am a sturdy girl, I told myself over and over between attacks of the gripping pain. I am a sturdy girl, I am strong enough to face anything.

Axel came in along with Louis and his brothers and cousins. Before long Maurepas and Vergennes and the other ministers had come too, and I began to feel very embarrassed. The huge screens that loomed up on all sides of the bed, hemming me in, shielded me from the onlookers to a degree but they also made me feel a need for air. I called for Sophie to fan me but Dr. Vermond sharply ordered her away. He also ordered Mufti taken off my bed which made me cry. She always sleeps on my bed. She comforts me. And she is so old now she surely cannot be a nuisance to anyone.

I could hear a buzz of conversation and the noise of many shuffling feet in the rooms next to my bedchamber and in the corridor outside. I knew the courtiers and visiting dignitaries were gathering, waiting to be admitted into the bedchamber. Between contractions I wondered idly which of the servants would win the lottery.

After an hour the pains grew worse, and I gritted my teeth and wrapped the rosary around my wrist and grabbed at the ropes that held the screens in place every time I felt a new spasm grip me. I heard Stanny and Josephine chatting about how hungry they were and when would they ever get to eat and I wanted to scream at them, can't you see I'm suffering?

Again and again the strong contractions tore through me, and I thought, this can't go on much longer, I can't take much more of this, or I'll surely die. I could see Count Mercy moving about in the back of the room, behind Axel and Louis and his relations and the ministers. He looked ill at ease.

"Can't you hurry it along?" Louis asked Dr. Vermond. "There must be some herb, some medicinal drink —"

"Nature must take its course," the doctor said, but he was beginning to look at me nervously and he tugged abstractedly at his waistcoat and ran his hands through his thin gray hair in a way that made me more anxious.

I reached out for Sophie, who wriggled past the doctor, ignoring his imperious complaints, and took my outstretched hand.

"Poor, poor thing," she said, "you are having such a hard time of it."

"What if I can't do this?" I whispered to her.

She held my hand tightly as another strong wave of pain passed over me, making me gasp and leaving me tear-filled and limp.

"You can, you can. But you may need some help. I'm going to get the midwife."

She left my side and went out. I was aware that more people had come into the room, and were murmuring and moving about. I thought I glimpsed Loulou, her pale face even whiter than usual, standing off to one side.

Presently Sophie came back with a large, capable-looking peasant woman.

"This is who she needs," I heard Sophie say to Louis. "A real midwife."

I felt a strange pair of hands running over my belly and feeling between my legs. I shuddered. Dr. Vermond was protesting loudly. Then, suddenly, I felt as if iron hands had grabbed my belly and were squeezing it unmercifully. I couldn't help myself. I screamed.

At once the atmosphere in the room grew tense and expectant. The murmuring voices were hushed. I could hear the fire crackling in the hearth.

"The head. I must move the head," the midwife said, and began prodding and pushing at me.

"Take that woman away!" Dr. Vermond shouted. "I am in charge here!"

"Then you had better shift the baby," the midwife told him calmly, taking her hands off me and wiping them on her skirt, "or they will both die."

Dr. Vermond blanched, and took a step backward. "I must consult with — with — my colleagues. This is a difficult case. I was not — adequately warned —"

The more he hemmed and hawed, the whiter and more alarmed he became.

Out of the corner of my eye I saw Loulou start toward the bed, then her eyes closed and she slipped to the floor. Immediately there was a commotion, and she was lifted up and taken out.

Louis was shouting at Dr. Vermond. "Do as she says! Shift the baby!" His voice was loud, but mine was louder as I felt another immense, prolonged, agonizing pain and screamed again.

"It is coming! The queen is having her baby!" Hearing my screams, the waiting crowd in the corridor outside was becoming impatient. Word was spreading rapidly that my baby was about to be born.

There was no holding back the crowd of nobles and courtiers who had been waiting for hours to be admitted to the bedchamber. They burst in a noisy flood through the single open doorway and came toward me, dozens and dozens of them, all at once. I thought at first they would knock over the screens on top of me and I would be smothered.

Suddenly the room felt unbearably hot, and I could not catch my breath. I was terrified, utterly terrified, and in such unendurable pain that everything, the people, the walls, the firelight, began to blur before my eyes.

Then I heard Axel's voice. Strong, commanding, reassuring.

"Sire," he was saying, "your accoucheur wants to consult a colleague. I have just the man." I struggled to stay alert. Through my dizziness I was able to see a man standing beside Axel, a pleasant-looking man in a black suit and with a neat bag wig.

"This is Dr. Sundersen, from Stockholm. He has delivered all the Queen of Sweden's babies."

The Swede bowed to Louis. "May I examine your wife?" he asked.

"Yes, yes. Somebody do something."

I was writhing helplessly, the sounds that were coming from my mouth were groans like the pitiful cries of wounded cattle.

Dr. Sundersen beckoned to the midwife, who resumed her painful manipulations of my belly while the doctor felt my pulse and took his gleaming metal instruments out of his bag.

He looked over at the woman, and addressed her. "I am so glad you are here. I often find that midwives know things of which we doctors are ignorant. Dr. Vermond, no doubt you were about to bleed the patient from the foot. Would you do so now, please."

I felt a painful cut as the French accoucheur, looking grateful to be of use, opened a vein between my toes and held a bowl under my foot while the dark red blood oozed from it.

Dr. Sundersen and the midwife worked smoothly and easily together, and I began to feel, despite my pain and weariness, that I was at last in good hands. Between contractions I tried to fix my eyes on Axel, who stood near Louis, a look of grave concern on his dear face. Even in those moments of agony I thought, he is dearer to me than anything, dearer than life itself.

"There," I heard the midwife say, above the increasing din in the room. "It will come now, the head is free."

"Your highness," Dr. Sundersen said to me, "I want you to concentrate now. I need you to stay awake. I want you to summon all your strength. You are going to work harder now than you have ever worked in your life. It will not take long. Shall we do this together?"

"Yes," I said, as loudly and bravely as I could. As I said it I knew that I would be able to bring my baby into the world.

"Push against my hand," the doctor told me, "as though you were lifting a tall building."

I did as he asked, no longer much aware of my pain, or of the undignified cheering and whistling that had begun in the room, or of the stifling airless heat. All my concentration, all my effort went to pushing up and out against the doctor's strong hand. The midwife too pushed down hard on my belly with one hand while with the other she held my arm and talked to me encouragingly.

I felt cold metal being put up inside of me, and a gush of warm liquid flowing out, and then excited gasps from the spectators, some of whom, I realized, had climbed up onto the furniture to get a better look at what was happening to my body.

"Here it comes now. Just a little more effort. Another lift of the tall building."

In those moments I did indeed work as hard as I ever had, and I grunted like a ditchdigger.

A cheer went up, applause began, and I knew that my baby was being born. At last, my son. The heir to the throne. The next king —

Suddenly, shockingly, the applause ceased and the cheering turned to groans.

Dr. Sundersen was smiling as he held the squalling, bloody, wrinkled baby up for me to see.

"Your daughter is perfect, your highness. A princess for France."

I fainted.

That was yesterday. Today I am recovering, resting in my bedchamber which is still littered with trays of half-eaten pastries and discarded orange peels and peanut shells and old newspapers left behind by Louis and the others. My chamberwomen are too busy gawking at the baby and bringing me gifts and messages of congratulations to do any cleaning. Mufti is sleeping on my bed and the pugs run back and forth chasing each other and barking frantically when visitors come into the room.

Through it all the baby sleeps quite peacefully, small and pretty and greedy for milk when she is awake. She is a terrible disappointment, of course. She should have been a boy. I am regarded as a failure, though Louis says I should pay no attention to what anyone thinks and that we must look forward to having sons.

No, I think. Never again. I will never go through such a terrible ordeal again.

But my little one, my Marie-Thérèse, is so precious to me. I love her far more than I ever imagined I would. My very own, beloved, dear child. I will try to be as good a mother to her as maman has been to me. Only I won't scold her or criticize her as much.

Axel came to see me this afternoon. Officially he was bringing congratulations from King Gustavus of Sweden, and a gift, a carved statue of a Christmas angel with gilded wings and a halo of lit candles on her head.

Others were present in the bedchamber,

so we could not speak as we would have wished to. But as he left Axel took my hand and kissed it, and we exchanged a fleeting look that held all our love.

"Thank you, Count Fersen," I said as he rose to go, "for all you did yesterday for France. You and Dr. Sundersen saved my life."

SIX

January 2, 1779
I feel stronger each day. I am taking burdock root, which is supposed to make me able to have another child quickly and my little Marie-Thérèse has a wetnurse so my milk is supposed to be drying up. Louis says we must have a son right away so no one will be able to say we are incapable of creating one together. He says royal daughters are a curse to the throne if there are too many of them, and I know this is true. Mother told me that when she had her first child, my oldest sister Anna, no one at court gave her any peace until she had Joseph three years later.

January 20, 1779
Sophie has brought me some garlic in a pouch and put it beside my bed. She says I must smell it every day. If one day I wake up and I can't smell it, then I will know that I am pregnant. I smell it every day and sometimes at night when I can't sleep or when Louis wakes me up with his loud snoring.

February 14, 1779

I have given little Marie-Thérèse the nickname Mousseline which was my mother's pet name for my sister Josepha. Her hair is starting to grow and it is a light blond like mine. Her eyes are gray and when she looks at me it is a very penetrating look. She does not smile yet. Her gums are not swollen or sore so there is no sign of any milk teeth coming soon.

I have taken her to Louis's levee and everyone crowds around to look at her, and also at me, for they are all expecting that I will soon be pregnant again.

February 28, 1779

Louis played a mean trick on me. He knows I sniff the garlic in the pouch beside my bed, hoping for the day when I cannot smell it and then I will know I am pregnant.

He took the garlic out of the pouch and put in asafoetida, which as everyone knows has a very different smell. A stink in fact. So I smelled the pouch and I knew something was wrong. My sense of smell had changed. It must mean I was pregnant.

I hurried to tell Sophie. I can't smell the garlic, I told her. I smell something else. It is horrible.

She smelled it, and made a wry face.

"Someone is playing tricks on you," she said. "It must be that impertinent girl, that Amélie."

But Amélie was nowhere near my bedchamber, and had not been near it for several days.

Then I saw Louis in the corridor, laughing to himself. I realized he must have been the one to replace the garlic with something else. He continued to study herbs and plants and kept a large supply of them in his attic rooms.

I said nothing to Sophie but that night, when Louis came to my bed, I reproached him and he hung his head sheepishly and admitted what he had done.

"It was only asafoetida. It didn't do you any harm. I thought it was funny." He chuckled.

"It's cruel to joke about important things."

"I have to joke about them," he said as he climbed into bed, his voice low and full of weariness. "Otherwise I couldn't go on. I do so hate pretending to be something I'm not."

"And what is that?"

"Why, king, of course."

"But you are the king. The sacred, anointed, rightful King of France."

"We both know that is only an act. Besides, as I have explained to you many times, it was my father who should have been ruling. Or else my older brother. It was never meant to be me."

"These are just excuses."

"That's where you are wrong. I have developed a theory. The Theory of Mistaken Destiny. I've only confided it to Chambertin and Gamin so far."

I said nothing. Louis's mind took strange turns. I have grown accustomed to them.

"In my theory, some men are thrust by fate into positions for which they were never intended at birth. Such men are cursed never to fulfill the destiny foisted upon them. It is a tragedy, really, when that happens. A tragedy worthy of the pen of the great Racine."

I sighed. "Well, that's as may be. But leave my garlic alone from now on. And as to our destinies, yours and mine, we must simply do the best we can from day to day, and not think too much about tragedies. Mercy is always telling me to try to remain positive and cheerful."

"Mercy treats you like a simpleton."

There was nothing I could say to that. Count Mercy, who had often shown me kindness when others were harsh, certainly considered me to be far more shrewd than Louis. And far more courageous.

"The count and I are on good terms," I said, and did not continue the conversation. I often find Louis's lofty reasonings tiresome. He is not succeeding as a king, he knows it, and he attempts to excuse it rather than attempting to improve.

If only he would listen to good advice!

April 1, 1779
General Krottendorf is very very late and I cannot smell the garlic. I think I am pregnant again. I feel ill in the morning. Already I dread the pain to come but I have made Louis promise to hire Dr. Sundersen again, and the skillful midwife Sophie found or another good one.

We have decided to wait to announce my pregnancy, just as we did with Mousseline. Next month is soon enough Louis thinks. I can hardly wait to write to maman. If only I could tell her in person.

Louis jokes that we should call our boy Garlic.

May 2, 1779
Yesterday I got very sick and lost the baby. Sophie was with me every minute. When she emptied my chamberpot she saw the blood

in my urine and knew right away that my pregnancy was over.

"Probably it was a boy," she told me. "When babies are lost it is more often a boy, the midwives say, and they know."

"But that is terrible," I said through my tears.

"No, it is good. It means you can make boy babies as well as girls. The next boy will be stronger. He will have a chance to survive."

I pray that she is right.

August 16, 1779

Louis's youngest brother Charlot came today to take me to the races. He drove up with a furious clatter in his new green carriage, which nearly tipped over in the courtyard. It is very light and fragile, with thin high wheels and no roof and hardly any sides.

Louis would never have let me ride in it if he had seen it. But Louis is away hunting, so I can do as I please.

"Your majesty," Charlot called out as I approached the carriage, "it is The Devil, at your service." He was all in white, from his elegant wig to his embroidered brocade doublet to his white satin shoes with diamond buckles. I could tell he had been drinking because he swayed back and forth as he stood, holding the reins of the restless horses in his hands.

I smiled. He nearly always makes me smile and laugh. The postilion helped me up, and I felt the delicate frame of the carriage shudder under me as I sat on the narrow upholstered seat and Charlot sank down beside me.

"And are you really the devil, or is that only a vile rumor?"

"Not me, your majesty, this wondrous vehicle. She is The Devil Incarnate, because she is so dangerous! And so fast, and so tempting!"

I held on tightly as we raced along the dusty road, the carriage dipping and swerving at every rut and hole, our escort of mounted guardsmen thundering along behind us.

The races, when we reached the racetrack, were not nearly as thrilling as the ride there and back in The Devil, and Charlot has offered to take me again next week.

I said I would go if he promised not to tell Louis.

He snorted. "He'll find out sure enough. There are always people eager to tell him everything you do and everywhere you go.

You know the stories that are being spread about us, that we are lovers, that you are my partner in debauchery, that together we spend more money than all the tax farmers can collect."

"Foolish gossip, nothing more. Besides, it is well known that I prefer older men, like the Comte de Giverny." We both laughed at this. The count was over seventy.

I got down out of the shaky carriage and said goodbye.

"I'm off to Paris," Charlot called out as he flicked his whip over the backs of his horses, "for another night of wine, women and song!"

He cheered me up, and I am much in need of cheer. He cannot guess that his companionship is a great boon to me. As long as tongues wag about my supposed affair with Charlot, they are silent about my real love, Axel. Our precious times together remain secret, except from loyal Loulou and discreet Yolande. Sometimes I think Louis knows and accepts that Axel and I love each other, for Axel is one of the very few men Louis feels he can turn to for friendship and advice. But Louis and I have never spoken a word about my feelings for Axel. And I may be wrong. Louis may not realize or suspect a thing.

September 3, 1779
Today Mousseline said very clearly "Mama."
Only she said it to the wetnurse.

October 13, 1779
I have decreed that all the women at court
will wear feathers. Ostrich feathers, peacock
feathers, parrot feathers. Within a few hours
of my announcement every shop in Paris
was sold out of feathers, of course. The birds
in the royal menagerie have been removed to
a secret safe place to protect them from
feather-hunters with guns.

December 13, 1779
Nearly a year ago my little girl was born.
How I wish I was now carrying her little
brother inside of me.

December 27, 1779
Cold weather has forced the workmen to
stop their labors at the Petit Trianon, where
I am having renovations made. No fires can
be lit in the fireplaces because new over-
mantels are being installed. So the house is
extremely cold. Carpenters cannot work
with chilblains on their fingers.

The bills have begun to come in for the
redecoration and they seem unusually
high. I questioned the architects and they

were evasive. After some thought and a few inquiries I guessed the reason: the architects are receiving a portion of each sum charged to the royal treasury!

I was very angry once I realized this and I went to inform Louis about it. He was up in the attic, in the room where he makes his locks with the master locksmith M. Gamin. He spends more and more of his time here, away from people and hiding from the ministers.

He looked up from what he was doing as I came in and greeted me, but did not stop. He was sitting at his workbench, bent over a complicated piece of machinery. Bits of metal were spread over the bench.

"Louis, I must speak with you."

"Very well."

"The renovations are costing too much. The architects are overcharging. I have caught them at it."

"I don't doubt it."

"But — something must be done! This must stop!"

"Just send the bills to M. Necker."

"Yes, I know you think M. Necker will solve all our financial problems, but he has been receiving bills from these architects for four years, and he has paid them!"

Louis wiped his brow. He was preoccupied with inserting a small piece of metal between two larger pieces. He paused while he completed the task, after several failed attempts.

"If he has paid the bills, then we must owe the money. I wouldn't worry over it." I recognized the edge of exasperation that came into Louis's voice when a subject irritated him.

"You are the one who used to always say 'Economy, economy!' "

"That was before."

"Before what?"

"Before I found out what a hopeless quagmire our finances are."

"And now?"

"Now I leave everything to the genius, the wizard. M. Necker."

"Then I will go and complain to him."

"Complain away, it won't make any difference."

I left him there, bent over his intricate constructions, and returned to my apartments. The following afternoon I summoned M. Necker who bowed to me with an amiable smile when he was ushered in. I had seen him often, but had never had a conversation with him. He is a large, portly man, of imposing appearance, with a prominent jaw and a comical monkeylike face. He looked sleek and smooth, well fed and accustomed to his comforts. I had heard that he possessed an immense personal fortune.

"How can I be of service?" he asked.

I handed him the most recent bills from the renovations to the Petit Trianon.

"These bills are too high," I said simply. "The architects are overcharging."

He took them and rapidly looked them over, his expression grave. "I see nothing amiss here."

"But the amounts are twice the initial sums named when the renovations were begun."

"Estimates are usually exceeded. One comes to expect that. It is impossible to anticipate every contingency."

I was having difficulty keeping my temper.

"If you will look more carefully at the bills, you will see that the architects have added fees of their own, for work they did not do."

The financier shrugged. "They supervised."

Something in his manner put me on my guard. He was being just as evasive as the architects had been when I confronted them. Why? I watched him, putting the bills into a neat pile and setting them aside. The thought came to me, he's in league with them. He's being bribed. There is no one we can trust to honestly do what is best for France.

M. Necker met my gaze. An understanding passed between us.

"Madame," he said after a pause, "the architects supervise, and for that they are paid. I supervise the royal finances, and those who send in the bills, and for that I am also paid. The real question is not, how large are the bills, but rather, how will the funds be raised to pay the bills. That is where I am useful."

He walked over to a carved cabinet where I keep a collection of fine porcelain figurines. He contemplated them, as if assessing their value, then turned back to me.

"I know the bankers. We speak the same language. I can persuade them to part with funds when others cannot. Therein lies my value. In the same way, the architects know the builders and decorators. They speak the same language. They can assure that work gets done, well and on time. Therein lies their value. I believe I have made my point. I wish you joy of your renovations."

I saw that it was pointless to talk further, and ended our interview.

March 17, 1780

All the gardens of the Petit Trianon were illuminated tonight in honor of the visit of King Gustavus to our court. Fires burned in a deep ditch that encircled the groves and lakes and beds of shrubbery. Candles in thousands of little pots threw a flickering light on the trees, making them glow pale green and luminous. It was a fairytale scene, eerie and magical. The Temple of Love shone with an unearthly light, its marble gleaming as if lit from within.

Through it all walked Axel, in all his splendor, so fair, so noble in his features and his carriage. He came to me as I sat on a carved stone bench beside the lake.

The air was warm for March, and perfumed with the scents of lavender and jasmine from blossoming plants brought from the greenhouses. Reflected firelight sparkled on the surface of the lake, and shone from the gold buttons of his white uniform and the row of gold medals that hung from colored ribbons across his chest.

He sat beside me and took me in his arms. I thought, I have never known such complete and perfect happiness. For an hour and more we sat there, no one near us, wrapped in each other's arms, while the lights played across the trees and buildings, gradually dimming as the stars brightened and the moon rose.

April 7, 1780

King Gustavus is leaving in two days. This afternoon he came for his final audience with Louis, accompanied by Axel and several others. Louis received him in the Chinese Salon, and I was present with some of my ladies.

Louis gave Gustavus a medal making him a Knight of the Golden Lily, and I gave him some beautiful Sèvres vases and tapestries from the Gobelins works.

He thanked us for our hospitality and then took us completely by surprise. "I would like to invite your majesties to visit me, at my court. To help me in the creation of my Swedish Versailles."

"Perhaps one day we shall," said Louis curtly.

"Oh, sire, you misunderstand me. I would like you to come very soon. This summer."

"Impossible," said Louis. "I am needed here."

"You need not stay longer than a few weeks."

"It takes a few weeks just to get to your faroff country. No! I cannot."

My thoughts were whirling. Sweden. Axel. Time with Axel.

King Gustavus looked over at me, then back at Louis. "How regrettable that your majesty cannot be spared. But perhaps your gracious queen could make the journey? I would so greatly value her advice in the decoration of my new palace. She has such exquisite taste."

I smiled. "And I would love to visit your beautiful country."

I could tell that Louis was quite taken aback by this turn of events. His mouth worked nervously, and he narrowed his small eyes. All was quiet in the room while he pondered his decision. I dared not look at Axel.

Finally Louis blurted out his answer.

"Yes! Yes, she shall go — but only for a month or two. She must be back before the weather gets cold."

But the weather is always cold in Sweden, I wanted to say, then checked myself.

"Your highness is most generous," King Gustavus said, and then addressed me.

"We will do our best to make you feel at home in Sweden, my dear." He kissed my hand, bowed to Louis who nodded back, and then took his leave. One by one the members of the king's entourage kissed my outstretched hand — last of all Axel, who as he straightened up, smiled at me and winked.

SEVEN

June 20, 1780
Here it is, the middle of the night by my clock only outside my window the sky is light. Not the bright light of noon, but light enough to read by. What a remarkable place this is. And what remarkable changes it is making in me!

I have been here at the palace of Drottningholm in Sweden for nearly three weeks. Each day I consult with the chief palace architects and decorators on the repairs and renovations being done. King Gustavus asks for my advice constantly, on a great variety of matters, not only the design of the palace but such things as how the royal dining table is set at Versailles and how many courses are served when the public is admitted to watch King Louis dine. In my small traveling party I brought along engineers, carpenters and gardeners. They have answered hundreds of Gustavus's queries about palace drainage and the repair of outdoor fountains, the usefulness of sunflowers in keeping mosquitoes away and methods of thatching and repairing roofs.

In all my life, no one has ever turned to me so constantly for advice and help. And I am finding that I like it very much! Louis relies on me a good deal, of course, but his pleas for help are only now and then. Long intervals pass between his spasms of panic. And what Louis needs, I cannot really provide. I cannot stiffen his backbone or shore up his confidence in himself. I can only provide the support of my presence and my concern, both of which hearten him until the next wave of fear strikes.

I must try to sleep, but it is hard, even with the curtains closed against the brightness of the midnight sun.

June 27, 1780

Every afternoon this week Gustavus has called together a group of officials or learned men to talk over important issues. He has invited me to be present. Axel is there to help in the discussions and also to learn, as Gustavus expects him to become his principal adviser one day. The men speak in French for my benefit, but it is a strange sort of French, and I cannot always understand them, especially when their speech is hurried. Axel has taught me a few words and phrases in Swedish, so that I can count to ten and name the days of the week and say "Please" and "Thank you" and "I'm very glad to meet you."

I don't understand why this is happening. Why all these deep matters are being aired in my presence. Gustavus says he wants to know, what do the French do? What do the French think? And he looks to me for those answers. I point out that I am not French but Austrian. He says that I am French by marriage.

I think Gustavus wants to impress me as much as consult me on French ways and attitudes. Axel says I am right to think this.

July 1, 1780

I miss my little Mousseline but it is better that she is not here. She is delicate and the weather here is very changeable. I receive news of her every two or three days and Chambertin writes with news of Louis. Louis himself has only written me three letters, all very brief. In the last one he included a vial of syrup of poppy, to help me sleep during the long light nights. I don't know why he sent it, unless he thinks Sweden is such a backward place that the apothecaries have no syrup of poppy. But that is nonsense. The shops here are well stocked with all sorts of medicinal remedies, as well as beautiful furs and carvings and warm knitted jackets and hats and mittens.

July 4, 1780

King Gustavus is to be occupied with the Riksdag, the Swedish Parliament, in the coming days and Axel has invited me to his estate, Fredenholm, which means the Place of Peace.

July 6, 1780

We arrived here yesterday after a long journey through deep woods and across snowy fields. Even though it is July, it snows here and there are areas where the snow never melts, from one year to the next.

The countryside is very beautiful, so un-touched and with so few people living here. Vast forests of fir and pine, many small blue lakes, larks and finches swooping and diving in the air. The purity and freshness of the air overwhelm me. I keep filling my lungs with it. I cannot get enough.

Axel's estate is really a large working farm, six hundred acres, and he rents out the fields to ten families who have been here since the 1500s. They were serfs at one time but his grandfather freed them and now they are tenant farmers, though they still look on Axel as an overlord and come to him to solve their problems and settle their disputes.

I decided not to bring any servants with me so I dress myself and arrange my own hair very simply. What a relief, not to have to endure the tedious hours-long toilette and all the time in front of the mirror with my hairdresser André. I feel more myself, more alive.

July 7, 1780
I awoke this morning to the sound of an axe chopping wood and when I went to the window I saw Axel hard at work, the sleeves of his linen shirt rolled up above his elbows, quartering logs. While I watched he methodically finished chopping the pile he had in front of him and brought them into the house where he soon had a warm fire going in the immense tiled stove, black with soot. The house is small enough that one stove warms it all, while providing hot water and a hot oven for cooking our food. We breakfasted on fresh bread and reindeer cheese and fish caught last night in the lake, plus a mound of sweet cloudberries from the bushes beside the door.

This afternoon we packed a basket with food and went walking in the hills. It is hard to say how long we walked because the light did not change. By the time Axel looked at his watch it was past six o'clock and we spread out our blanket in a dry spot overlooking a lake and sat down.

"So, my little angel," he said as we ate, "how do you like it here?"

"It is very beautiful, and very peaceful. And above all, very simple. That I like best."

He nodded. "So simple it is bleak. But there is something here, some pristine quality, that draws me back again and again. I have been spending my summers here ever since I was a boy. I love the solitude, the serenity. I have cousins living near by, and my sister the schoolteacher runs the school in the village. She does a lot of good there."

"As do you."

He shrugged. "I don't know. I follow in my father's footsteps. He was a soldier, a diplomat, and a statesman. I will never reach his eminence."

We were silent for awhile, watching a flock of geese land in the lake. It was a sight I had never seen before, hundreds of black, gray and white birds, all identical, landing in the water and floating as if in formation, honking harshly and pecking at each other.

"It's good for me here," Axel said after a time. "It renews me. All the outdoor work and fresh air. While I'm in Fredenholm I don't regret yesterday and I don't anticipate tomorrow. I live in today, and revel in it.

"Maybe that's why my father retired here in his old age. For the enjoyment of each day. He was very ill, at the end, dying of pthisick. He could hardly eat anything and had a terrible cough. Yet he liked to sit out among the trees, in the summer weather, with his big wolfhound at his feet. He was at peace."

Axel laid his head in my lap and I stroked his fair hair. He had never talked to me so intimately before, of his family. I had often talked to him of maman and my brothers and sisters, especially Joseph and Carlotta.

One name hung in the air between us, as yet unspoken: Louis. We didn't mention him, but I knew he was in our thoughts as, hand in hand, we made our way back along the hill path in a worsening drizzle toward the warmth and shelter of Fredenholm.

July 9, 1780
I am learning all the names of the mushrooms. Also which ones we dare not eat.

There are so many different kinds, chante-relles and Nun's Cap, gray Stink Horn and the poisonous Jack-my-lantern that glows in the dark only it is never dark so how can we tell?

Every day that I spend here I am feeling better, happier and more relaxed.

July 11, 1780

One of Axel's tenants got married yesterday and we went to the wedding. I asked to borrow a red skirt and white shirt of the kind the peasant women wear and the clothes were brought to me, along with a pair of soft felt boots and a garland of roses to carry.

We joined the hundreds of guests that had come from surrounding villages. Two bands played lively music and we danced with all the others, doing our best to follow the steps, stumbling and laughing. The women sang in a style I had never heard before, making an eerie sound like cats fighting. It was all very raucous and joyous.

I felt so free. No one had any idea who I was, only that I was a foreign noblewoman who was a friend or relative of Axel's. That I might be a queen must have been the far-thest thing from any of their thoughts. When I moved into the center of the circle of dancers and took my turn dancing a solo (which, I admit, had more steps of the quadrille than of a country dance), they all clapped and cheered.

What a time I had! Twirling in my borrowed red skirt, my borrowed boots clomping on the rough stones and tough meadow grass, my hair free of restraints and tossing in the pure summer air. And Axel nearby, clapping, dancing, smiling his approval of me.

Barrels of strong local cider and aqvavit were broached and the heady liquor flowed abundantly. The bride, a hefty blond peasant girl of sixteen, filled my glass again and again. We ate caviar and drank red wine, and every few minutes, it seemed, the crowd started to whistle and clap and would not stop until the bride and groom kissed. Kissing here in Sweden is loud, with lots of lip-smacking.

Sometime in the middle of the night a peasant drove us back to Fredenholm in his wooden cart that smelled of hay and manure. Axel held me in his arms while the cart bumped its way along the rough track. I leaned against him, swooning from the wine and cider, tired from the dancing, in love with the world. I thought, this is the happiest night of my life.

July 16, 1780

Two days ago we started out to return to Drottningholm. I was very sad to leave. We rode to a town, then went southward by coach, through mile after mile of deep forest. The weather turned very cold, on and off it rained. Twice the coach had to be driven onto a large ferry to cross a lake.

Toward the end of the day the coach broke an axle and we had to walk in the rain to the only shelter near by, which was a small tavern with a cracked sloping roof and walls that leaned inward at an odd angle. I felt sorry for the poor horses that had to stand patiently in the hard rain with their heads bowed while the repairs were made.

Axel and I sat at a low scratched table by the fire and ordered wine and bread and cheese.

We drank our wine, waiting for the coachman to come through the door to tell us that the broken axle was mended. But an hour went by, and then two, and he did not come. The rain continued to beat down on the roof of the tavern, and an old man came in, wet and bedraggled and walking with the aid of a stick. He was blind, his sightless eyes were turned upward toward the ceiling. He felt his way to the fire and spread out his hands toward its heat.

"Here, old father, drink this and warm yourself." The tavern keeper guided the visitor to a table near us and set down a tankard in front of him.

"There are a French lady and gentleman here to keep you company," he added. "See that you guard your language."

"A fine French lady and gentleman," the old man said, speaking French for our benefit. "Well then, God bless them. I have done them a service in my time. I fought for the old French king, the old Louis, at Fontenoy and Raucoux, and I won for him too. That was not how I went blind, though. No, I lost my eyes in prison. In a fight. Haven't seen a soul in thirty-seven years. Now, what would you like to hear, my lady and gentleman? A French battle song? A dirge? I have the second sight, even though I lost my eyes. My second sight tells me, it ought to be a dirge."

I shuddered at his words. No, not another death!

Axel gave the man some coins and he drank his beer and wandered off. Eventually our coach driver came to say that the axle was repaired and we went on.

July 17, 1780
Last night a thunderstorm broke and we

could not get to the estate where Axel had arranged for us to stay. So we took shelter in a peasant house and were shown what hospitality the family could offer.

A thin, bent old woman welcomed us, her eyes shining and her gums nearly toothless. Her drab skirt was worn and patched and a rag covered her sparse gray hair. She motioned us toward the immense stove, where some twenty people lay on sleeping platforms. From several cradles in one corner of the room came the wails of infants.

I stepped into the large, warm room and gasped, the smells were so strong. Smells of fish, cabbage, garbage, tobacco and open sewer drains like the ones at Versailles. And smells of bodies long unwashed dressed in dirty clothes.

A crowd of faces stared at us as we made our way to a table where the old woman served us cabbage soup with fish heads floating in it and a loaf of coarse black bread. The eyes of the dead fish staring up at me, the grease on the surface of the soup, made my stomach turn. Out of politeness I ate several spoonfuls of the soup and a morsel of the bread. Axel, I noticed, ate heartily, as if he were dining at King Gustavus's table.

As I did my best to eat I could not help looking over at the people lying on their sleeping platforms. They were wide awake — our arrival had apparently awakened them — and they kept their eyes on our food, watching every spoonful and every chunk of bread. Their faces were thin, and they all had the same vacant look, even the children. Several of the men drank from a metal cup that they passed from hand to hand. The reek of alcohol was in the air, along with the smell of burning wood and human waste. While I watched, large black cockroaches crawled over the threadbare blankets and across the floor at my feet.

The old woman who had greeted us and brought us food was busying herself making a bed for us. She brought several long benches over by the stove and laid planks of wood across them. On top of the planks she laid a very old, very dirty featherbed and piles of rags.

I soon had my fill of the food, and realized, to my horror, that I needed to relieve myself. But there was no privacy. The others, I could not help but notice, made full use of the reeking chamber pots beneath the sleeping platforms, in full view of everyone in the room.

"Madame," I said to our hostess in my very crude Swedish, "is there somewhere I might —" I pointed to one of the chamber pots.

She nodded her understanding and, reaching for my hand, she led me outside. It was still raining very hard, and we splashed through mud as she guided me toward a barn. She took me to an empty horse stall with straw on the earthen floor, and pointed. Then she left me.

I realized that she was being respectful — and kind. This was the very best she had to offer. Solitude, and relative cleanliness. The stable, with its rich scent of manure and animal breath, smelled much better than the house. But it was extremely cold. I soon did what I had to do and returned to the warmth of the stove-heated room.

In my absence a fight had broken out. The people had climbed down from their perches and were squabbling over the remains of my food. One man was hitting a woman and shouting drunkenly at her. I saw a boy with a snarling, feral face pick up a yellow cat and hurl it against the brick wall. In the midst of the melee an old woman stood, head bent, reciting a prayer. I could understand two phrases, which she seemed to repeat again and again.

"The wrath of the lord is come upon us! Preserve us from the wrath of the lord!"

Shocked, I watched the squalid scene, desperate to intervene yet helpless. I felt tears running down my face. The one thing I could do, I did. When the injured yellow cat came staggering toward me, I picked it up and held it close to my chest. I felt it claw me but I ignored the sharpness of its claws, determined to protect it.

Axel was hurriedly thanking the old woman for her hospitality and giving her a handful of coins, which she examined so closely that she did not see us go. Snatching up one of the ragged blankets from the makeshift bed that was to have been ours, Axel draped it over me and the cat and led me outside into the rain.

I was too numb to speak or think. I let him take me along the muddy road, reassuring me that we would surely come to another shelter before long. It was still raining, though not as hard as before, and after we had walked for half a mile or so we came to a deserted old farmhouse and spent the night there, curled up together on the wooden floor, wet and cold, with the cat huddled against us for warmth.

July 20, 1780

My precious time with Axel is almost at an end. In two days I must return to France, having stayed away longer than I thought I would. I miss Mousseline very much. When we arrived at Drottningholm there were five letters waiting for me, telling me that Mousseline has begun to say "give me" and "no" and "do it" and to say the name of her little pug dog which I named after my dear old Mufti.

Chambertin writes to say that Louis has been fretful without me. Twice he locked himself in his workshop with a basket of pastries and refused to come out for several days. No one could persuade him. The ministers were mortified because important talks were under way concerning the American War and the king's presence at dinners and receptions for the ambassadors was essential. Chambertin says only I could have made Louis do his duty. When I am there he is less timid and rebellious and much more willing to do what is required of him.

King Gustavus took Axel and me through the palace rooms he is renovating, so that I could see the final outcome of my suggestions. The artisans have been very busy and the results of their work are very fine indeed. Gustavus favors Roman and Greek design with fluted columns and Pompeian friezes and mosaics made of shards of glass. One room I helped to plan was nearly finished, and the effect was very striking. Deep blue walls, white Doric columns, carved white plasterwork in an antique pattern of flowers and fruit. There will be deep blue carpets to match and a ceiling painted by an Italian artist from Verona. He arrives next week but I will already be gone and won't be able to meet him.

While walking through the immense, expensively decorated rooms one thought nagged at me more and more. Why should a king live on such a lavish scale while his people spend their lives with many families packed into one dirty, stinking room with bare walls and a leaking ceiling? My few hours spent among the peasants have affected me deeply. Even as I walked amid the tranquil splendor of King Gustavus's palace I could not rid my mind of the images of the dark rooms I had seen, the hungry faces, the squabbling and brutality I had witnessed at first hand.

I turned to Axel. "Those people we ate with, the day it rained so hard," I said, "what can be done for them? They are so poor —"

To my surprise, Axel only laughed. "Those were rich peasants. They had a large house, animals, food. You should see how the poor ones live."

King Gustavus was curious about our exchange and Axel explained to him that we had been forced to take shelter with some farmers.

"You have never before seen how peasants live, I think," the king said to me.

"Only from a carriage window."

"Life is very harsh for those born with so little."

"Is there no way of improving their lives then?"

"King Gustavus has improved their lives," Axel said loyally. "He has abolished torture. No one is put to death any more for crimes they have committed. He has reformed the state finances. Taxes are lower, and the peasants now are able, if they can afford it, to buy their lands and own them as free men."

"Yet there is so much misery, even so!"

We walked on, through the Malachite Dining Room, its walls covered in panels of the brilliant green gemstone, and into the Crystal Salon, where dozens of glittering chandeliers sparkled in the sunlight and threw reflections on the gilded walls.

Axel seemed thoughtful. At last he shrugged. "I love and admire the peasants, and have lived among them, from time to time, all my life. But they are like children. They wander through life ignorant and weak, unable to rise above their station. Unable to accomplish anything but hard labor. For most of the men, drink is their only consolation. For the women, it is religion."

"Come now, Axel. You are too pessimistic. The countryside is changing, even here. Farming methods are improving. Crop yields are increasing. People are eating better and living longer. If only nature cooperates, giving good harvests, there will be much progress in our lifetimes. More health of bodies and minds. Meanwhile, my dear," Gustavus said to me, "you may donate your pearl earrings to the poor."

I felt my earlobes. I was indeed wearing pearl earrings, though not my most elaborate ones.

"Only you mustn't do that," said Axel, "because if you do, they will murder each other to get the pearls. It only causes harm, you see, to cast pearls before swine."

I didn't argue with Axel or the king. But I have promised myself that when I return to Versailles I will arrange to send some money to the Swedish peasants. And I will double the amount of bread Abbé Vermond distributes at the palace gates.

EIGHT

November 27, 1780
My dearest, dearest, most beloved maman is dead.

December 13, 1780
I can hardly write anything, I am so wretched. I look in the mirror and see someone I don't recognize. A woman with a pinched face and gray cheeks and sad sad eyes. Will I ever eat again? Will I ever be able to think, and move, and take delight in anything?

I sit day after day in my darkened rooms, black velvet curtains covering the windows, unable to do anything but weep and read my Bible and light candles for maman's soul. Poor Mousseline cries. She doesn't understand the change in me.

Abbé Vermond comes to pray with me but I am beyond all consolation. I read and reread the letters from Joseph and Anna, telling me of maman's last days. She had wanted to die for a long time. In the final week of her life she sewed her own shroud, of white silk embroidered with the imperial emblem.

If only, instead of preparing for her funeral, she had written me one last letter! If only she had praised me for doing my best in a difficult life! How I would cherish that proof of her love and approval.

December 25, 1780
It is a sad Christmas day. The palace is still in mourning for the great empress and our usual celebrations have been subdued. We go to mass daily and I light a candle for maman and repeat my prayers with Abbé Vermond, who has been very faithful to me during my grieving.

Sometimes I simply feel nothing. I am empty of all feeling. It is terrible.

January 4, 1781
I try to busy myself with a project I began before maman's death. I decided I would do more than talk about the misery of the peasants. I would sell my most valuable possession, the great yellow diamond called the Hapsburg Sun, and have the money distributed to the poorest of them. I have ordered the diamond brought up from the palace vaults where my jewels are kept.

In the past few days I have been haunted by the memory of the blind old soldier Axel and I met in the tavern in Sweden.

He wanted to sing us a song, and said something like, "It should be a funeral dirge." Did he have a premonition about maman's death? How could he have known?

The yellow cat I brought back from Sweden is growing fat and sleek on thick cream and sweetmeats. He is deaf in one ear and one of his legs is crooked but otherwise he has recovered. Maman had a yellow cat that always sat on her desk. This one reminds me of her.

January 6, 1781

I am recovering from a great shock. I sent Sophie for orange-flower water and ether to calm me.

Something terrible has happened and I don't know who to turn to. Axel is away. If only Joseph were here! But I am thinking, I don't dare to tell Joseph. So much damage could result if the truth came out.

It may not be safe to write this in my diary. But I have thought it over, sipping my orange-flower water and ether, and finally decided that I need to set the truth down somewhere.

I am fairly certain that while I was away in Sweden last summer, Louis took the Hapsburg Sun and pawned it to a rich

Genevan moneylender whose acquaintance he made through Necker the banker. I found out because when I had the jewel brought up from the vault, and summoned M. Christofle the jeweler from Paris to appraise it, he told me that the stone was not a diamond but a paste imitation!

At first I couldn't believe it. But when I questioned the head guard of the vault, he finally told me that in June of last year the king ordered the Hapsburg Sun brought to him and he did not return it to the vault for over a month. What was returned must have been a paste replica.

I confronted Chambertin, who knows nearly everything Louis says or does, and he admitted that the controller Necker brought a Swiss man of business to Louis's levee and that a package was later delivered to that same man under guard.

Chambertin is trustworthy. He will tell no one about this. I must be certain none of the other servants find out, or suspect something. If a rumor started that Louis had pawned my celebrated jewel, it would be assumed that the treasury was empty and the government unable to repay the huge loans M. Necker has been taking, loans of millions of francs. It would be interpreted as an insult to the Austrian Empire, which could anger my brother Joseph, who is now emperor. And it would cause a great personal scandal around Louis himself, who would be seen as a thief.

Indeed he is a thief, and I intend to tell him so to his face.

January 9, 1781

After much searching I found Louis at last up in the attic, crouching on the floor, picking the lock of a long-unused door. It was very cold in the attic and he had put on his father's old black coat, so worn and threadbare it has faded to gray in places.

When he heard my angry footsteps he turned toward me, shrinking back in fear, a cowardly look on his face.

Ignoring etiquette, which I usually do when we are alone, I walked right up to him and glared down into his frightened eyes.

"I know what you did. You stole the Hapsburg Sun. You pawned it. And you put a bit of paste back in the vault. You stole the most valuable thing in my dowry. You deceived me. And you risked scandal, and dishonor, and the alliance between France and Austria."

He wept, sitting on the dusty floor in the old overcoat. His face crumpled, like

Mousseline's when she has been disobedient and knows she must be punished.

His weakness made me angrier. I began to pace up and down.

"Stop it!! Stop acting like a child and stand up and talk like a man!"

With a huge sigh and an immense effort he heaved his large bulk off the floor and leaned against the door. He wouldn't look at me.

"I have so many faults I cannot answer you. I am ashamed of what I did, but I had no choice. Necker and the others came to me. The interest on the loans was due. They said they had miscalculated. There was no money to pay the interest. The loans were about to go into default. I couldn't let that happen." His voice was mournful, plaintive.

"But the crown of France has many treasures of its own. Chests of gold, your mother and grandmother's jewels, paintings, statues —"

"I have been selling crown possessions for six years, ever since I became king. Before that my grandfather sold a great deal. Many of the art works on display are copies. Many of the jewels are paste."

"You had no right to take what was mine, without asking."

He raised his eyes to my face. "And if I had asked, would you have given me your precious gem?"

"No. Never."

"Of course not. I had to take it by stealth. I was assured the copy I had made was of excellent quality. I thought you would never find out. I would not have chosen the Hapsburg Sun to pawn except that Necker knew a man who had always coveted it. A Genevan, a rich trader on the stock exchange. He offered to pay all the interest on our debts in return for the gem. At the time I thought we had a chance to pay him back, to get the jewel back, in a year or two at most. Now I doubt it."

I was furious. At Louis, at M. Necker, at the ministers who hate me and who must have felt a private delight in the plan to rob me of my treasured gem.

"I want it back," was all I could think of to say. "Get it back — somehow."

I left Louis then, the image of wretchedness, and began to walk away. I made my way back to my apartments, still full of resentment and exasperation, and it took me several hours to compose myself sufficiently to meet with Loulou and Sophie and give the necessary orders to my household.

January 13, 1781

I have been thinking long and hard about Louis's deception in pawning the Hapsburg Sun and after much thought I realize that I have been selfish.

Yes, Louis was deceitful. He should have come to me to explain why he felt he had no choice but to pawn the jewel. And he waited until I was gone, far away in Sweden, to do what he did. Yet I too was engaged in a deception, traveling with my lover, relishing the time we had together. Although the risk was small, I too was risking scandal. Indeed had Axel been less careful when we made love, I would have been risking the succession itself. Dear maman, if she were still alive and knew the truth about Axel and me, would say that I am an adulteress, and that I should be brought before the Chastity Commission to be reprimanded.

Father Kunibert would say I should be sent straight to hell.

Louis is a thief, and deceptive, and terribly weak. But I am an unfaithful wife, and just as deceptive as he is, and weak for giving in to the force of my love for Axel.

Are we not equally to blame?

January 14, 1781

Yesterday I made my confession and then went to Louis who was taking a nap. I took him in my arms and told him I forgave him for pawning the Hapsburg Sun, and asked his forgiveness in turn for any wrongs I may have done him.

He wept in my arms, and I wept a little too, for in truth I am very fond of Louis and pity him in his miserable and unwanted role of king.

January 18, 1781

Axel is taking his regiment to America. Before he left he came to me to say goodbye and we both know there is a chance I may never see him again. Many officers die in battle, or of wounds or illness. Many more are maimed or crippled for life.

"My darling, I am going to say something that may shock you," he told me just before he left. "After I'm gone, think about it seriously, and remember it."

"It is this: Louis is not well. His mind is weak. Such people are fragile, and their apparent sanity can shatter at any time. It happened to King George in England not long ago, and could very easily happen here.

"If Louis should become worse, and the

doctors decide he must step aside to allow Prince Stanislaus to rule, I want you to remember that you and the Princess Royal" — he meant Mousseline — "will always have a home in Sweden. With me."

He gave me a piece of paper. On it was written the name of a military contractor in Paris. I could always get a message to him through this man, he told me. And in case of urgent need I could always go to the court of King Gustavus, who would gladly make me welcome.

"Joseph would make me welcome too, in Vienna," I reminded Axel.

"Unless Austria and France are on better terms than they are at present, you would be well advised to go to the Swedish court."

Saying goodbye to Axel was like tearing out part of my heart, yet I was glad he was going — going, not only to war, but out of my life, at least for a time.

I will try not to miss him too much, or worry about his safety, or think of his dear mild eyes, his warm touch, his kisses — I will try my best to be a good and faithful wife.

I will try.

March 10, 1781
My cheeks are pink again and my face looks

more like myself. In the past week I have become very hungry and have sent Eric to Sweden to fetch reindeer cheese of which I became very fond while I was there. I would have sent for cloudberries too only they are not in season yet.

Louis brought me a basket of his favorite pastries, full of sweet cream custard and sugared almonds and rich chocolate icing. Together we ate every single one, and we both got sick afterwards.

March 21, 1781
I am pregnant again. Hardly anyone knows, only Dr. Boisgilbert and Sophie and Loulou and of course Louis. Count Mercy, who has spies in my household, and who constantly tries to get information from Dr. Boisgilbert, may know as well because whenever he sees me he smiles to himself.

We will make the announcement soon, perhaps next month.

April 22, 1781
Joseph is coming for another visit in a few months. He is very pleased that I am expecting another child and says it must be a boy this time.

If only I had news of Axel.

May 12, 1781
Charlot came to the Petit Trianon in his green carriage and offered to take me to the races but I told him the ride would be far too rough and I might lose the baby. He visited awhile and admired some renovations I am making to the upstairs rooms in the Pompeian style. He told me of some exciting experiments being made by a M. Montgolfier who is able to make an immense linen bag rise up into the air and sail over houses and fields and then come down again. He wants to attach himself to the linen bag and go sailing through the air with it.

June 3, 1781
Finally I have heard news of Axel. He is safe, and has been in the Carolinas where the British have seized important towns. He is now in Virginia.

June 20, 1781
Mousseline sang all of Frère Jacques today and threw her bowl of soup at her nanny. I have been telling her that she will soon have a little brother or possibly a little sister (pray God no!) and this upsets her a good deal. She frowns a lot and disobeys.

If maman were here she would be shocked at how I fail to discipline my daughter. Maman was always very firm with me and my sisters and brothers. If we disobeyed we were shut out on a landing of the staircase with our hands tied behind our backs for hours at a time, and then given only bread and milk for supper. Mousseline is reprimanded, but never very firmly, and is never deprived of food or restrained in any way. I only hope she will grow out of this rebellious phase soon. Louis says he was completely unmanageable as a child. Probably she is just like him. Will my next one be equally hard to manage?

Louis has gone off to hunt and collect plants in the forest of Compiègne, taking only Chambertin and a secretary and a valet with him. He invited me to come along, but I said no. I know he would ignore me most of the time and I would have very little to do. He imagines that I would enjoy helping him collect his plants and that we would read his books on forest flora together. How little he knows me! And after so many years of marriage.

I told him I must prepare for Joseph's visit instead.

July 1, 1781
A large packet of letters arrived for me today

from Axel! He has been writing to me every week but had no way of sending the letters until April, when he was able to send them with an officer returning to France aboard the *Valkyrie.* The ship ran aground off Brest and the officer was drowned, but another soldier found the packet and sent it here to Versailles.

I read all the letters through twice, in order. He misses me. He has suffered many hardships and is worried that the British will win the war after all. I treasure these dear dear letters and I weep as I read them.

August 2, 1781
Joseph is here and to my great surprise he has brought my sister Carlotta with him!

I could hardly believe my eyes when the huge traveling coach drew up in the outer courtyard of the palace and Joseph, looking older and more important as he is emperor now, got out and then helped a very fat, very richly dressed woman to alight. I looked closely at her — and realized that it was Carlotta, whom I have not seen in eleven years!

I ran to embrace them both, forgetting that I am six months pregnant and that I must be very careful as I am carrying the heir to the throne — or so I fondly hope. We hugged and cried and laughed and hugged again.

Joseph, wearing a long golden coat, pince-nez and a gray bagwig, has taken on an air of gravity that he did not have when he was here last. He is less the raffish man of the world and more the kindly old uncle. He shows signs of strain, and no wonder, after all he has been through, leading a regiment against the Prussians and attempting to conquer new territories, saying a last goodbye to dear maman and taking over all the responsibilities of being emperor and head of the family.

Carlotta, who I must admit has gotten way too fat, has four chins and is very unfashionably dressed. I must bring Rose Bertin to court and order her to make a new wardrobe for my sister. Her hair has gotten thin and is not well arranged. When I brought her into my apartments all my ladies-in-waiting tittered and hid their smiles behind their fans. She has also gotten quite sour and critical. In this she reminds me of maman.

I had Mousseline brought in by one of her nursemaids and Joseph and Carlotta exclaimed over her.

"She looks just like you did when you

were a baby," said Joseph, who was thirteen or fourteen when I was born and remembers me well. "A little blond sprite."

Mousseline is a pretty child with curly hair and light blue eyes. Her rash is all gone and her skin is very white and smooth. She enjoys being admired but wails and has tantrums when she is thwarted.

August 5, 1781

Joseph has gone hunting with Louis at Compiègne and I have had a chance to spend a lot of time with Carlotta. She was very much the critical older sister at first but after a few hours of talk she broke down and cried and confessed that she has been very unhappy. She quarreled bitterly with her husband and he sent her away. She went to Schönbrunn and has been there ever since, under Joseph's protection. But she feels lost and homeless, and misses her children.

Her husband has brought his favorite mistress to live in his palace, replacing Carlotta. It is a scandal but no one dares to speak up about it. Carlotta has a sharp tongue and is not in any way an adornment to the court so I imagine everyone was glad to see her go, except her children of course.

I was touched to see that she still has the net purse I made for her when I was pregnant with Mousseline.

August 11, 1781
Charlot invited M. Montgolfier the inventor to Versailles to fly his remarkable balloon. It is made of linen and is very very large — the size of a large ballroom. A fire was made with bundles of straw underneath the linen and slowly — miraculously — the giant bag began to fill up with vapor and rise into the air! It traveled over the garden, carried by the wind, and floated on and on, getting smaller and smaller, until it finally came down in some trees. The ropes were tangled in the branches.

Charlot is excited and begged to be allowed to tie himself to the bottom of the balloon so that he could fly with it. Joseph wants to bring M. Montgolfier to Vienna to fly his balloon for the Scientific Institute there. Louis asked M. Montgolfier many questions about his invention. What made it fly? Why had no one thought of this before? What made it come down so quickly? He kept asking and asking until the poor man was exhausted and begged to be allowed to leave.

We have had a very fine day. A large

crowd of people gathered to watch the amazing sight and most of them were very respectful to us though a few were rude and one very shabby-looking man spat on my shoes. The weather was perfect, quite warm with a completely cloudless blue sky. I wish I had brought Mousseline. One day, long in the future, she may be attached to a balloon herself. By then it may be so common that everyone is doing it. Imagine the sky full of balloons!

August 13, 1781
I have confided in Joseph about Louis and his pawning of the Hapsburg Sun. It felt very good to confide in my brother, especially as Axel is far away and I have been alone with my secret for many months.

August 25, 1781
I have said a very sad farewell to Carlotta and Joseph. Carlotta looks better now, in her fashionable gowns and high-piled hair filled out with false hairpieces by André, who I must confess is very skillful. She gave me a charm to put under my pillow to protect me and the baby from any black magic anyone might try to use against us. We hugged each other and I wept. Joseph too embraced me and wished me a safe delivery.

"Send a swift courier as soon as the baby is born," he said. "Don't wait even an hour. We will be eager to hear the good news."

"And wear Ste. Radegunde's girdle throughout your labor!" Carlotta called out from inside the coach. "Mother would want you to."

"I will, I will," I cried as the heavy traveling carriage lumbered off, its great wheels raising thick clouds of dust.

I miss them. I miss home. No matter how long I live in France, I think I will always be an Austrian at heart, in exile from the place where I belong.

September 14, 1781
Word has come that Axel and his troops have been marching with the Americans to attack the British in Virginia. I wonder how Axel is at this moment, whether he is safe. Many officers have been taken prisoner by the British.

I know that wherever he is, whatever he is doing, he is thinking of me.

September 17, 1781
Dr. Sundersen has arrived to attend me and has brought a very large and strong-looking Swedish midwife along. When I saw the doctor I felt my legs start to give way under me, for my first glimpse of him brought back

terrible memories of pain and fear and the suffocating feeling I had during my labor with Mousseline. When he bowed and kissed my hand, however, I began to feel reassured, remembering how skilled he was and how when he said to me, shall we do this together? I felt certain I could complete my labor successfully, and sure enough, together we brought my beloved Mousseline into the world.

Louis grumbles that Dr. Sundersen is asking a very large fee. I respond that the safe delivery of the next king of France is surely worth a large fee.

September 26, 1781

Dr. Sundersen has ordered me to stay in bed from now on as he expects my labor to begin within the next few weeks.

I have another packet of letters from Axel! Thank heavens he is safe and has been ill but is now fairly well again. General Rochambeau has sent him to confer with General Washington a number of times because his English is good. Axel says General Washington is a very cold man. Not all Americans are cold, I know. Mr. Franklin was charming and jolly when he was here, everyone enjoyed him. I have met a number of other Americans though I must say some of the women were frosty and dressed so badly that they looked much older than they were. Of course I have met mostly American aristocrats and diplomats and their wives, not military men such as General Washington.

October 6, 1781
Charlot has flown in a balloon. M. Montgolfier attached a very large basket to the bottom of his linen bag and put a sheep in it and some other animals. He made the balloon fly and the animals flew with it. Then, after it came down, the animals were taken out of the basket and Charlot got in — Stanny tried to stop him — and it went up and Charlot flew from the meadow almost all the way to the village of Saumoy.

When the balloon came down and the basket bumped hard on the ground Charlot hurt his wrist but apart from that he is fine. All the villagers were there, screaming and cheering. Charlot came to see me and told me all about it. His wrist was bandaged. I have never seen him so full of good spirits. He says I am as big as a balloon.

October 29, 1781
A week ago today my labor began, early in

the morning. I had sharp pains, not an ache like last time. Sophie was excited and worried and went to get the midwife, who sat beside me and felt my belly each time the pains came.

Dr. Sundersen arrived, laid out his instruments and said, "Now then, it will not take so long this time, I think." That made me feel relieved. Being awakened by strong pains had frightened me. The doctor told me once again that a second baby is usually easier than the first.

I wished for Axel to be there. All the family came in, and eventually all the ministers. No one else was allowed in, though there were many people in the corridor outside. Louis was very nervous. He kept jumping up and pacing around the room, saying, can't she have more air, give her more air. I was not complaining, I was quite comfortable and there was plenty of air, and no noisy crowd of spectators climbing on the furniture.

The pains kept getting worse, and the midwife helped by rubbing my back. Louis kept wanting to give me some syrup of poppy for the pain but the doctor said no, it would put the baby to sleep and he might not breathe after he was born. Besides, I was able to bear the pain. I know it helped that I had been through it before, and knew that I could endure it all the way to the end. I kept the girdle of Ste. Radegunde on, and I prayed to the saint, and I know the blessed girdle gave me strength.

My memories of the last few hours of my labor are vague, because the pain became terrible and I felt faint a lot of the time. I remember calling for Loulou and Sophie and Carlotta (though of course Carlotta was not there, she had gone back to Vienna with Joseph months ago) and gripping their hands tightly. It hurt when the midwife pressed down on my belly and when the doctor, who kept telling me to work hard, lift up, raise the building like last time, put his instruments inside of me.

I screamed then, and I remember hearing Louis say, don't hurt her. For the Lord Jesus's sake don't hurt her!

I remember tears, pain, and liquid flowing out of me.

Then I remember nothing, until I saw, quite distinctly, the face of M. Genet, the keeper of the seals, standing beside the bed. He looked overjoyed. He said, quite loudly, "A son, a son has been born to France!"

There was a great cry of joy in the room. I heard Louis shout "God be thanked" and someone, I think it was Stanny but I'm not sure, was swearing.

Dr. Sundersen held up the little red creature for me to see, and then swatted him on the bottom until he began to cry. It was a weak little cry, like the feeble sound made by a very small, undersized puppy. The midwife washed him and wrapped him in a beautiful blanket embroidered with fleurs-de-lis and crowns and laid him in my arms. He was warm and very small, smaller than Mousseline when she was born. His eyes were closed, he had no hair at all. I kissed him and then I must have fainted, because I don't remember anything else except dimly hearing Louis's voice say, "Madame, you are the mother of a dauphin."

I am, indeed, now at last the mother of a dauphin. God be thanked.

NINE

December 14, 1781

My son is worshipped almost as if he were a god in human form. Envoys from foreign courts, officials from many parts of France, influential Parisians and the royal ministers and courtiers all approach his cradle as if it were a holy shrine, and gaze on him as they might gaze on a saint or a relic of the true cross.

We have waited so long for an heir to the throne to be born, so many long bleak years. Now that he has come at last he seems almost a miracle, an unexpected boon from heaven. I could not be happier to show him off, except that he is so very small and so much less alert and active than Mousseline was.

Hardly anyone is aware of this. The visitors who come to touch his cradle in awe only catch a fleeting glimpse of him and cannot really tell anything about him. To them he is just a tiny baby wrapped in woolen blankets in a golden cradle, France's precious dauphin. To me, however, he is more. He is my beloved boy, my

Louis-Joseph. But he is also a lethargic little infant, quiet and uninterested in his surroundings. He does not wave his arms and kick his legs like other babies do and though he is almost two months old he is not yet able to raise his head from his silken pillow.

I am always careful to lock this diary and I keep it in a new place now, where no one would ever think to look for it. No one must read what I write here about the next king of France.

February 2, 1782
I am so worried about our little Louis-Joseph. Three specialists have come to examine him, all the way from Edinburgh.

February 17, 1782
Loulou found me crying today and did her best to comfort me, but I am beyond comfort.

More specialists have seen my little Louis-Joseph and they all say the same thing. His back is crooked and he will never stand up straight or walk by himself. Louis has paid them well to keep silent on this matter. No one must find out — only his nurse knows so far. I keep him swathed in blankets so that visitors — I almost wrote "worshippers" — only see his face.

February 28, 1782

Axel is alive and well. He is a hero! Finally I have more news about him. I had not heard anything in so long I was afraid he had been wounded or even killed.

He was with General Rochambeau and the Americans when they besieged the English General Cornwallis and Cornwallis finally surrendered his sword and turned his forces over to the victors. During skirmishes with the British Axel fought bravely and saved many men, both French and American. General Rochambeau decorated him and General Washington shook his hand and thanked him and made him a member of the Order of Cincinnatus. I am very proud of him and will tell him so when I see him. Oh, when will I see him again? It has been so long.

Of course I could not know it but these skirmishes and the surrender of the British happened right before Louis-Joseph was born. My stars and Axel's must be in alignment, as Sophie would say.

April 3, 1782

I am writing this in the grotto at the Petit Trianon, a safe and private place. Eric is standing guard nearby, at the entrance to the grotto. Ever since Louis-Joseph was born

Eric has hovered near me and the baby, almost as if he and not Louis were the father. I am glad of his protection, and have told him so.

I need the privacy and solace of the grotto on this afternoon. We have had yet another discouraging diagnosis from the physicians. They say that the baby has had a chest disease that has turned from his lungs into his shoulder and back. They say that his little back and shoulder must be probed by the surgeons so that the illness will not return to his lungs and kill him.

I do not understand this but the head physician said it in a very solemn voice and he appears to be a skilled physician. Everyone says the best doctors are from Edinburgh and that is where he has his practice. On the other hand, I have heard people say that Edinburgh is almost as dirty a place as Paris and that people throw their filth into the streets with abandon. The Scots are said to be very hardy, however.

April 24, 1782
Yesterday the surgeon came to the palace to carry out the orders of the Edinburgh doctors. Louis-Joseph is now six months old and the doctors say he is old enough to undergo

the pain this procedure must cause.

Eric was there and stood outside the room in the corridor the whole time. I heard Amélie shouting at him and I know she has been more angry at him than ever in recent months. Sophie keeps telling me I must dismiss Amélie, who is disrespectful and insolent, but I am afraid to. She knows too much about me. I know she makes fun of me behind my back. I hear the younger girls laughing and they smother their laughter when I come into the room. Some of them look shamefaced, and I know that deep down, they love me and are loyal; Amélie has not turned them against me.

I did not want any of the servants present when the barber-surgeon did his work on Louis-Joseph so I had Sophie send them all away for the day, all but Eric. Sophie, Louis and I waited for the barber-surgeon to arrive. I held Louis-Joseph in my arms and he was sleeping peacefully.

I watched while two burly men came in with a small armchair on a platform. Then the barber-surgeon himself came in, a scruffy-looking man with a scraggly black beard, a cheap coat and tricorn hat. He nodded to us briefly and got to work.

A bowl of water was brought for him to wash his hands and I noticed that the wash water was very dirty when he finished. He laid out his instruments, then motioned for Louis-Joseph to be brought to him, and for his little flannel gown to be removed. Then he strapped the baby into the cruel-looking chair, with his poor little back and shoulder exposed. He took a long, sharp-looking steel needle and began jabbing it into his small white back. Louis-Joseph screamed, and I was so shocked I screamed with him. Blood dripped from the wounds as the cruel probe moved up-wards and over into the poor baby's shoulder.

It was all over quickly, but I could hardly restrain myself, I was so upset. When the barber-surgeon finished, and his assistant began swabbing the wounds with an oint-ment and bandaging them, Louis asked the man gruffly, "Is it necessary to hurt him so?"

"Of course it is necessary. The muscles are weak. They must be strengthened through stimulation. That will be fifty francs," he added.

"Send your bill to the minister of fi-nance."

"I require to be paid now."

For a moment I thought Louis might strike the barber-surgeon, but he did not.

It was unheard-of for a physician or trades-man or merchant to demand payment of the sovereign. But Louis, perhaps realizing that it had become a well known fact that many of our bills go unpaid for months or years, restrained his initial impulse. He paused, then went out into the corridor. I heard him speaking to Eric. Presently he came back in the room.

"I have sent for the funds. If you will wait —"

The barber-surgeon bowed. "Your majesty."

The wailing Louis-Joseph was released from his confining straps and I took him in my arms, wrapping his blanket around him. I took him to the nursery and rocked him until he finally slept. But he woke again during the night, several times, and each time I applied oil of sassafras to his wounds, which had turned an ugly red.

Today he is fretful and has cried a lot. His back and arm are swollen and he feels hot to the touch. I wonder when we will see some evidence that the treatment has had a good effect.

May 10, 1782

Poor Louis-Joseph still has a swollen back and arm and it seems to me that he cannot easily move his arm now. He developed an abscess and it had to be lanced. I held him while the barber-surgeon cut open the abscess in hopes that my holding him would soothe him, but he cried anyway. I wonder, is he becoming accustomed to pain?

Sophie wants to bring an astrologer to court to cast his horoscope. She says it may give us hope for his future. But surely it might equally make us despair. I said no.

June 30, 1782

Despite our best efforts it has become impossible to keep Louis-Joseph's condition our family secret. He can barely sit up and cannot crawl like a normal child his age and this cannot be concealed. He rarely smiles and never laughs. Toys and dogs do not interest him. My preoccupation with him and my anxious look and Louis's frequent visits to the nursery are in themselves revealing. Mousseline is jealous of all the attention her brother receives and has become harder to manage. She is very temperamental and will not behave herself. I confess I do not know what to do to control her.

July 9, 1782

I have discovered, to my horror, that my bedchamber women are betting on when my son will die, the same way they bet among themselves last fall on when he would be born. Loulou and Sophie have orders to stop this morbid wagering.

August 2, 1782
Since the physicians and barber-surgeon have not been able to cure Louis-Joseph I decided to give in to the urgings of many at court who praise the healing gifts of the Neapolitan who calls himself Count Cagliostro.

He claims to be a healer and I have met people who say he took away their disease or their pain. He also claims to be three thousand years old and this of course I cannot believe. Nor do I think he learned his healing arts from the ancient Egyptian pharaohs or that he was raised among Arabs at the holy shrine of Mecca.

People are so gullible, they will believe anything if they are desperate enough. Their common sense goes out the window. Still, I believe there are some people who possess powers that cannot be easily explained and this Neapolitan may be one of them. If he can help my poor son I will be grateful.

I have summoned him to my apartments and he promises to come tomorrow evening.

August 4, 1782

Count Cagliostro came last night, a tall, robust man with penetrating eyes and a very theatrical manner. He wore an immense red cape and kept flourishing it as he strode through my salon, where some twenty people had gathered to witness his treatment of the dauphin. Loulou was there, and Yolande, and my sisters-in-law Josephine and Thérèse and even Count Mercy.

Cagliostro began speaking in some strange language and told us he was praying to the Egyptian god Anubis. He talked at length of his many memories, of the eras of Greece and Rome and the Middle Ages. Count Mercy snickered and I certainly understood why. It was evident to me that this Neapolitan was trying to impress the gullible. He had no more lived in the time of Socrates and Caesar than I have — although there are some who say we have all lived many past lives, and I suppose it is possible. Besides, as Charlot remarked to me about Cagliostro, "You do realize, dear Antoinette, that the man may be a poseur and also possess genuine powers." I was willing to wait to see the genuine powers work.

Eventually the count took a flask from an inner pocket and pulled out the stopper.

A very pungent, musky scent filled the room.

"I shall now invoke the power of the ancient healer Batok, priest of Thoth," he said solemnly. "Do not be afraid. Batok is a benevolent spirit. Should he appear to you, be assured that he is entirely harmless."

He came over to Louis-Joseph's cradle — I was sitting next to it — and after asking my permission, he put a drop of the liquid on the baby's forehead, murmuring some incantations as he did so.

A whitish fog rose from the cradle and seemed, just for a moment, to form itself into a vaguely human shape before it dissipated and was gone.

"Do not be alarmed, your majesty," Cagliostro whispered to me, bending low and touching my arm reassuringly.

The onlookers gasped and I gasped with them, but it all happened so quickly that I did not have time to react and snatch Louis-Joseph away from any danger. I looked down at him as he lay in his cradle, and saw that, very briefly, he opened his small blue eyes and for once, he seemed to actually see what was around him instead of looking vacant. The flicker of interest appeared to pass as quickly as it had come.

His eyes closed and he was soundly asleep again.

Cagliostro was applauded and there were shouts of admiration and approval. With a twirl of his red cloak he was out of the room and gone.

I did not know what to think. I watched Louis-Joseph for an hour and he continued to sleep peacefully. Then, leaving Sophie to watch him, I sought out Louis who was in his library, eating pastries and reading. I told him all that had happened, and he laughed.

"A white vapor, you say? An old magician's trick. They use a preparation called Vaporous Phosphor. It makes a puff of smoke. He probably hid it under his cloak, or it was in his flask. Batok, priest of Thoth indeed. What rubbish."

"And yet some people swear he has helped them, that they are well because of him."

"They have persuaded themselves into getting well," Louis said. "But that only works for adults. Don't expect any improvement in Louis-Joseph."

Today, this morning, Louis-Joseph seems no different. Did I only imagine that he had a momentary mental awakening? I don't know. At any rate, Sophie came to tell me that Count Cagliostro left in his coach at midnight last night, bound for Italy. A small crowd came to see him off, tossing rose petals in his path and begging him to return soon.

September 12, 1782
I have had my fill of healers and charlatans. First there was Count Cagliostro, then a trio of water-gazers from Martinique who claimed to see maman's face in a bowl of water, then the Irishman who sold us Hamlin's Wizard Oil to ease Louis-Joseph's pains, then Sophie's astrologer (I finally said yes to an astrologer) who predicted that Louis-Joseph would live to be ninety and have seven children.

None of them were any help to us, though the Hamlin's Wizard Oil did seem to ease the pain in the baby's arm some-what and I thought he moved it more easily after I rubbed it on.

September 20, 1782
Joseph has sent a doctor from Vienna who is able to repair crippled limbs and backs. Using the tools in Louis's workshops he has made a small stiff brace for Louis-Joseph's back. It has to stay on night and day, though sleeping in it is quite difficult and I'm sure

Louis-Joseph will never be able to learn to walk until the corset is taken off.

September 22, 1782
I have not slept in three days and Louis-Joseph has not either. He has cried so much he is hoarse. The stiff contraption to correct his back and arm is too tight. I'm certain of it. But the doctor says no, it must stay as it is. The baby will adjust to it. Unless it is very tight it cannot work.

September 23, 1782
Exhausted and bleary-eyed, I went to Louis today, taking the weeping Louis-Joseph with me, and begged him to send the Viennese doctor away. I showed him the deep cuts on the baby's back made by the cruel corset.

He refused to consider my request at first, but I was stubborn, and Louis-Joseph's piteous faint scratching wailing sounds eventually became too much for him. With a great oath he threw the piece of machinery he was working on against the wall and said, "Bring him over here." Taking his sharp cutters he cut away the stiff corset and gave the order for the Viennese doctor to be dismissed. I will write to Joseph and explain what happened.

October 18, 1782

For many months devout people have been advising me to take my son to a healing shrine, such as St.-Martin or Chartres. Pilgrims are cured at these shrines every day, they say. Why not the dauphin?

Eric told me about a series of healings that have taken place recently in St.-Brolâdre, a village not too far from here. There is an ancient spring near where a hermit lived many centuries ago. A chapel was built nearby over the hermit's grave. People go there to pray to St. Brolâdre and many are cured. Amélie's aunt and cousin are both alive today because of the healing powers of the saint.

"Her family lives in the village," Eric said. "She grew up there."

"I wonder why she did not tell me this herself."

"I imagine, your majesty, that she was afraid you might blame her if you took your son to the shrine and he was not healed."

I looked at Eric, his fine blue eyes as clear and earnest, his face even handsomer now than it had been when I first became infatuated with him when I was a girl so many years ago. We are both parents now, he a mature thirty-two or thirty-three, I nearly twenty-seven. We are both dissatisfied in our marriages, Eric quite miserable and I more or less resigned to Louis's limitations as a husband, yet made happy by the knowledge of Axel's love. I wondered whether Eric had found someone to love, a woman he could not marry but who made him happy. I hoped so.

We both knew that what he had just said about Amélie was a polite lie. We exchanged glances, wordlessly letting the lie hang in the air, unchallenged.

"I would be honored to escort you to St.-Brolâdre if you like. I know the curate there very well. He could tell you far better than I of the many remarkable healings performed by the saint."

"Perhaps a small traveling party, a single coach with an escort of five or six guardsmen," I said, thinking aloud. I was remembering the times maman took us to the shrine of Ste. Radegunde, to pray with the villagers and the pious Viennese who made the pilgrimage often, taking their sick relatives and even their animals.

Maman had dressed in the plain black gown of a penitent for these excursions, and had refused to display any signs of her high birth and imperial power. She herded us all into a modest coach, crowded in together, and ordered the driver to take us to the point where the well-worn pilgrim path began. Then, taking us little ones by the hand, with my older brothers (Karl was still alive then, in my memories) and sisters walking on ahead, maman had walked amid the crowd of commoners, singing hymns and chanting prayers as the others did. Once at the shrine she had knelt in the dust, humbling herself, and prayed for those in need of healing. We witnessed several remarkable cures at that shrine, though Joseph was always skeptical of them; I remember him telling me that people are suggestible and any cures they undergo are due to their own self-hypnosis, not divine power. This is exactly what Louis says.

I thought for a moment, then smiled at Eric. "I will talk to the king about this," I said. "If he agrees, we will go, and we will be grateful for your help."

Eric kissed my hand and left me, saying nothing further about Amélie.

November 5, 1782

We have been to the shrine of St.-Brolâdre, but our journey did not turn out at all as we had expected it would.

In order to reach the village we had to

travel through the outskirts of Paris. It has been years since I was there. I had forgotten how nasty and overcrowded the streets are, filled with rotting garbage and death-carts hauling away corpses and open sewers flowing down the center of the narrow old alleys. Far from welcoming us, the Parisians we passed looked askance at our carriage, which was clearly a nobleman's vehicle even though it did not bear the royal coat of arms. Eric and six uniformed guardsmen rode beside the carriage and two postilions led the way.

We had hardly gone any distance along the city streets when we began attracting a crowd. Looking out of the carriage window, I could see a variety of faces, some blankly staring, some excited and smiling, many frowning and surly. The carriage slowed to let a herdsman drive some pigs past, and I clutched the sleeping Louis-Joseph more tightly in my arms.

I felt the coach rock slightly as something hit the door. A second jolt and a third soon followed. I realized that people were throwing clods of earth — I hoped they were not clods of filth — at the vehicle. Eric rode up alongside my open window, shielding the opening from the bystanders who were closing in around us, shouting and singing.

Bring them down
Haughty bastards
Bring them down
Every last one!

Drive them out
Damned aristos
Drive them out
Every last one!

"Stop that singing!" Eric rode into the crowd, shouting orders in his Austrian-accented French. But he, and the guardsmen and postilions, were all pelted with mud and at one point a dead dog was thrown through the window of our carriage, landing at my feet.

Louis, enraged, took the stinking thing by the tail and threw it back out the window.

"Whoreson pigs!" he shouted at the leering, singing demonstrators. "Poxy devils!"

The carriage began to speed up, the road obstruction had passed. I heard our driver shout to the horses and crack his whip, and the crowd parted, melting away in the path of our advance.

I was trembling. I wondered whether we would be able to reach the shrine of St.-Brolâdre in safety. We went on, through the narrow, dark streets, greeted by stares and the occasional shouted insult. I heard Louis swear under his breath.

Eventually we came out through an ancient portal into open country. Eric informed us that we were on the highroad to the vicinity of St.-Brolâdre. In a few moments I felt my anxiety recede somewhat. I turned to Louis.

"These crude Parisians have no idea who we are," I said to him. "If they knew you were the king they would bow in reverence."

"And have they no reverence for their betters? Does a nobleman have to be king to be treated with dignity, as he ought?"

"People say it is the Americans who are to blame. They are levelers. They despise crowns and titles. They have infected the Parisians with their ideas. Yolande says she doesn't dare come into the capital at all any more."

But it was not only the Parisians who gave us an unexpected reception. When we arrived at St.-Brolâdre some hours later the village appeared to be deserted. No smoke rose from the roofs of the cottages. No horses whinnied in the barns. No dogs barked. Not a single face peered from a window. The silence was unnerving.

I have heard of villages so devastated by

cowpox or plague that no one is left alive there. St.-Brolâdre was like that, a place so empty it might have been swept by a lethal disease. Eric took us to the chapel built over the saint's tomb and there we met the curate. When we asked him where everyone was he looked shamefaced. He said the villagers had gone to a festival in a nearby town, but I could tell he was lying. Besides, even at festival times there are some villagers who cannot travel to distant celebrations: new mothers, the very old and very sick, the dairymaids, the blind and the simple. Here in St.-Brolâdre there was absolutely no one at all except the curate — or so it seemed to us.

After we laid Louis-Joseph before the saint's tomb and dipped him in the sacred spring flowing from a rock we went to see the house where Amélie's family lived. Her cousin, the curate told us, had become crippled and could not walk, yet after praying to the saint she was restored to health and strength. Amélie's aunt had suffered from a bloody flux and was also miraculously cured. Eric took us up to the door of the cottage and we knocked and peered in through a window. There was no response.

"They've all gone to the festival," the curate told us. "They won't be back for several days."

Just then I saw the edge of a curtain twitch.

"There's someone inside," I said.

Eric knocked loudly on the door.

"Come out! It is your king and queen who have come to call on you. Come out at once!"

We waited, and presently a sheet of paper came sliding out from under the door.

Eric snatched it up and handed it to me.

"Grievances of the Village of St.-Brolâdre," I read out loud. "The inhabitants affirm and declare that they have no grazing for livestock, that they pay heavy taxes on the sale of their produce, that their land is dry, stony and infertile —"

"Enough!" Louis shouted. "Break down that door! Arrest everyone inside!"

The guardsmen kicked the door in and rushed into the cottage, swords at the ready. They found no one, only a few pieces of homemade furniture, some pots and pans hanging on the wall, bare cupboards and, on a table, a candle, a few books, some paper and some quills and a bottle of ink. It appeared that whoever had been sitting there had drawn up the statement of grievances. But he was gone now.

We heard a crash and the sound of foot-falls and rushed around to the back of the cottage. There was a barn and pigsty and beyond them, open fields, muddy and bare, their crops having been harvested months earlier. In the distance we could see, quite clearly, the retreating figure of a youngish woman, running as fast as she could across the dark stony ground. The white froth of her petticoats was visible with each nimble step she took. On her head was a bright crimson cap, of the kind the Parisians call a cap of liberty.

The guardsmen in our party gave chase, and ran across the fields shouting for the woman to stop. But she was fleet; she outran them. At the edge of the village, where the open fields gave way to a copse of trees, she paused, and turned to look back in our direction. It was in that fright-ening moment that I recognized her. It was Amélie.

TEN

June 4, 1783

I was up before dawn today, watching eagerly from the roof for Axel to come riding into the courtyard. He sent a message saying he would be in Versailles by midmorning, and just in case he came earlier I wanted to be the first to see him.

So many riders came and went that by nine o'clock I was very impatient. But then I saw the white horse and the fair-haired rider in his dusty white uniform — and I knew at once that it had to be Axel. I ran down the staircase and through the long corridors and nearly collided with Axel, who was hurrying along in the opposite direction, on his way to me.

"There she is!" he cried out. "There's my little angel!" Three startled pages, sitting on a bench in the corridor near us, quickly got up and left. We were alone. We hugged and kissed and cried and laughed and hugged again, until my gown was covered in dust and Axel's coat was stained with my rouge.

"How thin you are! And how brown!"

"You, my dearest one, are more lovely than ever. Motherhood becomes you."

We spent the next hour together, secluded from curious and spying eyes, holding hands and kissing and talking. I saw Axel's scars from the two wounds he received. His skin is not so soft as it was. All those nights sleeping on the hard snowy ground in cold tents, all those days with no shade from the hot Virginia sun. He has lived an outdoor life, rough and unsparing, and it has toughened him.

What bliss it is to have Axel here. If such a thing is possible, I am more enraptured with him than ever.

June 22, 1783

I have begun a new fashion at court. Axel brought me a box of beautiful pale calfskin gloves scented with rose perfume. I wear a new pair each day. All the ladies of the court imitate me.

July 6, 1783

Louis talks to Axel for hours at a time about his years in America and his other travels. Louis has never been anywhere and he longs to go on long voyages — or so he says. In truth I think he is too timid to go very far. And how could he bear to be without his cooks and his daily feasts, the soft feather-beds we sleep on, his workshops and plant samples and library? He could never feel safe anywhere, except in his beloved forest of Compiègne, without the guardsmen who protect us.

The other afternoon at dinner, when we were all eating together in my apartments, Louis and I, Axel, Chambertin who occasionally joins us at Louis's insistence, and the two children, Louis was telling Axel how he has drawn up charts and navigation routes for a voyage around the world.

"Do you imagine that you might lead such an expedition some day?" Axel asked politely.

"I'm no mariner. I get sick sailing up and down our canals. Have I told you about the canals I am helping to design?"

When he said this I thought, oh no, not the canals again. He does so love to go on and on about them. But Axel, patient, kind Axel, did not betray any irritation even though he has heard about Louis's canals many times.

"I am always intrigued by your majesty's waterways."

"One of them I am going to call 'Canal La Reine.' To honor my wife." He reached over and patted me on the arm. "I owe you so much, my dear. Especially now that you have given France a dauphin."

Little Louis-Joseph sat up at the table, his nurse beside him, his entire upper body twisted to one side, his head inclined toward his shoulder and his face contorted in pain. I confess that I cannot see him without tears coming to my eyes. He has learned to feed himself after a fashion, and he says a few words. But he is a sad child, and in constant pain. He is a Walking Sorrow. That is how I think of him, though I never say the words aloud. He walks unsteadily, holding onto things. I have not seen him walk more than a few feet without holding on to something or someone.

How he wrenches my heart! I have changed, I know it. When I look into a mirror I no longer see the girl I was, a very pretty girl, always ready to laugh. Now the mirror shows me a woman, much filled out in figure (though far from being fat like Carlotta or hugely fat like Louis), with eyes that still hold ready laughter but also greater knowledge of the world and its temptations. There are lines at the corners of my mouth and eyes, small lines as yet. Sophie calls them wisdom lines.

She says her mother began to get her

wisdom lines at about the age I am now, nearly twenty-eight, after she lost three babies in a row. One was born dead, another one died of the cowpox and the third one, the one she loved the most, fell into the street from a window and was struck by a butcher's wagon. After that happened she came to my mother's court and went to work in the kitchens. Eventually all her children became royal servants. Sophie was appointed to my nursery, and in time she became my principal dresser.

I am glad Sophie has told me her mother's story. Servants, even when one strives to be kind to them, as I do, always seem as though they are part of the palace, as though they had always been there and always will be there. It is good to be reminded that of course they have lives of their own, and sorrows and losses like those we all must bear. Sophie understands my sadness over Louis-Joseph and often comforts me.

July 17, 1783
Louis is going to take Axel and some of the ministers to see the new Canal La Reine he is building in my honor. No one really wants to go of course.

I am reading the book everyone is

talking about, Jean-Jacques Rousseau's *Confessions*. It is like the *Confessions* of St. Augustine which Abbé Vermond has read me portions of, only Jean-Jacques's confessions are more real and more believable. Reading this book has made me cry. Or it may be that I am always ready to cry these days, because of my overflowing sorrow about Louis-Joseph. He has gotten very thin and coughs a lot.

August 2, 1783
By good fortune our route to the Canal La Reine passes near Ermenonville, where Jean-Jacques is buried. I told Louis I want to visit his grave. I feel close to him after reading his beautiful honest *Confessions*.

Poor man! What a strange sad life he had. But reading his *Confessions*, I truly felt as if he understood me, especially my feelings. He claimed that he was unique, that no one like him had ever lived before. He made me realize that I too am unique, that no one else could ever fully understand what I am living through. Especially not my terrible anguish over Louis-Joseph, and over why God gave me such an afflicted son.

I cannot possibly write all the thoughts and emotions Jean-Jacques has stirred up in me, but he has affected me deeply. I feel in a curious way almost as if he were my friend, someone I know well. So I want to go to his grave and mourn.

August 29, 1783
Our journey to visit the Canal La Reine was very dull, all except for one afternoon when I went to Ermenonville where Jean-Jacques is buried and at Louis's request Axel went along as my escort.

There at Ermenonville, having sent the carriage away and needing no guards or servants, Axel and I were alone as we were in Sweden long ago, able to talk freely and affectionately without any fear of being spied on or overheard.

It felt so very good to be with him, as if we had never been apart and no time at all had passed. We walked hand in hand along the winding path that leads to the grave, the tomb set in a copse of trees on a small island in a lake. We met no one and were aware of the silence that surrounded us, heat rising from the warm stones under our feet and clouds drifting slowly over-head.

I sat by the tomb and put my hand on the chiseled marble. I said a sort of prayer, not for Jean-Jacques but to him, as if he were still on earth. I can't explain it.

Axel sat under a nearby tree looking thoughtful. After a time I joined him, not caring whether the grass stained my pale gauze gown or my pink slippers.

"I admire him too, you know," Axel said. "He treasured simplicity, as I do. He struck through all the needless complexity, to find the truth."

I nodded, at a loss for words. We sat quietly, and I rested my head on Axel's strong shoulder.

"One simple thing I know for certain," I said at length. "I love you."

He kissed my forehead. "And I love you, little angel. Always."

Since that sweet afternoon I have been thinking, especially during the long nights when I sit beside Louis-Joseph's little bed, trying to soothe his broken sleep. It seems to me that there are really only a few things in life that truly matter. Love. Nature. Hope. To love those around us. To seek comfort amid nature. To live in constant hope.

Wouldn't Jean-Jacques agree?

October 7, 1783
My household has grown smaller by one. Yesterday Amélie was taken away to be im-

prisoned in the Bastille. Her crime was rousing the villagers of St.-Brolâdre against the king and compiling a list of grievances on their behalf.

Louis has had the entire matter looked into with great care. It seems that Amélie, unknown to any of us, even Eric, has been corrupted by the radical orators and pamphleteers who preach and write ugly lies about Louis and me. She hates me anyway, because of Eric's devotion to me. No doubt she imagines that we are lovers, though we never have been. In any case, she has become one of those who are demanding change, and trying to force it to come about through dramatic action. She has been secretly attending meetings and listening to rabble-rousing speakers and allowing herself to be corrupted by the things they say about Louis and about the government. For a year and more she has been pursuing this dangerous secret life, learning to read and write and even teaching others and spreading the new gospel of change among others of low birth like herself.

Knowing that we intended to take Louis-Joseph to be blessed at the chapel in St.-Brolâdre, she went there, harangued the villagers (whom she knew well, having grown up among them), and convinced them to make a statement to Louis and me by their absence on our arrival. After much discussion the villagers formulated a list of grievances and she wrote it down.

Her mistake came in staying on in St.-Brolâdre after the others had left. No doubt she wanted to observe our surprise and unease when we got there and found no reception prepared, no crowds to greet us. So she stayed — and was captured. Now she is receiving her just punishment.

I am sorry for Eric and his two children. I don't imagine that Eric misses Amélie, but I'm sure her children do. How Mousseline and Louis-Joseph would suffer if I were to be taken from them!

I have intervened on the family's behalf and Louis has given the governors of the Bastille a special order to permit Eric and the children to visit Amélie once a week for an hour.

November 20, 1783

My autumn melancholy is with me again. Axel has told me that he must leave Versailles for some time, in order to accompany King Gustavus on a tour of Italy. He will be gone many months. I have had him with me for far too short a time. I am already missing him and grieving his departure to come.

It is not only Axel's leaving, and the bare lifeless trees and short dark days and cold winds of autumn that are lowering my spirits, but the flood of ugly writings that are sold not only in Paris but right on our doorstep, as it were, here in Versailles.

Right below the terrace of the palace is a ramp leading to the road. A bookseller has set up his stall just at the end of that ramp, so that visitors to the palace, once they pass through the outer and inner gates, must walk right by him on their way into the galleries and salons. There are thousands of these visitors, and a great many of them, I am told, buy the filth from this bookstall and read it.

Terrible, wicked things are written about me. That I am guilty of practicing the "German vice" (loving women instead of men), that I have lived the life of a prostitute, that I have no morals whatever and even seduce young boys and girls. Copies of these horrible books and pamphlets have been found in the palace, papers that picture me as a monster who can never have enough sex, always seeking new victims to seduce. Ugly caricatures of me are horrifying. I am portrayed as a greedy, grotesque demon or a harpy, feeding off the flesh of the poor while I indulge in every kind of sexual excess.

Louis says there is no way to prevent these publications from being sold. Hundreds of them are seized every week by the authorities but the printers just keep on printing more. As long as there are people eager to buy this filth, printers will print it and sell it. The bookseller near the palace has been arrested several times yet each time he is set free eventually he comes back and opens his stall for business again.

January 14, 1784
A new year has begun and before long Axel will be going. Louis-Joseph has a rheum in his chest and is being treated with plasters. I have had three of my back teeth drawn. Afterwards I could not rest or sleep for five days, the pain was so terrible.

February 19, 1784
Sophie came to me this morning during my levee and whispered to me that there was a woman to see me. She said "a woman" and not "a lady" and she implied that I would want to see this woman in private, not during my levee when the room was full of others milling about and my every word and deed would be scrutinized.

I told Sophie to bring the woman to my sitting room just before mass, when I could see her alone.

When I entered the room I saw, seated on a sofa, a middle-aged woman of ample proportions wearing a whimsically eccentric gown of red and orange silk and a jaunty hat with an orange feather. When she stood and curtseyed to me, hurriedly removing her hat, I saw that her brown hair was streaked with gray. Evidently she did not bother, as so many other women over thirty do, to dye her hair or cover her gray strands with false hair. Her pleasant, round face was smiling benignly and I could not help noticing, even through her layers of silk, that her body was strong and muscular.

I sat down on a sofa opposite her, and two of my pugs jumped up beside me. Absently I stroked their heads.

"Your royal highness," she said, smiling, "I am Eleanora Sullivan. We have a mutual friend in Count Axel Fersen."

My eyes widened, but I said nothing, and kept my outward composure. This was the woman who had been Axel's mistress for many years, the former acrobat. I knew that she lived in Paris and that he still saw her, though she had a liaison with some wealthy American financier who was her benefactor and protector. I thought, so this aging woman has been my rival all these years.

Remembering my manners, I invited her to sit down.

"Thank you for receiving me, your royal highness. I would not have come, except that I have heard how gracious you can be and how you place a high value on simplicity and sincerity."

"I place a high value on honesty, Miss Sullivan."

"Mrs. Sullivan, if I may correct you. I was married for many years to a wonderful man, when we were both performers in the circus."

"Very well then, Mrs. Sullivan. Why have you come to see me?"

She leaned forward, and the look on her face was very earnest.

"Because you are standing in Axel's way."

"In what sense?"

"His very great love for you is preventing him from living the normal life that would be best for him."

I wanted to blurt out, how do you know what is best for him? Surely I know him best. He is happiest when with me. We could not love each other more. But I held my tongue. Queens do not quarrel with circus acrobats, no matter how far they may have risen in the world of Paris society.

"Did he tell you that he has been looking for a wife?"

I was nonplussed. Finally I managed to say, "No. He didn't."

"At his sister's urging, and knowing it would have been his father's wish, on his last leave from the American War he went to many balls and dinner parties in Stockholm. He met Margaretta von Roddinge. She is twenty-three, pretty, charming and warm, well educated, from one of Sweden's finest military families. Her father is a general in King Gustavus's cavalry. Axel likes her, and she admires him, as any young woman would. The family had another match in mind for her but they are not pursuing it. They are waiting for Axel to propose."

She waited a moment for all that she had told me to have its effect.

"I have met Margaretta," she went on at length. "Axel brought her to see me. I believe he wanted my approval, though heaven knows why he would feel he needed it. I liked her very much, and wished them both well."

I felt faint. I longed to call for my orange-flower water and ether. I fanned myself rapidly, and reached out for my pugs, which were panting and licking themselves. Then my courage rose.

"Then why doesn't he propose?" I asked Eleanora Sullivan defiantly.

"Because of you, your highness."

"There have always been other women in Axel's life, as long as I have known him," I said, trying to sound as worldly-wise as possible. "Yourself among them."

"Forgive me for speaking so straightforwardly, but we both know that he has never loved another woman as he loves you. He is bound to you by ties too strong for him to break. But you can break them, if only you will."

"Are you asking me to send him away?" I could hardly say the words. Send Axel away? Send away the love of my life?

When she spoke, her voice was flinty. "Release him. Let him go home, marry, become the father of a family. Let him do it wholeheartedly, with no lingering hopes that somehow you and he will one day make a life together."

Upset as I was by all that this odd and unexpected visitor was telling me, I was yet able to study her expression, in an effort to understand whether she was being entirely truthful, and what her motives were in coming to me with her devastating news.

There was sympathy in her wide brown eyes, and determination in the set of her generous wide mouth. I saw no malice or envy in her, though she might well have envied me on account of Axel's deep feelings for me, feelings which, I was sure, had long since driven her to the margins of his emotional life. I felt instinctively that she was speaking the truth about Axel's considering marriage, and about the girl Margaretta. He would marry, I thought, out of duty to his family, and because it was the conventional thing to do. He would choose a good woman, an exceptional woman. But he would always love me best.

"We both want Count Fersen's happiness, Mrs. Sullivan. France is grateful for his service — a service that my husband needs now more than ever. For a man of Count Fersen's ability and achievements, matters of state must always come before personal considerations."

My words were cold and formal, the words of a queen. I was certain, however, that Eleanora Sullivan could guess the feelings that lay behind them. I was telling her that I would not let Axel go.

I rose and smiled, I hoped graciously. The interview was over. Eleanora Sullivan also rose, and curtseyed deeply.

"I hope you know, your highness, that you are breaking his heart," she said, then left, her heavy-footed tread loud on the parquet floor. When she had gone, and I heard the door close behind her, I clutched the dogs and wept as if my own heart would break.

May 4, 1784

When Axel came to tell me that he was at last leaving for Italy with King Gustavus he found me on the grounds of the Petit Trianon, in the area set aside for the cottages I am building there. Four of the cottages are nearly complete and ready to be occupied, and I was giving instructions to the painters to paint crooked black lines on the plaster walls, to look like cracks. I want the cottages to look charmingly weathered, as if they had been there for a hundred years. I had Louis-Joseph with me, walking unsteadily along, holding my hand. He loves coming to this little hamlet and visiting the white lambs and white goats in their pens. Only here do I see him smile.

Of course I have not told Axel about

Eleanora Sullivan's visit to me or her revelation about Margaretta von Roddinge. I thought we were so close that there would never be anything we couldn't talk about. I was wrong. I don't know what to say about his marriage, or possible marriage. It is as if the entire subject lies outside the closed circle of our love. Perhaps that is how he sees it as well. I have never asked him about the other women in his life, though he has talked of them from time to time. He knows that I have no lovers. That I am his, body and soul, for life. He fully understands my marriage to Louis, a blend of duty, good will and affection. It may be that he looks on Margaretta von Roddinge the same way I look on Louis, as someone with whom he can fulfill his family's expectations and share affection and children. But his heart, like mine, will remain in another realm entirely, a realm we share together.

Nothing could have been more tender than our leavetaking. He could hardly tear himself away from me, and promised to write often from Venice and Florence and Rome, sending couriers to Versailles with his letters. He stayed on until evening and we supped together upstairs in the Petit Trianon, relaxing before the fire in the room we have shared so often, the room I keep only for him and never use except when he is with me.

We stayed up most of the night, loving and talking of many things — but not of his plans for the future. I worry a little. Will Margaretta steal him from me? I am nearly thirty years old, no longer the beauty I once was. The tensions and sorrows of my life are there to read on my brow and in the lines beneath my eyes. My body is too ample. The corsets I once shunned, I need now. Axel says he sees only loveliness when he looks at me, and I believe him.

He promises to ride in a gondola in Venice on a moonlit night and dream of me.

June 11, 1784

Eric has come to me to beg me to use all my influence to have Amélie released. He says she is suffering terribly, that her small dark stone cell is full of rats and that she is not given enough to eat. She is not allowed to wash and her clothes are torn and filthy. He says the children cry when they see her, and are upset for days afterwards.

I know she deserves to be punished yet I intend to talk to Louis, to see whether a milder prison can be found for her.

I have had no letters from Italy.

August 23, 1784

I have not yet said anything to anyone but I believe I may be pregnant again.

September 9, 1784

We have made the long journey to Fontainebleau and I am sick to my stomach every day. There is no doubt that I am going to have another child. It cannot be Axel's baby as I had my monthly flow as usual after Axel left for Italy.

Louis is very happy and as a sign of his good will he has arranged for Amélie's imprisonment to be less harsh. Her food ration will be increased and Eric will be allowed to take food to her each week. He is also allowed to take her some bedding and new clothes. She is taken with the other prisoners to the scullery once a week where she can use the water in a common trough to wash herself.

November 7, 1784

I am still so sick I can barely bring myself to write in this journal. I was never so ill with Mousseline or Louis-Joseph. I feel tired and dread having to undergo the lengthy daily court ceremonies. Even sitting through mass is an ordeal for me, and I become very irritated with Louis and Charlot who tease each other and talk loudly throughout the celebration.

January 3, 1785

Dr. Sundersen says it will only be a few short weeks before my baby is born. I am very large and can only wear my loose-flowing tunic-style gowns, the ones I call my "Aristotle" gowns. I look absurd in court gowns. I am so large I might be having twins, only there are no twins in my family or Louis's that I am aware of.

Our holidays were somewhat spoiled by all the criticism of me. In Paris it is being said openly that I have created a "Little Vienna" on the grounds of the Petit Trianon and that I have spent millions of francs on my little hamlet. It was expensive, I admit, to divert the stream that runs the mill, and to create the lake. But the eight cottages were not very costly and I have built them, along with the barns and orchards and animal pens, as an act of charity. Eight peasant families were brought here to live in the cottages, but three of the families moved out almost immediately complaining that the chimneys were clogged and that they could not grow grain in the poor earth.

The hamlet is not yet a complete success but we have harvested many sacks of oranges and my two prize cows, Brunette and Blanchette, give rich milk which Louis-Joseph drinks greedily. The ground is fallow now but will be planted in the spring and by fall there will be grain to grind in the mill. Or so I hope.

February 16, 1785

I have a large bundle of letters from Axel, who is glad about my having another baby and hopes it will be a boy.

"Gustavus is enraptured with Italy," he writes. "He talks of nothing but how warm it is in Florence now and how cold it would be if we were in Sweden. He cannot quite believe that it rarely snows in Florence and never snows at all in Rome. We are going south to Rome soon and will stay there several months before going on to Naples."

I am dismayed. It sounds as though Axel will be away for a long time. I need him.

Thankfully I have had no further visits from Eleanora Sullivan.

April 1, 1785

I cannot say enough about my dear new son,

my big healthy bouncing boy. After being sick so much during my pregnancy I expected a long and painful labor but he surprised me by being born quickly and easily — God be thanked!

He is taking the wetnurse's milk greedily and almost never cries. His body is perfect, round and pink and soft. Thank heaven I am capable of having a healthy son. Now if poor little Louis-Joseph were to die (everyone whispers about it) there would still be an heir for France.

April 20, 1785

Joseph sends me congratulations on the birth of my little Louis-Charles but says nothing of his violations of Austria's treaty with France. Joseph is so aggressive, so unlike our mother who was wise and content with the large domain she inherited from her august father. Joseph always wants more. Now he covets some lands in the Low Countries and our ministers are threatening to go to war over this.

The ministers seek out Louis every day or so because of some crisis, either the constant lack of money in the treasury or a diplomatic issue like this trouble caused by Joseph, or some other difficulty. Louis goes hunting to avoid them, so they come looking for me. They came this afternoon.

April 22, 1785

I dislike meeting with the ministers because I cannot possibly understand all of France's treaties and interests abroad, and because the ministers all hate and resent me, they do their best to make me feel ignorant. But I see through this (how could I fail to, after all these years?) and stand firm. I ask them to explain, slowly and clearly, what the problem is and what our choices are. Then I say, I am going to consult my husband. Then I wait awhile, summon the ministers and give a reply.

It is all a pretense, of course. I would gladly consult my husband but he will not listen. He runs away or puts his hands over his ears. You decide, he tells me. And the worst of it is, the more I do decide, and the more adept I become at standing up to the ministers, the more excuse Louis has to leave everything to me.

I cannot extricate myself from this dilemma, and it weighs heavily on me.

Meanwhile, on this matter of Joseph's breaking the treaty, I have decided that France should give way on this issue of the Dutch lands. We will not threaten war —

but I will write to Joseph and tell him that he must pay the Dutch a large compensation and that if he breaks other treaty promises I will tell the generals to take our troops to the borders and be ready to attack. I hope this will not be necessary as we have no funds to pay the troops. Our enemies do not realize this, but unless new loans are raised, France cannot even afford to defend herself, much less attack.

June 1, 1785
Count Mercy cautions me that someone has been reading my journal again and passing on information in it. He thinks there are spies in my household. Ever since Amélie's arrest he has been more worried than ever. I must not write any more until I have found a more secure hiding place. The count was very angry at me for being careless in writing too candidly of things that could endanger the safety of my brother's government and also that of France.

December 16, 1785
At last I feel I can write safely in this journal again. I have found a new and more secure place to keep it. It has been six months since my last entry, but I have been jotting down short messages on scraps of paper and

hiding them in a big yellow Chinese jar that no one ever looks in or lifts up to clean because it is too heavy.

I am now going to list the most important of these messages:

First, two hundred of my servants have been dismissed in order to reduce the expenses of my household. Some of those dismissed were caught stealing things. Second, I am pregnant again. Third, we have had a great deal of rain, far more than usual. Fourth, there was a terrible balloon crash in the Channel between France and England, the waterway we call the Sleeve. Everyone was shocked and grieved. These are the most important things.

February 2, 1786
I read Axel's most recent letter with dread. "Dearest little angel," he wrote, "I will be returning to Stockholm with Gustavus in May. I must attend to family matters that I have been neglecting for far too long."

What could he mean, except that he intends to marry Margaretta von Roddinge? I am heartsore.

He will marry her, they will settle down together. He will grow to love her and I will become only a lovely dim memory. They will have children and he will become a devoted husband and father. I will never see him again.

April 24, 1786

It does me good to walk through the hamlet at the Petit Trianon and help with the spring planting. My belly is very big with the new baby, who is due to be born in three months, but I can still walk in the ploughed fields with my peasant tenants and throw out the seeds. The air is full of the scent of apple blossoms, and I remember how, as a child, mother took me in her arms and walked with me in the palace orchards when the trees were in full bloom. Under the eaves of the cottages swallows have built their nests and the baby birds are just starting to hatch out.

Everywhere there is new life, growth, expansion. But inside the palace, all is rot and decay. My apartments, which I redecorated before Louis-Joseph was born, are still beautiful and striking, yet if I look closely I can see, even there, peeling paint and bare patches where gilding has been scraped off with a knife to be sold. Scratched floors and chipped furniture have never been repaired. Carpets are stained. A musky odor hangs over everything, especially when it rains.

My apartments are quite livable, as are

the grand salons and reception rooms, but most of the hundreds of rooms in the great palace of Versailles are all but in ruins, full of mold, with rats running over the marble floors and mice chewing on the brocaded sofas and carved table legs. Holes in the roof let in all the winter rains. Each year more rooms have to be abandoned. Palace officials and servants have to find expensive lodgings in the town, and landlords take advantage of them shamefully. Something should really be done about all this sad decay but without enough money for repairs, nothing can be undertaken.

May 21, 1786

The word whispered throughout the court this spring is bankruptcy. No one has any money, everyone is borrowing from everyone else. The servants' wages are unpaid, so they think they are justified in stealing furniture and curios and objets d'art, even the lace trimmings from gowns. All the gold curtain tassels have been gone for years. Steel shoe buckles and steel buttons are coming into fashion, not only because they are "republican" and therefore stylish, but because the servants have stolen most of the gold buckles and jeweled buttons. The thieves cannot be found and punished, there are far too many of them. Thievery is an unpleasant fact of life, and spreads mistrust and suspicion.

Despite all the bankruptcies and complaints about lack of money, the court is lively, there is a frenzy for new fads, new styles and colors. Sophie and Loulou amuse me by showing off the new gowns with ruffs at the neck in the style they call "Henry IV" after the cynical Renaissance king. Louis's pet zebra, a gift from the King of Senegal, has been made the emblem of fashion and his black and white stripes are on everything from hats to stockings. Charlot has a zebra-striped balloon which draws crowds when he sails in it over the palace rooftops.

André has created whimsical hairstyles called African Zebra and Hedgehog and Fat Goose to match the revived color Goose-Droppings that everyone is wearing.

It is all very amusing. We cannot be anxious and gloomy all the time. Besides, I must keep a positive attitude for the sake of the little one I am carrying inside me. I secretly hope it will be a girl this time, a pretty blond angel like my Mousseline, who is temperamental but beautiful. I wait in hope.

ELEVEN

March 6, 1787
God help me, but there are times when I wish I were dead.

More nasty vicious unsigned letters have been sent to me, and I could not help but read them. People are so wicked, so monstrous! When will they stop trying to torment me? I am only trying to help Louis, to do my best.

March 17, 1787
This accursed Assembly of Notables — it should be called an Assembly of Nobodies, Stanny says, and I agree with him — is proving to be a miserable failure. I am being blamed, as usual, for wrecking it, but the truth is, the delegates themselves are to blame. It was the controller-general Calonne who urged that a gathering of "notables" from all over France meet in Paris to promote reforms. He organized it, and he tried to influence its discussions. When the notables rebelled and were reduced to arguing and squabbling, Louis dismissed Calonne. It was his idea, I had nothing to do with it, no

matter what Calonne himself says.

I wish someone would come to my defense. It is not my fault that France can no longer raise loans or that Louis is running out of officials to appoint. He has nightmares that the English fleet will invade our shores and conquer us. He cries out in his sleep, "I surrender! I surrender!" When this happens, Calonne is not there to comfort him, or all the Notables. I comfort him. I reassure him. And the next day I meet with the ministers, at Louis's insistence, because he cannot bring himself to meet with them as he should. I am the only one he trusts. I cannot let him down.

April 6, 1787

The Assembly of Notables limps on, and I limp on too, though the demands of my four children are often too much for me. My littlest one, my tiny Sophie, I can hardly bear to write about. She was so small and weak when she was born that Dr. Sundersen shook his head and patted my arm in sympathy. No words were necessary. I knew he thought she would soon die. Yet to everyone's surprise she managed to suckle, and she is still here, though tiny and feeble.

I sit beside Sophie's cradle at night and rock her and sing to her, and sometimes

Louis-Joseph climbs up into my lap and nestles against me. Louis-Charles, my healthy son, delights me with his strength and vigor, yet he fears the dark and cries out for me at night. And Mousseline sometimes needs soothing and comfort as well, even though she is going on nine years old and very much a young lady.

I need sleep. I am often worn out during the day. Dr. Boisgilbert says my body has been overtaxed with four pregnancies. Yet peasant women often have ten or twelve pregnancies by the time they are my age, nearly thirty-two, and still have the strength to till the fields and harvest the crops alongside the men. I think I am overtaxed from worry.

May 26, 1787
Yesterday the new principal minister, Archbishop Loménie de Brienne, dismissed the Assembly of Notables and sent them home. They were very angry and I'm sure we have not heard the last of them. The real question is, can the new government raise new loans?

June 12, 1787
It has been raining for a week and I have not been able to go out. All my usual vexations irritate me. Sophie refuses to nurse.

June 15, 1787
Sophie still will not nurse and cries a lot. I stay with her.

June 17, 1787
All I can do is pray. Please, dear lord, don't let my little girl die.

June 23, 1787
Two days ago we attended the funeral mass for Sophie and buried her in the lemon grove at the Petit Trianon, next to the stone I put there in remembrance of my miscarried baby all those years ago.

Hardly anyone came to Sophie's funeral. She was of no importance to anyone but me, even though she was a princess of France. She did not live quite a year. May God preserve her precious soul.

July 13, 1787
I have hardly left my room since Sophie died, and I have no appetite. My children are my comfort, especially my little chou d'amour, as I like to call him, Louis-Charles, who is two years old now and cannot keep still, he is so full of high spirits. Mousseline and Louis-Joseph play cards, chou d'amour chases the pugs and runs laughing along the corridor with Sophie chasing him. Abbé

Vermond has been very kind to me. His presence is always a consolation. I realized recently that he has been my confessor since I was twelve or thirteen years old — nearly twenty years. He has been with me, at my side whenever I need him, all that time.

August 2, 1787
I have come to St.-Cloud with the children. Louis is at Compiègne. There is nothing but bad news from Paris, and I don't want to hear it.

September 9, 1787
A miracle has happened. Yesterday I was in the forecourt of the palace, which was crowded with coaches and wagons and carts, all assembling for the annual trek to Fontainebleau. I was supervising the loading of the wagon with Louis-Joseph's things, something I ordinarily leave to the servants. I just happened to be there, standing in the dusty courtyard, when I saw a great white coach with the arms of King Gustavus drive in through the main gate. I knew at once that it must be Axel.

When he stepped down out of the coach he looked different, not only because he has abandoned his powdered wig and wears his own blond hair tied back off his face but because the set of his features is more resolute. Something has changed in him, I can sense it.

I was overjoyed to see him. I had been imagining that I would never see him again, and trying to resign myself to having lost him to Margaretta von Roddinge. Louis was very happy to see him as well, and that night at dinner, Louis began telling Axel all about his book on the plants and animals of the forest. (He has returned to writing his book *Flora and Fauna of the Forest of Compiègne*.) Axel told us of his military duties, of the war that is going on just now between Sweden and Russia and the troops he has led into battle. He said nothing about his family, and I did not raise the subject. Only the next day, when we met at the Petit Trianon, did he speak of his personal life.

"When I left you last to go to Italy with the king, I thought nothing would ever be the same between us again. I thought I would force myself to marry and give up my roving life, set aside my great love." He kissed me and stroked my cheek.

"I tried — but I found I could not do it. Not honestly. Not wholeheartedly. You were always in the way." He smiled. "A lot of people were angry at me when I finally made up my mind not to marry."

"Not to marry! But I thought it was all arranged."

"Not quite. I never actually made the girl an offer."

I felt giddy, lightheaded. As though I were about to lift off into the air, like one of Charlot's balloons.

"And all this time I thought — I thought I had lost you."

"You could never lose me. You never shall lose me."

We embraced then, long and lovingly, and talked no more of anything but how sweet it was to be together again.

September 20, 1787

Axel is with us at Fontainebleau but goes to Paris from time to time to attend to King Gustavus's business and military affairs. When he returns from Paris his jaw is always clenched in anger.

"The whole city is in chaos!" he burst out two nights ago when he returned from his last trip and came to see me. "My carriage can hardly move, the crowds are so thick in the streets. And the things they shout! They threaten us all. You are 'Madame Deficit,' as you know. Louis is 'Louis the Chicken-Hearted' or 'Louis the Triple-

Chinned.' They join hands and sing, and dance around bonfires, looking like the savages I watched dancing around their campfires in Virginia.

"Even well educated people, cultivated people, have caught the fever of criticizing the government. I went to a dinner party, and all I heard was 'There is no government any more! We need a new government! We need the Estates-General!' "

"What's that?"

"Some medieval assembly, I suppose. They like the idea of it because it sounds like the English Parliament, and you know how Parisians like everything English at the moment!"

It was true. There was a vogue for English dress, English hairstyles, even the English way of walking, which was very strange and undignified.

"The alarming thing is, the entire city is alive with this ferment of political talk. There are clubs and debating societies in every coffeehouse, everybody seems to belong to one. Walls are covered over with political slogans and ugly caricatures. Paris is holding its breath, waiting to explode."

I talked to Archbishop Loménie de Brienne about all this when he came to bring me some papers to sign for Louis.

He said he was aware of the unrest in Paris but that it was only a temporary madness, stirred up by a few troublemakers. It would pass, he assured me. He told me about an earlier time in French history, over a hundred years ago, when King Louis XIV was a boy. There were great crowds in Paris then too, and terrible rioting, and criticism of the government. But in time it passed and tranquillity was restored.

Later I read about that violent time in one of Louis's histories. The more I read the more troubled I became. The revolt in Louis XIV's childhood, called the Fronde, began over the government's lack of money. The people rebelled, the parlement of Paris rebelled, and eventually the queen, who was ruling on behalf of her son, had to give in to the will of the people.

I could not help but think, sitting by the fire and reading, that our situation was like that earlier one. Our government is out of money. The people are rebellious, and Louis is always saying how obstinate the parlement of Paris is. Will I, the queen who must often take my husband's place, have to give in to the will of the people?

November 2, 1787
I have little time to write anything in this

journal these days but will write a few lines today to mark my thirty-second birthday. How terribly old I have grown! Sophie keeps finding gray hairs here and there among my blond ones and trying to pull them out.

December 8, 1787

We are attempting to economize. More of my household servants have been dismissed and over half the gardeners at the Petit Trianon as well. I was very sorry to see them go, and worried too. How will they feed their families? There was one in particular, a giant of a man who has planted and weeded and raked in my garden for many years, to whom I said a heartfelt farewell. He nodded to me but did not smile. Who will hire such a huge menacing brutish man? How will he survive? I don't believe he has ever worked anywhere but at Versailles. I wanted to give him a purse of coins but Abbé Vermond cautioned me against it.

"If you reward one you must reward all," he told me. "Otherwise you will do more harm than good."

I cannot possibly give them all money. I don't have enough. If only they knew the severe measures I am taking to spend less. I have ordered no new gowns for spring from Rose Bertin. Instead, four seamstresses are at work mending and sewing new lace and trims on old gowns. (I call them "old" but of course most of them appear new, as most of them have hardly ever been worn and have been kept carefully preserved, packed in lengths of taffeta in my wardrobe trunks.) Mousseline's spring gowns are being made from my old ones. It takes only a few ells of cloth to make her a gown.

Loulou has sent several large boxes filled with my satin and brocade slippers to be resoled. I have been wasteful with my slippers, and will not be wasteful any longer. Instead of wearing each pair only once — as with my gloves — and then discarding them I will wear them until they need repair. At least two or three times.

December 18, 1787
Our Archbishop Loménie de Brienne is too ill to continue as chief minister. (The other ministers are reluctant to work with him, so he has been taking much of the responsibility for the running of our extremely shaky government.) He must retire soon. What will we do when he is gone?

February 1, 1788
All our troubles seem to be descending on us

at once. Louis-Joseph is feverish and terribly thin, and spends most of his time in bed. His poor back hurts him and he looks up at me with his large, grave eyes and says "I'm sorry maman." It breaks my heart.

Louis has ordered the disobedient Paris parlement to disband and once again there is rioting, not only in the capital but in other cities. Axel is urging me to counsel Louis to abdicate and let Stanny govern as regent until Louis-Joseph is old enough to reign. Stanny would not let this unrest go on unchecked, Axel says. He would bring in the troops, make mass arrests, and force the rebellious part of the people to obey.

I know Louis would never agree to this. He hates Stanny too much. Besides, Louis imagines that, despite all his fears, and his dread of confrontation, deep down he understands his subjects and can be a good ruler to them. Axel says this is a dangerous delusion and provides proof that Louis is not fit to be king.

April 3, 1788
For some time now Axel has been living in an apartment just above mine, an apartment I ordered renovated for his use. It is heated by an enormous Swedish tile stove, and Swedish servants are in attendance. It is very

easy for us to spend time together now, easier than ever. Louis says nothing but of course he knows that Axel and I are lovers and I sense that he accepts the situation. He trusts me. He knows I will not desert him. I believe that he wants me to be happy. He also trusts Axel and relies on Axel's love for me to benefit the entire royal family. Needless to say, Louis does not realize that Axel would be only too glad to see him step aside as king.

Officially, Axel is the representative of King Gustavus of Sweden at the court of France. Just as Count Mercy is the representative of my brother, Emperor Joseph. Unofficially, Axel is our friend and adviser, and far more of one than Count Mercy has been in recent years. That Axel is also my lover is of no significance — except to me of course.

April 15, 1788
Last night Axel and I were sitting in a swing in the palace rose garden, just at twilight. It had been a warm day, and the evening was pleasant, the air scented with the sweetness of the first early blooms. My head rested against Axel's shoulder, and he looked across at me and smiled. We did not speak, we were too caught up in enjoying the quiet

beauty around us, and the slow fall of night.

The sound of heavy footfalls made me tense. In a moment Louis came into view, walking by himself along the path toward us.

"Ah, good evening," he said when he had gotten quite close to us. "Yes, a lovely evening. I just came out to check on the ardura japonica. It usually begins to bloom just about this time, in mid-April. There are specimens in Compiègne Forest too, you understand. But they bloom earlier, around the first of April."

"Won't you join us, your highness?"

"Ah — I suppose so, yes. Just for a moment." He sat on a nearby bench, making the old wood creak and groan under his weight. There was an awkward silence. Suddenly he got up again.

"You must excuse me. The light is failing, and I must take my samples from the trees while I can still see them clearly."

"Yes, indeed you must," I said. "I believe I'll stay out here a little longer."

"Of course, if you like. Er — whatever your pleasure is."

He shambled off, whistling, in the direction of the cherry orchard.

May 16, 1788
A battle is being waged, a battle for

Louis's soul. At least, that is the way Jean-Jacques would have seen it, and written about it.

It is a battle between the time-honored way of ruling and a new and untried way, untried except in England. Louis knows only the time-honored way, the way followed by his grandfather Louis XV and my mother and most of the kings of Europe. The king's word is law, the king is absolute. Long live the king.

But the new royal councillor Malesherbes is trying to convince Louis to adopt the English way. Malesherbes urges Louis to write a constitution and offer it to the people. Share power with them, he says. Only in this way can the monarchy be saved.

The battle rages.

June 11, 1788
It has been unbearably hot. We sit by the open windows but the air is perfectly still. My maids of honor fan me constantly and I try to rest. The children suffer.

June 12, 1788
This morning an extremely high wind blew up out of nowhere and trees and bushes were uprooted in the gardens. I sent Eric to

the Petit Trianon to help the villagers and try to secure the animals. The sound of the wind was like a great waterfall or onrushing torrent. A fearful sound.

We quickly shut all the windows and tried to get everyone into the cellars where the wine and ice and foodstores are kept. We could hear windows breaking all over the palace. Louis is out hunting. I hope he will be safe.

June 14, 1788

Everyone is saying God sent the great storm to remind us all that man is not in charge of events on this earth. Some say that the disobedient Parisians are being chastised for their disloyalty to the king.

Reports of enormous damage are arriving by messenger from as far away as Ghent in the north and Tours in the south. The great wind destroyed the wheat crops and fruit trees and thousands of animals and birds have been killed by giant hailstones. There will be famine.

How much more can we bear in this terrible year?

June 29, 1788

The storm is long over but the damage lingers. Prices have fallen desperately low on the stock exchange, and the comptroller-general has had to put his own money into the fund to help storm victims. The Comédie-Française is also giving a performance of *Athalie* for the benefit of those who lost their crops and homes.

I have been officially informed that the treasury is in arrears by 240 million francs. It is an unimaginable sum.

August 8, 1788

The Parisians are furious and no one in the capital is safe from their fury. Loulou went there on necessary business and when she came back she was white-faced and terrified. Eggs had been thrown at her carriage and garbage hurled inside. She told me she thought she would never get out of the city alive.

What happened was that an announcement was made about the government's debts. The treasury is empty and as a result, no more payments are to be made in cash, only in slips of paper promising to pay some time in the future. No one trusts the government to honor these promises. The Parisians feel cheated. Now they have one more reason to hate us.

August 23, 1788

I feel guilty, being so deeply happy and content with Axel while the rest of France is in such turmoil. I have known all the joy life has to offer. How lucky I am! I say this even though I have known sorrow and distress, and there may be more sorrow and distress to come.

Never mind. I am the happiest woman on earth.

September 1, 1788

Louis has yielded to all the criticism and destructive rioting and to the advice of Malesherbes and many others. He has declared that the Estates-General will be summoned next May. Archbishop Loménie de Brienne has resigned, and we have heard that the Parisians flocked into the Palais-Royale in the thousands when they learned this news and rejoiced noisily. Necker has been restored as finance minister. Within twenty-four hours of his appointment, they say, he had begun to raise loans and restore the government's credit once again.

TWELVE

April 15, 1789

Things are happening too fast. Often I feel lost in the whirl of events. I have not thought it safe to write much because twice I discovered servants reading my journal. My old hiding place for scraps of paper in the yellow Chinese jar is no good. I have a new hiding place now. Axel knows about my journal and so does Chambertin. Should anything happen to me, I have decided that the journal must be preserved. It will go to Louis-Joseph and his heirs. I want them to know the truth about me, not the endless lies my enemies tell.

The delegates are gathering from all over France to attend the Estates-General about which there has been so much talk and debate all last fall and winter. They are coming here to Versailles, away from all the unrest and disturbance in Paris. The residents of Versailles are delighted, because the deputies need accommodation and all the rooms in the town can be rented at high prices.

We have summoned yet another specialist from England to examine Louis-Joseph, who has not gotten out of bed for three months and has a very bad sore throat. Sophie has been giving him tea made with cold water root and bathing his feet. He wears a wool scarf even though the air is mild. He complains of an odd taste in his mouth and constant pressure and pain in his side and back.

I sit by his bed and sometimes, when it has been a long time since I've slept, I find myself staring at Louis-Joseph's small white hand. It is so pale in the candlelight that I can almost see right through it. The veins stand out blue and spidery, the long fingers are very narrow at the tips, like the fingers of a fine violinist. As he sleeps, coughing often, his breath catching in his throat, his fingers jerk and twitch, and I clasp his fragile small hand between my two big stronger ones, as if trying to give him what strength I possess.

April 30, 1789
The English specialist says Louis-Joseph's lungs are slowly collapsing because his spine is becoming more twisted as he grows older. There is nothing he can do.

We continue to do our best for him, yet he vomits most of what he is given to eat.

Sucking ice helps a little to prevent this. His cheeks are red with fever but he smiles at me and I know he is glad I am there beside him. Louis cannot bear his suffering and only stays by him for a few minutes at a time. He quickly becomes overcome and weeps, and does not want the servants to see his weakness. Sometimes he gets very angry and kicks at the walls or the door. His left foot is swollen and sore and Dr. Boisgilbert has put a poultice on it.

Tomorrow the Estates-General assembles officially.

May 6, 1789

Yesterday I accompanied Louis to the first meeting of the Estates-General. I drafted his speech and helped him decide what to wear. He was very nervous but performed well I thought.

We entered the chamber just as the bells were tolling the noon hour. At once the ushers knelt and all the deputies and spectators fell silent, so silent I could hear the shuffling of Louis's feet in his gold court slippers and the clanking swords of the Gardes du Corps who formed our escort.

It was an impressive sight, the immense room with its severe Doric columns, balconies and painted ceiling. Louis sat on his red velvet throne, and below him the hundreds of deputies were arrayed, the clerics in their black gowns and white lace-trimmed aprons, a few wearing the scarlet hats and toga-like wraps of high churchmen, the nobles in their swords and multi-colored finery, jewels flashing from their hats, shoes and fingers, and the common people, the Third Estate, in their plain black suits and white wigs.

There were a few shouts of "Vive le roi!" from out of the silence, but not many. I was told afterward that Necker, when he came into the room earlier, had received very loud and prolonged applause.

Hard though it was for me to concentrate on what was going on, as my mind was on Louis-Joseph and I had not slept much the night before, I managed to listen to the speeches. Louis spoke in a kindly, fatherly way, squinting at the delegates because he couldn't see them very well without his glasses. Necker droned on and on for three hours, his speech as long as a long sermon. I was very uncomfortably hot and nearly fell asleep several times.

When we left a few people shouted "Vive la reine!" and I curtseyed to them. This made them cheer louder and I curtseyed again, lower this time.

May 10, 1789

Again today I heard much talk at court of the extraordinary white lights in the sky at night, the lights they call the aurora. Axel says they are quite common in Sweden, but they are hardly ever seen in France. They are said to be an omen that an extraordinary time has come.

There has been another omen. About a week ago Louis climbed up on some scaffolding high above the inner courtyard of the palace. He was watching workmen make repairs. He missed his footing and nearly fell to the ground. He would have been killed for certain had he fallen all the way. By good fortune he was saved from falling by one of the laborers who managed to grab his coat and haul him up to safety.

The freak white lights in the sky, Louis's near-fatal fall, plus Louis-Joseph's sickness all happening at the same time are frightening. I have written to Joseph about all this.

May 22, 1789

My dearly loved son is only a shadow of a boy, pale and ghostly lying on his white sheets. He tries to speak but makes very little sound. Sometimes when I come into the room he turns his face to the wall. I bring him horehound candy to suck on.

The doctors examine his urine and shake their heads and say "very ill indeed" or "exceeding dangerously ill."

I pray to St. Job and have fastened a medal around Louis-Joseph's neck with the name of Jesus. "Suffer the little children to come unto me," Jesus said. My hair is turning more and more gray.

May 29, 1789
I was holding my sleeping Louis-Joseph in my arms today when they came to measure him.

"Why?" I cried.

"For his coffin, madame," I was told.

June 2, 1789
Prayers were said today in all the churches of France for the preservation of the dauphin's life. Even the deputies stopped their quarreling and disputes over voting long enough to bow their heads and pray for the boy who should have been Louis XVII.

He has been given the last rites.

June 12, 1789
I have come to my quiet place, the grotto in the Petit Trianon, to mourn. Louis-Joseph was interred four days ago. We were not al-

lowed to attend his funeral, being a state funeral for the heir to the throne. Etiquette forbids it. Louis and I mourned in the chapel, privately, and Abbé Vermond came to see us. He was in tears for he had loved Louis-Joseph for his meekness and his goodness.

Must all those who are good and meek die? What are my prospects, I wonder? I have some goodness in me, I know. I continue to distribute food, not only here at the gates of Versailles but in Paris as well, where bread prices have gone up quite alarmingly in recent weeks and there is much hunger and want.

Yes, I have goodness in me. But I am certainly not meek. Quite the opposite. When the ministers come with their bundles of papers for Louis to sign (really for me to sign), and leave the bundles with me, I complain loudly.

How can you come to us at such a time? I ask. Can't you see that we and the entire court are in mourning?

I rant away, and the ministers and their deputies avert their eyes and lay down their papers and depart in a hurry.

I cannot possibly read all the papers they bring me. I could not do it even if I were not exhausted, and in low spirits, and grieving for my son.

Thank goodness for my refuge here, in the grotto. I sit on the soft green moss and listen to the sound of the stream. Eric guards me. I am safe and protected.

June 17, 1789

I sat Louis down this morning and as forcefully as I could, I told him that he must act at once if he is to save the monarchy.

Louis was disheveled and feeling ill, as he had eaten and drunk too much last night. I gave him some wintergreen and camomile to chew on to settle his stomach.

The situation in Paris is more serious than we had been led to believe. I have heard from many sources that the deputies of the common people are gaining the upper hand in the Estates-General, encouraged by the Parisians, who no longer respect any law or tradition. The deputies are going to try to take over the government.

"Everything rests on the soldiers now," I said, aware that my body was tense with urgency and that my jaw was clenched. "You must order them to disband the Estates-General, break up the subversive political clubs, and impose a curfew in Paris and in every other town where disturbances have occurred."

Louis sat chewing on his herbs, his small eyes downcast. I was well aware that he did not like what he was hearing, that he dreaded having to act with firmness — military firmness — against his subjects.

"You must not delay," I went on. "Every day is costly. The soldiers have been loyal so far, but they have not been paid in months and they see what is happening more clearly than anyone. Because you fail to act decisively, the soldiers are the only government France possesses. They do their best to keep order, but how can they when the voices of dissent grow louder and louder? The soldiers are only human. They want liberty, good government, a hopeful future. They are being led astray by all the radical political talk.

"Axel and the Marquis de la Tour du Pin — who, in case you may have forgotten, is in charge of our defenses here in Versailles — have just come back from reviewing the French Guards in Paris. They say half the men have become republicans, and do not want a monarchy any more! Their loyalty may be only an illusion."

"Then how can I order them to disband the Estates-General, if I can't trust them?"

"Count Mercy says the way is to bring in

the regiments from Brest and Rennes and Longjumeau. The west of France has not yet been infected by the anti-royalists. Bring in the western soldiers, thousands of them, and all the police within fifty kilometres of the capital. Let them shoot the delegates if necessary, and the rioters. That will quiet the dissent soon enough!"

"And what of the promises I made to the deputies only two weeks ago? In the speech you wrote for me? I promised to be their faithful friend and good father. I am their father —" He broke down, reminded no doubt, as I was at that moment, of Louis-Joseph.

I ignored his emotionalism, though there were tears in my own eyes as well.

"Then be a good father and reprimand them for disobedience! Don't let them take all your fatherly authority away!"

"I've never been good at punishing the children, you know that."

"Now is the time to learn. I will help you. Count Mercy too, and the marquis, and Axel —"

Louis waved his arms in the air, as if warding off blows. "I can't — I mustn't — I need time to think."

"The time for thought is past. Now is the time for action."

I wished, at that moment, that I were a man, a strong man, strong enough to lift my husband to his feet and force him to summon the generals, to give the orders. To bully him physically as well as with my angry words.

"My head is cloudy," he told me. "I must go out, walk, and clear my head."

I knew what he meant to do. "Don't go hunting today. These hours are precious."

But he was already on his feet, stumbling along the corridor, headed away from me and away from all that called him to stay and do what needed to be done.

I called him back, in a voice that sounded in my own ears like my mother's voice. But he was gone.

July 15, 1789

Events have overtaken us. Louis did what he felt he could, sent some troops to form a ring around the capital. But he decided against forcibly disbanding the Estates-General. Despite all my angry speeches and even some pleading, despite the urgent messages from the ministers and from several of the military commanders, he could not bring himself to use violence, or the threat of violence.

The consequences are truly terrible.

Paris has been taken over by a governing committee answerable to no one. All the troops have withdrawn to the outskirts, but only temporarily, for the Parisians are starving and cannot hold out forever. People are breaking into gunsmiths' shops and arming themselves. The Estates-General has turned itself into the National Assembly, and the lower classes are in charge. Yesterday a crowd attacked the old Bastille fortress, where Amélie was imprisoned, and killed the commander. Amélie is free. Eric says he doesn't know where she has gone. She didn't come home to him or visit the children.

July 16, 1789

Everyone is leaving. Charlot has gone, and Yolande, and Madame Solange, and my dear Abbé Vermond, and dozens of others, all vanished so suddenly, in such haste and fear. There aren't enough horses and wagons and carriages to take away all those who are fleeing Versailles, so some have set out on foot, hoping to buy horses and wagons when they get to the next village.

The most terrible rumors are being spread. Versailles is about to be invaded. Armies of the Third Estate are on the march, coming this way, vowing to kill

Louis and me and all those who hold noble rank. The English are coming, and our soldiers will not resist them. There are new rumors every hour.

I don't know what to believe, but we must leave, of that I am certain. Several times a day I am called out onto the balcony to show myself to the noisy, hostile crowd of demonstrators in the courtyard.

"Give us the queen! We want the queen!" they shout. Sometimes they demand to see Mousseline and Louis-Charles along with me, and I dread exposing them to the angry faces and ugly words. I know I am the one they hate; they point their muskets at me, not at the children. Each time I show myself I think, this time they will surely kill me.

July 18, 1789
All is confusion. People rush from room to room, packing, clutching each other, the women weeping, the men cursing and quarreling. Everyone forgets to eat, sleeps in odd snatches. We are awakened at all hours by ringing bells and firing muskets.

I have lost my battle to convince Louis to leave and go to the eastern fortress of Metz, across the border, where I'm certain we would be safe. Charlot has gone there, on his way to Italy, and so have many others. The foolish ministers want Louis to stay and go to Paris to face the rioters and lawbreakers there who have formed an illegal government.

"If you will not go, sire, at least send your wife and children to safety," Axel told Louis. "The Swedish government will guarantee their protection. I will escort them myself."

Louis appealed to the ministers, who pointed out that Louis-Charles, as heir to the throne, could not leave France without appearing to abdicate his rights, any more than the king himself could.

To me their arguments seemed foolish and self-serving, and I told them so.

Louis could not make up his mind. In the end he listened to the ministers and to Stanny, who has not yet made up his own mind to leave.

"Is this what you want then?" I shouted at them, "that I and the children should become targets for the drunken angry mob in the courtyard? Where is your honor, gentlemen? Where is your chivalry? Shame on you all!"

I left them open-mouthed, and a good thing too.

July 21, 1789

Sophie came to me today and brought me word of the strange and unexplained things happening in the country districts. In Nantes, dragoons were seen approaching the town but none ever actually arrived. The citizens were up in arms to defend themselves. In Ste.-Maixent bandits were seen, hundreds of them, on the far horizon. Many people saw them, yet the bandits either passed by very swiftly or they were an illusion. Reports of the same kind are coming in from all over, Besançon and Vervins and even faraway Marseilles and the villages nearby.

Adding to the panic are attacks on castles and murders of landlords by their peasant tenants. Is there no restraint, no decency left anywhere?

I have appointed a sensible and trustworthy woman, Madame de Tourzel, to be the children's governess. She will not panic, she is loyal and levelheaded. She will remain prepared to take the children to safety on very short notice. Sophie has packed my trunk and I am ready to go. Chambertin has secretly made preparations for Louis to leave in a hurry if need be, though Louis has not authorized him to.

August 11, 1789

We wait here from day to day, never going out, receiving bad news hourly. My sister Christina sent me a long letter and the messenger who brought it committed it to memory and burned it before crossing the border into France. He knew he would be killed if the new government of the National Assembly discovered the letter in his possession. Christina says what Joseph and Carlotta both say: leave France at once, while you still can.

August 25, 1789

Louis insisted that I stand with him and receive the Parisians who always come to Versailles on this day, his Name Day, the feast day of St. Louis, to celebrate with him. I am surprised that this feast day is still observed by the Parisians, given all the traditions that they have discarded in the past few months, but I agreed.

Louis asked me to dress in my simplest clothes and to wear the tricolor cockade, the symbol of the National Assembly, in my hair. He always wears the cockade in his hat as a gesture of benevolence. Since I do not honor the National Assembly or the Parisians, who have, in effect, become the governors of France for the time being, I refused to pander to them.

I wore a fine silk dress in a color I call Frozen Tears and I also wore around my neck the false Hapsburg Sun, which twinkled almost as brilliantly as the real one used to do.

It was the first time I had formally received the Parisians since the convening of the Estates-General so I told Loulou to have the ushers bring them into the Green Salon, next to my bedchamber. The Green Salon has furnishings of silver and gold and the special gilding called "green gold" which is unique to Versailles. Woven hangings of hunting scenes adorn the walls, the colors brilliant, the figures and animals lifesize and almost living and breathing in their intensity. Pilasters of gold stand at the corners of the room. It is altogether quite magnificent.

The twenty or so shabbily dressed Parisians who were admitted stared at me, and at the decoration of the room, quite rudely before the mayor bowed to me (he should have knelt, his bow was disrespectful) and said a few words.

As he spoke, talking chiefly of the hunger in Paris, I found myself looking at a woman standing near him. She was dressed in a dirty white petticoat and ragged cloth jacket, and her thin arms and legs poked out from the sleeves and from beneath the skirt. A scarf covered her hair and partly hid her face, which she kept averted from me as the mayor talked on. Unlike the others she did not gaze at the tapestries and furnishings of the room, but kept her eyes on the mayor's back, or on the red, white and blue cockade she held, twisting it between her fingers.

At last the mayor concluded his remarks and Louis thanked him graciously. As the delegation prepared to leave the woman I had been curious about tore off her scarf and looked me full in the face.

It was Amélie!

She approached me. "Your highness," she said, inclining her head ever so slightly, not really nodding, "perhaps you recall one who served you for many years in this very room, one whose firstborn is your god-child?"

Shock constricted my throat, but I managed to say, "Of course I remember you, Amélie. I remember that you were taken to the Bastille, and imprisoned for treason."

At the mention of the Bastille all the Parisians burst out in exclamations of amazement, and stared at Amélie with something like reverence. Ever since the day the angry crowd from the Faubourg Saint-Antoine seized the ancient fortress and began to tear it to pieces anyone associated with the Bastille has been treated as a saint or a mystical being.

"She is a heroine!" someone shouted. "She deserves honor!"

Amélie smiled, approaching me more closely and holding out the cockade she held. "I have been liberated, thanks to my fellow Parisians."

Everyone in the room, even Louis, cheered — except me. Several of the people shouted "Down with tyranny!" and shook their fists.

As the shouting began to die down the mayor, visibly nervous, said "Our business here is concluded. We are needed at the Hotel de Ville."

"One moment, your honor." Amélie kept her steely gaze fixed on me. "I'm certain that before we leave, the queen would be pleased to receive this cockade to wear in her hair." She held out the hated red, white and blue thing to me and I did not take it.

"Take it, take it," Louis whispered loudly to me. I stood still, and returned Amélie's gaze with a look of disdain. After what seemed like a long tense minute or two

Louis reached over and took the cockade from Amélie.

"I am glad to accept this on my wife's behalf," he said, squinting at the entire shabby group. "And I thank you all for coming."

They began to file out, and I heard murmurs of "Haughty Austrian bitch!" and snatches of a song about "Madame Deficit."

Amélie was the last to leave. As she sauntered toward the door, rudely turning her back on us, she said a few parting words.

"Thank you, your majesties, for all those pleasant months in the dungeons. And if I were you, Austrian, I would sell that damned jewel you wear and buy bread for your people!"

The ushers grabbed Amélie but Louis signaled for them to release her. She smirked and chuckled as she left the grand room, running her nails down the gilded molding of the doorway and leaving a long deep gash in its burnished façade.

September 19, 1789
Louis still refuses to leave and will not listen to any of us who try our best to persuade him. However, he is strengthening the de-

fenses here at Versailles and will bring in more troops to defend us if need be. Axel has gone to report to King Gustavus in Stockholm and will bring back more Swedish troops when he returns.

I hear the tramp of the soldiers of the Flanders Regiment outside my window and feel a little less anxious. A detachment of the Gardes du Corps is always in the corridors outside my apartments. Eric too stays close to me. I told him about Amélie's insolence and he said she had never attempted to contact him or the children since her liberation from prison. He has sent the children to safety, to live with his parents in Vienna. But he refuses to go himself, saying his place is with me. I am very touched and tell him so.

September 23, 1789

We have harvested the last of the fruit and grain at the Petit Trianon hamlet and I sent it to the Mayor of Paris personally, to be distributed to the hungry people. We were very short-handed in the harvest, as all but one of the peasant families living in the cottages have left. The animals are not being tended and I have told Chambertin to arrange for them to be sold. I said goodbye with sorrow to my two dear cows Brunette and

Blanchette. Blanchette is pregnant. I fear I will never see her calf.

September 26, 1789

I am worried because the Marquis de la Tour du Pin has made the rounds of the sentry posts that guard the palace and says that we must be absolutely certain that all the gateways to the palace courtyards are locked at all times. Our security depends on this.

He has detected a vulnerable spot between the Cour des Princes and the Cour Royale where only one man stands guard. The guard must be doubled or tripled there, and the loyalty of the sentries must be checked and double-checked.

The marquis suggests that Louis and I and the children withdraw to Rambouillet which is much easier to defend. Louis says he will consider it. The marquis cautions me that many of the palace servants are compromised and have been won over by the disloyal Parisians. They stay on at Versailles because they hope to receive their back wages but once they are paid they will leave. Meanwhile they are not to be trusted.

September 29, 1789

Last night I persuaded Louis that we all

should go to Rambouillet and the wagons were loaded so that we could leave this morning. But when we awoke Madame de Tourzel told us that Mousseline was ill and we decided to wait a few days until she recovered.

October 5, 1789

I wish we had gone to Rambouillet. I have a very uneasy feeling. This afternoon I went with Louis-Charles to the Petit Trianon and he was playing in the grotto. Eric called up to me and said, come quickly, there is a message from the palace. I picked up Louis-Charles, who has gotten quite heavy now that he is four and a half, and went slipping down the moss to where a valet in livery stood waiting with two horses.

The valet knelt in the mud — it had begun to rain quite hard.

"Your highness," he said in a high, frightened voice, "the palace is under assault. I have been sent by the Marquis de la Tour du Pin to tell you that you must come quickly. They are closing the gates against the attackers."

We mounted the horses, the valet taking Louis-Charles, and galloped off through the rain toward the huge bulk of the palace, veiled by the mist of rain. Soldiers of the Flanders Regiment surrounded the walls.

I thought as we drew closer, how will they be able to fire their muskets and their cannon when everything is so sodden and wet? Axel had told me what difficulties he and his men had in the American War, trying to fire their weapons when the weather was bad.

We dismounted and I hurried inside, carrying Louis-Charles who was protesting and squirming. The soldiers quickly surrounded us and led us along in the direction of Louis's apartments. As soon as we entered the palace we heard an uproar. People were shouting, running, colliding with one another in their haste. No one was in charge. The ushers who normally kept order were rushing here and there in as helter-skelter a fashion as the others. People stood in knots of three and four on the landings of the staircases, exchanging news. Some dragged half-empty satchels or baskets along the corridors, bound for hiding places or exits. A few managed to drop to their knees as I passed, but many were so intent on their own business that they ignored me, their eyes never meeting mine.

And I too was intent on reaching safety,

and on finding out what was happening. I had seen the angry crowds massed in front of the main gates leading to the Court of the Ministers but there was nothing unusual in that, they were there every day, milling and complaining, waiting for the food we distributed and then demonstrating in their noisy disruptive way. Where were the attackers? Clutching Louis-Charles, and with four of the soldiers of the Flanders Regiment escorting me, I hurried along the winding corridors and up the old staircases to Louis's apartments, which were crowded with people, all talking at once.

Louis was not there, he had gone hunting and was not expected to return for several hours. I handed Louis-Charles to Madame de Tourzel who had brought Mousseline up to Louis's private study and was doing her best to comfort her. I hugged her and told her not to cry, that there were many soldiers to protect us and that we would be kept safe no matter what happened. I sent a valet to the kitchens to get as many baskets of food as he could, for us and the others, and after an hour he returned with bread and fruit and cold chicken and wine.

A breathless, red-faced messenger arrived and the clamor grew louder. He had ridden hard to bring us news. He shouted that a mob of women was marching toward Versailles, armed with pikes and swords and scythes, demanding bread and threatening to kill the king and queen.

"I have just come from Sèvres," the man said. "They passed through there like a cloud of locusts. They took all the bread from the shops and most of the other food too. And I tell you, some of those women were not really women. There were plenty of men among them."

"How many? What arms did they have? Why did the National Guard not stop them?" The messenger was questioned ceaselessly, but all he knew was that the crowd was loud, wet and angry, and that they were only a few kilometers away.

When Louis finally returned from his hunting trip, throwing down his coat and satchel, flinging his heavy belt on the floor and tossing his bloody hunting knife to Chambertin, who had accompanied him, he faced the courtiers and servants in the room and looked weary, leaning on the back of a chair for support as he was told of the approaching crowd.

The ministers gathered around him, all of them, except the ever sanguine Necker, urging him to go to Rambouillet at once and take us with him.

He sat down heavily and I brought him some of the food from the kitchen, which he proceeded to eat in silence.

"Your majesty, there is no time!" said the Marquis de la Tour du Pin when the tension in the room had become unbearable. "You must go at once!"

"I do not wish to compromise anyone," was his response. "I do not wish to become a fugitive from my own palace, my own home."

One of the ministers, I don't remember which one, said "Do you wish to become a corpse then?" and Louis reprimanded him sharply.

"My subjects would not harm me. I am their father. They look to me for leadership."

"With respect, sire, they may not harm you, but they are threatening to cut the queen's throat," the messenger from Sèvres put in. "I heard some of them say, 'We'll tear her skin to bits for ribbons!'"

"I will protect the queen. Now, let me eat my supper in peace."

He went on eating, while around the table the ministers kept up their debate. All but Necker were agreed that we should leave. I spoke up too and reminded Louis that we had been ready to go for weeks, and that Madame de Tourzel had prepared all the children's things.

Just then, however, we learned that General Lafayette, who is in command of the Paris soldiery, the National Guard, was coming to the palace and Louis said he would not leave before consulting with Lafayette who was surely in the best position to advise him.

I was very tired but felt that I had to go to my own apartments to talk to my household servants — at least to those of them who were still there. I found them in my Grand Cabinet, in a state of great alarm. I addressed them, as calmly as I could, hoping to reassure them by my own hopeful and confident attitude. I was calm, as my mother would have been, and I looked each one in the eye as I talked, encouraging them to show bravery and not let a group of violent lawbreakers frighten them.

"They are not true Frenchmen and Frenchwomen, these bandits who threaten us," I said, uncomfortably aware of my German accent. "They are renegades, who deserve to be put in prison."

I pointed to the detachment of the

Gardes du Corps that was posted just outside the window and told everyone to go to bed — as by this time it was quite late — and do their best to get a good night's sleep.

But as it turned out, I spoke too soon. General Lafayette arrived at the palace about midnight, and I went up to Louis's apartments to hear what he had to say. All the ministers were still there, and many courtiers as well, dozing on the furniture or on cushions on the floor. Madame de Tourzel had put Louis-Charles and Mousseline to bed in the guardroom adjacent to Louis's study, the safest room in the entire palace.

Lafayette came in, looking roadworn and very weary, his boots caked with mud and his uniform wet and dirty. He had with him two delegates from the National Assembly, also looking much the worse for the weather and from lack of rest.

"I have brought twenty thousand men," the general told Louis, "plus some Parisians who are pledged to protect you. From what I have seen, I don't believe they are needed. There was a rabble of women in the vicinity, but they seem to have melted away. We saw no armed mob."

The delegates from the National Assembly requested that Louis move to Paris, where he would be safer and on hand to ratify the Assembly's decrees.

He ignored this implied challenge to his supreme authority and politely agreed to consider their request. Then Lafayette dismissed most of the troops, including the comforting detachment of the Gardes du Corps that had been positioned outside my window, and we all went to our beds.

I hope I can sleep tonight. As I write this, I can hear the troops marching off, going back to Paris or to their barracks at Rambouillet twenty-five miles away.

October 6, 1789

At daybreak this morning I was awakened by a low rumbling sound which became louder and louder and then changed to a fearsome mixture of tramping feet and screaming and shouting.

"Your highness! Your highness! Get up! Run! Leave as quickly as you can!"

My lady-in-waiting Madame Thibaut, still wearing the gown she had on last night, had run into my room. I could tell she hadn't slept, but had been keeping watch.

Through the open door I could see into the salon beyond. Eric was there, with several of the Gardes du Corps. They were guarding the outer door. Suddenly I heard loud thuds. Someone was trying to break down the salon door.

I heard musket fire, and many women's voices, shouting "Where is the whore? We want the Austrian whore!" The shouting became a chant. "Whore whore whore. Where is the Austrian whore?"

My hands trembling and my heart pounding, I hurriedly put on the overskirt Madame Thibaut held out to me and grabbed a dressing gown. The salon door burst open and I saw Eric and the soldiers lunge at the first of the intruders, trying to block the doorway with their bodies.

As long as I live I will never forget what I saw next. How can I write it! My hand trembles now, as I struggle to hold the pen.

A huge man, dressed from head to foot in black, thrust himself into the room, holding an immense axe whose blade was smeared red with blood. He swung the axe, and cut off the head of one of the soldiers. A cheer went up.

"Headchopper! Headchopper!"

More people began pouring into the room through the gap in the doorway and I heard Eric call out, "Save the queen! They want to kill the queen!"

The axe swung a second time, and I screamed.

"Eric!"

I stood paralyzed, unable to move or act, so filled with horror that I forgot to breathe.

Madame Thibaut tugged at me. "Madame, you must come. Remember your husband, your children —"

She pulled me along, stumbling, out the far door of the room and along the passage that connected my bedroom with Louis's, a passage no one knew about but the two of us and our most trusted servants and the pages who often slept on benches in the corridor.

I ran, blindly, the noise from my apartments loud in my ears. I felt torn. I wanted to go back, to kneel beside Eric and mourn him. In one horrible instant he had given his life for me, he had loved me that much. And once, long ago, I had loved him.

When we got to the door that led into Louis's apartments it was locked. We banged on it and screamed and finally a frightened Chambertin opened it, just an inch at first, then all the way. After we were inside he slammed it and bolted it and moved a heavy wardrobe against it.

Louis was in his nightshirt, unshaven,

sitting at a table. There was a plate of food in front of him but he had eaten little. He looked up at me as I entered the room and said, "I did the wrong thing last night. I did the wrong thing." He shook his head and looked down at the table.

I went to Madame de Tourzel and was assured that the children were all right. Thank heavens they had not seen what I saw, I thought. I said nothing about it to anyone, though I heard Madame Thibaut describing the scene in the salon to all those in Louis's room.

For the next several hours we waited in terror, barricaded against the invading mob, hoping that the soldiers who had not been sent away last night would be able to restore order. We heard musket fire from time to time, and through the windows we could see, in the muddy courtyard below, hundreds of people thronging and exulting together, some with blood smeared on their faces and hands, others dragging severed arms and legs, gruesome trophies of their savagery.

I watched in horror as one of the dead soldiers of the Gardes du Corps was carried out into the courtyard, his corpse hacked to pieces before my eyes. The palace was being stripped of everything of value. People carried gold plates and goblets, jewel casks, lengths of fine fabric, hangings and paintings out into the courtyard and loaded them on wagons, unimpeded by soldiers or any of the Versailles servants.

At about one in the afternoon we heard a pounding on the door to the outer corridor and a desperate screaming. The door was opened and one of my chambermaids was admitted, a young girl of only eighteen. She saw me and rushed to me, sobbing and holding her arm which was bleeding. I wrapped some linen around her arm and held her until she recovered herself somewhat.

"Your highness, it was Amélie," she was eventually able to say. "She came after us with a knife!"

"Don't worry. She can't hurt you now."

The girl began to cry afresh. "She said — she told us — she was coming for you."

"As you see, I am safe."

"She bragged to us that she had unlocked the gate to let the murderers in."

"Amélie has much to mourn this day. Her husband has been killed."

"Oh I know. She watched him die. She says she's glad he's dead."

"Her children will mourn him, as will we

all. He was a fine and loyal man."

I did not let the girl see how shocked and saddened I was to learn of Amélie's betrayal. But later on, when I was alone, I wept.

In the afternoon Lafayette came to tell us that he was bargaining with the leaders of the mob, and that they agreed to leave the palace if Louis went out on the balcony and confronted them.

"Don't go, sire," Chambertin urged him. "You will be killed for certain."

"My people will not harm me."

I admired Louis then, even though I felt that he was denying the reality of his danger. He told Lafayette to announce that he would appear on the balcony in half an hour, then asked one of his valets to shave him and dress his hair. He borrowed breeches and a shirt and jacket, and put a red, white and blue cockade on his lapel. I went to sit beside him while he was shaved, and held his hand. He smiled at me. When at last he was presentable, he stood up and bent over to whisper in my ear.

"If the worst happens, my dear, promise me you will guard the children with your life."

"You know I will."

He nodded then to the servant who was

holding the window open that led out onto the balcony. As he stepped out we heard the commotion increase. "The king to Paris! The king to Paris!" came the shouts. I thought I heard Louis try to say a few words but his voice was drowned out by the clamor below him.

I waited for a fatal musket shot to be fired, but heard none. Eventually there were a few cries of "Vive le roi!" Soon the shouting became a new chant. "The queen! We want the queen!"

Having faced the crowd before, I knew what a terrifying experience it was. My knees felt weak, and for a moment I thought I might faint. Madame Thibaut came up to me as if to help me, but there was nothing she could do. I had to face this ordeal alone. Or did I? On an impulse I went into the guardroom and held out my arms for Mousseline and Louis-Charles, who ran to me and embraced me.

"I need your help now. Will you help your maman?" Both children nodded wordlessly and clung to me.

When Louis climbed in from the balcony, I stepped out, lifting Louis-Charles and helping Mousseline through the window. We walked to the railing of the wooden balcony and stood there, in the rain, the children holding my hands. They had been trained almost from infancy to stand up straight and hold their heads up high on public occasions, not to show emotion but to be dignified as became a prince and princess. They did so now, and I was proud of them. I was sure they could feel me trembling.

We stood there for what felt like half an hour, but in reality must have been only a few minutes. The hubbub had died down slightly when the children came out, but now it rose again.

"No children! No children!" came the renewed shouting. "We want the Austrian bitch alone!"

Now I saw, for the first time that afternoon, muskets raised and leveled at me. I turned then and helped Louis-Charles and Mousseline climb back inside, into the arms of their waiting father. My last hope is gone now, I thought. This is what they came for, to make a sacrifice of me. In that instant of time many images raced through my mind, images of my mother's face, young and beautiful, of Axel, lying naked and smiling at me, of poor Louis-Joseph and Sophie, of the green hills of Fredenholm and the stables at Schönbrunn where the starlings built their nests under the eaves.

All but overcome by these tumbling memories, with tears in my eyes I turned and walked slowly to the edge of the balcony once again. All at once I was aware of how I must look, a stout, wet, bedraggled woman in a wrinkled yellow dressing gown, without rouge or powdered cheeks, my graying hair uncombed and loose around my shoulders. This was no queen, I thought, but an exhausted and pitiful woman.

I shut my eyes, said my prayers and waited.

And waited.

The rude chanting continued. I heard cries of "Shoot the Austrian bitch" and "Kill her, kill her!" Yet no muskets were fired. After a few moments I opened my eyes and looked out across the courtyard, across the sea of faces. Tears and the rain blurred my vision, but I could make out some in the crowd. I thought, is Amélie among them? To my astonishment I saw one of the women cross herself. Another knelt in the mud. Then a man stepped forward. "Vive la reine!" he shouted. Immediately he was struck and pummeled by those around him, but his cry was taken up nonetheless.

"Vive la reine! Vive la reine Antoinette!"

I heard Chambertin calling to me through the window. "Come in, come in," and I turned and reentered the chamber. Almost at once I fainted.

When I revived Madame Thibaut was sitting on the cot where I lay, with a tray of food and a bottle of wine. She told me that we were going to be escorted to Paris, and that Louis and the children were already on their way to the waiting coach. I ate greedily and swiftly, washed and dressed, and then joined them.

I slept most of the way to Paris, with Louis-Charles sleeping on my lap and Mousseline leaning against me. It was very late when we arrived at the Tuileries palace, but I felt restless and couldn't get to sleep in the bed that had been made up for me there. Too much had happened on this eventful day. I had to write it down.

Dawn is breaking. I can see, through the dirty window, the first steaks of pinkish light on the horizon. The household is beginning to stir. There is no one here to light the fire in my room, and I am cold. Autumn is here, and winter is coming. What is to become of us?

THIRTEEN

November 1, 1789
I cannot sleep here. The old bed they found
for me, a bed last used by Louis's late
mother, is hard and lumpy, with a frayed
canopy and no proper bed curtains. All our
featherbeds at Versailles were torn apart by
the mob from Paris. The whole palace was
full of feathers. So there was no bedding to
bring with us here to the Tuileries palace. I
lie on a pile of blankets over a straw-filled
mattress that stinks of the stables.

I cannot sleep — but not just because I
am cold and the bed is very uncomfortable. I have nightmares. I dream of Eric,
my handsome, faithful Eric, with his head
being severed by a single savage blow and
blood shooting up out of his neck and onto
me. I dream of being chased, endlessly, by
a howling, rampaging crowd of grinning
women, who get closer and closer until,
just when they are on the verge of tram-
pling me to death, I wake up screaming.

The nightmares wake me up, and then I
spend hours fretting, listening for noises in
the corridor outside my bedroom, imag-

ining that a new attack will come, worrying about Louis-Charles and Mousseline, and how I will ever manage to keep them safe. I think of waking Sophie, who sleeps on a pallet at the foot of my bed, and asking her to keep me company, but I don't have the heart to disturb her. At times I miss the familiar sound of Louis's loud snoring. He is sleeping far away in the guardroom, on Lafayette's orders, surrounded by dozens of soldiers.

Tomorrow is my birthday. I will be thirty-four years old, yet I know I look forty at least. Thank goodness there is no mirror in my bedroom.

November 16, 1789

We are prisoners here. There is no other word for our condition but captivity. The Gardes du Corps, our loyal bodyguards for so long, have been ordered to leave and have been replaced by the surly National Guard, who are more our jailers than our protectors.

They take pleasure in goading and offending me, making coarse jokes about me loudly enough for me to hear, laughing and snickering when I pass by and belching or worse in order to annoy me. They listen to my conversations and I'm sure they would want to know what I write in this journal if they knew I kept a journal. Probably if they ever did find it they would tear it to pieces.

They drink and then they become rowdy and start fights with the palace servants. Lafayette cannot control them, and they pay no attention to anything Louis says. Their rude staring and sullen, hostile looks frighten me.

Sometimes I don't know which are worse, the angry, rude soldiers or the excitable loud crowds that keep up a constant chanting and shouting in the courtyards and under our windows. The din starts at dawn and continues until after midnight, the demonstrators carrying torches and warming themselves over bonfires that they feed with shrubbery from the palace gardens. Even now, as the weather is turning quite cold at night, they keep up their noisy vigil, calling for Louis or for me, threatening us, and singing the fearsome new song that has become their rallying cry, the Ça ira.

I hear it in my brief troubled dreams, that terrible song. "It will happen! Yes it will!" they sing gleefully. "Hang all the aristocrats from the lampposts!" Raucous singing, drums beating, artillery booming — the National Guard is forever testing its cannon — it is enough to drive anyone mad.

December 9, 1789

I have injured my leg again and this time our new doctor, Dr. Concarneau (Dr. Boisgilbert emigrated with Charlot), says I must stay in bed until it heals. It is merely sprained, not broken. It hurts very much.

December 16, 1789

Thank heavens Axel has returned from my brother's court. As a representative of King Gustavus he is able to go and come freely while French subjects are often detained at the border by the National Guard. The assembly is more and more suspicious of anyone who is wellborn. We are all hated and mistrusted.

Axel has rented rooms in the rue Matignon near the palace and the assembly meeting hall which is in the palace gardens. He has given up his military posts in order to devote himself to helping us and no longer wears the uniform of the Swedish Regiment. I like him better in the sword and white stockings of a nobleman of rank. How I wish he could be with me during my long sleepless nights!

He says Joseph is very ill but still cantankerous and difficult. Joseph did not give Axel the money I asked him for, much to my great disappointment. Axel says Joseph thinks the upheavals here in Paris are only temporary, and will soon pass. He thinks it is all the result of court factions fighting one another. He hasn't seen what I have seen, what I see every day: the triumphant, leering faces of the poor Parisians, jeering at us and eager to do us harm. If he could see these faces with his own eyes Joseph would be as frightened as I am.

January 5, 1790

I am allowed to walk for half an hour each afternoon. My leg is getting better. On afternoons when it is not too cold or rainy Louis and I and the children put on our thick coats and cloaks and walk in the gardens. It feels good to be up and walking. I was very tired of lying idle all day, resting my leg, being read to and hearing Sophie's stories and playing whist with Mousseline, who is learning well.

One thing I did accomplish, though it was sad. I sent away all my pugs and my old yellow cat to Naples, with a friend of Carlotta's who offered to take them. Much as I will miss the dear little dogs and my sweet yellow companion at least I will not be fearful every time one of the hateful guards starts to tease them and kick at them.

January 28, 1790
This afternoon we went walking in the English garden near the riding school. I was walking ahead, with Loulou, and Louis-Charles walked between us, skipping and jumping and now and then dashing into the bushes and then rushing back to us. He made a game of this and we became accustomed to hearing the sound of rustling branches as he wove in and out of the evergreen foliage that lines both sides of the path.

Louis and Axel were some twenty or thirty paces behind us, along with four soldiers of the National Guard who strolled along in a most unsoldierlike way, neglectful of their task — which was to protect Louis — and preoccupied in talking among themselves, their conversation interrupted often by unpleasant laughter.

I knew what Louis and Axel were discussing. Axel was preparing to leave for Spain, supposedly on a diplomatic mission for King Gustavus but really to try to persuade Louis's cousin King Charles IV to give us some money. Axel believes he must go at once, as quickly as possible. Louis can't make up his mind when Axel should go. They have been debating about this for several days. When the soldiers are nearby they pretend to be talking of horseracing, of all things.

"Sire, I must impress on you most earnestly," I heard Axel say, "to run that horse in the very first race. He is ready. He will win for certain. If you delay —"

At that moment we heard a heavy rustling in the bushes and a tall man stepped out, reached for me and thrust a knife toward me. In a vivid flash I saw the blade go past me, just missing my cloak.

"Maman!" Louis-Charles cried out. I ducked to pick him up, and in that instant avoided another thrust of the deadly knife. I was barely aware that Loulou had fallen to the ground in a faint, so intent was I on holding onto the screaming Louis-Charles and beginning to run back down the path toward Axel and Louis and the soldiers. I could not run very fast because of my leg. With every step I felt a sharp stab of pain.

In a blur Axel ran past me, sword raised, shouting.

"Stand aside! Throw down the knife or I will cut you in two!"

Louis, dazed, stood where he was, open-mouthed. I kept on running, nearly colliding with the four soldiers of the National Guard who were moving — far too slowly I thought — to Axel's assistance, ignoring me entirely.

I ran back into the palace, gasping for breath when I got there as Louis-Charles was very heavy, and practically fell into the arms of Chambertin, who appeared to be on his way out to join our walking party.

"Help! Call the guards! Call Lafayette! A man attacked me!" Taking Louis-Charles from me, Chambertin hastily called out for aid and then, satisfied that Louis-Charles and I were unharmed and that the commotion in the garden had died down, led me up to my apartments.

I was shaking. I am still shaking now, as I write this, with twelve guardsmen in the corridor outside my door and as many more standing just outside my windows, watching for any intruders. I am safe, but for how long?

February 12, 1790
Today after eating my midday meal with Axel I suddenly began to feel terribly ill, so ill that I had to lie down immediately. I clutched my stomach and moaned.

"Get Dr. Concarneau," Axel shouted to

one of the pages, who ran off at once. To Sophie, who was bending over me, feeling my hot forehead, Axel said, "Did you change the sugar in her sugar bowl today? Tell me the truth."

Sophie hung her head. "No. I meant to, but —"

"I told you to change it every single day, without fail!" I had never heard him speak so sharply to anyone.

"Don't you know what danger the queen is in? Anyone could put poison in the sugar bowl! Anyone at all!"

I saw a man enter the room, youngish and florid-faced, carrying a bag.

"Who are you?"

"Sir, I am Dr. Concarneau's new assistant. He was called away on an urgent case."

I moaned again. The pain was growing worse. I thought, they've poisoned me for certain. I'm going to die.

"Get Dr. Concarneau now!"

"Sir, he is an hour's ride from here, in Saumoy. One of the Duke de Penthièvre's tenants is ill."

"What is he doing attending to peasants! He is needed here!"

For a few seconds Axel paced the floor in exasperation. Then he turned to the young man.

"Damn it then, come over here. She's been given poison."

Ill as I was, and doubled over on my couch, I felt a new sensation — fear — as the young physician assistant approached me.

"Axel —" I called out, holding out my hand to him.

"Yes, my darling, you'll be all right now. He'll give you something to counteract the poison."

"You do have an antidote, don't you?"

The young man, evidently flustered, fumbled in his bag.

"Yes, yes sir, I do."

"What is it?" The question was asked in Louis's booming voice. He entered the room with a brisk step and came up to the physician, who had put his bag down on the carpet and was kneeling beside it, rummaging for something.

"What is the antidote?" Louis demanded again.

"I — I can't remember, your highness. Something Dr. Concarneau gave me —"

At that moment a glass vial fell out of the man's pocket, and with it a red, white and blue tricolor cockade, the revolutionary symbol.

"Seize him!" Louis shouted, and a

guardsman and two valets rushed forward to take hold of the physician's assistant.

With surprising quickness Louis snatched up the vial that had fallen onto the carpet, took it to the window, and held it up to the sunlight. Then he smelled it.

"Poison!" he cried. "A distillate of mercury! Take this hateful stuff away and throw it in the fire," he said to one of the grooms, who enfolded the vial in his lace-trimmed handkerchief and left the room with it.

"Sweet almond oil!" Louis said. "That's what she needs! That's what physicians use when someone has taken poison."

"Do perfumers use it too, by any chance?" I heard Axel ask urgently. I heard him — as if from a distance. I was nearly fainting, now, from all the pain.

"Yes, yes."

Axel ran out. The would-be poisoner had been dragged from the room, struggling and protesting.

Sophie sat at the foot of the sofa, rubbing my feet and legs. Louis knelt beside me, holding my hand and patting my shoulder.

"Poisons work very swiftly," Louis was saying to me. "Whatever is making you ill, if it hasn't killed you by now, probably it won't."

His words were not very comforting. I felt as if an acid had been poured into my stomach and was corroding me from the inside.

After what seemed an hour, Axel came in with a small flask and a cup. He poured out thick oil from the flask into the cup and handed it to me.

"This will cause you to empty your stomach," he said. "I got it from a tradesman I know who mixes perfumes."

Axel held my head while I drank, and kept on holding it when I vomited into the basin Sophie held under my chin. Slowly I began to feel better. The pain receded and in a while I was able to stand. Louis patted my hand and left.

"From now on there must be fresh sugar brought to the table with every meal," Axel announced to my servants. "No exceptions. No excuses. It might be wise to appoint a food taster."

Feeling more myself again, I tried to make light of the situation.

"A food taster?" I said. "No one would want that position."

"What does it pay?" came a cheeky voice from among the servants who had gathered in the corridor outside during the crisis. I laughed as heartily at this as everyone else, and am still chuckling as I write this now, though I sip at my water glass cautiously, and have decided not to sweeten my drinking water any longer with sugar from the sugar bowl.

February 20, 1790
The man who attacked me in the garden was a professional killer brought from Rome, we have discovered. He was hired by a rich man with an accent but he did not know the man's name. Axel is satisfied that the guardsmen have gotten all the information out of him that they can. He will be turned over to the National Assembly for punishment.

The poisoner who posed as Dr. Concarneau's assistant managed to escape the guards and has disappeared. I fear he may come back and try again.

For many weeks now, ever since I was attacked, I have been arguing with Louis about our leaving the country. We must go. I am absolutely convinced of it. Everyone at court assumes that we will go, secretly, and we receive many private offers of help.

Dr. Concarneau, who is a Breton, assures me that in his part of France Louis is loved and revered and that if we took refuge in Brittany we would be protected. He offers to help us in any way he can.

Axel has a plan all ready. He wants us to disguise ourselves as servants, Louis as a very portly valet with an eyepatch, me as a chamberwoman or laundress (he says I would make a very charming laundress). He will arrange for us to be brought, along with a group of other genuine servants, to his rooms in the rue Matignon and from there we would be taken by a secret route which he has arranged to Normandy and from there by ship to Sweden or England or Italy (where Charlot and Carlotta are) if we prefer.

Everyone is pressing us to leave, but Louis is stubborn.

"I will not be chased out of my own kingdom by a band of rebels," he says. He insists that before long foreign armies will invade France, arrest or kill all the deputies in the assembly, and restore order. Many people say that there will be warfare within France, between the assembly and National Guard and soldiers from the provinces, where Louis is still revered and the Parisians are hated.

"Whatever happens," I say, "we are bound to be in greater danger than ever for as long as the fighting lasts. We cannot affect the outcome by remaining here as hostages."

"I am no hostage," Louis mutters when I say this. "I am King of France, as my forefathers were. As my son will be."

Whenever he begins talking in this vein I know it is useless to argue further. I leave him to his pastimes, writing his book on the forest and making his locks (he has brought all his lockmaking equipment here from Versailles) and playing cards with Stanny, who always wins.

I sometimes think how strange it is that Louis, who never wanted to be king and who used to talk so often of his Theory of Mistaken Destiny, should now defend his crown so stubbornly. And so blindly, refusing to see the danger we are all in.

March 16, 1790
"There is an old priest to see you."

Sophie told me this late last night, just after I had gotten Louis-Charles to sleep at last. Like me, he has nightmares, and dreads going to sleep because he knows he will be awakened by fearsome dreams.

The last person I wanted to see was some old priest, no doubt one of the many visionaries who come to see us here and insist on telling us about seeing the face of the Virgin Mary on a wine cask or hearing the voice of Jeanne d'Arc saying

"Save my beloved France!"

Yet the old man who leaned on his cane in the doorway of my salon was not some troublesome visionary, but Father Kunibert! A much older, stooped, enfeebled Father Kunibert, his thick eyebrows now snow-white in his wrinkled forehead. When I went forward and kissed his dry cheek and led him toward the fire I saw that he had tears in his eyes, though when he spoke, his voice still crackled with condemnation, and the tears soon dried.

"Why in heaven's name are you still in this accursed country?" he asked when he had warmed himself. "Can't you see that the devil and all his demons have been unleashed here?"

"I know, Father Kunibert," I said, sitting beside the old man who stared at me quizzically. "But Louis will not leave. Not yet."

"Then you must go without him."

His words chilled my heart. Though I had never admitted it, I had been thinking the same thing.

"Do it now. Come back to Vienna with me. I have a large coach. I can conceal you and the children. I am a person of no importance, just a weak old foreigner with a clerical collar. The National Guard will not bother with me at the border. They will let me pass, especially if I rant and shake my fist and curse at them. They will laugh and wave me on."

I sighed. My shoulders slumped. Part of me longed to follow Father Kunibert's advice, to walk away from the din and turmoil of the Tuileries, the battles with Louis, the fears and nightmares, and take refuge in a carriage leaving for my homeland, where my family would embrace me and protect me. I am weary. Father Kunibert was offering me rest.

"Louis feels that before long we will be rescued," I said, my voice low and tremulous. "He wants to wait."

"Who is going to rescue you? Not your brother Joseph. I have come to bring you the news that Joseph is dead. Not even Count Mercy knows yet. I wanted you to hear about it first."

I could not stop the tears. I bowed my head and sobbed like a child, while the logs in the fire hissed and snapped and even the buzz of voices in adjacent rooms, usually annoyingly loud, seemed subdued.

Joseph is dead! I knew he was ailing, Axel had cautioned me of the gravity of his decline. Yet I had been thinking that he would be there for as long as I needed him, as I surely did now. My crusty, blunt, worldly, humorous brother, gone!

And who was now emperor? My brother Leopold, of course. Joseph had no children that lived — no legitimate children at least. The next oldest male in our large family, Leopold, would become his successor. Had become his successor.

Leopold had always been a cautious, rather colorless man, and I had never been close to him. He cared little for me — though he must care about the honor of our dynasty. And about preventing the spread of anarchy from France to other countries. No doubt he would offer us assistance.

I raised my head and wiped my tearstained face with my handkerchief.

"Have you brought me a message from Leopold?"

"No. I want to talk to you ABOUT Leopold, to make certain you understand your true situation. I tell you plainly, Antonia" — his bushy white eyebrows rose and he fixed his watery pale blue eyes on me — "he will not help you. He persuaded Joseph, when Joseph was dying, not to send you any troops or money. Leopold hesitates. That is his nature, to be hesitant."

"But surely, once he knows that we are

captives here, that we have seen our splendid palace of Versailles wrecked and our servants murdered before our eyes —"

"He is quite aware of what has gone on here."

I let the full meaning of the old priest's words penetrate my mind. What he was saying was, your family will not come to your aid. You cannot count on them, ever. Not unless you leave France. Perhaps not even then.

"There is someone else I can rely on," I said at length, my voice low. "Count Fersen. He will never forsake me."

Father Kunibert snorted his disapproval. "Your liaison is common knowledge. I advise you to repent and ask the lord and your husband for forgiveness. However, under the circumstances, I am glad you have a protector you can count on. I'm certain that if he were here now, with us, Count Fersen would want you to go to Vienna with me."

"Yes he would."

"Where is he now?"

"He has gone to Spain, to try and persuade King Charles to send us money and soldiers."

"Spain! Joseph used to call it the weakest kingdom in Europe. You'll get precious little help from Spain!"

At that moment I felt so tired and dejected I wanted only to sleep — a dreamless, nightmareless sleep.

"Ah, Antonia! You have much to bear. You always were a stalwart girl, the best of Maria Theresa's daughters. And the one with the truest heart."

"I never knew you thought well of me, Father."

"I couldn't very well tell you, could I? I was your confessor. My role was to chastise you for your sins, not praise you."

"I still keep the journal you asked me to write in."

He smiled. "I only wanted to make you think a little about what you were doing. I knew if you had to write down your sins that you would ponder them — at least for the time it took to clean your pen."

He reached over and patted my hand, then took his cane and I helped him to his feet.

"Tomorrow I will go to Count Mercy. The next day I leave for Vienna. You can send a message to me through Baron Goulesco in the rue des Maturins. Think carefully about all I have said, and think of your children. Come to Vienna with me!"

I have not yet decided what to do. If only Louis would agree to leave with us!

April 7, 1790
The National Assembly has done nothing to punish the Italian assassin who attacked me, I am told. He was allowed to leave the country and return to Italy last week, without so much as a reprimand from the deputies.

I am doing all I can for poor Father Kunibert, who was arrested shortly after he left the Tuileries palace on the night he came to see me. When the guards who arrested him asked him to explain his reasons for wanting to talk with me he became indignant and spoke out against the assembly. Immediately he was taken to prison and so far neither my attempts to have him released or Mercy's have had any effect.

June 4, 1790
We have come to St.-Cloud to spend the summer here. How good it feels to breathe country air instead of the stench of Paris! St.-Cloud is a summer palace, open to the outdoors, with few fireplaces in the rooms and views of the lovely gardens from all the windows. I walk in the fragrant, flower-filled

gardens and feel the cool mist from the Grand Jet, the great spout of water, ninety feet high, that erupts from the pool at the foot of the cascade. Throughout the gardens there is the constant sound of water plashing and trickling and rushing over rocks, a refreshing and soothing sound. And no shouting and chanting crowds to keep us all on edge with the ceaseless clamor.

St.-Cloud is my house, my very own. Louis made it over to me six years ago. I wanted to tear down the old chateau and build a new one from the ground up, but the cost was too high. So I had the house enlarged and added new façades, and remodeled my apartments in white paneling with delicate gilded ornaments. It has turned out well, I think, and if only our lives were more peaceful we would be able to enjoy it to the full, for the game is plentiful in the park adjacent to the house and Louis enjoys hunting and riding here and I cannot get enough of the sweet country air.

To be sure, we are not very far from Paris and can see the city in the distance, and hear the faint sound of the tocsin ringing, calling the people to be on alert. An ominous sound. Whenever I hear it I feel a shiver of fear.

Only a year ago, in the first week of June, my precious Louis-Joseph died in my arms. So much has happened since then!

July 20, 1790

I agreed to receive the Comte de Mirabeau, the most powerful member of the assembly, with great reluctance. Axel thinks Mirabeau will be able to help us in our escape plans and told me quite bluntly, "Mirabeau can be bought."

He is said to be grossly immoral. According to rumor he slept with his sister and has seduced hundreds of women. At least one of them, an honorable married woman whom he led astray and all but destroyed, died after he abandoned her. Scandal follows him and he has been in prison at least three times.

I received him in the orangerie, away from the house and without the servants present, as he has come in the greatest secrecy and does not want any of his assembly colleagues to find out about his visit. I had heard that he is very ugly but did not realize until he crossed the threshold of the long, narrow orangerie that he is also quite deformed. His head is grotesquely large, his body massive and fleshy. He has a monkeylike face, with small, bright restless eyes set in a mass of olive skin deeply pitted and scarred from smallpox. There was a disturbing grin on his face as he approached me, yet much to my surprise he was holding out to me a bouquet of fragrant narcissus, one of my favorite flowers.

"For you, madame," he said in a grating voice, his thick southern accent very noticeable and disagreeable to me as I am accustomed to hearing Parisian speech. He held out the flowers and I took them, smelling them and enjoying the rich scent.

"These are quite the fashion in Paris at the moment. Women wear them pinned to their liberty caps. You must have a liberty cap, no?"

"I would be glad if you would state your business, Count Mirabeau."

"Plain Monsieur Mirabeau, if you please. We have recently abolished all noble titles."

"Including mine?"

"Yours first and foremost. Yours and your husband's."

"Whatever your assembly may do, or attempt to do, I am who I am. Nothing can alter my heritage — or yours."

"I have not come here to debate our social standing, but to offer you my assistance."

"At a price, no doubt."

"Naturally. Now that we former aristocrats have no more lands and patrimony, we must work for a living. I am an advocate for the people, that is my profession." He sat down on one of the wrought iron benches among the orange trees, leaned back and crossed his legs.

It was a bold, indeed a shocking gesture. No one had ever before sat in my presence, while I was still standing, without asking my permission. And he seemed perfectly at his ease doing it.

"As an advocate for the people, I offer you a bargain," he was saying. "I will help you leave France, and in return I expect a pension of six thousand francs, and the position of chief minister in a new constitutional government, of which your husband will be titular head."

"Why aren't you speaking to him about this?"

"We both know why."

He is no fool. His directness and his intelligence are refreshing, even if his manners are appalling.

"What makes you think the king" — I deliberately called Louis "the king" rather than "my husband" — "would agree to leave? No one has yet been able to persuade him that it would be in his own best interests, or that of the country, for him to go."

"I am well aware that you are anxious to go and that he is reluctant. Don't bother to deny it — your conversation with the priest from Vienna was overheard and brought to my attention."

"I want that priest, my old confessor, released."

"I will see what can be done."

Mirabeau was a formidable sparring partner. I was not at all certain that I could match him, stroke for stroke.

"I will ask you a question, madame. THE question. What will it take for Louis Capet to read the handwriting on the wall? Do you remember that passage from the Bible about King Nebuchadnezzar? A mysterious hand wrote words on the wall. The message read, 'You have been weighed in the balance, and found wanting.' The monarchy, madame, has been weighed in the balance, and the people find it wanting — in usefulness. I don't happen to share that view. I believe that a king can serve a useful purpose in France, provided he is willing to make himself the servant of the assembly. He must do as we say, and not the other way around."

"You must realize that he could never agree to that. He would work with all his strength — as would I — to see you destroyed first."

"Spoken like an ex-aristocrat. I would take off my hat to you, if I were wearing a hat, or if we still observed those outworn customs. But I must say once again, and I urge you to listen to me, what will it take to make your husband see reason and emigrate? Anarchy throughout the country? Civil war? Another assassination attempt — on his life this time?"

At this I felt frightened. I had been able to escape the Italian assassin and the poisoner. Louis might not be so lucky.

"It could well happen, you know. He goes out hunting often, does he not? With only a few huntsmen and a trusted friend or two? He could easily be abducted, taken to some lonely place in the forest and killed."

It was true. Louis was very vulnerable — and so were my children.

"I must not stay," Mirabeau said. "I am watched, just as you are. And my visit here, if it became known, would harm my position and make it harder for me to assist you."

His leavetaking was as unceremonious as his arrival had been. He rose, turned his back on me and slouched off heavily toward the door of the orangerie.

"Don't forget," he called out over his shoulder. "I am your best hope."

And don't you forget, I retorted under my breath, that you are dealing with a Queen of France, and the daughter of Maria Theresa.

September 1, 1790

I have done all I can to prepare for our departure. New wardrobes for all of us have been made up and sent to Arras, along with a large armoire containing everything we are likely to need, from caps and combs and supplies of my orange-flower water and ether to games for the children and a traveling altar for saying mass.

With Axel's help I have ordered a spacious new traveling carriage with a stove and dining table so that we can eat on our way. It is a large and handsome vehicle painted dark green and yellow with upholstery of white velvet.

Axel points out that it would be better for us to travel in farm wagons, so no one would look twice at us. Better still, he says, we should not travel as a family at all, but as individuals. He can send the children to the Normandy coast with one of Eleanora Sullivan's trusted servants, an old Italian tightrope walker no one would ever suspect of hiding the dauphin and his sister the princess. King Gustavus will send a ship to pick them up. I can pretend to be one of the hundreds of cooks who serve the Royal Swedish Regiment. When the regiment goes back to Sweden, I can travel with it. Or I can join the thousands of farm laborers who come up from the south to harvest the grapes, and when the harvest is over I can leave with the others and cross the border into Italy.

Louis is the most difficult to disguise, because of his size and because it will be hard for him not to insist on being treated as a king. But Axel thinks he can arrange for Louis to dress as a huntsman in the service of a Hungarian nobleman, Count Olezko, who could go hunting in the forest of Compiègne and leave Louis at his hidden retreat there. Chambertin would be waiting to accompany Louis by wagon, both of them disguised as farmers, on the journey north toward the border. As long as they kept to the forest paths and stopped only in small villages Axel thinks they could reach the border at Fourmes

where he can arrange to have troops waiting.

Either way, whatever plan we follow, we
must go, and soon. My carriage will be
ready before long. Perhaps, as Mirabeau
thinks, some new terrible shocking thing
will happen and Louis will suddenly
change his mind and decide to go after all.

October 17, 1790
I have thought of a clever way to save
Mousseline. We will arrange her marriage to
a foreign prince. She is old enough to be be-
trothed, and she is still a princess of France.
(Whatever Mirabeau may say about titles,
she has the royal blood of the Bourbons and
the Hapsburgs in her veins.) I will write to
Carlotta and Leopold and Louis's cousin
Charles to see what can be arranged.

December 1, 1790
I am at my wits' end with Louis. Sometimes
I feel so exasperated with him that I could
scream. I do scream, in private, when only
Sophie and Loulou can hear me. I am at my
worst at times like this when Axel is away (he
has gone to Turin where Charlot is attempting to gather an army of emigres to rescue
us) and there is no one but Chambertin to
help me cope with Louis's tantrums.

He is as unmanageable as an unruly child. He curses at Lafayette when he comes to report on the soldiers. He even slams the door on me now.

"Emigration, emigration, all this endless talk of emigration! I'm staying here. I'm never leaving! Ever!"

His irritation makes no sense, because he hates the Tuileries palace as he often says and has begun to hate the Parisians too, for all his fine talk about being the loving father of his people. He wears around his neck a medal they gave him not long ago. It says "Restorer of French Liberty and True Friend of His People." Stanny laughs at it, which only vexes Louis more.

January 9, 1791

I have been ill. All the fear and tension we experience daily and my futile efforts to change Louis's mind about leaving have exhausted me and brought on the fever and cough that have kept me in bed for so long.

At first I was worried that I might have been given some sort of slow-working poison, the kind that weakens a person gradually day after day until they finally die. Dr. Concarneau has decided that is unlikely. He thinks it is a rheum in my chest brought on by cold weather (the palace is very chilly and our supply of coal is low this winter) and my general weakness. I am too thin. My cheeks used to puff out but now they are sunken inwards and my bosom, once quite large, has shrunk and all my gowns have had to be taken in a good deal. Axel says he quite likes my white hair, but I know he does not admire the dark circles under my eyes or the deep lines that are etching themselves into my skin. I look like what I am: an ill woman marked by anguish and worry.

"My dear, my dearest dear," Axel said, taking my face between his hands when he returned to the Tuileries from Turin to find me ill in bed, "all this trouble is destroying you with worry. You have been carrying France on your shoulders. I long to bring you peace. I must get you out of France, somehow."

I put my arms around his neck and buried my face in his shoulder. I felt so glad, so relieved to see him. He had just arrived, and was still in his travel-stained clothes, his breeches spattered with mud and wet with rain. He had his big wolfhound Malachi with him — he takes the dog everywhere he goes now — and Malachi too came up to us and pushed his warm pointed nose into my hand.

Axel sat with me awhile, talking to Dr. Concarneau when he came in to see me and hugging the children when Madame de Tourzel brought them in to say goodnight. I told him that my efforts to arrange a betrothal for Mousseline had come to nothing.

"They will not let her go," I said. "The Spanish king was willing to make an offer for her hand, to marry his son. But the assembly has forbidden any of us to leave French soil. They say this decree is for our safety, to prevent us from being kidnapped or held hostage. But the truth is they want us for hostages of their own. We are more useful to them here!"

"Mousseline is so like you," Axel said when Madame de Tourzel had taken the children to their rooms. "And Louis-Charles too. We must make your cheeks rosy again like his."

He told me that his meetings with Charlot in Turin had been disappointing. Charlot was gathering men and had managed to raise a small amount of money. But he was many months, perhaps even years, away from assembling a force large enough to invade France and defeat the National Guard.

"Your brother Leopold must join in, and

bring his Austrian troops," he said. "Otherwise the forces opposed to the revolution will have no chance whatsoever of succeeding."

I sighed. My bad leg had begun to ache, and I felt very tired. I lay back against the pillow and gently Axel tucked me in, pulling the blankets up around my chin.

"Never fear, little angel," he said, kissing me on the forehead. "I have another plan. Give me a month and it will be ready. Then we will put the bloom back into those cheeks again."

February 24, 1791

I went to Axel's rented house and there, waiting in the courtyard, was my beautiful green coach!

Of course I was eager to go inside and I was amazed at how large it seems, and how spacious it is. A lever is touched and a dining table comes up out of the floor. There are cupboards and a larder for food and a stove for warmth and for cooking.

I climbed up beside Axel on the coachman's seat and we set off along the Vincennes road.

"Where did you learn to drive a carriage?" I asked him as the horses gathered speed, the rhythmic clopping of their hooves loud on the dirt road.

"My father's coachman, old Sibke, taught me when I was just a boy. He started me off with ox-carts and then went on to four-horse rigs and finally carriages. But this heavy thing is the largest coach I have ever attempted to drive. I pity the poor horses, dragging such weight. They will have to be changed every fifteen miles, you realize, once the journey is under way. It may be difficult to provide that many strong fresh horses at such frequent points along the route. If need be, I will buy them."

"You have already been too generous."

Axel shrugged.

"Many others have made contributions. The king of Spain, Italian princes, well-wishers in Vienna and St. Petersburg and Stockholm. Even a certain former circus acrobat who told me to tell you she hopes you will be safe and prays for your swift emigration."

"Thank Mrs. Sullivan for me."

"I will."

"There is one thing I must ask of you, Axel," I said as we turned into a park and began the long return journey to Axel's house.

"Yes?"

"Don't come with us."

"But you need my protection."

"General Bouillé promises to meet us with his troops and escort us across the border soon after we leave the outskirts of Paris."

"But you may meet with outlaws, renegade soldiers, bands of revolutionaries."

"We will be armed. Besides, the smaller our party is, the less likely we are to attract attention."

"This carriage," Axel replied, patting the seat beside him, "cannot help but attract attention. You can be certain of that."

"I want you to leave France by a different route than the one we take. If the worst happens and our escape fails, you must remain free, not captured along with us and most likely executed. I am selfish about this. I could not bear to lose you. I would die. I know I would.

"Besides," I went on, "you must travel alone and by a different route so that if we should be captured, you can continue to work on our behalf. We need you."

"At least let me drive you out of Paris, to make certain you leave the palace safely."

"All right. But then you must go on alone."

"It won't be long, you know. Soon we'll

both be out of France, no longer answer-able to this monstrous assembly which has taken over everything." He took my hand and raised it to his lips.

"Soon, my little angel, all this long nightmare will be over for us both."

March 2, 1791
Finally, after much effort, I have convinced Louis to agree to Axel's escape plan. He is in very low spirits and frightened, yet he has seen letters from both my brother Leopold and his own cousin Charles telling Axel very frankly that they will do nothing until we are out of France and cannot be held hostage by the assembly. So Louis realizes that we now have no choice but to leave.

He is angry that the assembly has now decreed that he should no longer be called king but "Chief Public Functionary."

June 19, 1791
Tomorrow we go. I have been afraid to write in this journal for the past several months, fearing that if it should fall into the wrong hands and be read, our escape plan would fail. Now, however, we are ready to leave and so far we have been fortunate.

"Are you ready for the play?" I asked the children tonight when they came to me to say goodnight.

Louis-Charles giggled. "I get to be a girl, and wear a dress, and have ribbons put into my hair."

"And you mustn't laugh," Mousseline told him. "We have to be onstage all the time, just like in a play, and do a good job of pretending."

"And who am I?" I asked them.

"You are our governess. You give us our lessons."

"And how do you address your governess?"

Louis-Charles looked puzzled.

"We call her madame," said Mousseline. "We do not call her maman."

"What do we call papa?"

"Monsieur Durand. He is M. Durand, the valet."

"Now, who is your maman, just for tomorrow?" I asked.

"Madame de Tourzel is our maman," said Louis-Charles staunchly. "Only her name isn't Madame de Tourzel any longer. It's Baroness Korff, and she comes from Russia."

I embraced him and kissed him. "Perfect!" Then I embraced Mousseline, my beloved daughter. My heart aches for her. If only I had been able to arrange a marriage for her, and send her away to some foreign court!

All is in readiness for tomorrow. Axel was here earlier, bringing us our official passports and making one last check on our timetable for departure. If all goes as we hope, in two days we will be across the frontier and on friendly ground, surrounded by troops loyal to the monarchy, out of danger and with all the troubles and fears of the past two years behind us for good.

FOURTEEN

June 27, 1791

I am going to set down here, while it is all still fresh in my mind, the details of our journey, a journey unlike any other I have ever taken, and one whose outcome I could never have foreseen.

We started off after midnight on the night of June 20 in the greatest secrecy, having managed, through much cleverness on Axel's part, to elude the palace guards. Once we were all safely in the carriage we rode as quickly as the horses could carry us past village after village, stopping only to exchange our weary horses for fresh ones. It was very dark and the roads were bad. We dropped into deep ruts and had to stop several times while the postilions got down and moved fallen trees and branches out of our path. There was no moon. The children slept, leaning up against me, but my fears kept me awake. I kept thinking of the Committees of Search that were said to ride along every road and imagining that I heard hoofbeats approaching in the distance.

Madame de Tourzel was very brave, keeping up her role as the mistress of the traveling party and looking very elegant in her borrowed finery. (She is of noble birth but has never been well-to-do, and had to borrow a black silk traveling gown from Loulou, who is about her height.) Louis, in the dark overcoat and plain black hat of a valet, with no shiny buckles on his shoes and no jeweled ornaments on his hat or rings on his fingers, drank from his brandy flask and then proceeded to doze quietly as the hours passed. I sat nervously on the edge of the white velvet seat, watching out the window and praying that nothing would happen to impede our progress.

The night wore on, the sky began to lighten and we stopped at the town of Meaux to change horses. I covered my face with the veil of my brown hat to ensure that no one would recognize me. Louis kept his head down on his chest, either sleeping or pretending to sleep. The people in the vicinity of the post-house stared at our carriage, because it was very large and expensive-looking, but did not look rudely in the windows as the Parisians customarily did and did not appear to be suspicious of us. Some of them, I was glad to see, wore the white cockades of the pro-monarchist party in their hats. Accustomed as I was to seeing only the red, white and blue cockades of the republicans, the sight of the white cockades cheered me and I wished I could tell the good citizens of Meaux who we were. But of course I did nothing to betray our true identities, and before long we were on the road again.

The children were hungry and I fed them some veal and bread from the large carriage larder, which I had ordered filled before we left. Louis awoke and ate too, and Madame de Tourzel nibbled on a wedge of cheese. I could eat nothing, I was far too anxious.

"Only a few more hours," Louis told us all. "Soon we will be at Châlons and from there it is only a short way to Pont-Sommevel where the cavalry will be waiting for us. They will take us the last fifty miles or so to the border. No one will be able to stop us."

I sat back against the soft padded cushion of the seat and sighed. Only a few more hours. I hoped I could nap — or at least rest.

But I had hardly dropped off to sleep when I felt a tremendous jolt and heard the horses neigh shrilly. We shuddered to a halt. I jerked awake and looked out the window. We were on a narrow bridge above a swift stream, with expanses of forest stretching away on both banks. The horses had fallen, the carriage leaned to one side and I guessed we had broken an axle. Louis was swearing. The coachman and all three postilions were struggling to free the horses where they were pinned under the broken harness.

All was confusion and it took an hour at least before we were able to go on, slowly, to the next village. It was a costly delay. We were very late reaching Châlons, and even later reaching the next village beyond it, Pont-Sommevel, where we expected to be met by the cavalry detachment.

Something had gone terribly wrong. If the cavalry had been there, they had chosen not to wait for us. But what if they had never been there at all? What if they had met with a Committee of Search and had turned around and galloped away? We had no way of knowing. Were we in danger? Should we turn back? Or would we meet the horsemen further on?

We decided to go ahead, but Louis got out his musket and loaded it and kept it on his lap, beneath the folds of his coat.

The day was very hot, and the dust of

the road blew in through the open carriage windows, making us cough. We coughed our way through the next village, and the next, aware that we were drawing more and more attention to ourselves. I kept my veil lowered and Louis kept his large round hat pulled down low over his face, but by the time we reached the village of Ste.-Ménéhould we were so alarmed and tense that our agitation was noticed and the villagers began to stare at us curiously. I saw not a single white cockade in the village, only the tricolor republican cockades everywhere.

There were soldiers scattered here and there, some of them quite drunk. One officer came up to our carriage.

"Nothing has gone as arranged," the man whispered hurriedly. "I cannot be seen talking to you, or we will be suspected."

He moved off quickly, but not before we had, in fact, drawn the suspicion of some of the villagers. I saw them staring, muttering, becoming all the more curious when some of the soldiers mounted their horses and began following our carriage as we rolled on through the village.

We now had an escort, albeit a very small one, and we were getting closer to the border with each slow mile we traveled. But it was getting dark by this time, and the road turned hilly and the ascent was difficult. Our coachman was tired, having been driving since midnight the previous night, and our own nerves were worn thin. Louis-Charles was fretful, Mousseline sick to her stomach and complaining.

I brought out fruit, beef and cheese and a bottle of wine and we ate in anxious silence, as the carriage lurched and lumbered through the gathering darkness.

We knew that we were in a very hostile area, one patrolled by German and Swiss mercenaries in the pay of Austria who preyed on the villagers and bullied them, demanding food and liquor and money. Axel had warned us before we left the palace that all travelers coming from the direction of the capital were routinely stopped and questioned in this region, and we were prepared to be questioned.

We were not prepared, however, for the road to be blockaded and our forward progress halted completely.

We arrived in the village of Varennes and found that some of the local officials had closed off the road so that we could not pass on through. There was a hubbub in the street. Late as it was, people were coming out of their houses and raising the alarm. I saw National Guard soldiers mustering, holding their muskets and standing to attention. I wondered whether our own small cavalry escort would gallop off into the woods and abandon us.

"It's no good," Louis said to me in an undertone. "Someone has betrayed us."

An official came up to the carriage, opened the door, and began to question us, holding a candle up to our faces and demanding that I raise my veil and Louis remove his hat. They ignored Madame de Tourzel entirely, and I saw that she had quietly begun to cry.

"Who are you, and what is your destination?"

"I am Monsieur Hippolyte Durand, valet to Baroness Korff," Louis asserted, attempting to brazen out our imposture.

Our questioner snorted. "You are not! You are Louis Capet, Chief Public Functionary of France, former king. I recognize you. Your fat face is on the worthless promissory notes issued from your treasury."

He looked over at me, and I could not return his gaze. I felt sick. My stomach churned, there was a terrible pain in the back of my neck and I suddenly needed to relieve myself.

"And you, lady, are the Chief Public Functionary's wife, the one who has been robbing us for years, taking bread from our children and spending our money on diamonds for yourself! Tell me, where are all those diamonds now? Are they in this carriage?" He began rummaging under our seats, pushing us roughly aside while he searched for treasure. I clutched Mousseline, who clung to me, her eyes wide with fear.

"Your trunks will be searched," the official said. "And you will not be allowed to proceed further. Get down out of this carriage now."

With a sigh Louis heaved his large bulk out of the carriage, which rocked and lurched with each of his heavy steps. The musket he had been keeping on his lap fell to the ground, and the official picked it up.

"Was it your intent to fire on the people's representatives?" he demanded to know.

"I would have protected my family, had the need arisen."

"I believe it was your intent to incite a counter-revolution. I believe the Chief Public Functionary has become an enemy of the people of France."

In response to this Louis reached up and

pulled out, from under the collar of his plain linen shirt, the medal he wore on a chain around his neck. He held it out to his questioner so that the man could read the inscription: "Restorer of French Liberty and True Friend of His People."

"This was presented to me," Louis said with dignity, "by the people of Paris."

"Some friend you are! Attempting to flee the country, leaving your people to the mercy of the cruel troops who harass us! Abandoning France in her hour of need!"

"Please, sir," I could not be quiet any longer. I was doubled over in pain and badly in need of my chamber pot.

"Yes, yes. Madame Sauce!" he called out loudly. "Take this woman inside before she becomes a nuisance."

A stout gray-haired woman in a nightgown and white mobcap stepped out from the ever increasing crowd of villagers.

"Come with me," she said brusquely and helped me out of the carriage. The children and Madame de Tourzel followed. The woman led me into a dark shop where barrels of goods were arrayed in front of a wide counter.

"Maman," Louis-Charles said, his voice uncertain. He had never been in a place of this kind before.

"It is all right, papa will come soon. We will be all right here."

To my great relief we were shown up some narrow stairs into a small bedroom lit by a single candle. The children lay down and Madame de Tourzel tucked them in bed. I went into an adjoining room and made use of the chipped porcelain chamber pot the woman handed me with evident distaste. Afterwards I bathed my face and hands in a washbasin and asked Madame de Tourzel for a willow bark powder for my pounding head.

Outside, church bells had begun to ring and more and more houses were lit up. The whole village had come awake, dogs were barking and roosters crowing. I lay down next to Louis on a hard narrow bed, hoping the pain in my temples would grow less if I tried to rest.

Presently I heard a noise at the window. I got up to open the shutter. On a ledge outside was a young cavalry officer, his white uniform smudged and stained. Evidently he had climbed up from the alley below, which was dark and deserted, all the villagers having assembled in the street facing the front of the houses and none in the back.

"Madame, I must speak to the king."

I shook Louis out of his drowse, and drew him over to the window.

"Sire, come quickly. I have twenty men waiting to take you to General Bouillé. He is only eight miles away. Give me your son and I can hand him down to safety. We have horses ready for you. But you must come now, at once."

Louis squinted at the young officer. "Is that the Duc de Choiseul?"

"Yes, sire."

"You are a good young man, like your father before you."

"Thank you, sire. Now please! Do not hesitate!"

"Go! Now!" I pushed Louis toward the window. "I'll lift Louis-Charles out after you have gone."

"But —"

"You must do this. It may be your only chance."

"But — the soldiers — the National Guard —"

"We can outrun them, sire. Our horses are faster."

"Surely they will raise an alarm, fire at us."

"That is the chance we must take. But we will surprise them. We will be gone before they can take aim."

Prodded by me, Louis had put one leg over the windowsill.

"What about you?" he said, turning back and looking at me. There was no affection in his eyes, only bewilderment.

I shook my head, impatiently. "I am not important. You are. You and Louis-Charles. Besides," I added ruefully, "I am the one they really want. The one they hate."

I heard a whistle from the alley. A signal, I assumed.

"Hurry, sire. Hurry!"

Louis started to climb out on the ledge, then stopped.

"No," he said quietly, and began to climb back in.

I knew he was afraid of heights, but what a time to give in to his fears!

"Go on!" I said, as loudly as I dared, not wanting to alert whoever was in the shop below us. "Don't stop now! You can make it!"

"I will not leave my family."

I knew that tone of voice. It had a terrible finality in it.

Louis was now back in the room, brushing off his brown coat.

"Ride to General Bouillé on my behalf," he was telling the young officer. "Tell him to bring his entire force here, as swiftly as possible."

"But sire, what if —"

"Go now."

There was no countermanding that regal voice. Crestfallen, the young duke agreed and began going back down toward the street, from which came another shrill whistle.

"Be safe!" I called down after him. "And thank you."

Two hours, I thought to myself. With fresh, swift horses and a good road, he can be back with General Bouillé and his men in two hours. By then it will be dawn. What will they do with us then?

With a sudden unexpected gesture Louis reached for me and embraced me, pressing me to his heart in a way he seldom did. I crumpled in his arms, and wept.

Together we waited, counting the minutes, praying for General Bouillé and his men to come, while more National Guardsmen poured into the town and the restive, chanting crowd sang the hated Parisian song "Ça ira" and beat against the walls of the shop with sticks in a very unnerving way.

Dawn came, and with it the distinct sound of hoofbeats. But there were not many riders, not General Bouillé and his hundreds. Only two. They came galloping up to the knot of officials standing in the street outside our building and I heard one of them announce in a voice of authority that he was Captain Romeuf, aide-de-camp to General Lafayette, and that he was carrying important papers from the National Assembly. The other rider was also an officer, but I did not hear anything he said.

The newcomers conferred with the officials, while I kept thinking, two hours must have passed by now. Where is General Bouillé? He must come soon. I stood at the window, looking down, clenching and unclenching my fists.

The official who had questioned us was addressing the crowd.

"As you know, the Chief Public Functionary is here among us." At these words loud boos came from the crowd. "He has been stopped here, by the loyal citizens of Varennes, before he could reach the frontier. By his attempt at flight, he has shown himself to be a deceitful traitor to the people of France. I took from him this musket." The official held up Louis's old gun, and at the sight of it the crowd booed again, more loudly this time. I could hear cries of "Shoot him with it!" "Death to the Chief Public Functionary!"

"This enemy of the people, who has been conspiring to harm the people of France and their National Guard, has been ordered arrested by the National Assembly. We will carry out this order, and the Chief Public Functionary will be returned to the capital."

Loud cheering and applause erupted. Captain Romeuf and his deputy conferred briefly, then we heard them coming up the stairs to the room where we were, their boots thumping loudly and their swords banging against the walls of the narrow stairwell.

Oh please, I prayed silently. Please, let General Bouillé come now!

The door to the room burst open and the two men came in, with the official who had harangued us earlier behind them.

"Chief Public Functionary!" the taller of the two officers said loudly, "I am here to arrest you and your wife by order of the National Assembly. You are to collect your possessions and come with us immediately."

"As the restorer of French liberty and true friend of my people, I will accompany you." Louis moved to follow the men down the narrow stairs, and, unable to think of anything else to do, I gave a little cry and fell to the floor, pretending to faint.

There was a small commotion. I was laid on a bed, Louis slapped my face in an effort to revive me, restorative drinks were brought and a very unpleasant doctor curled his lip in disgust as he examined me and pronounced me to be perfectly well.

"She only fainted out of fear," he remarked to the two messengers from Paris. "These aristocrats have no stamina. The least disturbance shatters them."

I wanted to strike him but restrained myself. Presently I sat up. I had succeeded in postponing our departure by perhaps half an hour or so. General Bouillé had not come. Either he was not coming, or he might pursue us and overtake us on our return journey to Paris. I tried to cling to that hope.

Of our long, dispiriting, wearying trip back to Paris I will write little. Angry, insulting villagers surrounded our slow carriage every mile of the way, even when it began to rain and they were soaked through. We were not allowed to raise the carriage windows but were obliged to keep them open, so that everything we did and said was witnessed and commented upon, by the National Guard who kept watch over us and by the hostile crowd around us.

"Hang them all, fucking pigs!"

"Dump them in the ditch!"

"Long live the people's assembly!"

"Rot in hell, miserable fat hog, and your pig wife and your ugly piglets!"

I put my hands over my ears but it did no good. The nasty chanting voices echoed in my head like a deafening wave of sound, so strong and intense it was almost a blow. I was so tired. I longed for sleep, but the voices, the hideous, jarring voices kept me awake.

"Austrian bitch! Whore! Sow! Ugly hag!"

I will never forget the sight of those dirty, leering faces staring at us through the open windows, grinning at us, waving their pitchforks and scythes, threatening us. Had the National Guard not been there I'm sure we would have been pulled out of the carriage and murdered.

I will not write here of the worst humiliations of that endless hot, dusty journey, save to record that I was ill, and that my every act was watched and remarked on gleefully. In the end it was all I could do to keep my dignity, sitting back against the cushions in my dusty gown, desperately in need of a bath and a long night's sleep. What had begun in hope was ending in a nightmare of shame and failure. My one shred of satisfaction was the knowledge that Axel was safe, across the border in Brussels, waiting for news of me.

FIFTEEN

July 28, 1791

As usual in Paris in July, it is raining. I have moved to new quarters in the Tuileries, since the Parisians came in and ransacked my old apartments — a scene of horror I will forbear to describe. I sit now at an old desk in a small room on the third floor, a room that does not overlook the gardens where crowds continually gather.

While writing this the rain has begun to fall harder and harder, driving against the windows and running in a great cascade off the roof. I long for a cup of hot tea as the room is chilly and my silk wrap is thin — but most of my servants have been arrested and taken away and there is no one I can call on.

I try not to think too much about our future. Our one friend and ally in the assembly, Mirabeau, is dead and the new name on everyone's lips is Robespierre, an odd little man from Arras.

I hope that my new guardians will let me walk in the gardens on sunny days. My leg is weak again but I can walk quite a long way if I use a stick. Louis-Charles needs the sun, he has grown a little pale of late. A boy his age ought to be out-of-doors, riding his pony and running with his friends. As my brothers did at Schönbrunn all those years ago. I remember the warm, bright summers at Schönbrunn with such pleasure.

Not at all like this afternoon, with the hard chill sheets of rain that beat down so savagely against the old windows, making everything a blur and leaving me lost in a hazy fog of thought.

September 3, 1791
Horror of horrors, Amélie has been placed in charge of me, as my jailer.

"Eat your bread!" she shouts when I leave my small half-loaf uneaten on my plate. "It's good for you."

"The pastrycook is a poisoner," I tell her. "I won't eat anything he bakes." It is rumored in the palace that the pastrycook is an avid revolutionary who wants me dead.

"Then starve, for all I care," she says, strutting around the room, fingering the small chunk of gray stone she wears on a chain around her neck, a souvenir of the Bastille. "And from now on you are confined to this wing of the palace."

"But my husband and children —"

"You must ask permission each time you wish to see them."

"I wish to see them daily."

"That will not be permitted."

All my old servants, except Sophie and Loulou (now demoted to a chambermaid), have been imprisoned or sent away. Amélie will not tell me what their fate is to be.

"The People's Chamberwomen will provide what service is appropriate for you," Amélie says. It is the People's Chamberwomen who bring me my small bowl of boiled meat and half-loaf of coarse bread and small carafe of wine at each meal. Sometimes, when they bring in my food or change the linen on my bed, they dress in my gowns and put my fine feathers in their greasy hair. They strut from one end of the room to the other, imitating me, calling out obscene remarks.

"We know you have thousands of diamonds," they say, coming close to me and hissing like snakes in my ear. "Where are they? Where have you hidden them? Those jewels don't belong to you, Citizeness Capet. They belong to the people of France."

I do my best to ignore the chorus of ugly

voices and the ugly words they say, confident that my jewels are in good hands. I sent my jewel case to safety with André my old hairdresser when he emigrated. He took it to Stanny, who now has it, in Coblenz. Stanny and his wife made it to the border on the night we were arrested in Varennes and sent back to Paris. They crossed with an escort and are now with Charlot, raising an army.

Irritating and hostile as the People's Chamberwomen are, Amélie is far worse, especially when she deliberately wounds me with reminders of Eric.

"His body was never found, you know," she remarked to me. "My husband's body I mean. There were so many corpses in the palace that day he was killed — and most of them were without heads — or clothes. How could anyone tell one man from another?"

At this the People's Chamberwomen burst out laughing.

"Would you have recognized Eric's naked body without his head, citizeness?" Amélie asked me.

"Of course not."

"I wonder. He wasn't faithful to me, you know. He had several mistresses, in addition to you."

"Eric and I were never lovers."

The People's Chamberwomen hooted and jeered, and began singing the latest awful song about me.

> So many lovers
> So many men
> She wants to bed them
> Again and again.
> She is voracious
> Not hard to get
> All the men love her
> Marie Antoinette!

I do my best to remain above it all — the restrictions and punishments, the cruel taunts and painful talk of the man who was dear to me. I have nothing but contempt for Amélie, and all the more contempt because I know she does not mourn for Eric, who was a good man and died heroically in my defense. But then, she never was worthy of him.

October 4, 1791

I spend so many hours writing letters that I have little time or energy left to write in this journal. I write to my brother Emperor Leopold, and Louis's cousin King Charles, and to Stanny and Charlot, and to Count

Mercy. I urge them to send an army as swiftly as possible. I tell them frankly that only force can save us now. We have no political allies. Louis has lost nearly all of his authority and I believe it is only a matter of time until we are eliminated entirely.

They will not kill us, of that I am certain. To kill us would bring on a terrible revenge. More likely they will imprison us more narrowly than at present. The Tuileries palace is our prison now. In the future we might be shut up in an old chateau in some provincial place, and all but forgotten. Louis feels abandoned and forgotten now. He is inactive and leaves all the work of corresponding with our friends and allies to me.

October 12, 1791

I am still allowed to receive visits from my dressmaker Madame Rondelet (my former dressmaker Rose Bertin emigrated long ago), and this morning she came with her workbasket full of gifts for the People's Chamberwomen and Amélie.

She passed out the presents as soon as she arrived: warm red, white and blue woolen scarves, red aprons, blue and white striped petticoats. The gifts provided a distraction. Madame Rondelet handed me a petticoat she had made for me and my guards did not bother to examine it, as they were so busy admiring themselves in their new clothes. The petticoat has secret pouches sewn under the ruffles. Letters are concealed there.

When Dr. Concarneau comes to treat me he brings bread and cakes (made by a pro-monarchist pastrycook) and messages are often hidden in the false bottom of my bread plate.

Recently he came and delivered a basket of muffins. "From a well-wisher in Brittany," he said. I bit into one of the muffins and nearly broke my tooth. Something hard had been baked into it. I spat out the object and discovered that it was a diamond ring. Quickly I put the ring back into my mouth, then told the doctor I had some pain in my gums and asked him to examine me. (I am not allowed visits from a dentist.)

With great presence of mind he saw the ring in my mouth, palmed it, and then rubbed my gums with a medicinal salve until he had a chance to conceal the ring in the bread plate.

"Send it to Stanny," I whispered. "To help raise money for the army."

November 18, 1791

My leg has become ulcerated. Dr. Concarneau comes twice a day to apply salve to the wound and put on new bandages. He brings letters hidden in his medical bag and takes mine away. I know he takes great risks and I am very grateful to him. I have confided to him that I no longer have my monthly flow and he says it is a result of all the worry I experience and also my lack of sleep. I stay up at night, often until past midnight, writing my letters. Sophie helps me. When I look out of the window at that hour I occasionally see the eerie lights in the sky, the aurora. White, green, sometimes violet lights.

"The end of the world is coming," Sophie says. "These lights are an omen."

I wonder if she could possibly be right.

December 31, 1791

Tonight the old year ends. Such an atrocious year for us all! If only we had managed to reach the border in safety, we would be in Coblenz now, living in hope. I would see my beloved Axel again, most beloved and most loving of men, and most self-sacrificing. Once again I would be in the shelter of his arms, surrounded by the protective circle of his love.

I am so glad he is safe. I feel his love

even from far away. Troubled as I am, the thought of him brings me joy and warms my heart on this cold night.

I pray that we will be rescued in the new year.

February 2, 1792

I pray daily for rescue — and yesterday fresh hope of a rescue came.

A dark-haired young laborer wearing a tricolor cockade on his shirt and carrying a basket of tools came into the small room I am using as a bedchamber after showing Amélie and the People's Chamberwomen his special pass. Without looking at me he walked to the window and began scraping away at one corner of the frame, saying something about having been sent to repair a leak. He seemed to know what he was doing, and the women did not challenge him.

Something about him intrigued me. I watched him work and after a short while, when the others had drifted out of the room, he dropped a small square of paper at my feet.

"Excuse me, monsieur, but you dropped this," I said, picking up the paper and holding it out to him.

"Sh!" he whispered. "Read it!"

Immediately I turned away from him and placed the paper in a book which I pretended to read. Once I was certain no one had overheard our exchange I furtively unfolded the paper and read:

"I am the boy you once rescued from Prince Stanislaus's beatings. You sent me to Vienna, where your brother Joseph enrolled me in a military academy. I am now Lieutenant de la Tour in the Austrian army, principal commander of the Knights of the Golden Dagger. We are four hundred men of noble birth here in Paris, pledged to guard and defend the king and his family. We will not fail. Look beneath the candleholder. Burn this paper."

I reread the message, then crushed it in my hand. Lieutenant de la Tour took a plain pewter candleholder from his tool basket, stuck a candle-end in it, and lit it, placing it on the table in front of me. The afternoon was growing dark, and he needed the light to work by. Yet when he completed his repairs he left the candleholder on the table, and I burned his message in the dying flame. After the candle burned out, I turned the candleholder over. A tiny golden dagger was stamped into the metal — and when I touched it the entire base of the candleholder dropped open to reveal a hollow tube. Inside was another message, and when I unrolled it I was astonished to see hundreds of signatures, each followed by the words "To the death."

These surely were the signatures of the Knights of the Golden Dagger, the men pledged to safeguard us. Tears ran down my cheeks. So many names. Such honor. Such bravery. Quickly I rolled up the paper and put it back inside the candleholder, refastening the hinged bottom.

I did my best to disguise from Amélie and the other women the delight I felt and the upsurge of hope that swept over me during the evening when for a precious half-hour I was allowed to join my family. I wanted to tell Louis what had happened but several of the National Guard were lounging in the doorway and of course I did not dare breathe a word about Lieutenant de la Tour's visit. I played whist with Mousseline, and Louis read aloud to Louis-Charles from a storybook. We laughed and hugged each other.

When Amélie came to get me to take me back to my apartment I kissed Louis goodbye on the cheek and whispered "I have good news." I can hardly wait to share it with him.

February 14, 1792

Axel is with us once again. Despite all my warnings and entreaties, in my letters to him, that he not risk his safety and his freedom by returning to France, he is here. In our precious moments alone he kissed me hungrily and told me that he could not stay away, that he is continually anxious about me and devotes all his time and thought to freeing me and my family from the trap that is closing around us.

Though he is still beautiful, as beautiful as a carved statue, he now looks like a hunted man. His face is thinner and his dear warm loving blue eyes are wary. His hair, drawn back republican-style and tied with a black ribbon, is shot through with threads of silver.

He comes here as a representative of the Queen of Portugal (a disguise of course) and wears an immense black cloak and oddly shaped black hat of the kind Portuguese noblemen wear. He has dark-haired Portuguese servants and brings his big gray wolfhound Malachi with him wherever he goes. Axel says Malachi is the best bodyguard he could possibly have, quite mild and affectionate most of the time but able to tear out the throat of anyone who might attack him in a matter of seconds. I could not help noticing that Malachi growled whenever Amélie entered the room during Axel's visit.

He stayed with us most of the day yesterday, telling us, in low guarded tones, what we most wanted to hear: that sincere efforts are being made to deliver us from these monstrous men of the Legislative Assembly, which since last fall has been the governing body of France.

I dare not put down all that we were told, but King Gustavus has been our most faithful ally, as it turns out. He has done much more than Stanny and Charlot who are slowly raising a small force of soldiers at Coblenz. Gustavus made a daring effort to send almost the entire Swedish fleet to Normandy last fall (I knew nothing of this) with the intent to land two thousand soldiers and then march toward Paris, gathering support in the loyal western provinces of France along the way. Had he succeeded in this grand plan I have no doubt the Swedes and the loyal French would have conquered Paris. The revolution would have collapsed and all the wicked deputies would have been locked up and tried as the traitors they are.

That would have been a great day!

Gustavus is preparing to launch a

second invasion but in the meantime he can smuggle us out of the Tuileries if we will agree to go one at a time. Louis continues to resist any escape plan. He has given his word to General Lafayette that he will not attempt to leave the Tuileries and he intends to keep it. Axel told me he thinks Louis is being foolish and stubborn (when was Louis ever not foolish and stubborn?) yet he respects his integrity.

February 17, 1792
A false spring has made the trees bloom early outside my window, and I too am blooming a little after my long winter of ceaseless letter-writing and weary vigilance. With the connivance of blessed Dr. Concarneau, who managed to convince the new head of the Legislative Assembly that I am very ill and need warmth and rest, I have managed to spend a few days with Axel at St.-Cloud.

February 19, 1792
Wrapped in Axel's strong arms, with the world kept at bay, here at St.-Cloud I am hardly aware of the passage of time.

When he kisses me it is as thrilling as the first time. I am lost in him, lost in a daze, a dream of happiness.

"My dearest little angel," he murmurs, stroking my cheek, kissing my lips, my cheeks, my forehead. "We have been through so much together."

"You have risked everything for me — your career, your family life, your life itself."

"If only I could have done more," he said tenderly, wiping away the tears his words caused me to shed. "Don't you know by now that you mean more to me than my life?"

Was any woman ever so loved as I am loved?

We make love, we sleep, we eat, we talk, we stroll hand in hand through the gardens in the unusually mild weather. It is as if, though surrounded by a sea of hostility and danger, we two occupy an island of serenity and love.

I passed a long mirrored panel this morning and dared to look at my reflection, something I rarely do as the sight of my old pinched, pale face depresses me. To my amazement I saw a radiant, happy woman with a faint blush of pink in her sunken cheeks. My eyes were bright and there was even a glint of the mischief I used to see there.

Oh Axel, you work such miracles in me!

February 27, 1792

Axel left for Brussels this afternoon. We are full of hope that within the next few months either King Gustavus or an army raised by Stanny and Charlot will liberate us. In the meantime we can call on the Knights of the Golden Dagger for protection. Lieutenant de la Tour, who continues to work as a laborer at the palace and keeps a close watch over me, assures me that some fifty of the four hundred knights, disguised as Parisian revolutionaries, are always in the vicinity of the palace and have worked out a series of signals so that in the event of an emergency they can be at our side within a few minutes. I keep the pewter candleholder by me and use it to send out and receive messages.

March 22, 1792

Today I called Sophie in to help me dress and with her aid I put on a stiff sort of corset made from twelve layers of thick taffeta.

"But you have always disliked corsets," she said as she fastened the bulky garment in place. "Besides, you are so thin now you hardly need one." Sophie has become quite tart in her speech and brusque in her manner. Amélie and the rough, coarse People's Chamberwomen despise and mock Sophie constantly, and though she

does her best to remain ladylike and un-
perturbed in the midst of their hostility I
know that their cruel remarks and taunts
disturb her and keep her on edge. I urged
her to emigrate months ago but she would
not leave me. I value her loyalty far more
than I could ever tell her.

"This is not just any corset," I said. "I've
had it specially made."

When she finished fastening the thing
tightly around me I went to my wardrobe
and took out a knife that I keep concealed
there. Telling Sophie to close the door and
lock it to keep Amélie out (she bursts in
unannounced so often!) I handed Sophie
the knife.

"Now, stab me," I said, shutting my eyes
and standing in front of her bravely,
waiting for the blow.

"What?"

"I said, stab me."

She swore in German, an oath I will not
write here.

"As your mistress, I order you to drive
that knife into my chest, with all your force."

With a cry unlike any sound I had ever
before heard Sophie make she struck me
with the point of the blade — only to break
it against the stiff armor of my protective
corset.

I laughed. "You see, Sophie, I am not mad, though you must think me so. This corset will keep me safe. Not even a musket ball can penetrate it. And I have had one made for Louis as well."

I heard a snuffling sound. Sophie was crying, head in hands. I was astonished. I had never before seen my sensible, practical, capable Sophie in tears. I realized that I had been thoughtless in demanding that she prove the reliability of the corset by trying to thrust a knife through it. I had known that she could not harm me, but she had not.

"Oh, your highness," she said through her tears, "I am so afraid for you!"

I realized then, in that moment, how worried she was about my safety, and how bravely she had borne her worries, keeping them hidden from me under a mask of impatience and irritability.

"Dearest Sophie," I said, hugging her. "How I rely on you! How grateful I am to have you near me. But you mustn't worry, really you mustn't. We are close to being rescued, I assure you. It won't be long."

We heard raucous singing in the adjacent room. The People's Chamberwomen have added a new song to their repertoire recently, a song introduced by the men from

Marseilles who have been pouring into Paris to help defend the city.

"To arms, citizens!" they sang. "Form your battalions! Let's march! Let the tainted blood spill out over our fields!"

I groaned at the off-key singing. "Oh no, not again!"

Sophie smiled a little, then she looked at me seriously.

"If your wise mother were here, your highness, she would tell you to put no faith in corsets, or in phantom rescuers from across the border. She would say, go away with that man who loves you."

"Axel."

"Of course."

"We did go away, last summer. Remember? Only we didn't get far enough, and the National Guard caught us and brought us back."

Sophie lowered her voice. "I think you know what I mean. Go away, with that Swedish man, by yourself. I'll take the children. Leave the king to his fate."

"And if I did that, Sophie, could I ever forgive myself?"

"The king would want you and the children protected."

"In all this weary time, since the earliest days of our danger, he has never once come to me and urged me to go without him."

Sophie pursed her lips and said nothing, but her eyes were full of disdain.

"I will say nothing against my sovereign. However, there are times when I wish he showed better sense."

There was nothing either of us could say to that, so I asked Sophie to help me out of my heavy corset and put it away in the wardrobe with my petticoats.

I have noticed that for the rest of the day today she has been less tart with me.

April 15, 1792

Mercy has sent me a secret message to say that my brother Leopold is dead and his son, my nephew Francis, who is only a boy, is now emperor. What will this mean for us? Axel will know. I await his next letter.

May 10, 1792

The Parisian savages have a horrible new device for executing criminals which they call the Blade of Eternity. It is like a gigantic chopping block. A heavy razor-sharp blade falls with a thunderous loud rattling sound on the neck of the poor criminal and cuts off his head instantly. The bloody head falls away and there is a fountain of red blood.

Louis says great crowds gather to watch the killing machine at work. It is thought to be very fair and in keeping with the ideals of the revolution which are Liberty, Equality and Fraternity. The Blade of Eternity makes all men equal in death, whereas in the past noblemen were executed by the sword and the common people were hanged or died under torture.

I shiver at the thought of how much easier and more mechanical it is to take life with this device. It is all so cold and precise, so lacking in feeling and dignity. Amélie reads to me from a newspaper called *The People's Friend* and in it a writer called Marat says that if France is to be calm again, two hundred thousand heads must be cut off.

Such ridiculous statements have become more and more commonplace. Amélie forces me to listen to this sort of monstrous rubbish but I try to shut my ears to it. This Marat is even uglier than Mirabeau and has some sort of repulsive skin disease that makes him stink. According to Dr. Concarneau all the men in Paris are trying to make themselves as dirty and smelly as possible in order to be true to the revolution. They wear long untrimmed moustaches, ragged loose trousers and wooden shoes. And, of course, the red, white and blue cockade and the red cap of liberty. The doctor has taken to wearing loose trousers because if he wears the tight breeches of a nobleman he is spat on.

May 15, 1792
We are all in a state of great excitement because we are at war and the Austrian armies are advancing with great success. The French soldiers have no courage at all and run like rabbits at the sight of true Austrian arms. When the French met our Austrian forces at Lille they were so frightened and confused that they murdered their own commander!

Soon the Austrians will be in Paris and we will all be safe. Meanwhile the Parisians are becoming more and more suspicious of each other and use their terrible killing machine to cut off each other's heads.

June 7, 1792
Lieutenant de la Tour has cautioned me that my journal may be used by the revolutionaries to condemn me as an enemy of the people so from now on I am writing on little scraps of paper which I stuff into the candleholder on my table.

Axel has sent word to me that King

Gustavus, our great friend and benefactor, is dead, stabbed by a nobleman who, Axel says, resented him for his liberal ideas. Axel is now without a protector and benefactor although he is very active in supporting the Austrian and Prussian troops which will surely be here soon. He may lead an army himself in support of the Duke of Brunswick who is in charge of the combined forces.

I dream of Axel, proud and handsome on a tall white horse, riding at the head of hundreds of strong warriors thundering into the courtyard of the palace and conquering the National Guard and all the hateful Parisians. The dream is so vivid that when I wake I still think I hear hoofbeats.

June 28, 1792
Something has gone wrong. The Austrian army is not yet here and I cannot understand why.

July 3, 1792
My poor darling Mousseline has become a woman. I have done my best to prepare her for this day and to make her welcome the changes her body is undergoing. I hope that she looks forward to becoming a wife and

mother. If only we lived in normal times she would have been betrothed by now, or even married. She is nearly fourteen and very pretty, though I have to confess that she has something of her father's heaviness of manner and she lacks charm though not affection.

Looking at my dear daughter I see the future, and some of my hope is restored. Some day I will hold my grandchildren in my arms and tell them about these terrible days we are living through, and how we were saved and the king's rightful powers were restored to him.

Some day . . .

July 21, 1792
Yesterday Amélie and six of the People's Chamberwomen took me roughly by the arms and dragged me into a cupboard where brooms and mops and workmen's tools are kept. I called for help but they covered my mouth with their dirty hands and threatened to lock me in the cupboard with no food or water if I screamed again.

They tore off all my clothes, even my old patched and stained slippers, and left me in my chemise, shorn of its valuable lace which they cut off. Amélie, in triumph, ripped out one of my gold earrings, cutting my earlobe which bled a lot.

It all happened very quickly, and with much commotion, as the cupboard was small and the women kept yelling at me and bumping into the walls and over-turning buckets and boxes. I don't know what more they would have done to me if the cupboard door hadn't been flung open and Lieutenant de la Tour, dressed as usual as a laborer, hadn't stood there, his presence putting a temporary stop to their assault.

He pretended to be looking for a box of nails he kept in the cupboard and Amélie, who has been very flirtatious with him in the past, ordered the chamberwomen out so that he could find what he was looking for.

There I was, blushing, in my torn che-mise, barefoot, bleeding from my ear, frightened and trying to hide my shame. To his great credit the lieutenant did not react to the scene with the anger I'm sure he felt but went on poking about in the cupboard, taking scant notice of me but calmly removing his jacket and holding it out to me to put on as if the gesture was the most natural thing in the world.

"Ah! Here it is," he said as Amélie watched him search the shelves of the small room. He held up a metal box and smiled at Amélie, who smiled back.

"May I escort you back to your chamber, madame?" he said to me calmly, "or perhaps you were on your way to your husband's rooms?"

"Yes, I was," I managed to say, quite loudly and decisively before the surprised Amélie could object. It was all done so smoothly that within seconds I was out in the corridor with Lieutenant de la Tour, clinging to his arm, being taken to Louis.

"Thank you, thank you," I whispered. "They might have killed me."

"We will not let you be harmed," he whispered back. "Remember, we watch over you constantly."

He delivered me into the protection of several of Lafayette's officers who were in Louis's small apartment. To their credit, these men acted as gentlemen should, not as the unruly soldiers under their command so often did. After one shocked glance at me they averted their eyes, offered me blankets to wrap around myself and even handkerchiefs to bandage my ear. Louis was nowhere in sight.

"If I may say so, sir," Lieutenant de la Tour said to one of the officers, "the women who serve this lady have shown excessive zeal on behalf of the people. Perhaps they might be of greater service to the revolution somewhere else. Meanwhile I trust she will be in good hands here with you."

"Of course. Now get on about your work."

I watched the lieutenant leave, sorry to lose my rescuer yet more aware than ever that if I needed him, he and the other Knights of the Golden Dagger would come to my aid.

August 9, 1792

The alarm bells keep ringing, hour after hour, a maddening sound that keeps us awake and reminds us that Paris has become a scene of chaos.

Clang, clang, clang, it comes and goes, a tinny sort of sound. A warning. A call to arms. From every quarter of the city we hear it, and then drums start to beat and we know that one more group of militiamen has been summoned to readiness, with their pikes and knives and axes.

The midnight hour will soon be here and from my window I can see the bright blaze of massed torches moving on the streets near the palace. The commotion started in the St.-Antoine district, where the factories are and the hungry workers with no jobs and no bread. Then it spread to the Cordeliers district on the Left Bank, where all the radicals are, and then from the quarter they call the Quinze-Vingts, the most radical of all, where a week ago the citizens began demanding that Louis's crown be taken from him.

No more king! That is what they want, these wild creatures, these Parisians who hardly deserve the name of humans any longer. They will have no more God, no more priests, no more laws and no more king.

It was hot today, and nightfall has brought no relief. I sit by my window, fanning myself, listening to the bells ring ceaselessly, hearing the drums beat and watching the commotion in the torchlit streets. Paris is rising.

SIXTEEN

August 10, 1792

We did not sleep at all last night. Even if we had tried to sleep, the noise of the bells and the drums and all the marching and shouting would have kept us awake. That, and the waves of alarm that swept through the palace every hour or so, keeping us keyed up and frightened with each new message arriving from the assembly or the city officials or the riotous Parisians who, overnight, have taken into their own hands the government of France.

I am past weariness now, I have been up for so long that everything around me seems slightly unreal, and I have to pinch myself to know that I am truly awake and somewhat alert.

Last night, however, I was very sleepy at times, and the bells startled me out of a sort of trance. I remember walking into the guardroom where the children were resting with Madame de Tourzel and twenty soldiers around them, and having the feeling that I was about to drop from fatigue. But I kept my eyes open and went on with what I had to do, though my leg ached and my poor wits were sorely taxed.

The long night began with a change from our usual routine. Louis decided not to hold his nightly undressing ceremony because of all the turmoil in the city. Instead of preparing for sleep he kept his shirt, breeches and jacket on, though the Pages of the Bedchamber had his silk nightshirt and kerchief and white satin slippers ready in case he needed them. He put on the red sash of the Order of St. Louis for luck, and kept his wig on, uncombed and slightly askew.

Despite my pleading he would not put on the thick padded doublet I had ordered made for him to protect him from knife-thrusts and bullets, but I put mine on and still wear it now, though it pinches my ribs, as I write this.

Just after midnight we heard that the Mayor of Paris had run away out of fear of the Parisians and soon afterward a messenger was sent to warn us that no one was in charge any more. There was no law, no authority, only the soldiers and many of them were laying down their weapons and mingling with the citizens who were banding together into militias.

In vain I watched through the windows,

hoping against hope that my nephew Francis might arrive with his imperial troops or Stanny or Charlot might appear with a force of mounted men, or even, as in my dreams, Axel might come, invincible and victorious, on his white horse.

One defender we had, Lieutenant de la Tour, who as the night wore on stayed with us, dressed in a red uniform he borrowed from one of the Swiss Guard, a long saber and a golden dagger hanging from his sword belt. Chambertin too was there, looking after Louis, and Dr. Concarneau who was ready with bandages and medicines and smelling salts for Loulou when she felt faint.

Sometime deep into the night another messenger came into the palace courtyard, shouting above the din from the streets, telling us as we leaned out our second-story windows straining to hear him that a group of Parisians had formed a Commune and declared themselves to be the government.

"Nonsense!" I cried when I understood his message. "The king is still the king!"

"There is no king! There is no king!" the messenger cried, his voice turning into a melancholy wailing as the renewed clangor of bells and drums, now accompanied by the popping and bursting of brilliant fireworks, drowned it out.

So sudden and so great was the commotion in the palace after this news arrived that I could do little but reassure myself that the children were all right and that Louis, who sat open-mouthed and staring, was with them.

Sensing that we were all in great danger now, people were panicking and running away, climbing out of windows, running through the gardens, melting away into the darkness, abandoning us. The commander of the National Guard, an officer named Mandat, remained with us for a time, and so did another loyal friend, the public prosecutor. But the guard officer Mandat was summoned by the new self-appointed Commune and we learned that as soon as he left the palace he was arrested and killed by the mob. When word of this began spreading among those who remained with us, there was more panic and I heard running feet in the corridor outside the guardroom.

By this time it was nearly dawn and we ourselves had to make a decision. Should we stay and risk the wrath of the Commune, which had declared Louis deposed and might order us arrested, or should we seek refuge in the building that housed the deputies to the Legislative Assembly, as the public prosecutor advised us.

"If we go," I told Louis, "it will look as though we are giving in to the Commune. As for me, I would rather be nailed to the palace walls than abandon the Tuileries."

Louis, torn between the prosecutor's prudent but cowardly advice and my conviction that we should stay and fight, could not seem to make up his mind. But he urged all the remaining courtiers and servants to leave, not wanting any of them to be harmed. Only the soldiers of the National Guard and the company of nine hundred Swiss mercenaries that had been called to Paris from Courbevoie and Reuil should stay, he said.

The prosecutor urged us to think of our children, and send them, together with Madame de Tourzel, to the assembly hall. I was about to agree with this when Lieutenant de la Tour, who had been standing in the doorway of the room, stepped forward.

"Before you make any decisions, your highness," he said to Louis, "I would like to present to you the members of your faithful bodyguard, the Knights of the Golden Dagger."

He stood aside to let a group of men file into the room, each of whom wore at his waist the golden symbol of the fraternity, a gleaming dagger.

They were an oddly assorted company, some old men though still spry, some boys as young as fifteen or sixteen. To judge from their clothing, which ranged from the threadbare to the elegant, they varied a great deal in rank and income, though all bore themselves with the dignity and confidence of noblemen. They were the old France, the France to which I came as a young girl when I married Louis. And now they were pledging themselves to defend the monarch of that imperiled kingdom.

Each man and boy knelt before Louis, kissed his outstretched hand, and repeated his own name, followed by the pledge "To the death!"

On and on they came, this parade of sworn warriors, while we continued to hear the sounds of departing servants and, from the city, the clamor of marching feet and shouting.

A messenger burst in, interrupting the impromptu ceremony.

"The Communards have crossed the St.-Michel bridge!" he said. "The National

Guard has not fired on them! They are coming this way!"

Louis stood up then and spread his arms wide, as if in benediction.

"I thank you all, noble knights. Trusting in your protection, and that of my soldiers, I will remain."

"To your posts!" shouted Lieutenant de la Tour, and at once most of the noblemen ran out, presumably to join the National Guard and the Swiss mercenaries. A dozen or so stayed with us, as bodyguards.

I felt proud of my husband at that moment. The blood of the Bourbons rose in him, and gave him courage, and he showed his mettle. Even as he spoke, however, we heard the first shots in the distance, and I saw his face crumple in fear.

I looked out the window and saw the Swiss Guard, in their red uniforms, loading their cannon and drawing up in formation behind the thick palace walls.

In what seemed like no time at all the cannon began firing, and through the thick dirty yellow smoke I could discern the first of the Parisians entering the Carrousel square just across from the main courtyard of the palace. They carried long sharp pikes and wore their red caps of liberty, and in among the forest of pikes were large silk flags with stripes of red, white and blue — their banners held aloft.

"Come away from the window, your highness." It was Lieutenant de la Tour, leading me firmly back toward the opposite side of the room where Louis stood with his arms around the children, Chambertin and Madame de Tourzel at his side.

That is the last clear memory I have before we were swept up in all the chaos and confusion, of Louis holding onto the children, his back to the wall, his face a stark mask of fear.

Then, a split second later, the bombardment began.

All the windows in the guardroom where we were were shattered and the tremendous noise made Mousseline scream. There was glass everywhere, and warm freshly-spilt blood and I realized, in a sudden flash, that the lieutenant had probably saved my life in pulling me away from the window.

Led by a group of guardsmen and knights we ran into the corridor outside where servants and officials were cowering, not knowing where else to go. Down along one long corridor after another we ran, our way blocked by soldiers and frightened members of our household dashing here and there, trying to escape the onslaught from the courtyard. We heard more smashing glass and felt the floor shake violently under our feet as cannonballs struck the palace again and again. The screams of horses and wounded men reached us and we could smell the reek of gunpowder. My throat was dry from all the smoke in the air but I could not stop to get a drink, or to help Louis, who ran slowly and clumsily, or to aid those who held out their hands to me as I passed, in mute entreaty.

We ran into one of the grand galleries but stopped abruptly at the scene of horror it presented. There was blood everywhere, on the floor, on the carpets, on the furnishings, on the walls and hangings. Bodies were sprawled throughout the room, and a sewerlike stench assaulted us, for the bodies were surrounded by ordure. Some were headless, some were half-naked. I saw bloody women's torsos with the breasts all but completely hacked off, men's bodies without genitals.

The utter savagery of the unspeakable scene was beyond anything I had ever witnessed or imagined. I felt nauseous and so did Madame de Tourzel, who turned her head away and clutched her stomach.

Louis went to the window, which gaped open as the glass had been shot away, and threw up into the garden.

"Don't look," shouted one of the knights or guards. "Don't think about what you see here. Follow us, and hurry!"

Blindly I did as they asked, as the sounds of musket fire and the loud booming of the cannon and shaking of the palace floors and walls intensified. From every room we passed came piercing screams and harsh shouting and through open doorways we caught brief glimpses of the savage invaders at their bloody work.

We ran down little-used hallways and through decayed and vacant rooms, finally climbing a dusty old staircase that led to my apartments. The soldiers and knights went in first, swords and sabers and muskets out. They surprised a large group of Parisians who were looting my wardrobe chests and flinging gowns and chemises and petticoats onto the floor, ripping my beautiful furnishings to shreds. Some of the looters were shot where they stood, others cut down as they ran toward us, eyes wide and bloody pikes and knives raised in murderous attack.

Animal cries came from their throats as they rushed toward us, chilling and terrifying. I clutched the children to me, not wanting them to watch what I was seeing only too clearly. For the savages, who reeked of wine, were monstrous, and in their drunken mayhem they had made a shambles of the room.

I can hardly bear to write what I saw there. Bodies writhing on the floor, stabbed in the belly, bloody intestines in ropy strings, brains spattered across the parquet floor, satin gowns covered in blood and innards, bodies of uniformed servants and officials intertwined, caught in a grotesque embrace of death. Faces with ghoulish expressions of surprise, horror, anguish, pain. Groans of the dying, cruel laughter of the butchers, exultant in their atrocities. Men and women waving reddened knives, drunk on the royal wine from the cellars, drunk on revenge, unleashing a lifetime of grievances on their hapless victims.

And the blood, all the blood. Streams of it, torrents of it, pouring down the yellowing marble staircases, red blood, dark blood, the maroon stains of dried blood, blood that added the metallic reek of iron to the strong odors of smoke and gunpowder and wine in the stale air.

Flies buzzed in their thousands over the

heaps of mutilated corpses, the flies of a hot August day, the feast day of St. Lawrence the Martyr. I was so overcome with the shocking sights around me that for a long time I became fascinated by the flies, and fixed my gaze on them, watching them land on the severed limbs and corpses and then rise up into the air. It was as if, by watching the flies, I could somehow block out everything else in the room, everything I could not bear to see and hear.

Once again it was Lieutenant de la Tour who took my arm and shook me out of my trance. With a deft movement he pushed me and the children toward the doorway and stood in front of us, defending us against a fresh onslaught of attackers who were running at us with their pikes pointed at our chests, screaming "Death to the king!" and "Death to the Austrian bitch!"

I felt the jolt and clash of arms as the soldiers and knights met the oncoming pikes with their own weapons. The Parisians were so close I could smell their foul wine-sodden breath and see the hate in their eyes. We will die here, I thought. We will surely die here. Nothing can save us. I heard Louis cry out and could not tell whether it was a cry of fear or of pain. Had he been wounded? Was he dying?

With a groan one of the Knights of the Golden Dagger fell back against me and collapsed, then another and another. There was blood on the floor, my shoes were slipping in it. Louis-Charles, who had been very brave until that moment, began to sob.

Suddenly a huge man came up behind us and spoke to me. I turned and recognized the giant gardener I had been forced to dismiss some months earlier. He swung Louis-Charles up onto his broad shoulders and held Mousseline close to his side. Both children clung to him and Louis-Charles stopped crying.

"Come," he said to me, "I know a way out." I called out to Louis, who followed us, and to poor brave Madame de Tourzel who had picked up a knife from the hand of one of the fallen Parisians and was brandishing it with all her vigor. Lieutenant de la Tour brought up the rear, protecting us from attack from behind as we made our way through a narrow opening in the wainscoting into a dusty passageway that led us eventually to a storage room and then to the looted kitchens. From there we quickly crossed through the gardens to the building where the Legislative Assembly was in session.

We were allowed in but were told to remain in a small room with barred windows where the secretaries customarily sat to record the proceedings. Even with the secretaries gone and their desks removed, it was too small a room for us all, and we had to stand. I felt like an animal in a cage, on display. Through the iron bars I frowned at the deputies, who hardly took any notice of us, they were so worried about their chamber being invaded by the armies of Parisians who were rampaging through the palace.

For hours we stood there, trapped in our little boxlike room, relieved to be alive but so desperately uncomfortable and tired and wishing the horrible day would end. We were given water and some cheese and fruit which we shared out among us all while outside the uproar from the palace continued and the deputies quarreled, shaking their fists and shouting vociferously.

The whole world has gone mad today, I thought. And I am at the center of all the madness.

I am too tired to write at length about the rest of our endless day. Finally we were permitted to go to a safe location and were given food and basins of water to wash in. I feel as though I can never wash away the stains of this terrible day, the Feast Day of St. Lawrence the Martyr. I remember the story of St. Lawrence, burned by the Romans on a grill, and I cannot help but think of the many butchered martyrs I saw this day in the palace. Had we not been protected by the guardsmen and knights, we might well have been martyrs ourselves, piled up among the other corpses in a gruesome heap, to be thrown into carts and burned in a lime pit until, like St. Lawrence, there was nothing left of us but ashes.

August 20, 1792
I cannot sleep. If I try to sleep, the nightmares come. There is a doctor here in this dungeon where we are imprisoned but he is rude to me and will not give me any orangeflower water and ether to help me sleep.

I dream red dreams. Headless bodies stagger toward me. Heads, open-mouthed, drift past. I am chased along dark corridors and I run as fast as I can but the hideous things that pursue me are faster. Just as they catch up to me I wake screaming.

August 27, 1792
We live now in the smallest tower of

Charlot's old mansion called the Temple. We are heavily guarded here, and surrounded by hostile people. When we were first brought here Chambertin, Sophie, Madame de Tourzel and Loulou were allowed to come with us. But they were soon sent away and imprisoned. I have tried very hard to find out where they are being held but no one will tell me.

It is very hot in these rooms and there are rats everywhere. Louis-Charles likes to trap them and set them free in front of Mousseline who shrieks when they run over her feet.

My thick taffeta corset was taken away from me but I still have the girdle of Ste. Radegunde that mother sent me to wear during my labor and I wear it now for protection. Since I have begun wearing it I am able to sleep though the terrible red dreams still come at times.

Officially France has no king any longer, yet that is nonsense, and I don't care who reads these words or hears me express myself on this subject. My husband is the anointed ruler of his people, crowned in a sacrament and chosen by acclamation. He is now and will always be a king, Commune or no Commune, Robespierre or no Robespierre.

This arrogant little lawyer Robespierre claims to be the voice of the people yet anyone can tell at a glance that he is too strange and disturbed to be anyone's voice. I watched him when he came to the assembly hall on that awful day when we were imprisoned there. He spoke loudly for such a small man and people did listen to him instead of ignoring him as they did most of the other speakers. He was very peculiar, however. He kept walking back and forth on his high-heeled shoes, like a nervous woman and not a strong or forceful man. He had a nervous tic in his cheek and the muscles there kept jumping convulsively. He kept biting his nails and pulling at his clothes and smoothing his collar, and his ugly skin was full of scars and looked like the color we used to call Goose-Droppings. Altogether he made me shudder.

I cover these words with my hand, smearing the ink a little, because there is a representative of the Commune in the room with us and I suppose he might ask to see what I am writing. So far he has not.

September 7, 1792
My heart is pounding so fast I can hardly

catch my breath. I have just seen something I almost can't believe, yet I know I have seen it with my own two eyes and it is not a nightmare.

A group of Parisians, chanting and waving banners, came into the open area in front of the guard barracks here and began parading noisily in front of our windows. They had a severed head impaled on a pike and brought it close enough so that we could see whose head it was.

I felt my skin crawl. It was Loulou! My dearest friend, my confidante. Next to Sophie, the woman I trust most in the world. Her mouth was open, her eyes staring. Her hair floated out behind her.

I cried out and covered my eyes, but not before I caught a glimpse of another lump of flesh impaled on a pike. It was a woman's genitals.

I ran from the window and flung myself down on my bed. I cried for a long time, then decided that I must leave a record of what was done to the loveliest, most faithful, dearest lady I have known. So I have set down here what happened to her. It is too hideous to think of. Once more I will write her name, a small memorial to one I loved very much:

Marie-Thérèse de Savoie-Carignan,
Princesse de Lamballe
1749–1792
Requiescat in pace.

SEVENTEEN

October 1, 1792

Each night a lamplighter in a dark cloak and pointed hat comes through our apartments and fills our oil lamps and trims them, then lights them. Until tonight I had taken little notice of him. But tonight he nodded to me when he entered the room and placed a familiar-looking pewter candleholder on the table in front of where I was sitting, my knitting on my lap.

I looked up into his face. It was Lieutenant de la Tour! I gasped but prevented myself from crying out. The Commune representative who always sits in our common room, overhearing all our conversations, had nodded off before the fire and so noticed nothing. Even Louis, who had Louis-Charles on his lap and was drawing a map of the French provinces for him, did not look up at the sound of my sudden intake of breath.

The lamplighter completed his task, lighting a lamp in each of our rooms and leaving us candles for the night, then left. I waited until it was fully dark, then retired to prepare for the night, taking the candle-holder with me. Once in my room I quickly turned it over and searched for a message inside, and found one — from Axel!

I have not heard from him for months. Now he sends word that he is with the Austrian army and has been since July, though he was captured once and later wounded at Thionville. His wound is healing and he is once again with the army which is about to begin an assault on Lille. He says they have had some setbacks and he thought the Austrians would be in Paris long before now but he remains hopeful they will be here soon.

"Take heart my dearest girl," he writes, "my little angel, my love. With every breath I think of you."

I kiss his dear letter, and my tears fall. I know I should burn it but I can't bear to destroy this precious paper he has held in his hands, these precious words he has written. I will sleep tonight with his message under my pillow, hoping to dream of him and praying that our liberation will come soon.

October 2, 1792
This morning before dawn I was awakened

roughly by someone shaking me and shouting in my face. In the dim lamplight I could see that it was Amélie, dressed in a new, well-made red and white gown in the current Parisian fashion and with the chunk of gray stone from the Bastille on a chain around her neck. From her ears hung earrings made like miniature guillotines — a fashion I had been told about but could hardly imagine to be real.

"Get up, citizeness," she said briskly. "You are to be examined by the Committee of Vigilance."

I clutched my pillow, feeling for the letter that lay beneath it and trying to think, how can I destroy it, where can I hide it?

"Will the Committee allow me time to dress?"

"Dress quickly then." She made no move to leave, to allow me any privacy.

"If the Committee will permit me, I would like to change my linen —" I began.

"Do you really think anybody cares about looking at your bony old body?" Amélie said impatiently. "All we care about is that you are under suspicion as an enemy of the revolution. Never mind getting dressed. Stand in the center of the room."

I did as she asked, holding my pillow and the letter, concealed behind my hand.

Amélie motioned to companions in the adjoining room. "We'll talk to the old bitch in here." Two women and two men came into my small bedroom, bringing a lamp which they set down on a low table. They were young, younger than Amélie whom I knew to be around my age of thirty-six or a little older. The men I judged to be perhaps twenty-five, the women closer to twenty. They stared at me.

"Citizeness Capet, the Committee of Vigilance for the Commune, the Temple section, demands that you answer the following questions. Have you any valuables?"

"Only my wedding ring."

"Will you take an oath to defend the revolution?"

"I took an oath to obey my king and husband, at his coronation. I could hardly forswear that oath now."

"She refuses. Write that down," Amélie said to one of the men, who began looking around for a bottle of ink and writing paper. There was a brief commotion while these materials were found, and I took advantage of the distraction to slip Axel's letter inside the linen pillowslip.

"Will you swear that you have had no contact with any foreign power whose aim is to destroy the revolution?" Amélie asked next.

"I have written letters to my sisters and brothers," I said truthfully, omitting to mention the hundreds of other letters I have sent, in code, to a dozen foreign princes and governments. "They are not in sympathy with the revolution."

"In fact your nephew Francis is at war with France."

"If you say so, citizeness. I am not permitted to read any newspapers."

"It matters little what you say," Amélie snapped, walking in a slow circle around me, the little metal guillotines in her ears sparkling in the candlelight. "We know everything you are doing. Every lie you are telling. It is only a matter of time before you are summoned before the Revolutionary Tribunal and condemned as a criminal."

She came closer and looked at me knowingly. "Just as your great friend Loulou was."

Her words sent a frisson of horror down my spine. I saw once again the ghastly head of my dear friend, the private parts, exposed for all the world to see, and imag-

457

ined the awful fear and panic and suffering Loulou must have endured at the hands of the communards before she died.

"We took our time with her," Amélie went on, speaking matter-of-factly and watching my reaction as she continued. "With her, it was not a quick slitting of the throat or stabbing in the gut, as with the others. No, your friend Loulou, the princess" — she gave the word a mocking emphasis — "deserved a long slow death.

"We woke her up very early, just as we did with you this morning. Then we dragged her outdoors, and made her stand in the cold between two stacks of dead bodies while we stripped off her clothes and Niko and Georges here" — she indicated the two men — "raped her, was it twice or three times?" She turned to the men as she asked this. The men shrugged. I could not help myself. I began to sob.

Amélie laughed and continued to circle me, partly walking, partly skipping.

"Let me see, then we cut off her breasts and threw them to the dogs, and I think we made a bonfire between her legs, and used one of her arms as a torch. Then we cut out her heart and roasted it and ate it. By that time she was dead, of course. So we cut off her head and her cunt (both of which we knew you would recognize) and put them on pikes and marched around with them for awhile."

I was shaking and unnerved yet I held tightly onto my pillow and was careful not to let Axel's letter slip out of the pillow-case. I have never, in the whole of my life, wanted to kill anyone as much as I wanted to kill Amélie at that moment.

She ordered her companions to search my room which they did, throwing the bedclothes and thin mattress onto the floor, opening the chest in which I kept my few remaining possessions and flinging the contents out, spilling the water from my washbasin onto the floor. Fortunately they did not examine the pewter candleholder very closely or they would have discovered its hollow center.

When they were finished Amélie addressed me once more.

"Citizeness, the Committee of Vigilance will recommend that you be kept on the list of suspects. You will be questioned again. Meanwhile, here is a souvenir, from your late friend."

She reached into her pocket and pulled something out which she laid on the table in front of me. It was a shriveled human ear.

November 14, 1792
I am afraid for Louis.

Louis has been betrayed, and by a long-time friend. The locksmith Gamin, who taught him lockmaking and worked alongside him for so many years in his attic room at Versailles, has denounced him. Gamin told deputies of the new assembly about a secret hiding place for documents that he built in Louis's rooms, with a large locked box inside. He took them to the palace and showed them the hidden niche in the wall.

The box was full of important papers, some of which proved that Louis had been sending and receiving messages from other sovereigns. The irony is that I am the one who sent and received nearly all the messages while we were at Versailles, not Louis. Yet to the Committee of Vigilance and the Revolutionary Tribunal that would probably seem an unimportant detail.

I have heard nothing further about the progress of the Austrian army but it is too late in the year now for any large army to advance. Wherever they are, they will stay in their winter bivouac until spring.

December 18, 1792
Snow is falling. We huddle by our hearth

fire, wrapped up in shawls and jackets because of the cold wind that blows in through the ancient chimney. The room is always smoky yet our guards do nothing about it and I know better than to ask for any help from the local Committee of Vigilance. They are not at all vigilant about our wellbeing.

Seven days ago Louis was tried before the new governing body, the Convention. Today he talked about it for the first time.

"It was nothing more than a formality, my trial," he told me. "It lasted barely a quarter of an hour." His tone was resigned yet dignified, with no trace of self-pity.

"They accused me of crimes against the revolution. Then they adjourned, and I was brought back here. No one argued for or against me. I was not questioned. I merely stood there, feeling surprisingly calm, and listened to what the prosecutor said.

"It hasn't happened since the days of Charles I, you know," he went on after awhile. "Not for a hundred and fifty years. The judicial murder of a king."

"No, Louis, surely they would not dare!"

"You saw what they scrawled on the wall here the other day, in blood-red letters: LOUIS THE LAST. It was an omen."

"What's an omen, papa?" Louis-Charles

climbed up into his father's lap.

"An omen is a sign that something is about to happen. Usually something we don't want to happen." I got up and went over to where Louis sat with Louis-Charles on his lap. I put my hand on my husband's shoulder, and kept it there as he talked on.

"You remember the lessons I gave you about the English King Charles, the one who was killed by his subjects long ago."

"Yes, papa. He had his head chopped off by an axe. Just like this mice-killer Robert gave me." Robert was the son of one of the Republican Guards, a boy Louis-Charles's age. Louis-Charles reached into the pocket of his trousers and brought out a miniature guillotine, a small blade with a weight attached to it.

"Oh no!" I said, snatching the awful thing from his grasp.

"But maman, all the boys have these. We execute mice with them. Birds too, when we can catch them."

"You are not to have anything to do with such a terrible cruel machine," I told my son. Louis went on with his history lesson.

"Of course the English were wrong to kill their king. And they soon realized it, and gave the throne to his son, another

Charles, who was a very fine fellow, but a little too fond of the ladies."

Louis-Charles laughed. He is a sunny child, with a cheerful good nature. Even here, in this prisonlike place, he always manages to amuse himself and retains his good humor.

"Now, this is what I want you to remember. Whatever happens to me, I am still the true king of France and you are the dauphin. The throne belongs to you and your children. If I should die, you will be King Louis XVII."

"Yes, father. You have told me so many times. But you are not going to die."

Louis stroked our son's head affectionately. "Not quite yet, little king. Not quite yet."

I try not to think of what may happen to us this winter. I say my prayers and read and reread Axel's precious letter and wait impatiently for the lamplighter to come each night. Sometimes it is Lieutenant de la Tour, sometimes a different man. I never know. To calm my nerves I knit mittens and scarves and have begun embroidering a set of chair covers. Mousseline helps me. She is very good at embroidery and much more patient than I am. Tomorrow will be her fourteenth birthday. How I wish she could have known her grandmother and namesake, the great Maria Theresa.

January 20, 1793
The terrible terrible news has come. Louis is to die tomorrow.

He came to tell us, trying to be as dignified and as brave as he could, wearing his red sash of the Order of St. Louis and his prized gold medal inscribed "Restorer of French Liberty and True Friend of His People."

He kissed us all tenderly and embraced us and we wept together, without shame even though the guards and the representative of the Commune were there in the room.

Louis-Charles and Mousseline called out "Father, father" again and again, until even the rough guards had to turn their heads away, for the sight made them cringe.

"Now I shall never complete my history of the flora and fauna of the forest of Compiègne," Louis said wistfully. "I shall never see my beloved children grow up, or grow old with my beautiful wife, who has done her best to make me a better man."

He told us again and again that he loved us, and I could tell how great a strain it was for him to bear up under the pain of parting. When at last the guards came to take him away he held us close and then pulled me aside. He took off his wedding ring, kissed it, and put it in my hand.

"I release you," he said quietly. "Axel is a fine man. Marry him, and be happy!"

Tears blurred my sight as I watched him being led away, my noble, foolish, well-meaning, exasperating husband and old friend. I had always been at his side when trouble came. Now, in his final hours, I will not be near him. I cannot bear the thought.

January 21, 1793

I heard the drums beat early this morning and knew that Louis was being led to the scaffold. I hoped the children were still sleeping, and were spared the realization that their beloved father was about to die.

I knelt beside the bed and said a prayer for his soul.

This evening when the lamplighter came, he was Lieutenant de la Tour. We were able to exchange a few words without being overheard and he told me that he and other Knights of the Golden Dagger had been present in the crowd that came to watch Louis's execution. At one point several of the Knights attempted to rescue

Louis but the Republican Guard prevented it.

"He died bravely and well," the lieutenant told me. "He had no bitterness. He would not let them bind his hands, or restrain him in any way. He was willing to die.

"There was one odd thing, however. He insisted on wearing a torn old black coat, an antique. It made him look like a vagrant and not a king."

"Ah, of course. That was his father's coat. He treasured it."

"They made him take it off before they executed him. It was tossed into the crowd. People tore it to bits. He forgave them — for that and for everything else. He said, 'I forgive those who are guilty of my death.' "

"Yes. He would say that."

After the lieutenant left I stood for a long time listening for the sound of the newsboys in the street calling out the events of the day.

"Louis Capet Executed!" they cried. "Former King Dead!" "Madame Guillotine Marries Citizen Capet!"

March 2, 1793
They bring me a special soup every day now, because I am so thin. After Louis died I

could not eat, and soon my black clothes hung on me like rags hung from a pole.

My leg has started to hurt again and the prison doctor lets me have laudanum drops to take when the pain becomes too hard to bear. The laudanum makes my nightmares worse, and Mousseline, who is so good to me and watches over me almost like a mother, says she is sure my moodiness and sadness are made worse by the laudanum drops and urges me not to take them.

We all stay together at night in one room now, the two children and I. It comforts me so much to have them near me. I seldom leave this room except when our meals are served and we sit at the table in front of the hearth in the common room. Being there makes me sad, remembering Louis sitting in his large chair giving Louis-Charles his lessons. I prefer to sit on my bed, knitting, while Mousseline reads to me from novels or stories of shipwrecks or pirates.

When I comb my hair it comes out in clumps. It is all white now.

One of the guards amuses himself making sketches of us with pastels. He captures the children's likenesses very well. Louis-Charles is there on the page, plump-cheeked and with a look of liveliness and mischief in his blue eyes. Mousseline he draws very much to the life, making her look delicate and fair, pretty though not beautiful, her even gaze tinged with sorrow. But when he draws me, the image is that of a sour-faced, pinch-cheeked old woman, with dark circles beneath her eyes and deep lines etched into her skin. How could that possibly be me?

March 24, 1793

I fear they are trying to poison Louis-Charles. He is ill so often, his forehead is hot with fever and he cries and holds his side where it hurts him. Sometimes he has a bad cough and chokes if he tries to lie down, so I hold him in my lap and he sleeps leaning against me. I try to sleep too, but often my nightmares come and then I cry out and wake up and wake him up too.

I have a small supply of oil of sweet almonds that Dr. Concarneau gave me. I keep it nearby in case Louis-Charles becomes severely ill.

Louis-Charles, my precious boy, is now King Louis XVII. Of course the revolutionaries want to eliminate him. They are so heartless, so ruthless, they would not hesitate to kill a child. And if they can do it by slowly poisoning him, making it appear that he is dying of an illness rather than being murdered, then they will avoid any appearance of cruelty.

Only a few weeks ago he was fine. Now he is pale and in pain so often. How can it be anything but poison?

May 10, 1793

Louis-Charles seems better and I am puzzled. Are they putting poison in his food or not?

I have new messages from Axel but I don't dare write here what he tells me. My spirits are lifted by his news, and by the warm mild weather and the pink and yellow roses I can see from my window.

Is it the warm weather that makes me feel so tired? I am still living mostly on medicinal soup, and a little bread.

May 18, 1793

He has come. The Green Ghoul. The man they say is in charge of everyone and everything now. Maximilien Robespierre.

I heard a slight commotion in the hallway outside and then he stepped into my bedroom. I was reclining on my bed, resting, and Mousseline was reading to me. When she saw the ugly little man in the bright green waistcoat and trousers, his hawklike face a mass of pox scars, his strange light eyes looking huge behind thick spectacles, she cried out involuntarily.

"Do not be alarmed, Marie-Thérèse," he said unctuously, his voice high and nasal. "I am here to help your family."

"You helped my father to his death," my brave daughter snapped back. "Now you want to attack my mother. Can't you see she is ill?"

"Mousseline, dear, leave us please. Find your brother. I think he is playing ball in the courtyard."

"Your late father," Robespierre said, interrupting me, "was a victim of the Convention. I could not have prevented his death. But I did not call for it."

"I will never believe anything you say," Mousseline replied as she went out. "You want to kill us all."

My daughter's boldness made me afraid for her. But then, I live in fear for both my children.

The Green Ghoul — I cannot think of him otherwise — came further into the room, the high heels of his polished shoes clicking noisily on the bare boards, and pulled out a chair. He took a linen handkerchief from his pocket and carefully wiped the chair seat, then sat down. His movements were hurried. He was evidently very tense, and struggling to control himself. He bit his nails and I noticed the muscle in his cheek that kept twitching. From time to time he put one hand up to his cheek as if trying to make the twitching stop, but it would not stop.

"It has not escaped my notice that you are a clever woman, citizeness," he said to me evenly, his voice soft but full of menace, "and clever women, at this moment, are a threat to France. I think, citizeness, that you are working hand in glove with another clever woman, Citizeness Roland, my rival."

Jeanne-Marie Roland was the celebrated leader of the war party in the Convention, the Girondins. I had never met her, much less conspired with her. But the Green Ghoul thought otherwise. I said nothing, and he went on.

"You and Citizeness Roland are conspiring to destroy the revolution. Together you are in secret communication with the rebels in the West." (He meant the Vendéan peasants, who had been in open revolt for months.) "And with our enemies the Austrians." His voice remained low, but took on a sibilant hiss. He spoke through clenched teeth, the muscle in his cheek dancing convulsively.

"The enemies are at our gates, even within our gates. Never has the country been in greater peril. Never have you and your children been in greater danger."

I felt the menace of his words, and was suddenly terrified, almost to the edge of panic. Where was Louis-Charles? Where was Mousseline? Had this horrible man brought troops with him to seize my children?

Robespierre had gotten lightly to his feet and was pacing in front of me, biting his nails. "If you put an end to your futile conspiracy, I will spare your son. If not —"

I felt my heart in my throat. For one dizzying moment I thought I would die, but the moment passed.

"We have known for some time that the traitor Citizeness Roland and her pack of fellow-traitors want to turn the revolution backward, to restore the monarchy and enthrone your son as the next king. We are sworn to prevent that at all costs. We could simply send you all to the cold embrace of the Blade of Eternity. But I would prefer to use subtler means of gaining my ends, in order to keep my enemies guessing."

I was doing my best to fight against the awful fear that rose in me, fear that quickened with each shrewd glare of the little deputy's small light eyes. At the back of my mind, however, I understood that this vain, foppish, dangerous man, a man who wore lace at his neck and wrists, a powdered wig and high-heeled shoes in the old court style, had blundered. He was allowing his own fears to mislead him.

Slowly, as he spoke on in his high, nasal voice, I thought I understood what was happening. Robespierre, the Green Ghoul, was even more afraid than I was. Afraid of everyone, not only Citizeness Roland and her Girondins, not only of the rebellious peasants in the West and the phantom Austrian army (which, I knew from Axel's letters, was in full retreat), but of the fragility of his own power.

Fear of a terrible retribution hounded him, and would not let him go.

Very well then, I would use that fear to my advantage.

I got to my feet, feeling unsteady on my sore leg and holding onto the iron bedstead for support. Never had I felt more like the queen I once had been, the queen I still was.

"Release me and my children immediately, and once we are delivered to the protection of the Austrian army, I will divulge what I know and enable you to crush your enemies."

He laughed, a dry, horrible choking sound, more a cough than a laugh. He came toward me.

"Tell me all you know immediately, or I will order your son to the guillotine."

"You would not dare do that. All France would rise against you."

"All France, madame, would rise up and call me blessed."

Once again, mustering all my courage, I rose to my full height and straightened my spine. I realized, now, that even though I wore thin slippers and he had on high-heeled shoes, I was taller than Robespierre.

"Release us, or I will give the order for the destruction of Paris."

I saw him blanch, and felt a surge of elation. Axel would be proud of me! I thought.

At that moment a familiar figure in a dark cloak and pointed hat entered the room, carrying his flagon of lamp oil, his flint and tinder and his knife for trimming wicks. He was humming to himself, absorbed in his nightly task of lighting the lamps.

"Leave that," Robespierre cried.

There was a brief pause, then the lamplighter came further in, and walked up to the table near where we stood, Robespierre and I, facing one another.

"If you will allow me, sir, it is getting dark and I must light the lamps. I will only be a moment."

He stepped between us, so that he was only an arm's length from the exasperated Robespierre. I saw the muscle in Robespierre's cheek quiver.

"Stop at once! Don't you know who I am?"

The lamplighter turned, as if to look into Robespierre's face, and as he turned, he spilled his flagon of oil over Robespierre's immaculate green waistcoat.

"Stupid oaf!"

What happened next happened so quickly that I could not see it, but somehow the lamplighter, who was of course Lieutenant de la Tour, struck his flint and sent up a spark that lit Robespierre's waistcoat on fire.

I stepped back into the corner of the room as an unearthly scream came from the Green Ghoul's dry lips.

"Water! Water!" Robespierre cried as he slapped at the flames — which, I have to say, were far from all-consuming. One corner of his waistcoat had flared up, but there was much more smoke, and panic, than fire.

Three guards came running in from the outer room, carrying pitchers of water, and drenched the sputtering, smoke-blackened Robespierre. While they were putting out the fire, the lamplighter vanished. I did not see him go.

After assuring me, in a very angry and menacing tone, that I would be hearing from him again and from the Committee of Vigilance Robespierre left in search of the prison doctor, much bedraggled and sucking on his burned fingers. He did not appear to be injured, though his wig was singed and the costly lace at his neck and wrists was dingy with smoke and ash.

That night at supper, for the first time in months, I ate heartily.

July 5, 1793

They came for him quite early in the morning, four big burly coarse men from the Committee of Vigilance, bursting into the room where we all slept, Louis-Charles, Mousseline and I, and demanding that I hand over my son.

Of course I refused, and climbed out of

bed and threw myself between Louis-Charles and his kidnappers, fending them off and shouting at them when they lunged at me and tried to snatch him away.

I had no shame or pride. All I cared about was preventing these criminals from taking Louis-Charles away. I scratched them with my brittle, breaking nails, I bit one of them in the arm until he bled. I threatened them with the only weapon I possessed, a long ivory headscratcher. In the end, I pleaded with them, in tears, not to take my son from me.

It was all in vain, of course. They grew exasperated with me and finally told me bluntly that unless I handed Louis-Charles over to them obediently and at once they would kill both of the children.

I had to let him go. I have been crying ever since. I fear I will never see him again.

July 11, 1793

If I wait long enough, I see him. He is led past the small window in the guardroom on his way to the courtyard for exercise every afternoon. Sometimes they bring him out at one or two o'clock, sometimes not until four or five. I sit by the window and wait.

He skips past, singing, a red cap of liberty on his head. My beloved chou d'amour, my dear little king. One day, God willing, he will be crowned. How I wish I could be there to see it!

August 3, 1793
They gave me half an hour to say goodbye to my beloved daughter and pack my things. When I asked whether I would be returning to the Temple the official in charge just shook his head. I know what he meant. I know what my fate is to be.

At first I felt lightheaded and ill, but that passed. I had an unexpected fleeting thought, which was that perhaps I will see Louis again.

I sat down with Mousseline, just as my mother sat down with me many years ago before I left Vienna, and talked to her, both of us knowing that unless by some miracle we are rescued it will be our last conversation. We said the thing that matters most, that we love each other very dearly. She said — blessed, blessed girl! — that she wished she could give her life for mine.

"Take care of your brother," I told her. "One day the two of you will be freed. Be a mother to him."

Together we prayed for strength and for deliverance out of the hands of our enemies. Then the captain of the guard came for me and I was taken under heavy escort to the Conciergerie, where I was stripped of my clothing and inspected for diseases and most of my few possessions were taken away.

I am now officially Citizeness Marie Antoinette Capet, Widow, Prisoner 280, awaiting trial where I will be sentenced to die.

EIGHTEEN

August 11, 1793

It is barely dawn. The first faint light is coming through the one tiny barred window in this cramped room, and as I have no candle I write by this dawn light.

The guards who sleep in the room with me snore on, unaware of me. This is the only time of day I can have any privacy — now, and late at night when the guards have drunk themselves to sleep.

I have been ill, but am better now. The shock of this place, and the knowledge that soon I will be brought to my trial, weakened me and for several days I was at the mercy of the prison doctor and the maid they have assigned to me, a sweet, obedient girl named Rosalie. For those few days I was barely aware of being alive. I only remember seeing the doctor's face and smelling the lime-flower water he poured out for me, and also being fed by Rosalie.

The truth is, and I may as well admit it, I have become old. And being old, I am weak. Sometimes I am afraid of dying, sometimes I feel brave and fearless. My body has grown limp and slack, I am like an old tree in autumn that has lost its leaves and begun to wither. I was beautiful once, of that I am still sure.

I sleep badly here, and my mind is not always clear. Images from the past blur with those from the present, and now and then I am confused. This room is so small, so dark, so bare. It smells of mold and water drips down the stone walls when it rains.

August 14, 1793

After many months with no bleeding at all I have now begun to bleed without stopping. Rosalie takes away the old linens and brings me clean ones but I must change them often and only a thin stained screen separates me from the guards when I do so. I am often embarrassed. A dirty black-haired thief named Barassin, with a constant grin on his face, comes in at all hours of the day and night to empty my chamber pot. He also makes money by allowing visitors to enter my room and gape at me in return for a few coins.

I am quite a spectacle, I'm sure. The former queen, who once lived in a great palace full of gold and marble, crystal chandeliers and velvet curtains, now living in one small prison room with rotting walls and a few shabby sticks of furniture. I have only two dresses here, a torn black one and a plain white morning gown. Rosalie sends my one pair of dusty black shoes to the kitchen to be brushed each night. She whispers to me that many of the other prisoners here, most of them aristocrats, come to the kitchen to pay homage to my shoes and even kiss them in reverence!

A very touching and comforting thing to hear. Of course, I know that they are really paying tribute to my late husband, not to me. I am merely a symbol of all they have lost.

August 27, 1793

Wonder of wonders, I can hardly believe what has happened!

Last night at about nine o'clock, just as the guards in my room were getting very drunk and beginning to nod off, the hairy grinning Barassin brought a visitor in, with his large wolfhound.

"There she is, Prisoner 280, the queen that was. Won't be here much longer, they say."

The guards stirred slightly in their chairs as Barassin ushered the visitor in, but took little notice of him. They were accustomed to having me displayed.

I knew as soon as I saw Malachi, who came over to me and licked my hands with his wet pink tongue, that my visitor was Axel. My breath came quickly and I did not look at him. I felt the blood rushing to my cheeks.

He was laughing, a great broad laugh.

"So that's her, is it? What a sight! How the mighty have fallen, eh?"

I heard the chink of coins. Axel was handing out money, and plenty of it, to Barassin and the two guards.

"There now, why don't you all go down to the tavern and bring us back some wine? Have some yourselves while you're there."

"Thank you, sir. You're a generous man." The three went off, locking the door behind them and leaving Axel and me alone. He listened at the door, then, when he was sure they had gone, came over to me and enfolded me in his arms.

For a long time we stood there, embracing, and nothing mattered but the sheer comfort of his body against mine, his familiar smell, his warmth and vitality.

"We have very little time," Axel said after a few moments and led me to my small table where we sat down together. "On the night of September fifteenth I will come for you, at about midnight," he said. "There will be a farewell banquet in one of the cells in this wing. The Knights of the Golden Dagger will serve the food and be on watch. Your guards will be lured to the banquet, which will turn into a riot. You and I will slip away. I have bribed one of the sentries to let us leave the prison by the main gate."

"My children?"

"Lieutenant de la Tour will arrange to remove them from the Temple and bring them to where you and I will be waiting."

He held my hand and smiled. "You have nothing to fear. This time we will succeed. You'll see."

"Where will we go?"

"To Sweden. To Fredenholm. You loved it there, all the peace of the countryside. We will all be safe there, far from the madness of Robespierre and his Committee of Public Safety. He is insane, you realize."

"I know. I've met him."

"Your encounter is well known. You are the bravest woman that ever lived."

"Tonight, I feel I am the most fortunate."

"Do you remember the wedding we went

to in Fredenholm, on the estate?"

"Of course."

"When we get there, my dearest little angel, we will have a wedding of our own, shall we? Will you?"

I cried then, I couldn't help it.

"I will make such an old, broken-down bride."

"To me, beloved girl, you will be the most beautiful bride the sun ever shone on. Besides, we'll fatten you up on good Swedish cakes and pies and cloudberries and fish."

His smile, and the look of love in his dear eyes, are all I can think of now. He will come for me. I know he will. Only nineteen days to go. Anything can happen in nineteen days, I know. Still, I trust Axel. If only I could get word to Louis-Charles and Mousseline, so that they could share these days of joyful anticipation.

I am counting the hours.

September 5, 1793
Only ten days to go. He will come for me. He will come.

September 13, 1793
The time is so close now, I am frightened. I pray for deliverance.

September 17, 1793

It was all so very well arranged. Axel had planned everything, down to the last detail, and he is meticulous.

We could not have carried it out without the help of Barassin (who, as it turns out, is one of the Knights of the Golden Dagger, I was completely wrong about him), and several of the officials whom Axel had bribed well with Swedish and Austrian gold. We also had the help of Eleanora Sullivan, who lent Axel her carriage.

Rosalie Lamorlière, my maid, was told nothing of the plan. I did not want to put her in any danger. She has been good to me.

Barassin brought me my final letter of instructions, and a package, only hours before Axel was due to arrive, at midnight on the fifteenth. In the package was a pair of blue trousers and a red carmagnole jacket and black hat and black men's shoes — the uniform of a municipal officer. Also forged identity cards and passports for me and the children.

I was unbearably nervous all evening, and could not stop shaking. I told the guards I feared I had the ague and that made them stay as far away from me as they could in the little room.

At about ten o'clock I could hear visitors arriving for the banquet which was being held not far from my cell. Prisoners condemned to die often give banquets on the last night before their execution, it is a macabre ritual. So many prisoners are being condemned now, Rosalie tells me there are sometimes twenty executions in a single day. So it was not surprising that one of my fellow inmates should be saying goodbye on this night, no doubt with the encouragement of Axel and the Knights.

I smelled spicy dishes and was suddenly very hungry. Soon I heard singing and shouting. The banquet was becoming raucous. At about eleven o'clock by my gold watch (which I hang on a chain from a nail on the wall) there was a knock on my cell door and it was Barassin, saying that he and my two guards had been invited to dine. The guards shambled off, and Barassin locked the door.

When he opened it later, at around midnight, Axel came in, carrying a lantern and dressed in the black cassock of a priest, and I was waiting, having put on my disguise.

"Quickly," Axel said. "Follow me. Keep your head down. Don't show your face. If we are challenged, I will talk. You and I are on our way to visit the cell of a condemned man. As soon as we reach the courtyard, we will say we are on our way to the meeting room of the Revolutionary Tribunal, to inform them that we have met with the condemned."

I resisted the urge to take Axel's hand and, trying to walk with a manly swagger, followed him along the dimly lit corridor. When we passed the cell where the banquet was being held — the cell door was wide open — we saw my two guards, full plates in front of them, clearly intoxicated and paying no more attention to us than they did to any of the others in the corridor. I wondered how long it would be before my absence was discovered.

When we arrived at the innermost of the three gates to the prison we presented our passports and were allowed through. At the middle gate a guard shone a lantern in our faces and looked hard at me but he passed us through, and I thought we were safe.

As we approached the main gate, however, and saw that some twenty soldiers were posted there I heard Axel's sharp intake of breath.

"Our man is not there," Axel whispered. "We must go back."

We turned, crossed the open courtyard and ducked under a portico where some grooms were brushing horses. We stood in the shadows, conspicuous because of Axel's lantern.

What could we do? We were trapped. If we went back to my cell I might never get out again, and yet we couldn't get through the main gate because the sentry Axel had bribed was nowhere to be seen. This was in itself a worrisome sign; had he been arrested? Had he revealed Axel's plan, or what he knew of it?

As we stood watching, the grooms completed their task and led the horses away.

"Let's follow them," I whispered, and Axel, not knowing what else to do I suppose, agreed. The grooms led us, predictably, to the stables, from whose windows I could see carts and riders coming and going through a purveyors' entrance. Unlike the main entrance to the prison, this gateway, used by suppliers of provisions, had only a single guard.

I thought quickly. Axel was a good driver, he could drive a coach very capably. Surely he could drive a small cart. All we needed was a cart, loaded with empty flour sacks or barrels or boxes. We could pose as deliverymen.

"Have you a shirt under that cassock?"

"Yes."

"Then take off the cassock and try to look like a driver." He did as I asked, then we began our search for a suitable vehicle. Fortunately there were few grooms in the stables at that hour — it was by then after one in the morning — and no one questioned us as we searched from stall to stall, eventually coming across an old wagon to which we hitched a sleepy but serviceable horse.

"We requisition you in the service of the state," Axel said to the horse as he fastened on a harness from among the many hanging on the stable wall. Some empty feed bags, a large earthen jar, and a pile of blankets made up our cargo. We climbed in, Axel touched the horse lightly with a long stick he found in the bottom of the cart and we were on our way.

"To Gentilly?" the guard asked Axel as we came up to the gate.

Axel nodded, and we were allowed through.

As soon as the horse turned into the street I felt my stomach begin to relax. We headed along the road, the horse just beginning to gain speed, when I saw, at a distance of perhaps fifty feet, a structure looming up out of the shadows. As we came closer we could tell that it was a barricade, hastily built up out of bricks and lumber and pieces of old beds, tables and chairs, all piled haphazardly across the road. Our way was barred.

Axel turned the horse's head intending to go back the way we had come. But as the wagon made its slow cumbersome turn a line of people came into view, Parisians, communards, carrying lanterns and torches. They had evidently come up behind us silently, as we approached the barricade. We could not run them down. We were, once again, trapped. And in the middle of the line of people stood Amélie.

She stood triumphant, a frown of command on her implacable features, a pistol in her hand.

"Get down and show yourselves."

Axel jumped out of the wagon and helped me down.

"Remove that hat," she said to me. What could I do? I took it off, and my long white hair tumbled down my shoulders.

I saw Amélie's eyes widen.

"Fool!" she spat out. "Did you really think you could escape the Committee of Vigilance?" To the men nearest her she said, "I recognize this woman as Prisoner 280. Take her back to the Conciergerie at once and deliver her to the captain of the guard."

Axel stepped in front of me, drew his pistol, and pointed it at Amélie.

"Let her go."

"Take her," Amélie told the men again. They reached for me, coming toward me. Axel fired at them, and one of the men fell. Amélie fired at Axel, and struck him in the shoulder. I screamed. He went down.

I lunged at Amélie then, but several of the communards restrained me and began dragging me back along the road we had traveled, toward the prison.

"Don't worry, prisoner, he'll live," Amélie called out after me. "At least long enough for us to torture the truth out of him."

I spat at her. "When the armies of rescue come, you will all die. You will all die horribly."

Amélie laughed. "It is you who will die, Prisoner 280. And soon. We are the Committee of Vigilance. We do not let enemies of the revolution escape justice."

September 30, 1793

I have almost nothing left. A yellow glove

from my son, the little angel Axel gave me once, my wedding ring and Louis's, the girdle of Ste. Radegunde. And this journal, the record of my life.

But then, what do I really need? My time is short now.

A sparrow comes to my window every morning and evening, a little dark brown sparrow with yellow legs and an orange beak. He is thin, I see him shiver and fluff up his feathers against the autumn wind. I give him crumbs from my coarse black loaf. Food fit for peasants and sparrows, not for a queen!

If only he were a homing pigeon, and could fly to Axel. Axel is in Sweden now, I suppose. Free and happy there. I know that he was wounded but I think the wound has healed. He is sitting in a chair by a beautiful lake, with Malachi beside him. He is thinking of me.

Rosalie gives me so much orange-flower water and ether that I sleep most of the day. At night, though, I hear a lot of screaming. So many are being taken to their death, more and more each day. They are frightened. God bless them.

Note by Rosalie Lamorlière, maid to the Widow Capet in the Conciergerie

Prison, written on the evening of October 16, 1793 and added to this journal:

My mistress the Widow Capet, formerly Queen Marie Antoinette, was taken from her cell this morning by the members of the Revolutionary Tribunal who had condemned her and by the executioner Henri Sanson. I had helped her dress and put up her hair under her linen bonnet. She had saved the bonnet for this day, keeping it white and clean. But they did not let her wear it and they cut off her hair and bound her hands.

I followed her out into the courtyard. She limped because her leg was hurting her, but she didn't complain. I saw her mouth moving as she walked along and I knew that she was saying her prayers, and singing a little song from her childhood, "Soldier of the regiment, be strong, be brave." They made her ride backwards in a cart just like a criminal. It was cruel of them to make her do that.

I walked along behind the cart all the way to the square and stood behind the soldiers in a place where I could see my mistress, though I could not see very well for I was crying. She climbed the steps to the scaffold quickly and lay down under the blade. Some people say that she stepped on the executioner's foot and asked his pardon, but I did not hear that.

There was a loud rattling noise and the blade fell and I saw the executioner hold up her head and walk around with it, showing it to the crowd. They cheered and cheered and some danced and sang. A few were silent or sad and there was a line of men who raised golden daggers in a sort of salute as her head was thrown down onto the bare boards and her body taken away.

I will never forget her. She was a great lady, the sweetest lady I have ever known and very brave. I knew her better than anyone for many weeks and I can swear to how good she was. She wore white to her execution because she always said she was innocent, and I believe her.

My mistress made one final entry in this journal, in which she imagined what her death would be like and wrote of our late king's death and of her son and daughter and how much she loved them all. She was kind enough to write about me as well. Right up to the end, she never gave up hope.

Just before I began to write in this journal I found a note in her prayer book.

This is what she wrote:

The 16th of October at four-thirty in the morning
My God have pity on me!
My eyes have no more tears to cry for my poor children.
Farewell, farewell!
Marie Antoinette

Note to the Reader

The Hidden Diary of Marie Antoinette is a work of fiction, not fact — a historical entertainment, not an attempt at historical reconstruction. Readers who want a scholarly account of Marie Antoinette's life will find it in the author's biography *To the Scaffold*, and in the notes and bibliography cited there.

While Axel Fersen was a real historical figure, and one who loved Antoinette dearly, Eric is an invention, as are Amélie and Sophie and the bushy-eyebrowed Father Kunibert. So far as is known, Antoinette never went to Sweden; there really were Knights of the Golden Dagger, but of their actual exploits almost nothing is known.

Historians cleave to their historical sources, and do not (if they are good at their craft) deviate far from what can reasonably be conjectured from those sources, if not precisely verified. Novelists invent: scenes, dialogue, motivations, entire story lines. Yet the invention here is tethered to all that I know about Antoinette and those around her; it is tempered by decades of research into the late eighteenth century, a rich slice of historical turf which I have spent so many years exploring, blade by blade.

My hope is that through the magic of stark, simplified, dramatic fictional narrative, the long-dead spirits of Antoinette and her circle may live again.

The employees of Thorndike Press hope you have enjoyed this Large Print book. All our Thorndike and Wheeler Large Print titles are designed for easy reading, and all our books are made to last. Other Thorndike Press Large Print books are available at your library, through selected bookstores, or directly from us.

For information about titles, please call:

(800) 223-1244

or visit our Web site at:

www.gale.com/thorndike
www.gale.com/wheeler

To share your comments, please write:

Publisher
Thorndike Press
295 Kennedy Memorial Drive
Waterville, ME   04901